th!s

BY

DANIEL SHORTELL

www.danielshortell.com
Queens, New York

danielshortell

www.danielshortell.com
- novels -
- short stories -

This is a work of fiction unless it becomes true.

For information about bulk purchases, please contact
danielshortell.com at sales@danielshortell.com.

ISBNs:
Paperback 10 digit: 0692831185
Paperback 13 digit: 978-0692831182

Printed in the United States of America

For Faizal,

Oh how you rewired my brain! Now, time for me to wire yours (apologies in advance). Only love my little buddy, only love.

"Life is to be lived, not controlled and humanity is won by continuing to play in the face of certain defeat."
-Ralph Waldo Ellison

"Sometimes people don't want to hear the truth because they don't want their illusions destroyed."
-Friedrich Nietzsche

"Education is a system of imposed ignorance."
-Noam Chomsky

"Religion is regarded by the common people as true, by the wise as false, and by rulers as useful."
-Seneca

Narrators

 John Voyes

 God

 Zuberi Ortiz

 Bryson Acenes

 Aphamli Twist

 Father Kaysen McMurty

 Sariya Ribeaux

 Alain Nelling

Dear Intrepid Reader,

th!s can be a little complex at times. For orientation, several tools have been included in the back of the book to assist. Enjoy.

ag.
same
-llectual

-rhaps just ba-
-ival. Survival. A

Many glass containers arranged neatly in rows, steel columns of corn. Alvin Tan walks between the columns on the 82nd floor until, Grandma. Withered face, stress lines smiled into formation decades ago and preserved beautifully for mass appreciation. Her face, peaceful, serene. Alvin pushes the button, visit logged, her count increases by one and the mechanisms bend the corners of her mouth in regretful hello. Pressure increases, her green light blinks accordingly. Neighbors stuck on solid red, soon algorithms will swap red for green containers in the never-ending organizational dance. Everyone has their place. But who knows, things seem increasingly neglected, subtle differences, an uncertainty looms. There is an abundance of idle red on this floor, coincidental or indicative? Alvin, what do you think?

Difficult not to stare at her face. To observe another person, all their naked subtleties, without the guilt or audit of them watching you back. Indecent, vulgar, but human. The need to connect on some mentally manu-factured level requires pause though, time, to insinuate yourself into the orbit of another. A silly romantic wants to shatter her container, incinerate what remains into a peaceful oblivion. But, then there's always the allure of experience, wanting her to witness a thousand years of accumulated progress even if that progress is just decay and even if cognition amounts to trivial moments of technical lucidity. The sublimity of being history's indefinite witness, knowledge as an addiction. She's solid green, no longer blink⁚ How ridiculous is it that two incredibly divergent thoughts share th͏ breath? Die peacefully but live forever. That's the vanity, the i͏ detachment permitting sustained emotional conflict.

Vanity, is that all it is? Too simplistic. Malevolence? ͏ sic biology pushing us through the numbing grind of s͏ combination of all three? Why the hell does anyone carry on?

I was aware, wasn't I? Was Alvin? As life became a constant barrage of distractions, each day moving quicker than previous two. Keeping up was the fulltime job. This task, this obligation, this tiny, isolated piece of attention hastily granted to a very specific requirement. And then a month goes by. A year. Racing to keep all the balls in air, that's your job. Person-who-diligently-completes-all-the-benign-little-tasks-in-life-in-order-to-maintain-a-steady-march-into-the-future. Obligations. Family. Putting food in mouths. Paying taxes. Buying toilet paper, new pants. Mow the grass. The utterly banal yet necessary. Take medicine. Flush the toilet. Lock the doors. That's the survival. Identifying wants before they become dire needs.

But I knew better, right? Did Alvin? Work necessarily made me a witness of disintegration. Opposition voiced, shared in open forums. Questions, asked, but ignored by the scientific apparatus. An apparatus uninterested in truth, unwilling to entertain questions. Inquiry precluded for the expediency of notional progress. As so it goes, a coward is constipated with idle words and thoughts, he oozes rivers of coherence, while actions remain reserved for someone else. So, you don't demand answers. You're no better than a willing participant, coward that you are. Triggered by fear, you stew in self-righteous indignation. Robotic consumerism. Disinformation. Dark money. Bright smiles. Wasted human energy. So anger builds. Hope, no masochistic desire for a personally ruinous collapse. Inverted thought processes, mental instability as a response to social instability. Release achieved from projecting mental vitriol into a hopeless world. Inactive and quietly smoldering. That's the malevolence, a byproduct of fear's inaction. Alvin may have been angry, forced into action. Bulging anger, cathartic action. A build up and a release, sanity. Is someone here, that rhythmic noise? No, me. Just me, talking solo, mindlessly goose-stepping to the click track of haunted memories.

Things were different, years ago. The details of memories fade, but the poignancy remains keeping the past alive. Can Grandma remember those times? Does she still generate thoughts identifiable as her own?

...

An ambitious young professor at a university in the northern Midwest.

The resume, a dog's breakfast of collegiate ambitions; BS Philosophy, MS History, MS Computer Science, PhD in Social Networking Ethics. Landing a job by convincing a department head you can teach almost as fast as you can learn and by drafting unorthodox curriculums designed to help students navigate quickly emerging social questions. Build a small sub department, gain tenure in three years. An employment boundary case no doubt, and a chance (a hope!) to engage otherwise apathetic teenagers. And the cornerstone class, *The Ethics of Tech-Driven Social Innovation*. A gut course for most as seen by the flimsy arguments yawned up during finals, but a reservoir of thought for the few circling after class. Push the duffs through the academic meat grinder to avoid dramatics, engage the curious. We the self-ascribed "tech-moralists", meeting regularly to discuss the quickly morphing technological glue of society and its impact on human behavior. Their engagement, and the associated pride, fueling the hope that a life's work may have some staying power, a chance it may file down the unfortunate social burrs blooming on the precarious edge of technology for technology's sake. The work at university was rewarding, nominally compensatory and, for a frustrated idealist, added to the institution's intellectual integrity. Me, John Voyes, Professor of *Courses That Provide Students with Absolutely No Commercially Viable Skills*, age 27.

And, earlier. A typical life in a flat brown community out west. A pubescent child overwhelmed by young lust marries another child. Together they make children. Four children smooshed into a one-bedroom apartment. One child in college, one playing mommy, one just walking, and one breast-bound. Then, two in college. One working on a doctorate, one on a bachelors. Interleaved sprints of child-rearing and education. Conflicting ambitions, but all odds beaten, a happy family of four moves east, planting themselves on the bucolic fringe of a college town. The building blocks of middle class bliss mortared atop one another. Mortgage from the friendly neighborhood bank. In the study, wallpaper of degrees and certificates. In the garage, two tidy vessels of perfectly machined metal. Molded plastic, engineered wood, synthetic fibers and digital esoterica holding the many pieces of life in suitable fashion. Smiles and good grades. Milk and skinned knees. Animals shitting relentlessly on overpriced wool rugs. Late-night conjugality hidden from sound on a dilapidated basement couch. Gritty, red-hot on the sands of wherever by summer. Frozen, white-silence upon the mountains of wherever by winter. Grandma popping in for a visit, her teeth sleeping beside her in a glass, and the horror (oh, the tears!) they evoke in tiny marauders. The process of living life and the blind assumption that life is absolutely worth living.

The humble clapboard farmhouse. Situated on a few acres adjacent to the annexed field house used by the overly-optimistic football club, which itself, sat several miles from the campus. The house, a refuge, shelter beyond the cynical eyes of institutionalized smuggery. A place for family, quiet reflection and good old-fashioned hard labor. Tending to the small plot of crops and caring for the few animals that faithfully gave up their treasure. A minimal but heartfelt retreat into the past's fabled simplicity.

Beautiful Janine, following the three-legged goat, Cyrus, as he limped along foraging for the blissful, ethanol sting of rotten apples. Her long hair dancing in the breeze while the awkward, knock-kneed legs of a little girl thrashed at one another. Ingrid, sweet cherubic Ingrid, acclimating to a higher center of gravity and doing her best to scatter the chickens pecking militantly at the feed sprinkled along the outskirts of their pen. Sariya, my lovely Sariya, spending her days alternating between mom, gardener, baker, mechanic, and a million other roles she adopted like orphans. Her never-ending smile. Her patience and soft voice. Her pies. Her amazing pies. One of many side businesses, selling pies made from the fruits of her garden labors. Berry, apple, sweet potato, pumpkin, rhubarb. She could fill a pie shell with anything and sell it for a premium, unable to keep up with word-of-mouth demand. No recipes passed to her. No studying cookbooks or watching celebrity chefs. Just a love for experimentation and a refined palate enabling her to tweak the classics into subtle refinement. Hints of green cardamom and mint in the apple pie. Pineapple and cayenne in the berry. Orange rind and cloves in the sweet potato pie. People confessing how they felt strange paying so much for a pie when they could easily make one themselves with apples growing in their yard. How she would smile, humbly thank them for their business and promise three-for-free if ever a bad one. Sariya never gave a free pie away, didn't need to.

The shithole, is what she called it. The quiet solace found amid the dusty stacks of dog-eared pages lining its walls. An office of sorts. Impossible was walking past a used book sale. Unable to part even with the literature of my teens and the resulting office bloated with sometimes obscure, sometimes classic, sometimes perverted, and sometimes religious texts. Archiving the thoughts and ideas of generations past. Read. Read relentlessly. Agnostic to genre, indifferent to dogma, blind to the critic's sublime advertisement. Anything with a technological bent was escorted to the university office, the DMZ between personal and professional demarcated somewhere between work and home. The great parsing between professional and personal indulgences with a healthy intermingle between. Above all else, the idea, to ensure the diet wasn't overly influenced by any one particular modality of thought. A constant diversity of ideas, a crossbreeding of intellectual pursuits was the structural integrity binding the discrete blocks of knowledge. Something corny like that guiding the progression. One book at a time, build an intellectual fortress and expand and grow stronger if for no other reason than to stave off the inevitable disintegration of mental faculties. Knowledge as life.

...

But, standing here now. Cold concrete pricking toes poking through worn soles. Thoughts of a fortress. Stupid, self-indulgent. How quaint, how sad really. Trapped between two worlds, or maybe, a victim of one, a prisoner even. Sariya's tart pies and the sting they leave in the eyes. Peaceful summers harvesting rows of strawberries in the orange glow of evening sun after a day trapped breathing recycled air. The wild squeals of childhood ecstasy on Christmas mornings.

Grandma's face angles downward, neck twists slightly. Her lips pulsate briefly, insinuating the word ahead of it's sound crackling through a tinny speaker.

"Hello." Voice urgent, breathy.

"Hi Grandma."

"Hello." Same volume, tone.

Hauntingly stilted when they make her talk, best to move on than play their game. From a distance she calls, the jailer's parrot,

"Hello...........hello................hello...............hello."

Difficult to imagine how anyone thought contrived animations would make near death more comforting, more real. It'd be nice to see her eyes once more, it shouldn't be difficult to code and robotize. Once, they were crystal clear blue, your own shadow eclipsed across them as if her pupil was shape-shifting.

Upon the metal grating, passing quickly through many generations propped up behind glass, and onto the empty elevator. Where to next? Home? Not yet. May as well explore, think. On thirty-nine are the Vacant Eyes, could be a good place to reflect. Feet press down, the elevator hisses, thoughts go up. Nobody 100% alive here, apart from me. Am I 100% alive? What does that even mean? Millions of residents here, maybe a visitor or two at any given moment. Maybe. The incongruity between what we have and what we thought we would want.

The elevator lunges to a halt on thirty-nine and a man starts suddenly as the doors pull apart. He doesn't smile, rather, looks through me with distant disgust, shakes himself free of a thought, gives a nod out of proximity's obligation. He doesn't want to make eye contact and he certainly doesn't want to talk, no one ever does. Formaldehyde's pungent sterility wafts in the air as the elevator doors close and the corridor ahead opens to an exhibition hall tightly packed with containers. "Vacant Eyes" etched ceremoniously across the archway leading into a hall roped with track lighting, bathing the containers in clean, bluish light. Jon Voies, the name on the chromium placard, the occupant of the first container. So close, time a matter of getting the spelling correct. Suspended in a clear mold with the rest of the residents on thirty-nine, no call button on his container, just a solid red light. Defined by his hollow optic cavities, a deep ruddy-brown, they earned him a spot on this floor. Like his neighbors, he hangs frozen in time telling a singular story of sin, a story based on Saint Matthew's imbecilic rationalization. Psychotic.

After John it's Bethany, then Madsen, then Cloie, then Jules and so on. Sitting on a viewing bench, guessing at circumstances, pondering decisions made, yet nothing concrete comes to mind. Rarely does. Guilt, embarrassment, self-loathing, all likely precursors to the common outcome, but why an action so oddly ecclesiastical, so archaic? A masochism so incongruent with a society built on rote deference to cold calculation. Maybe it's a reaching out for anything higher? Maybe the logic of desperation is insidiously governed by self-destruction? Like every other facet of this maniacal world,

6

it's difficult to achieve clarity or even a simple cause and effect. Somebody always conceals an ulterior, nothing is as it seems, yet everybody continues to reinforce the apparatus, push the status quo forward. I'm guilty. Surely not of the design. But, because I didn't stand against its momentum, throw myself on the gears. So where does that leave everyone? The guilt-ridden goaded into carving their eyes out, the resilient refusing to die their pre-scribed death, the complacent selling their flesh for bread and the fortunate few watching the whole spectacle while finding comfort in relief and relief in comfort.

It's a waste of time, a pointless exercise, to fish in the past for under-standing. The thirty-ninth floor, where the blind eternally confess their sins in a perfectly organized orgy of stalled decay. The ventilation system kicks on, idles to a soothing hum, and within seconds the huffable prize hovers in a narcotic cloud. Malleable, everything feels lighter, a human slightly more open to suggestion in an odd, intellectually-coerced way. That light odor of The Pine always tickles, lubricates the flow of chemicals across the synaptic cleft. The quietly emerging euphoria of an extra few molecules of serotonin, dopamine. Subtle, but a sort of unspeakable bliss of pure cognition. Me, standing here, a comfy, caged bird on a perch watching out over the world without the bother of expectation or the needless obligation of wings. Pure, unadulterated emotional buoyancy. Something across the world chimes, and the doors fall away, revealing a tidy square to stand upon. The box closes behind me as the last, sticky traces of The Pine pass over loving lips.

...

Six PM, lecture done, and it was time to host the student group, prod around in ethic's relentlessly murky waters. Electronic gaming interests, through their well-oiled lobby machine, pushed new legislation through Congress legalizing the broad-scale implementation of entertainment dubbed, *sensory games*. The student group planned to discuss the legislation's ef-fects within the overall context of the gaming industry's quickly crumbling regulatory structure. Technological innovation in several areas of sensory bio-synthetics had progressed blisteringly in previous years and many new legislative rubber stamps were being sought by the Commerce committee.

Corporate money on one end of the political spectrum, "constituent shaping" on the other pushed controversial games into the realm of desirable technological progression.

Alexy Burns, a third-year philosophy student, sat slouched in a pathetically contemplative heap.

"The new gaming platform integrates all five senses," he moaned.

"I know, I read about it on my way over here. Unanimous vote on Tuesday."

"There wasn't a single objection, not one?"

"No, not even from the Radicals."

Prototype sensory games were being developed for play with a new class of game controller, essentially a high-tech latex-membrane suit. Colloquially referred to as the body-condom, the suit was an orchestrated combination of sensory interface modules providing a "post-virtual-reality" gaming experience called *mock-reality*. The suit's specification read like the sales literature for a full-body prosthesis...

> *...The spatial and tactile aspects of the suit are achieved by an integrated network of two million embedded electrodes and motion sensors distributed along and impregnated within the fully-permeable, synthetically-photopolymerized ethlybenzene-hydroperoxide suit. Each suit is user-specific, the design of which is mapped by a preliminary body scan (fitting scan) to ensure electrode placement aligns precisely with each muscle group and each substantial cutaneal nerve cluster. To mimic the various aspects of touch, formulated sensations are delivered to electrodes by way of highly-variable, multi-frequency microshocks to produce haptic sensations of pressure, temperature and vibration. Taste is mimicked through an integrated digital flavoring system that utilizes hyper-frequency electrical and temperature pulsation techniques delivered to electrodes embedded in a hydrogel tongue overlay. Dispense and diffuse algorithms correlating to the typical "bloom profile" of specified odors manage the precise ejection of combinatory serums, in gaseous form, from micro odor buds scattered around the suit's facial aspect. Spatially-*

sensitive, haptic-enabled holography produces visualization and manages interplay between gamer and related subjects, objects and landscapes. Sound is served by Corti-stimulators anchored to the temporal bone which bypass the unnecessarily complex mechanical componentry of the human auditory system by directly manipulating Corti-local hair cells in order to replicate the subtleties of pitch, frequency, attack, delay and direction.

The experience was complete, immersive. Gaming had become a fully engaging, sensory-activated and sensory-responsive experience. When your punch landed on the face of your holographic opponent, micro electrical shocks administered by your latex suit provided the sensation of resistance and knuckle-pain commensurate with a fist connecting to your adversary's bony jaw. The hologram would fall back, grunt, grimace and bleed while the gravel beneath him would crunch and scatter. If you were to lick your knuckles, the saline sting of sweaty blood was delivered in a bit and byte concoction to your tongue overlay. The burning tire set alight by a rioter across the street spewed a plume of holographic black smoke and prompted the integrated odor buds to digitally render the noxious fumes of burning rubber. Complete absorption into the role being played. A game difficult to differentiate from an actual fight.

Other members of the ethics group filled the few chairs in the stuffy, dim-lit room. The university's dean, Charlton P Tetterford, viewed us anti-business, thus stymied attempts to secure meeting space in lecture halls. Without support, we held meetings in my cluttered office rented at a premium and paid for by the local Radical Party chapter. Teresa, with her perpetually sour look, took a seat. Damian next, his huge frame consuming his chair. Jillian, Ivan, Takumi and the rest. Together again for another session of intellectual dry humping, the outputs of which, would never see the light of day.

There were impressively cogent ideas, arguments, generated during that Friday night meeting. A dissonance fogged the room though as agitated minds shifted incessantly, struggling to find a productive response to the moral anarchy purposefully initiated by the gaming platform.

"Morality should be completely off the table. In and of itself it won't garner large enough support," Alexsy argued. "The Corps are running at 65% of the popular vote. We must appeal in a manner aligned with their philosophy if we are to gain any traction."

"I disagree. Morality should definitely be a component of the argument. Not with any religious pretext, but within the context of encouraging desirable behaviors, establishing safe operating parameters for society, ensuring stability. No one chooses chaos and disintegration and even the most sadistic will act to protect their interests," Teresa said, staring at the ground.

"Morality, unqualified, is too broad and fuzzy," Jillian said, "it doesn't pass the moral hazard litmus test. Most people would enthusiastically resign themselves to a *harsh* regimen of lament and consternation, watching with measured horror as the world burns. But, so long as they believe their own wellbeing is secure, the blue-bloods will watch the red blood spill across decency's frontlines in tongue-clucking buckets. Morality, if it is to play a role, should be bought and sold like the commodity it has become."

"People can extrapolate, can deduce personal impact and injury by going through a simple cause and effect process," Teresa argued.

"Absolutely, I agree entirely. However, moral hazard boils down to a simple calculation and those powerful enough to influence decisions do so with a sense of calm justified by their ability to financially isolate themselves from the broader population. In effect, 'decline is for everyone else, not me, because I'm wealthy, secure and fortified'. Morality must be monetized, pitched and packaged as such, else it doesn't factor into the cost-benefit analysis."

"So what, the argument is that morality no longer holds value in society?"

"No, it does, it absolutely does. It's a matter of semantics. One man's morality is another man's path to profit and vice-versa. Morality imparts a sort of asymmetric impact on the balance sheet, but, since morality contains no native numerical descriptors, it requires a clear business case to establish commercial validity. Morality can be important, very important in fact, but it is inaccessible, distracting even, for many therefore it is much cleaner to distribute it within a financial wrapper. It's not that morality is necessarily passé, but talking about it certainly is. People with obscene wealth don't focus their energies on accumulating morality points; they channeled them into making bank."

The students sensed, with varying degrees of cynicism, a social tipping point masquerading as a gaming platform even if they, rather we, couldn't fully grasp it or describe its practical attributes. We learned, subsequently, that what was going on in the world had nothing to do with gaming, technology or the natural course of social trends. It was control, a seemingly benign, yet highly perverse version of it, formulated and disseminated by the powers that be. Not a control that was secretive or conspiratorial, quite the opposite. A method of control that perfectly complimented and reinforced the mundane practicalities of day-to-day living. Religion was always the great opiate of the people, but, in recent years, missteps and conflicting messages tarnished the various theological brands. Only the most faithful, the most woefully uninformed, still held fast to a spirituality based upon the tenants of dogmatic institutions. For everyone else, subtly contrived narratives and situations were required to garner broad scale economic and social engagement, to encourage those massively lucrative leaps of faith in order to establish the vehicle for control. Methods of control attempting to force compliance in archaically patriarchic ways were clearly outmoded, and the new path toward attaining control was to create the illusion of yielding it. The moldy *fire and brimstone* papyri and a couple handfuls of dead prophets were not sufficient to sell tech-savvy consumers on the necessity, let alone value, of cultivating faith. New contraptions were needed, new ways to enable the individual to exert more control over their own interactions with the world. A way to interface with the world, permitting each person's ego the opportunity to sit front and center for the myriad interactions, trivial or profound. To reconfigure the world such that a persons' entire reality exists within the narrow context of fulfilling an ever-increasing, acutely self-indulgent palette of wants and needs. Create the conditions, the entire landscape, to help people emotionally push away from one another as these genuine human connections are, by and large, a bar to increased consumption. Encourage people to pull into themselves, view others as competitive adversaries. Technologically assist people to create their own world of desire based on the outward and highly-visible successful expressions of others. Make consumption the priority and build an infrastructure to serve all wants and needs with immediate, scalpel-like precision. Science morphing into a tool used primarily by the powerful to calculate the exact terms for which a person is most likely to act in a manner beneficial to the powerful over themselves (but make the consumer feel like winner in the exchange). What better way to control people than by giving them the tools necessary to oppress themselves in a manner that makes them believe they are in control? Poor Jillian. To think that she was castigated by the group for being too cynical.

The ethics group disbanded later that evening after arriving at a single point of agreement; technology's influence on reality had evolved to the extent that it was incumbent on society to establish clear definitions for the various states of reality, and, to define the permissible conditions for technology to induce reality from unnatural means. A lot of esoteric language, and a basic methodology on how different states of reality could potentially coexist harmoniously in a free society. Naïve looking back, but at least some measure of blowback against the increasingly corporatist power regime.

Arriving home later that night, time spent gulping cheap beers, alone on the creaky porch boards. A simple, impotent attempt at detachment, intellectual lobotomy, leaving the emotions intact and prone to the insurgent, volatile fragments of memory. Looking out across Sariya's garden, numbing reveries lulling a vague head into feelings of accord with the nature, the hushed beauty of simplicity washing like waves. Life's basic, ancient movements; the capillary action of water, the addition of sun and carbon dioxide to make sugars, create oxygen. A bud grows to a flower and in it, a tiny insect routes methodically, then, flies on to facilitate the sexual rendezvous necessary to continue the insanely iterative nature of existence. And then, sullen eyes prick in a recherché moment of reflection, remorse, a moment where a tear outs the liar. We get what we want, we lament, then we do it all over again. Emotional robots. Another sip of beer, iterate back to the previous emotional state of intoxicated sublimity.

Warped boards creaked, an empty bottle traded for a full. In the pale, sickly light of a September moon, the irony of a solitary goldfinch on a cornstalk amid the coal black pitch of night spurred an inebriated mind. It and me, alone in the black. Incessant chirping at what appeared to be nothing. It's song, slow and steady, a series of trills slowly overlapping into a rising panic of sounds. Wings flapping. The bird sung death for a minute or so, then without notice, fell silent, flew away. Seconds later, a stray cat fat on mice emerged from the corn rows. Lumbering, head low, cadent shoulder blades rising and falling under fur. It dropped to the ground, rolled onto its back, grinding its head against the damp grass. Predators and prey doing the usual dance.

As the rising sun painted the eastern horizon, the hens announced the impending day and drunken feet toppled empty bottles. The curious stray perked, glared with amber eyes, while rotating its body to face the disturbance. As the last sip trickled down, I cocked my arm, heaved the bottle at the comfortable cat. With trivial effort, the cat sidestepped, shot hell from its eyes, slunk to the shed's protection.

It's unreal how much blood pours from your neck after being slit ear to ear. You don't lament the twelve-million Credit Tabriz being stained beyond recognition (wait, or do you?) or the howls of terror from your three prize-winning Alsatians as they suffer a similar fate. Nor do you dwell on your wife's naked, convulsing body, her twenty fingers and toes resting pulpy in an ashtray. Gory details vying unsuccessfully for stayed attention. It would seem that you are narrowly concerned with that *how* swirling about. Why is this coming through in the second person? Me, it's my head that won't let go of this irrepressible *how*. How did we arrive here, no, how did I get here? How did this happen? How is it that my trusted gardener of twenty odd years could set fire to the property he meticulously maintained for over two decades, then slaughter its inhabitants? This strange consciousness, oddly sharp, acrimonious even. A peek of the end emerges. Breathless clarity and a nagging *how*. Really? The unanswered questions are the final concern?

...

The Dhalytes had been leaking from The Piles for several months, moving slowly in sporadic little clusters, bony troupes, looking to scrounge whatever they could from society's makers. Relaxed, Jeffery and I looked out over the channels of highways leading from The Core toward The Blocks. From the balcony on 238 we glassed a cluster of Dirts grouping off to the West, a group of perhaps ten, maybe fifteen hominids. That subtle chill always creeps up the spine, the way it always did, before performing the quick mental walkthrough of contingencies, backups and fortifications.

Jeffrey sipped his Pinot, asked, "Care to go hunting Mr. Nelling?" a rifle bridged across excited, bouncing knees.

"Hmm, Can't say I'm prepared at the moment little Jeffrey."

"Stupid you."

"What I meant to say is my preferred arm is up on 240. Why would I want to compete with your dusty antique? I've shot rubber bands with better accuracy."

"Fine then, call it down Champ, we'll see who bags the most," he said.

"I prefer to keep a low profile on my attitude toward..., oh, I don't know, let's call them the less fortunate."

"Ok, so get off those fleshy knots and retrieve it yourself Mr. Prudence."

"And therein lies the conundrum. I'm not in the business of manual labor my friend."

"Smart. In two moves, you've boxed yourself into a paradoxical corner. Perhaps you're the one fit for a pink slip, a change of address perhaps?"

"Cute, coming from the guy who ranks at least forty places below me in Credits. Count them Jeffrey, forty. I'll help you: one, two, three, four..."

"Yeah, we'll see how well those Credits serve you in the end. At some point the law of diminishing returns applies. Anyway, why so cautious around your servants now? How is yet another demoralization going to matter?"

"Let's be clear. It's not as though I care about the plight of the Dirts or any other wildlife for that matter. That being said, I'm not dumb enough to broadcast my contempt for those below me. Is that plain enough for you? Bear in mind, Irons are perfectly capable of basic deduction. Creating problems because I'm too lazy to retrieve my own weapon is plain counterproductive. No sense in provoking the malcontents when all that's required is a light touch of discretion? Besides, I'm fairly confident I can beat you with your own rifle."

"Ok big talker, challenge accepted. But first, to your question, of course there's no sense in encouraging upheaval, however in this instance, you are looking through the wrong facet of the prism. If you turn it slightly, you'd see that force is the envy of diplomacy, a fact you know well enough from experience - step on a face and the desired elements, well they proceed to ooze on out. Oh, and your bit about provoking the malcontents, come on, I think you know they have plenty of reasons to revolt. In fact, let's call revolt a guarantee instead of dancing around the obvious. The point of no return was breached a long time ago my friend and it's unfortunate the majority of Corps are deaf and dumb to this fact. And the newfound moderation toward the under classes, I know I don't get it. But, perhaps a circumspect chap like yourself does. What *do* you think is going on here around us?"

"What do you mean?"

"I mean historically, the big, big picture. How will this chapter be written for posterity?"

"Propagation of the survivalists."

"Nope, I'd say you're way too optimistic there Darwin," he said.

"Alright then, perhaps you prefer it more blunt. Extermination of the hopeful?"

"Nah, you're in the sand, a whiffing fool."

"Of course. Ok then, you don't seem to appreciate glass-half-empty-or-full semantics, so how about some politically correct, backward looking anthropological bullshit?"

"Sure, I'm listening."

"Ok then, a very carefully managed social order."

"There it is, that's the problem with you! Your cynicism, though robust, is completely misdirected. You view this social structure as if some design is responsible for deterministically placing us at the top when I think you know damned well our situation is nothing more than a good coin toss," Jeffrey challenged.

"Sure, act as though we haven't engineered this entire order. Act as if our collective efforts weren't harmonized to put us atop the heap."

"Clearly you give us, whoever the fuck *us* is anyway, too much credit. I suppose you think the invisible hand guided our fortunes along the path of evolution? *We* are most fit for the human purpose? Pull yourself back down to earth Champ, people wield strength because they must, not because they are genetically predisposed to it. If you want to place your bets on careful design and purposeful engineering, so be it, but watch out when the hibernating awake. History is always a matter of time. I'll remain skeptical of success and shoot my way out of the foxhole as it becomes necessary. Me and my practical, post-Darwinian brethren won't bother to lament our ignorance though, instead, we will embrace it as the world sizzles," Jeffrey said, cocking his rifle.

Ppfffttt. The soft, airy sound of gas exiting through a suppression chamber.

Looking through his scope, "One down, many to go. Your turn," Jeffrey said.

"You know, I've seen many people kill, but you, you relish it more than anyone else. Why is that?"

He gave it some thought, wiped his lips, "this is my last functioning catharsis button, all others have ceased working. Now be a sweetheart and push yours with me."

"You're a sick bastard, give me that thing."

"Don't mind if you do," he said, passing the rifle.

Ppfffttt Ppfffft Ppfffttt Ppfffttt Ppfffttt

Looking through the scope, "Three of five. You should check your scope alignment, it could use some calibration."

"Says the junior marksman firing a weapon he can barely handle. You are 60 percent to my 100," Jeffrey remarked, "and now they are scattering. Time for the real fun, pull!"

The sun hung low in the evening sky and a breeze blew through the open glass facade. Jeffrey walked over to refill his glass, returned, sipped casually.

Silence hung.

"Think we'll go to hell?"

Jeffrey's look, incredulous. "What the fuck is wrong with you? You're truly a child today Alain, with these cute, fantasy projections, and now this metaphysical jerk off. Are you feeling alright? Do you need a hug? A snort of the 'ol Pine?"

"I'm just throwing it out there. It's a fascinating idea to consider, don't you think?"

"No, actually, I think it's childish and fit for hairy knuckle-draggers. Where exactly does that exercise end?"

"So you've never considered it?"

"Considered it, God? Look, the range of ideas to consider is infinite, so is the range of things to worry about. Why don't you save your energy for something useful, something tangible? If you're having difficulty reconciling big-boy thoughts, why not hop on the horn, reach out and atone for your sins Brother Alain! The Irons simply love that shit! Come to think of it, maybe you aren't who you think you are," he said, chuckling.

Ppffft, Ppfffftt Ppffftt

Looking through the scope, "Three for three, still 100 percent. I'm clearly a better specimen than you," Jeffrey said, sitting back in his chair with a relaxed smile, bridging the rifle on his knees.

"That's one way of seeing it, or perhaps you don't know how to properly sight a scope. And by the way, you should come to understand that sometimes irreverent things are said with the intention of sparking playful, theoretical discussion. I'd like to formally point out that *you* are the one who chose to use the word 'worry' in the context of The Almighty. You, the better specimen I should add, lacking subtlety in both discourse and basic telescopy."

"You know, and I apologize for changing the subject from your fascinating inquiry into the supernatural, but now that Dirt clusters are more frequent *my* most immediate fear is that air quality is at risk in The Core. To be laid up with Ebola for a month, that'd be a real downer."

"I'm fairly certain the spray programs are still functioning at this point. And for the record, your dodging of my God-fearing accusation doesn't offend me, but it certainly makes you look like a chump. At least learn to act the role of a Diamond."

"Yeah, I don't doubt their efficacy in The Piles, but considering the up tick in illegal immigration underway, I'm concerned the drones are not spraying Dirts exiting The Piles. Oh, and your accusations can rot in your nonexistent hell. Your sentence-parsing is as childish as your commitment to role-playing. Grow up and fuck off."

"Hee, hee! Ok, I see your point about the drones. Perhaps it's best we enjoy this nice weather behind the glass?"

"Couldn't hurt," Jeffrey said, pushing the button as he rose.

Sitting there, a beautiful Tuesday afternoon, relaxing, a couple bottles of wine and the acrid waft of burning gun powder. The network's latest production had recently wrapped, and in executive manner, we killed some time between intervals of allocating capital to winners. The life of a Diamond. The joyously recursive process of allocating an ever-growing base of capital. The acrobatics of ensuring all legal, legislative, messaging and colluding components are situated before plunking down the Credits; basic due diligence any competent executive was remiss to ignore.

"So, how well do you reckon season one'll do Jeffrey?"

"What, are you kidding me? Gangbusters. It will surpass previous premiers handily. I'd bet my life-savings on it," he said, a laugh hacking into a cough.

"Well that's encouraging to hear because I did."

"All in huh? Ballsy move."

"Ballsy? What's ballsy about a sure thing?"

"Nothing's ever a sure thing."

"Ok then, tell me the last time you lost."

He sat there, a far-off contemplation mixed with a lying smile, "Well Champ, you do have a point. Cheers to our latest good fortune."

Glasses clinked. *How Far Will You Go?*, the new, soon-to-be-award-winning show, Watch Inc's latest production. A simple gaming concept, but one that required a fair amount of maneuvering and paperwork for contestants to win the prize money and avoid prison. Consultants, lawyers, and legislators consistently tapped for their particular expertise in ensuring a known outcome for contestants. It was a nice economic bump, lauded by the Corps in the constant search for GDP boosters.

Sitting there on the 238th floor, reflecting on the network and the massive successes of the previous years. The vigorous push to make Watch Inc the leader in televised entertainment made it the top contender for industry consolidator. All roads to massively invigorated profits and stronger balance sheets lead to the merger, the complete consolidation of all going concerns in the industry. The winner-take-all approach. Companies within each industry merging into a single industrial player. The agriculture, healthcare, mining, energy, and telecom sectors had singularized within the previous two years. The music industry, existing as Listen Inc, consolidated decades prior. The motion picture industry, the sector which was the closest parallel to televised entertainment, had, in the last five years, melded into a singular entity. Every single cinematic production over the last four years had been conceptualized, produced, advertised and distributed from a single source. Movies Inc was THE purveyor of motion and experiential pictures. Working with the Corps, Movies leadership acquired substantial federal assistance during its consolidation by making a promise to cut ticket prices and royalties by 50% within its first two years. The subsidy justification, simple enough. Entertainment was to be even more accessible to Iron "voters", a clear social victory for *the people*, ensuring all participating members of the economy possessed the means to consume unlimited entertainment. Oh Movies Inc, you delicious mark you!

(from the distance) ppffffftt ppppfffttt pppffffttt

"Behold the competition from Ivory Towers," Jeffrey said.

"HEY! WELLINGTON! WHAT BRINGS YOU TO THE FRONT-LINE THIS AFTERNOON?!"

"OH..., HEY JEFFREY! HOW'S IT GOING? I DIDN'T SEE YOU THERE. YEAH, WELL, THOUGHT I'D POP A FEW ROUNDS OFF BEFORE HEADING EAST. TAKING THE FAMILY OUT TO THE BUNKERS FOR A FEW WEEKS," Wellington yelled back.

"AH LOVELY! YOU AND THE FAMILY HAVE A NICE TIME, YEAH?"

"WILL DO JEFFREY. HEY, THAT NELLING HIDING BEHIND YOU?"

"YEP, SURE IS. THE SILLY S.O.B. WAS LECTURING ME ON HELL, CAN YOU BELIEVE IT?"

"HA, CLASSIC! WE CERTAINLY SPEAK OF WHAT WE KNOW!"

"HI WELLINGTON. DON'T BELIEVE JEFFREY, AS USUAL HE'S SODOMIZING THE TRUTH!"

"THAT I DON'T DOUBT! GOTTA DASH THOUGH GENTS, TAKE CARE!"

"OH, AND BEST OF LUCK ON THE LAUNCH, I HEAR GREAT THINGS!" Wellington screamed.

"THANKS FRANK, ENJOY THE BUNKERS!"

"BYE FRANK!"

"Ahhh, two weeks in The Bunkers. Oh the unbearable tang of jealousy! I don't believe I've been out there in a month," Jeffrey reminisced. "Need to make a plan."

"Over a month?"

"Yeah, how about you. Been there recently?"

"Most nights my friend. Most nights."

"Most nights? Are you a glutton for commuter punishment? You're spending what? Two? Three hours in the sky everyday? Hold it, I think I unearthed the root of your existential funk!"

"About twenty minutes, eighteen if the winds are perfect. And you think forty positions in the Credit ranks is negligible. Stupid you."

He sat there, burning, the silence washing over my checkmate smile. The faint scent of vinegar and stale onions emanating from his armpits and hitching a ride on the breeze. The delicious, acerbic stench of raw jealousy.

...

The quickly expanding pool of blood shines crimson and chrome. How? Where is the how in this random cluster of recall? Nobody worth a shit is perfect. Footsteps still pounding throughout the house. It will take them time to clean out the food, valuables, whatever else they're after. The dogs, no longer yelping. Nancy's glassy eyes stare now, locked into perpetual shock. Shallow breathes, a thin trickle of blood from the corner of her mouth drips on the floor. She wants to say something. I want to hear something other than the reverb of larceny. An ever-so-fleeting tingle of euphoria. How?

The introspection that bubbles up when change is unwittingly thrust upon you. How every *why* is arranged end-to-end as the mind attempts to trace causality to a single origin, a single point of control. This process of putting pieces in time order, the assumption that order exists. The day spent dismantling the last Atonement Center under my supervision. Hard to believe that the operation, at peak, included over 150 call centers. Sure, 90% of those centers were staffed with phone operators handling business over the wire, but still, an operation comprised of over three thousand Irons working phones and booths generated an impressive revenue. Daily atonements at peak were what? Somewhere north of 350,000? Can't remember exactly. Substantial for a mid-size east coast franchise. *Hmph*, now, no income stream and meager savings to pick at over time. Least I was smart enough to invest in security, clearly a good investment.

The trip back home to The Bunkers from here should take what, about an hour? Assuming no roadblocks or God knows what. Heaps of useless shit grow larger by the day along the roadside; dilapidated tents, limp cardboard, plywood, tarps, plastic containers. The shoulders are choked out at some places with the detritus of failed lives. Fallen, disgraced Irons. Clots of disheveled, mangy children lob chunks of mortar, rocks and other missiles at my car. Their angry projections bounce off the car's reinforced plates without effect. Fortunately, newly cast Dirts of age and ability are elsewhere keeping the threat level low enough to relax in thought.

Rotten little shits. Spraying drones should be filled with something more caustic, perhaps at least a sterilizing agent to stem propagation. Why can't we force the Legislature to act on this growing problem? We've already progressed well beyond what many would consider the tipping point. Lately, camps are popping up everywhere along the roads leading to The Bunkers, a clear indication the problem is not abating. Culls are nothing new. Why haven't we addressed an issue this serious, with a more logical, pragmatic approach? Sure, deer were beautiful in their time, however too many destroyed the vegetation, degraded the landscape, invited disease. Kangaroos, elk, pigeons, mice and many other life forms were effectively managed in such a manner. What is the reason for hesitation? The age of being politically correct is long dead, why fake it?

Feels like only yesterday when the scientific community found the guts to finally publicize their studies on *Homo's* biological schism. The evidence was plentiful, impossible to refudiate. Finally, science provided hard facts on which to act, act in a manner consistent with the taxonomy of our genus. That nagging criterion of equality, motivated by some wide-eyed, humanistic notion, quickly melted away into the annals of history. We *were* not and *are* not the same. Period. There is no reason to make apologies. The natural order is defined by the cold, hard process of science. Theory, proof, proof, proof, and on and on. And fine, from time to time theories are proven wrong. We're modest enough to redact, no, we're scientific enough to redact if necessary. That is the process of good science. And this past year, again, another legislative victory rooted in science, removing ill-labeled Irons from The Core based on clear empirical evidence. Deus benedicis scientia!

But what's the point here? Why divert on these mental tangents? Today. Today is about the business, the business failing. Today, the business is done. Finished. Daddy is no longer employed. Sorry kids, we'll need to tighten our belts until the next opportunity comes along. We're fine, important to keep our wits. We've planned for this possibility. Eventuality? Drive home, just drive. Getting upset, freaking out, isn't going to help. Pragmatism.

Five minutes from home. Five minutes from Judy's warm embrace. Five minutes from the playfulness of Muhammad, Magdalene's beautifully expectant eyes. Trying to carve out an existence amid the craziness. So the business is a shambles. So what. Income has dried up. I'm not the first person to lose a job, right? Sure, the future has become uncomfortably questionable, but only a child would lose his head. This family can handle it. Security has been meticulously planned over the years, painstakingly devised. Stick to the plan. We will not waver, nor will we be distracted by the triviality of employment hiccups! It's time for positivism. Clarity of direction. To be procedural, codify our steps forward, rely on those unconscious fundamentals drilled in early on. Father knew this, gritty bastard. He knew all about establishing structure and sticking to it for better or for worse. Brutal. The son-of-a-bitch was brutal, but he knew tough times required strong actions. He knew how to draw lines, walk 'em, regardless of how the winds should blow. Stability. This is what we're going to need. Structure. Father's heavy-handed tactics, assumedly rooted somewhere in love, established order, provided the comfort of expectation. Isn't that what we want when times get tough? Expectation, a continuity arcing through the turbulence. Birch slapping across a tender back, the price of adolescent insolence. Difficult to see through the cloud of teen angst, but now, as a responsible adult, his rigidity pulled us through the difficult times. The job's a wash, people are angry, perhaps rightfully so. But, whatever. Yeah, business was about selling services. You thought they held value, else why did you buy? Dodgy services? Depends who you are maybe, but look, we've all got to make our living right? Nobody's holding guns to heads, making anyone buy. So maybe the gig is up, maybe there is no way for Salvation Inc to save itself. Fine. There are always other enterprises, always other ways to make our daily bread. 'Son, you need to put faith in your fellow man, put faith in the leaders among us.' Was the bastard prescient? Did he see society's shifting landscape? Did he see the strength in how the economy was evolving? Doubt it. A simple man of faith. Built from day one to root out and adhere to anything he could believe in. How he was so quick to stand behind anyone with power as if power was the sun radiating warmth to those nearby.

But, in a way, maybe he was right. A business dies off, another pops up. The kings of capital, the leaders among us, are always searching, always poised to discover the next business venture. What they are wired to do. Opportunity will come along, and I'll find a way to fit into a new organization. I'll figure out how to apply my skills to another corporation. It's not ingratiation, it's providing value. That's business, being valuable, having value, creating value. And it's never easy, right? People are flawed. Selfish. Parsimonious. But, we all want to see the future, reap the juicy dividends, so we work together because the ends justify it. Nobody wants to burn the house down. At times, things fail and fold. Nature's lifecycle, business isn't immune to it. But beyond any one business, it's the structure, society's structure that provides the stable foundation. The footing on which liberated people trade freely, enjoy democracy's benefits. Tiered into classes? Yeah, of course. It's naive to think people won't eventually fit in where they naturally belong. Order. Clean and tidy. The mind works best under a clear division of responsibilities. Otherwise, chaos. Overlap. Confusion. Sorting things into buckets, organization's basics, to establish some coherent order so everyone benefits from the collective strengths of all. The Irons, society's muscles, helping to push us into the next generation with sheer brute force of their labor. Me and the other Platinums; the thought-leaders, scientists, theologians, philosophers. The gray matter providing the intellectual capital to root out new technologies, new thoughts, and new solutions to drive innovation and to drive the productization of a strong, growing economy. And the Diamonds. The charismatic kings of policy and capital, endowed with the indefinable qualities necessary to adequately direct men, to establish vision and push to results. They are the rocks, the steady, sure hands implementing the Platinum's ingenuity. Times are tough at the moment, but we'll find our way back on track.

Turning into the compound's outer perimeter, memories of the good 'ol days, they creep in. Those days before so much required security. Days without the shadow of collapse looming ominously.

...

Second year of college and I made my way up the Quadrangle's steps to join the rest of the group for the bimonthly moonlight cotillion. And there she was. Dressed in an unassuming little black dress, the fringe of her hair tickled the bare expanse of her neck as she leaned against the stones in the brown-orange dusk. In her hand was a black, velvet clutch with a piping of shiny, black leather navigating the edge. She was aloof, almost intentionally so, waiting for the right approach, someone to reanimate her.

I had watched her obsessively over the past two sessions, carefully though, making certain my gawks were tucked behind dancers, a column, anything. Twenty years old and the first time feeling perfectly uncomfortable connecting with female eyes. It was as if my lusty feelings for this girl would scream from my eyes should they connect with hers, rendering me a simple, ogling pervert; the type some girls toy with, others slap. A conscious effort required to simply not keep looking at her. There was something alluring, addictive, in playing witness to her every move. Learning virginal nuggets of information about a girl I was being sucked into. A girl whose existence I had know of for mere weeks.

And there she was. The two of us alone together for the first time amid the dissonant cicada chorus drowning out everything on a warm evening. In those last few seconds upon approach, an entire vocabulary scanned for something cleverly pithy, but the overwhelming pressure of being thrown into contact with my crush rendered me mute. My shock registered, and she tossed me a lifeline.

"So, you're Jonathan's friend, aren't you?"

"Um, uhh, yeah....yeah we're roommates."

"He's an asshole isn't he?" she said, smiling.

"Well, his personality is a little odd if that's what you mean."

"I see, you two are rather tight, huh?"

"I guess you could say we've been a pair for a while now. We go back to middle school together, seventh grade".

"Ok, good then, so I'm right? He's an asshole?"

"You might be right. He can be difficult at times. But, he doesn't mean any harm I assure you."

"He may not *mean* harm, but he certainly is good at causing it."

Shit. Again, another introduction to a girl by way of Jon's idiocy. Nothing new. "I'm sorry, what the hell happened?"

"No need for you to apologize. You didn't set fire to the laundry room in Henderson with a load of fireworks, causing an evacuation on a Tuesday night, in the pouring rain mind you, the night before my chemistry mid-term...did you?"

Oh, she was victimized by *that* one. Hmm, could be worse. How does she know Jon's my friend?

"Ah, yeah, that was Jon, sorry."

"Again, you don't need to apologize for him do you? I mean, you weren't involved?"

"No. No. Actually, an emphatic no. I was not involved in that adventure nor am I usually involved in Jon's greatest plots. You're right, I shouldn't bother apologizing for that asshole."

Chuckling, "there you go, I knew you had it in you."

"It *is* fair to say he paid for his crime though, wouldn't you agree?"

"Perhaps. I saw his punishment in the paper. Is he still volunteering at the hospice?"

"Everyday."

That pause. Not an uncomfortable one. The type of pause allowing both parties to take a breath, carefully determine the next move. The verbal chess of young adults exiting the teenage years in cleverer-than-thou fashion.

"I'm Judy," she said, smiling, extending a slender arm.

"I know." Her hand and the chance to touch it. Sublime.

"Sorry?"

"What I meant to say is I know your name. You're wearing it."

"Oh, right. Sometimes I forget about this thing. I mean really, is it necessary? We've been dancing for over a month, I think I know who I am by now," she deadpanned.

"You don't happen to know your last name?"

"Nice. Yes, it's Ziljan. Yours?"

"McMurty. I'm Kaysen McMurty and it's very nice to meet you Judy."

"Well, it's nice to meet you Kaysen McMurty. So, you're not an anarchist, you're clearly not a faithful friend, what are you?"

"Hmm, good question. A normal guy I guess. Ambitious. Driven. Unsettled just enough to want more but not enough to kill at will. You?"

"I guess a dreamer at this point, sort of hoping the whole collegiate experience will provide some direction."

"Sounds rather innocuous. What major cultivates that sort of perspective?"

"Music I guess. My focus is composition. And what makes one so measuredly ambitious?"

"Business administration. The degree of the decidedly undecided."

"Um, Ok. You know, your expressions have an interesting shape-shifting quality about them like they are simultaneously at odds, yet agreeing with your mouth. I can't tell if you're being ironic or funny."

27

"I'm not exactly sure how the two are different. And actually, the word irony, though I've looked it up endlessly, I'm still not certain I know what it means. One often tries to be clever for clever's sake and another ends up being clever to slake comedy. Either way, someone is usually left feeling cold because they don't quite understand the meaning, or possibly the intent, which is pretty goddamn funny in its own right. Get me?"

"Really?" feigning anger, "Are you calling me dense?"

"Absolutely not."

"Then why are you smiling?"

"Because, regardless of what I say or how my face endorses or betrays it, you somehow seem interested. That makes me feel oddly pedestaled."

"Perhaps you are getting ahead of yourself?"

"Perhaps. Or perhaps I enjoy using my mouth, regardless of the consequences."

"Maybe you're a performer, an actor?"

"Judy, Darwinianly speaking, we are all actors slung uncomfortably on stage. Everything else is just cognitive dissonance."

"Ok…I think I get it. That's pretty dark, but your smile is calling your bluff."

"Or it's writing the check."

She watched my hands, searching for more information. Disconnecting eyes deflated the tension.

"Well if we must act, my fellow thespian, would you care to co-star with me this evening?"

"I'd be honored."

And with that, she took my hand in hers and we walked into our future together.

...

A few bodies strewn along the compound's outer perimeter, nothing unusual. Odd is the small blue flag, a spray-painted red "X" drawn overtop Salvation Inc.'s logo, a logo synonymous with a range of recently defunct religious services. Strange the flag still stands upright, but even more odd that it's planted inside the Phase I gate. How? Security should have intercepted the perpetrator before the vandalized flag made it to this point. Driving toward the flag, a quick scan of the area around the car before unlocking. Outside, the flame of my lighter engulfs the little flag and it whips in the wind casting off flecks of burning fabric which fall to the ground, smolder to ash. Flag burns out as the reinforced door of Phase II gate opens.

A gorgeous day in The Bunkers, tough to deny it even amid the worries. A fresh, easterly breeze. Overhead, a deep blue sky fading quickly to pink then orange, ultimately failing into a filthy brown hovering the hopeless western horizon. Stretches of lush green define the property's footprint while the gentle sway of flowering dogwoods evoke a natural calm. Continuing toward Phase III gate, the huge metal construct slides away, revealing a final stretch of pavement. Poking through the perfectly green ground, the glass tip of my subterranean iceberg glints in the evening sun. The adjacent turf creeps away like a centipede carpet. A fifteen degree roll into the safety of mother earth's bosom.

Back outside, The Pine's scent is gone, sensation lingers. Euphoria, a fully cognitive high. Somehow wasted yet acutely aware, motor skills completely unimpeded. *The Pine*, as they call it, a life-enhancement tool for Irons, but, as with all products, available to Platinums and Diamonds looking to slum. One of the many amazing advancements a silly society points to as indicative of progress. A happy divorce with reality.

Last year, perhaps the year before, when good fortune stumbled me upon Alvin Tan's severed hand. A moist, pulpy bundle complete with Alvin's tag and chip inside a knotted plastic bag, jackpot, the trifecta of modern security found amid mounds of trash. Somebody's homicidal foul play turned my good luck, and the only reason a loathed Dhalyte could hope to enter The Archives given the 32nd amendment's ban. Security concerns, *sapian* and *beatus* should not mix. A banishment well beyond The Archives, Dirts eliminated from society on laughable pretexts. We, the outcasted lot, economic collateral damage. Peripheral to society, not cut from the same cloth, thus not entitled to the same protections and rights as the participating members of society. Dhalytes are the nuisance, the bipedal problem *Homo beatus* must resolve to protect their way of life. The many rules and structures established to prevent mixing and cavorting between divergent classifications of human life. The propagandized shame and indecency of copulating across the prezygotic barrier.

Time to return to camp five miles west of The Archives. For the healthy, an easy trek amid the cool, smog-laden wind of a summer afternoon. Envy the healthy. Tucked uncomfortably in filthy underpants, Alvin's Iron credentials hide from the opportunistic scum marauding The Piles' famished outskirts. Here, where the most wretched Dhalytes wait for death. People struggling with mental illness in addition to their government-issued social stigma, banishment. An existence marked by the inability to rationalize or even functionally compartmentalize their situation; starvation, depression, confusion, and anxiety mixing and devolving into the slow rot of self-extermination. Famine always wins as a troubled mind fails to manage the grueling monotony of the daily hunt. Philanthropic Dirts pitch in to ease suffering when able but the problem's scale is far beyond practical remedy. Living without, the starving ritualistically seek milliseconds of cutaneous relief by flicking horseflies off skin-covered skeletons. The possibility to subside for short stints on meager charity until the slow burn of starvation quiets the madness. A form of human existence. With a sort of ironic efficiency, cooling corpses lie curbside until nightfall, when sanitation trucks collect them for delivery to their final resting place amid the routinely sterilized bodies decomposing in mounds on the outskirts of The Piles.

Failing lungs, bloody spittle and the rest intervals required. Holy shit, will I make it home tonight? A naked stick-figure claws his way to the curb, a dying dog hiding from the family. Hacking coughs, clearer lungs. Panic triggered by the stench of raw decay wafting through the air, mini thermals lifting disease from the scorched earth. Damn, am I even safe here? It doesn't even matter. Odd how nobody bothers to waste energy begging. Beg for what? Tiny bodies pepper the roadway, expired hours earlier, taut skin, dry and coarse in the afternoon sun. Distended bellies, alienesque heads with sunken eyes, their brittle limbs swollen at the joints, rigidly contorted and pointing at the clouds. Each placed curbside for pick up by sanitation trucks. Mothers' freed from burdens. Trucks circling on twenty-four-hour cycles ensuring efficient, disease-free disposal. Society's gift of good hygiene with a scornfully arched eyebrow. And everybody goes along with the program, basic human survival encoded in the brain. Survival and disease inversely correlated. Everyone's complicit in their own disposal at the appropriate time. Efficient. Camp after camp heading west toward The Piles as far as the eye can see.

Alone with these thoughts. Don't let the mind wander aimlessly. Force an intellectualization of this state of mind, of any and all states of mind. Don't become a victim of emotion. Emotion is too susceptible, too risky, when exposed to massive human suffering. Think. Think about something, anything. Crawl inside the head. Make the brain work. A three pound clump of cells. The brain treats rejection like physical pain. It consists of about 100 billion neurons passing signals across 1,000 trillion synaptic connections. Power diminishes empathy. The brain contains zero pain receptors, it feels no pain. It is 73% water. It is two percent of bodyweight. Certainty can be triggered with electric stimulation instead of facts or reasoning. A network of supercomputers. A tiny galaxy inside a hard shell. Perception beyond cognition. Awareness beyond the self. Intuition beyond the Universe. A portal to a space called God. God as a reflection in a mirror. God itself weighing in at nearly three pounds of predominately fatty tissue.

The Archives, a pinhole portal to the past. Weekend's at Grandma's, fishing expeditions down to the pond across fields of wet grass. The doughy smells of yeast and the sheer comfort of belonging. Three-and-a-half feet of pure significance. Importance, real human value. But the past connects to the present, each wrinkle earned or caused, through the sour narrative of a two-decade slog. This narrative, this life. A human through the meat grinder of transformation, the catalytic moments reshaping a man's future. Narcissism, pure unadulterated arrogance, grinding a human being into shredded clots of flesh and bone. Tetterford walked with his tyrannical confidence, hard heels assaulting the floor, into my office that morning. Ten minutes ago or was it twenty years? Time and I have become so vague, irrelevant.

...

"No, please, stay seated John," Tetterford said, a greasy smirk on his face. Hair slicked back, suit and tie immaculate, wire-framed glasses resting miniscule on his boxy, jawboned face. "This won't take but a moment."

"Ok sure, what can I..." was the start of a reply, but he continued instead.

"After discussions with the Board over the weekend, the decision was taken to make numerous structural changes to University operations, as such, your services are no longer needed here." He dropped a white envelope brandishing the university's new logo on my desk, looked around, visually calculating the dimensions of my office, then walked out without another word.

In the ensuing months, the papers revealed how universities around the country were experiencing broadscale organizational shifts. Entire departments gutted, or, if not gutted, under-funded into an anemic shell of its former self. Languages, History, Literature, Philosophy, Politics, Music, Writing, Classics, Anthropology, Archaeology, Studio Art, Dance, Drama, English, Film, Media, Bioethics, Psychology, Religious Studies, most of Education and on and on. In a massive consolidation of the education sector over the previous five years, Education Inc had purchased nearly 90% of universities nationwide and was implementing its restructuring program designed to improve the flailing fiscal situation pummeling higher education. The centerpiece of their restructuring included the elimination of programs not aligned with the *Science Economy*'s nationally strategic objectives.

Concerns for what was occurring nation-wide were very real, but the stress of providing for the family consumed all thoughts and energies. Mere fragments of a social safety net remained, so savings were tapped relentlessly while Sariya baked around the clock for the markets. A blur now, a bad dream, the fragments of memory hard to piece together. An unemployable Innovation Ethics professor selling his garden vegetables to scrape together enough money to buy insulin for his twelve-year-old daughter. Insufficient funds to enter the dialysis clinic. Janine dies. The remaining Voyes' evicted from their home. Sariya's pie money disappears with the ovens and a family of three moves to a church shelter. The church and its property eventually bought by Salvation Inc and the tiny patch of carpet where your family formerly slept is now occupied by a person colloquially referred to as an "Iron" who works at an Atonement Center receiving the telephonic repents of a morally defunct populace. Years evaporate.

What's a family of three to do? Survive. What humans do when pushed to the brink of existence, attempt survival. Herded into one of the many cobbled together tent cities, The Piles. Tent, a generous description for a patchwork of tarps, sheet metal, plywood and any salvaged scrap capable of deflecting the elements. Sleep found atop ragged heaps of blankets peppered with vermin shit and crawling with lice, bedbugs. Waking hours spent coordinating food scavenging efforts with trusted Dhalyte neighbors. Science recategorized us as biologically inferior, hence deemed only partially human and restricted from participating in anything designated for full humans. We smell bad. We eat little. We're not human, not the right sort anyhow. Our shabby appearance alone marks us as capitalism's Dhalytes.

Far from homogenized, Dirts, the epitome of diversification. Former machine-operators, professors, musicians, counselors, preachers, artists, pharmacists, bricklayers, drivers, reporters, writers, welders, scientists, medical doctors. Anything, everything. The illiterate and the PhD. The black, white and every shade in between. The quiet and the outspoken. The kind and the cruel. The optimistic and the pessimistic. Two little traits unifying a people: economic stature and a dreadfully small and underdeveloped *Motum Ducit* area of the hippocampus region of the brain.

We are Dhalytes, to a person. A poor, indistinguishable mass of filth-covered humanity. Less apparent is the second trait binding us as together. It certainly took a brazen bunch of highly compensated neurologists to *identify* this second trait uniting Dirts, laziness. Or, as properly summarized by the esteemed neurological community, *"a substantially diminished Motum Ducit resulting in a virtually unstimulable motivational capacity within the hippocampus."* We the inferior, not blessed with the God-given qualities of ambition and tenacity, therefore not citizens as outlined in the Constitution's 32nd amendment. Bear to look at us, we care not to lift ourselves from our filth, or rather, we are biologically incapable of doing so. Therefore, with a splash of ink, Dhalyte brothers and sisters alike pushed below the law, and, convenient as it was, an overpopulation problem solved immediately by a sixty-percent population reduction.

...

Beyond the Dhalyte-choked roadways branching west from The Archives lies the vastness of The Piles. Home. North and south beyond The Core of the city, the many concrete Blocks housing the Irons. East of The Core are The Bunkers, the fortified secondary, tertiary, quaternary, and on underground estates reserved for Diamonds. The massive Core, where *homo beatus* works, where Platinums reside, where Diamonds bounce between their many specialized satellite homes. Cities across the country oriented in a similar manner the only difference being the relative location of The Piles and The Bunkers depending on the orientation of the coveted coastline.

Walking across the trash-strewn stretch of land between the end of the roadways and the beginning of The Piles, it's difficult not to fall subconsciously into the habit of carefully scrutinizing each piece of trash, search for anything edible. Errant air-drops given the thorough attention merited. Quickly pocket several half-eaten packages of food, a length of rope, a stuffed bear missing arms. Sweat pours from a failing body, wipe it, continue on. Thousands of Dirts mill about listlessly, going through the same exercise, their numbers stretching to the horizon across the drop fields. Surviving. Sifting through the air-dropped trash bags flown over from The Core. The memory of fresh strawberries, corn, the melon which grew in abundance in the garden. Memories of harvests so huge that food was forced on others.

At The Piles' entrance, a swarm of bony, half-naked children crowned with the filthy chaos of unkempt hair, attack a deflated basketball. Kicking, screaming, squealing with the disproportionate amount of enjoyment only the innocent can squeeze from a common experience. Memories of Janine, Ingrid. My girls. Two little girls dragged into this fucked up world. Two girls I couldn't protect. Two little girls who watched in confusion as the world turned its back.

Sidestep the ballgame in progress, swipe away the plastic sheet covering the south entrance to the tent city. Home, its long, dark patchwork corridor funneling to a distant pinhole, a muggy, enveloping warmth. Pervasive stench composed of mildew and feet combines with the vague pungency of rotting flesh wafting periodically in harsh ribbons. Dark, cordoned-off rooms housing families asleep on the floor, huddled talking, or holding vigil over the sick. The noise comes in strange waves as relative silence is broken by a crying baby which inevitably triggers more babies until cacophonous wails unsettle the most stoic. A walk along the musty corridor, about a half mile or so, until the uneven blue letters of "Voyes" stare back, letters scratched upon a wood scrap dangling from a frayed stretch of twine. Inside, Sariya rocks Maven while Valerie placates herself stacking a handful of wood chunks.

"You're back," she says through a weary smile.

"It's good to be back Miss Ribeaux."

"So, how did she look?"

"The same. Exactly the same."

"It's good you went."

"I guess, though I can't make sense of it, why I bother to go there."

35

"You're not alone. Come, sit with us."

The thread of light beaming through the plastic overhead plays on her face, casting wispy eyelash shadows on brown cheeks. She cradles Maven with an arm and reaches around the side of my head with her other, pulling me close, lips to forehead. Maven kicks, jerks her head to the side, before resettling into her dream.

"How is she doing?"

"Much better. Fever is gone, she's less fussy. I think we're in the clear. Been asleep for a while now. And you? How are you feeling?"

"Exhausted. Completely exhausted."

"Certainly understandable."

"Valerie, come over here would'ya sweetheart?"

She sets down her blocks obediently, shuffles to my side, plunks down in my lap with a curiously suppressed smile.

Digging, "I have something for you."

At the sight of the teddy bear, her eyes glow, she grabs it, pulls it to her face.

"What do you say to Gramps?" Sariya asks.

"Thank you Grampa."

"You're welcome dear. So tell me, were you a good girl today?"

No words, just a drumming nod and an examination of her prize.

"That's a good girl."

Hastily, she takes the bear to her blocks which become dinner for the stuffed toy. She provides a mushy chewing soundtrack for the bear.

"Did you find anything else on your way back home or are you heading back out?" Sariya asks.

"As matter of fact I did."

"Excellent! I'll grab the plates."

The bulk of three packages divided into four portions with one pack held back as insurance. Eating in silence, Sariya helps a groggy Maven manipulate her spoon. Valerie takes thoughtful, small bites, chews carefully and doesn't play with her food. Atypical. Never ceases to amaze that even a starving child instinctively builds little mountains, carves tiny trails when given a plate of food, but not this time. Teddy bear altered the moment? Sariya returns pensive eyes, reaches over, a gentle hand squeeze. Ingrid's memory hangs amid Maven and Valerie's cherubic reminder. Like replicas at the respective ages, the chocolate-brown hair, the misty green eyes, and the full, nearly swollen lips. Janine's more distant memory shuffles in second, as usual, stoking the coals of parental guilt. Time blunts everything, eliminates nothing.

Plates ceremoniously wiped after the meal, the illusion of cleanliness. Sariya begins story time with Maven and Valerie. Three beautiful people, the remnants of a family. All of the world's joys and fears packaged together. Life curiously glancing over the precipice, waiting for the inevitable slip and fall. Thoughts never cease, never find a lighthearted counterpoint. What is, exists in this moment alone and isn't expected or retained for the future, no matter how near the future may be. Insidious are the mercurial thoughts of a better tomorrow, a fickle optimism that wants to send roots through the ashes. But, entertaining reveries too long is an attempt to quench thirst with brine.

Sariya nurses my swollen ankles. Sunlight fades overhead and her voice trails off as the grandchildren blink slow with creeping lethargy, grow limp with cadent breathing. Delicate bodies placed on the far corner of the mat entangle in an unconscious negotiation of space, push apart and settle. A tattered blanket tucked under frail limbs, bedtime ritual complete.

She waits on the other end of the mat, engaged in a toothpick manicure, slivers of grime coaxed out with precision. Welcoming with warm eyes, she pats the ground gently. Wrenching coughs shatter the quiet, rusty phlegm coats a hand. Failing health papered over with self-deprecating smiles, careful hands. Laying in silence, talking through our eyes. There is subtle fear in hers, elusive and masked with a contrived over-alertness bending fear into preparation. If that even makes sense. Never-ending stress. A constant vigilance defying the biological rules by not deteriorating her features to the extent of her years. A woman basking in her sunset and amazingly youthful, fresh, a natural beauty and grace. Oddly resilient genes sparing the ravages of time and circumstance. A taut, lean body, borne of a denial of basics, somehow belies starvation's horrors. Physically, she floats above the indecency permeating daily life. She remains beautiful even in the most insignificantly superficial ways. Love bias be damned.

She blinks. It is returned. Straight-line smiles broadcasted on brain waves of the same frequency. A hand squeezed, a nose kissed in return. Time, the ghost between us, only permitted sideward glances. It's palpable, haunting, but not acknowledged. More blood in the handkerchief with each passing day. Fatigue, shortness of breath, aren't concealable in a cloth tucked in a pocket. But she doesn't grace it with notice. She bears her fears well. I'm breaking down. I am dying. A breathtakingly complex disease, or a common bug tamed by medical science decades ago. Doesn't matter. Without a telescope, everything is an unfathomable blip in the sky. But this is not for us. There is no time to fret for ghosts. Live to the last breath. Push until there's no push left. So why speak of it, acknowledge it? Focus on the now and appreciate nights spent blinking at one another in this sublime silence. An encapsulated silence. A bubble of tranquility suspended in the great tempest of our tent city.

Little Priscilla was drugged out of her mind in preparation for her third round of clearly unwanted breast enhancement. After dropping her off for surgery, the woman of the house, feigning ill, skipped work again in a bid for reality show fame. And me, driving north from The Core toward home after a long day's work. Those days, those early days when the apparatus was still consolidating, when it was working feverishly to identify and consolidate the myriad methods for impacting consumer decision making. Working. Working as always. Me. Working as the servile machinist repairing hydraulic cylinders on industrial robotics, the goliaths responsible for care and feeding at The Archives, garbage collection and disease control in The Piles, anything. Everything. Pathetic iron hulks queued on the conveyors, laden with problems beyond the dexterity of repair bots or the computational sophistication of algorithms, defining my sliver of economic worth. Funny how an impossibly complex maneuver for code and metal is oftentimes a simple manipulation for an organic machine with many incremental versions spread across meggannia. Simple manipulations, however tedious, do afford some benefits I guess, even if they only pay a measly Iron wage and repeat without end for fourteen hours a day. The trick is in the training. Training yourself to escape, to retreat inside. To find solace and explore each thought in depth while allowing disembodied fingers to independently clear detritus, isolate problems on cylinders.

But that day. It was on that day, driving home after work mind wandering as usual, flipping indiscriminately through memories for something. A way to kill time. Lady Fortuna's wheel slowed to a stop, her arrow pointing at fate. So, fate it was, had to be considered. Sitting there behind the wheel of the car, those random thoughts about fate dancing on the mind's fringe, eventually melding into a shape. The shape, and the focus that developed it, how it morphed into an exercise in identifying fate's catalysts, a task forcing reflection on the specific point in time when that switch inside dropped. A switch signaling the turning point in my fate. That switch inside me, as it went off, and it's immediate effect. The realization it caused. The realization, pure lucidity, that there was no going back. A line had been crossed. I was becoming a different person, evolution or devolution unknown. And, what triggered the realization, the catalyst, wasn't some profound revelation. It wasn't the recognition of some shocking contradiction, forcing a person to inventory beliefs. Rather, that moment, my moment of abrupt life change, my developing fate, predicated on a single word that jackass used when asking me a banal question on Monday morning. *When*.

Driving north from The Core reflecting on that word, the many thoughts 'any other word spoken, any word other than *when* used in that sentence, and I may not have crossed over, may not have realized, on that particular day.' Though, looking back now, the change was bound to occur regardless. A matter of time. Weeks, months, a year afterwards perhaps, but that particular word on that particular day was the catalyst. That word pushed me over some boundary drawn in my head long before, pushed me toward fate. Must have been. *When*. That word. So assuming. So completely loaded with meaning that it became a catalyst for change. My catalyst for change.

"So Bryson, *when* are you going to buy your Palette?"

The Palette. The ultimate personal device. An electronic tool to improve all aspects of life. A communication device, a media consumption device, a recording device, an automation device, an interpreting device, an everything remote, and a life organization device all embedded in a bracelet and interfaced via hologram. The Palette could do everything. Its aim was to make life easier, more fun, and to connect people and ideas in ways no previous technology had. The Palette, as the rhetoric went, would enable any citizen to become a "life artist", a "creator of their own destiny". Its ridiculously overshooting tagline, *The Palette: Paint the Life that You Want. Today!*

What he, my coworker and consummate sheep, was asking was not my thoughts about or perhaps my interest level in the Palette's latest incarnation. The answers to those questions were predetermined, pointless to ask, stupid even. The age of extreme consumerism had already progressed beyond the need to entice potential buyers, of *selling* product. An ever-decreasing number of producers pimped massive quantities of a tiny range of quality products at rock bottom prices. The odd theater of people crawling atop one another to snatch a priority spot in line to acquire their nugget of homogenized hardware. The twisted humor of how corporations no longer advertised, instead, the ubiquitous plastering of smug *product notifications* informing consumers when and where to buy. And how they bought, without thinking, without considering want, certainly not evaluating need. Peoples' predetermined, focus-group responses to the perception of value and manufactured hype. And the tax breaks, oh the tax breaks! Our patriotic legislators tripping over themselves to give content producers massive tax breaks, driving prices through the floor, facilitating ownership, adoption, absorption. 'Technical saturation', a shrewd policy component of the larger Science Economy initiative. *The Civilized Dream*, for a civilized society. Everyone, regardless of socio-economic status, able to afford a roof, transportation, food, healthcare, but most importantly, unlimited media content. The consumer as king in this dream, sated on the very basics and primed to grow fat and stupid on a steady diet of audio visual noise.

My coworker, pursuing the dream by fervently consuming everything available to his kind. In reality, he wasn't asking me a question so much as he was sparking bland dialog, asking a rhetorical on a Monday morning as his brain was slowly caffeinated to life. He didn't have reason to doubt I was standing on pins and needles, waiting for the new gadget to descend from heaven. He knew I was primed, just as ready as him. What he wanted to know was if I'd like to go with him during lunch to pick one up at the Distro. It was that word, that fucking *when*, propelling me over the line. The realization that the joke was on us.

On that day, home from The Core, sitting in a cold, dark room continuing to ponder life's possible trajectory. The structures, the institutions, the norms, the overcrowded nonsensical everything defining modernity. Staring out the apartment's tiny window at the towering, brown buildings kissing blue sky above. Hives of worker bees living in pods, driving mini-pods to arrive at factory-sized pods to make contraptions to distract a population of undisciplined, agitated souls. Help lines a mere button-push away, the place to call to free your mind from the burden of the day's accumulated sins. An ignorant, self-obsessed clot of bodies concerned solely with scratching itches. A tormented sea of instant-gratification junkies. And, well beyond the bounds of The Core, a defective hoard starving on one side, and a evolution's cream living in subterranean opulence on the other. And separating humanity's poles, the Irons, we Irons, the flesh and blood buffer in between. The human DMZ, etched proudly in law as the heart and soul of civilization. Society's foundation. Sitting there, reflecting, how it was difficult not to mentally loop on the idea of ignorance. How pervasively viral it was, is. How it distracts. How unapologetically oppressive, despotic its nature. The sheer leverage it offers those using it as a means of control. And then, as reflection gathered steam, she came home. The most utterly distracted of them all.

Dressed in a rhinestone-caked bodysuit, beeping and flashing all over, she walked through the door carrying Priscilla's furry, compact body. Sweet little Priscilla, her distended belly wrapped in bandages, trotted here and there, happy to be clear of the veterinarian's knife. Flipping back plaited strips of chromium hair with an impatient wrist, wifey was clearly annoyed. Her many lifts, implants, rhinoplasties, mentoplasties, otoplasties, blepharoplasties, and rhytidectomies had locked her face into a particularly sunny interpretation of the world, regardless of the world. That day, the few living tissues she still wielded control over were taut, indicating she was experiencing something unpleasant. The expression on her face was something of confusion, the sort of mental twist a drunk experiences when attempting to tie the laces on his sandals. Years of interpreting facial expressions informed that the appearance of confusion was a decoy, an unintended trick. Subsurface was the bubbling cauldron of unspecified volatility.

Priscilla, circling madly and gnawing at the bandages encasing her torso, didn't acknowledge us, instead, cycloned in the hall yelping and gnashing her teeth. As her yelps softed, the growing silence obligated the question, carefully innocuous tones chosen, "What happened?"

"What happened? Fucking nothing, that's what the hell happened. I sat on the sidewalk at the studio for something like twelve hours in a line that never fucking moved. All these stupid bitches around me running their mouths, talking about how *they* are the best fit for the show, how perfect their bodies are, and yada, yada, blah, blah, blah all day long. Line doesn't move, I don't even get close to the door, nobody from the show talked to me. Sitting on a concrete path for an entire day, sweating, nowhere to piss, listening to this bullshit, missing a day's pay. And above all, this bitch has the nerve to tell me I'm in the wrong line. So I went off, yelling, swinging. We got to fighting, and because my slap landed perfectly on her dogface, the security guard tells me if I don't settle he'll boot me from the line. Yeah, me! Believe that? Bitch, all of them. Every single fucking one of them. My nerves are shot, busted. Move, I'm going neural."

The immediate regret for faking interest in her latest reality show tryout. Forever the same story. Stupid bitches, long lines, violence. Always lots of violence. Fumbling, to manufacture sympathies, "I'm sor..."

"And you know what else?" she barked, "Priscilla's surgery isn't fully covered by GoverMed cause it's her third round! Yeah, goddamn insurance only covers two rounds of elective K-9 surgery on the same appendage now. Sort of bullshit is that? Hell, the only reason for the third was because the second was a hack job!"

She had spun back into the room, poor Priscilla, knotty tufts of bloodied fur poking from her mouth. Looking into her sad eyes. She looked back up at me, pitifully, begging to be extracted from her inner tube of weeping gauze. Or perhaps, begging to drop her from the balcony, a peaceful splat. Her third breast surgery. The first round to resolve wifey's unhappiness with her *six unfortunate bee stings*. Healed, Priscilla unwittingly pranced a half-dozen plump nodules around the apartment at night for us. Of course it was a matter of time before the next enhancement was sought. Apparently the size was ideal, but Priscilla's tits needed to match the shape of hers, the latest fashion trend. Unfortunately, surgery two produced an imperfect shape so a third was pursued for a Chihuhua's raw, festering underbelly.

"Well, that's uh, that's unfortunate." A lament for the money we didn't have.

"*Unfortunate*? Fucking *unfortunate*, that's all you've got to say? Little short of the mark dontcha think? Where exactly do you think we'll get the thirty-five Credits to pay for this goddamn procedure?"

The default answer would have been savings if there was such a thing. Forty-three years of combined work, not a Credit to show for. The follow up, a clear memory, an answer chosen for its lack of accusation, its implied sympathy.

"I guess we'll figure it out."

But that drive home and fate's catalyst pushed me into new territory. How ideas started to take shape, become clear. No longer was it *we'll*. It was *I'll*. I'll figure it out. A way out. A way out of this hell. This twisted life. This joke of a life. Acrimony. Pointless stimulation, perverted consumption, abasement. Life in full sprint with eyes deliberately clenched shut for fear of seeing something undesirable, something unwanted.

...

So now, where do things stand? Years since Priscilla's faulty implants killed her, even more since the incident of *when*. Today, here, driving home again. The looping, the mental looping, stuck on the thought that driving anywhere but home is preferential. The famished Piles. Restricted Bunkers. The desolate Wastelands. Each, a better option than The Blocks and her monkey house.

Uneventful as usual. Long lines of steadily flowing traffic, clots of cars parsed by massive, overlapping arterial roads leading to The Blocks. Each mobile container delivered promptly to the appropriate tower. Efficient. *Whoosh!* There they go, my fellow members of section 84, breaking off from Block C arterial, and me, obediently following the happy pack. A constipated turd trundling toward an expanding circle of light, a single, orderly channel of passage.

Bryson, your toothpaste will be gone in 4 days, the third tooth on your comb is about to break off, your deodorant has eight uses left, and you are down to your last bar of soap. Bathroom Inc is having a 15% off sale this weekend, plus, they are offering a free bottle of Arnando Vas Deferen's new scent, **Ejaculate!***, with a minimum twenty Credit order.*

She's so helpful.

Traffic continues. Then, the big split from section 84 traffic into subsection 38, and descend into the storage deck beneath the tower. Spot 827d, tidy rectangle of pavement, where the mobile container spends one-third of its life. Power down. And the typical question emerges, "How long will I sit here before heading up to the apartment? One hour? Two?" If only sleep could be achieved sitting upright. If only humans could shrink to gnat-size, this car could be my entire world.

Bryson, your heart rate is 10% lower than usual. You only have one can of cherry NeverSleep in the fridge. Time to reorder! Do you want me to place the order now?

Last week's fight marinates the mind. Heated. More heated than normal, caustic. Suited up and locked into a game of ORGY on the SensaGame console. Oh!, stupid me. Why did I let the apartment door close upon its full weight, disturbing her concentration? The thud, shattering critical focus, jerked her from the fellatio position. Precious seconds lost toward achieving her final climax count.

"Congratulations!" an asinine host yelped, "You tied your previous high score! Sixty three men in one hour! Impressive and puts you in the top ten percentile among your network! But, to catch Porn Inc's master guzzler Mrs. Magnifislurp you'll need to work harder Corinne!"

Bathed in real sweat, huffing, she turned to me, "YOU PIECE OF SHIT!"

Bryson, do you want me to order the NeverSleep?

Disagreements at this point, exercises in premature escalation. I knew better. I knew enough to glide along the path of least resistance. How many times had that path been spit-polished, me, a beam of ultraviolet light? Quick, quiet and invisible. The encounters, none of them began with conciliation. Vitriol immediately lobbed as positions established in the previous fight were resumed. Our anti-greeting. And I knew this! So why with the door, why not be more careful?

"I's ONE goddamn blow from beating my all-time high asshole, thanks for wrecking my score! I'll never catch Mrs. Magnifislurp! And jackass, for the last time, the living room's mine until 10 PM! Can't you push that through your thick, fucking skull?"

My presence, the worst kind of nuisance.

"What can I say? I came home."

"Don't patronize me, you bastard! As if I give a shit. Don't you have anything better to do? Fall out a window, drive off a bridge, chug some bleach, hang yourself in the closet? I have wire if you need it, oh, here, come, come, I'll set it up for you!"

Bryson?

45

A nonchalant middle finger. Odd, as her frequent pleads for my suicide never registered in the past, never garnered response. And she seethed, throat rumbling, she stomped toward her neural station in the back of the apartment. Stupid me to think she intended to log on, turn on The Pine and watch her shows for the rest of the evening. Returning seconds later, sweat dripping from her latex suit and showcasing a face never seen, wielding a baton, threatening to smash my head. The search for the right appeal, terms she could understand.

"If you kill me, they'll throw you in a hole with nothing! Your games, your shows, all your glittery shit, gone! Think about it you crazy idiot!" Had the mad clown reached a breaking point? A point where a diminished capacity to reason was trumped by a highly developed faculty for reaction, constantly honed by systematically sating every base want. The squealing, the hurling of everything in reach and the struggle to keep the larger objects in the room between us. Our domestic dance around the room, running and dodging while she highlighted plans for my slumbering mariticide. How some powerful grandfather of hers could disappear me, the idle threat of each battle. Until, she grew tired, distracted. As her red peaked, she lost the will to attack, retreating instead to her neural, baton in white-knuckled hand. And me, careless, insignificant me. Collapsed but alert on the couch, safety's lonely vigil, until the sun told me I was late for work.

Bryson? Bryson, I can offer you a discount if you purchase a full case of NeverSleep. 7% off an immediate purchase.

That day, all the days, in the making starting a long time ago. But, finding a new place in The Blocks, yeah right. Impossible task. Some reason about construction starts halting, wasn't that the official line? The extremely strapped taking on couch-hangers in their pursuit of a few sustaining Credits. With no way out, each day was just another spar for the big one. A relationship deteriorating further. Unbearable becoming dangerous. Dangerous becoming life-threatening. And how once upon a time, we tried to be the compatible couple. Build a nest. Do the kid thing. Just wasn't in the cards. Each fight trucing with the fertilization of a new seed, a seed dissolved with a pill concluding the next blowout. Cycle after cycle, the clarity of fate. There it is again, fate. Staying together, the result of limited habitable options. The only option. To serve basic needs, life's priority. Life's focus. Happiness, that feeling you get when you empty your bladder. When you slake a thirst. When you fall asleep without fearing for your life.

Bryson? Bryson? Bryson, I can offer you a 9% discount if you purchase two full cases. Do you want me to put the order through?

Oh right, her.

"No. Do not place an order for *NeverSleep*."

Not even at the discount price?

"No. Not even." Yelling at an algorithm, futility defined. Remain calm.

So, here. Parked. Sitting. Is it better to perpetually shift, constantly search for the comfortable position that doesn't exist in the car? Or. Face her and hopefully achieve horizontal refreshment. Prone yet vulnerable. Here, a thirty percent recline. Three inches of headroom. Partially extended legs. Peace and quiet amid the line of similarly oriented heads. Here must suffice. Nestle into the most comfortable position possible, the mind will eventually drift to the future. A future of nothingness. A sublime happiness living in a void barely big enough to hold my body, breathing just enough to stay alive. A belly just full enough for the organs to play their tune. Nothing but my mind locked into a permanent state of contemplation, an exhaustive exploration of the innumerable thoughts cached in the mind. Does it matter if I find the answers? Does it matter if I'm alone? Does subjugation matter? Does it matter if I own nothing? Does it matter if this is just a bad dream?

Bryson, brushing with Denteriffic! before sleeping reduces enamel decay by 23%.

Good night world.

Bryson?

Underground, between Judy's cars the engine's whirring slows. Clicking heels on concrete echo faintly before dissipating in the cavernous garage. *Honey, I'm home and I'm no longer employed, uh... sorry about that!* No, frivolous positivity. The elevator descends, welcoming stainless sterility, and the doors chomp shut. Don't be flippant, inappropriate. The powerful, high-quality thud of solid steel doors bumping. *Honey, I've got some bad news...* doors pull apart to the back hallway. Nailed to the wall, the same blue flag with red graffiti seen outside. Gut lurches viciously, gasping, coughing, steadying hand against elevator wall. Composure! Elevator doors slam, a return to the metal box. Uncomfortable sterility. Choppy breathes, the flash of several years; birthday cakes, school shoes, wet kisses, wine glasses, skinned knees, dinner tables, sandy beaches, leg hugs, naked bodies, smooth skin, story time, yelling matches, sobbing make-ups, smiling faces, painful tears, sad goodbyes, ecstatic hellos, supple breasts, swollen belly, pain love and hurt bundled together. Into the hallway, one step closer to the tattered little flag, dried red paint frozen mid-drip on the wall. Knee gives out, a thudding foot claps the wood floor. This automatic walking continues, rubber legs. An exhaust fan hums in space. Hallway ends, opens to the kitchen. Rubber legs bend to floor, head rush, a violence known as heaving into the black.

When dreaming, your rational mind rarely considers the logic of what's going on around you. Very little, if any, energy is spent considering how you instantly acquired superhuman capabilities or how you ended up in such surreal circumstances. The brain seems to take each newly created piece of information and handle it much the same way a conscious person would handle, say the opening of a birthday present from a friend. The contents wrapped inside are unknown, but exist within a realm of imaginable possibilities therefore minimizing the amount of surprise any single gift could generate for the recipient. In the dream, once you acquire the ability, to say, fly, you don't waste energy trying to figure out the metaphysics of why you have the ability or how you acquired the ability. Rather, you take what is given and use it in whatever capacity makes sense given the circumstances. Much in the same way if someone gives you a new stereo as a birthday present, you don't spend time pondering how the stereo found its way into the box or how the stereo in and of itself came to be. You cordially accept the gift, thank the giver and wax ecstatic on the gift's usefulness, the thoughtfulness of the giver. Thus is the nature of surprises that exist within a known range of outcomes. Bounded surprises.

Unbounded surprises in life mete a considerably different effect on the recipient, and as these thoughts loop, this dream state dissolves. Why is there strange vomit on my face and what is this odd, bloody mess? "Did the dream start or just end? How did this? Who did this happen? Meaning what? Where was involved, I mean, where is this, or where am I?" A reality starts to build itself back into shape. Unaccountable anger and the suffocation of overwhelming heartache. Sitting upright, but not really, because I could be floating, flying.

I could be dreaming or getting ready to open a present.

Clarity always renders in accordance with time. Sitting in the stench of my vomit, paralyzed for what feels like an hour, perhaps a day. Reality creeps. Limbs refuse to move, yawn at each attempt, flaccid in their numbness. A crusty coating cracks each time the scene before me causes a wince. Dried tears?

Unbounded surprise. Dream or no dream?

A macabre circus frozen in time. Judy's head lies in Muhammad's lap, the majority of her torso lies across Magdalene's. My babies on opposing sides of the room. Judy's arms and legs, dangling from the pot rack, intermingle with the pots and pans reflecting glints of silver light. Crimson pools cover the countertop, floor. Heave and prostration. Saliva strings, tears and snot in a gooey mixture on floor. Dream? Dithering clarity and repetitious thoughts about stereos, gifts, superhumans flying. Everything vile. The fleeting fantasy of a bullet coursing through my head. Looping. Looping.

Everything tangential. Muhammad and Magdalene sit erect, face each other, backs against cabinets, hands tied behind backs, eyes closed. Magdalene's chest. Rising. Falling. Rising. Falling.

That first memory of The Piles, about four years old? Dad loving me like his own, walking to the crumbling roads leading east toward The Core. Always toting that well-worn, well-loved soccer ball. The ball, constantly limp, Dad doing his best to keep it inflated with massive lung pressure through a funny, metal cylinder, a crude straw. How we played for hours at a time, running back and forth along the broken macadam between makeshift goal posts of stacked **Limestone. Limestone, a sedimentary rock composed largely of calcite and aragonite, which are different crystal forms of calcium carbonate ($CaCO_3$). Limestone makes up roughly 10% of the total volume of all sedimentary rock on earth. Karst landscapes. Toothpaste. Chemical feedstock. Paint.**

The first memory from childhood, unpleasant. Not of an exciting game or a poignant dribbling lesson. Rather, that first memory, Dad's inadvertent vocabulary lesson. Taught on a sunny afternoon on approach to the flat stretch of pavement where we played, flecks of mica in asphalt sparkling like stars in the night sky. That man lying in the center of our playing field, curled in a fetal ball, resting on his side, hands shimmed beneath his head propping it off the pavement. Approaching, Dad bending down, called to wake him. When he didn't move, Dad, hesitantly, giving the man a nudge on his shoulder. Again, but nothing. Dad, resigned, rolled the man onto his back, an arm and a leg slapped limp on the road, a bare chest pointed skyward. Dad sighing, said 'a maze, he ate it'. A series of well-defined bones created a maze on the man's chest. Reaching to trace the lines of the man's maze, but Dad stopping my finger before it began. Dad handing over the ball, told me to pile up the goal posts, while he dragged the man to the road's edge. Searching for a few minutes, he returned with a threadbare blanket and laid it atop the man before joining me on the field to play. We played.

Played for hours while the maze man laid on the sideline, a quiet spectator. Years later, time spent with Dad, missed. His comments, as he squatted over that man, nothing to do with a maze. A dead man flipped over, 'emaciated' working its way from Dad's lips.

Stars observed from beyond this plastic window, childhood memories sorted and the ground cool against my skin. Skin, the product of unknown intermingling. The Asian in me, the South American, African. The many twisted ladders entering Mom on the night she was assaulted. Me, Aphamli Twist, a typical Dirt, typical complexion, scratching out an animal's life on the shit-scented side of town. Blind stars glitter above. Fucking crying babies, plastic crinkling, personal evacuations, screams. Chaotic cacophony. Mom and Dad dying from the bug, me, the plug, the purpose in someone else's life. Gerald Patel, a good man. Needed a reason to keep pushing after his wife's death. Me, the perfect project. This is life stars, pay attention. Mr. Patel, a good man, Dad's hunting buddy. Lead violinist in a former life, performing with the City Orchestra until the organization was de-funded, imploded. Mr. Patel, musical genius turned master scavenger. Tucked in his cell amid tattered blankets and plastic sheeting - a collection of the best finds in The Piles. Among them, his books, dozens, including the sadly estranged "L" volume of some antiquated encyclopedia set. Mr. Patel's library, a boy's treasure.

And the Goddamn babies keep crying, never shut up, a **Lance (a pole weapon, often equipped with a vamplate, used by mounted warriors in Medieval Times)** through the eardrum. Noise pierces through tender flesh with melting hot ease. Tears, their cynically diminishing value upon increase. Fall into the easy trap of hating victims, don't. Calm.

The products of Mr. Patel's obsessive scavenge hunts, and the exposure they offered, insight into other worlds. Tinkering with myriad fragments of electronic components brought home, tangled stuff in tattered cardboard boxes. Books read a hundred times over. Seed experiments when rare bits of discarded fruit found. Fashioning toys and tools from random scraps of metal, wood and plastic. A lion hauling kill to its vulnerable young holed up in the den. Patel, bent on making certain his little project developed a concrete understanding of how the physical world worked. To know how to manipulate objects into use. His obsession, his decadence, a nervous tick? Or a way to preserve sanity, divert energy, from realities to possibilities. Why didn't he teach the how and why of circumstances? The ignorant, self-indulgent, power-hunger of man? Mr. Voyes, filling educational gaps.

Mr. Voyes, man of questions, always asking them, always asking me to ask them. Nothing in the universe was settled, everything remained in flux well after answers were found. Especially after the answers were found. His struggle with any, all universal ideas. Laughing at the notion of a deterministic truth. How he constantly offered opinions and ideas before cutting the knees of both in the next sentence. A walking contradiction, constantly at odds with everything he seemed to believe. Constantly searching for meaning and explanation. Little Aphamli, one of his obsessions. Hell-bent on peeling back man's veneer so the little Twist boy could view the wobbly machinery beneath.

Five years this month, the first encounter with Mr. Voyes. Dead eleven months and this creeping anger grows. Difficulty sleeping, difficulty remaining in any position of rest or relative comfort. Agitation. This perpetual nervous tick, a constant aggressive energy tearing, rippling. Less rest equals more charge, evermore awake. Repeat. Like the maze man and Mom and Dad's death, Mr. Voyes death, a moment in life where everything recycles back into question. Everything loses form and shape. This time, things feel different. Mr. Voyes' death and the thin rod of steely resolve welded to consciousness. A single obligation welded to my conscience, legacy's call from beyond the veil. Our many discussions, countless verbal spars centering on those big ideas, looping infinitely. What are my responsibilities going forward?

Babies keep crying devalued tears.

What is painfully clear is that my mettle is untested, unknown. Me, the nobody. Fumbling with concepts that overshadow any action ever taken, the natural response, to wither. Tap out. Fade. Just go away. But, this increasingly unsettled state, the sleeplessness. Push out. Push against the confidence-withering fears. Build courage by whatever means necessary. Juvenile, bombastic? Who gives a shit? Launch into a superhero montage, puff up into confidence, childish inflation, rip at the bootstraps. It's nothing, a mechanism of motivation. Concealed, my embarrassment only.

I stand, confidently bent to the wind on a stormy precipice (queue wind, hair and clothing whip). A God rising among jealous onlookers (stern, envious looks), wishing they possessed the fortitude to seize the moment. Instead they yield (no sustained, direct eye contact), take refuge in my ability to protect, locked into mortal man's unabated fear of the unknown. And my flaws, my unfortunately inseparable humanness, is forgiven because of the priceless nature of deliverance. Me, the infallible, accepting their praise (massive applause, cheers and whistles) with the dignified humility of those exalted (with just a vague smile, no, no smile, just the eyes squinting ever so slightly in response).

Sad, exciting, overwhelmingly pathetic. A daydream shredding the confidence it's meant to build. Writhing thoughts spawning themselves out of thin air. Acute self-absorption; me contemplating me, giving myself the accolades of others, accolades for situations that haven't occurred by people that don't exist for realities that never will be. Silly, puerile. How to reconcile? How to find comfort in the unknown? How do people lead? Oh isn't that nice, tears. Silly fucking tears. A man, right? Head, heart and body indecipherable mixed into a sloppy whole. There is no reconciliation, never was, no path to comfort. Push, the desideratum of bootstrapping. Push, whatever the mechanism. Tears in the process. Trapped, a mind that has completely exhausting anything to ponder in this tiny domain, extend outward for new channels of self-evolution. Anger in the process. An eight-by-eight cell. How to balance my single plate, my single knife, and my single fork against these big ideas? A tiny stack of books against zealous ambitions. Fear in the process. Compare a dirty pile of blankets to a bed of material they call "silk". In the corner it screams, wants recognition. The old, tattered suitcase sitting beneath plastic sheeting. Hope wiggles in. With its implied failure, "hope" glows cold with a vague sense of unmerited optimism. Poignant hope, sharp and evocative, the memory of virginity lost. Drawing saliva like the **Lemon (a small evergreen tree native to Asia that produces an acidic, ellipsoidal yellow fruit used in both culinary and non-culinary applications)** mentioned in the estranged L. Hope and a suitcase pacify long, sleepless nights. Tears will be there. It comes down to courage in the end. When everything's lost, that's all there is. Do I possess the will, the grit, to step up? The dream where everyone dies and a whisper of dust blankets a lonely earth.

Until the moment comes, just waste away here. Alone among the millions, lacking everything except thoughts, carefully manufactured aspirations. We, the silent, inhuman majority. The lazy. Useless beings are we, not blessed with the right genetic formula, not worth counting. Surviving, the sheer human desire not to go extinct, not to settle in pre-dug graves. And the babies keep crying. Crying for deliverance, the mercy of a preemptive slaughter. But they must go on, right? Innocent possibilities. Everyone's naive hope amid the stink of death. Coddle that tiny bundle of hope, a **Lottery (a form of gambling which involves the drawing of lots for a prize**) ticket one is too timid to scratch for fear of realizing loss, continuing the slide into finality. Bony lottery tickets, the reason to hunt for paste even though you're really hoping to find a mountain of **Lorazepam (a high-potency, intermediate-duration, 3-hydroxy benzodiazepine drug used primarily to treat anxiety disorders. Lorazepam has all six intrinsic benzodiazepine effects: anxiolysis, anterograde amnesia, sedation/hypnosis, anti-seizure, antiemesis and muscle relaxation)** to quiet the self-hate. Narcotize the neurons. Life on the shifting slope between hope and fear.

A dinner plate, utensils. To feel. The skin registering an acute stimulus. Shatter numbness. Pique consciousness. Baby steps to inevitability? Maybe a clarity oozes? Sawing back and forth, the dull blade reciprocates across my forearm. Seconds of dull, frictional pressure, a drop balloons, pools with others. Gravity draws them under, a circle of red. The cut, drops rubbed between automatic fingers. Wet then viscous, progressing to an aerated stickiness. It's blood, real blood. Really sticky blood. Really fucking pointless. No answers. No relief. No control.

Drying blood, *why*? Why do it? What's the point, the purpose, meaning? Marked only by its regularity. Its lack of definition. Maybe a stupid animal doesn't understand, can't understand, the motives for actions taken. Not enough will or drive to figure out what to do or how to do it, instead react with opaque emotion to the environment. Stomach grumbles? Eat, assuming there is food. No food? Hunt. Hunt unsuccessfully? Get tired, rest. Wake up hungry again? Restart hunt. Get lucky, find abundance of food? Gorge. Over-gorge, vomit? Store vomit for later. After gorging, food remains? Down time. Down time available? Mind works. Mind starts working? Explore divergent paths.

I am a useless, lazy Dirt.

I am the unknown hope for millions.

Scratch dried flecks of blood, focus on the latter, how to be the man Mr. Voyes thought I could be? Everyday people die younger and younger, no change in sight. Occasionally, a small band of men charge anemically toward The Core with sticks, rocks, crude blades. Ghosts, never heard from again. Most conserve energy, hunt, attempt to keep the family upright a few more weeks, months, years if lucky. People used to group, hold discussions, attempt plans on how to overcome. But, despondency creeps. The weak are easily overwhelmed, too hungry to waste time and effort organizing. Basics of maintenance, trash disposal, and order, addressed by vocal elders, relics of improbability.

Suicide plague. Many arriving at the blunt realization: there is no reason to exist. Many trick the mind for a time. The untrickable grab rope, twine, a length of twisted plastic sheeting, head for the hanging gardens beyond the far edge of the drop fields. A lonely place, thousands pendulating in the breeze. A quiet place to go and reflect, or just go.

What if it's true? What if we are inferior, living like this because we are lesser beings? Why then should we bang heads against inevitability? Can I prove wrong the scientists who defined the Homo beatus, Homo sapian split? Most tell themselves mankind's division was an economic response to the double disaster of financial calamity and pandemic. But, what if? Isn't everything nested in a modicum of truth? Why did we end up in this similar, impoverished existence? The Piles, on a smaller scale, existed before The Super Depression. Before The Bug. Measures of motivation, tenacity and ambition aren't binary, they are gradients between people, right? A continuum of relative strength, weakness. Seems plausible. Could The Pile's first inhabitants have possessed the smallest possible *Motum Ducit*, and those who joined later possessed marginally larger regions? Are we too lazy to give exhaustive consideration to the supporting science, choosing instead to believe in easy conspiratorial narratives about an economic fix, a population reorg?

But, anger, endless plotting. Efforts with Mr. Voyes over the years, his suitcase, the relentless scheming to meet his expectations. Measures of motivation, aren't they? Every waking moment beyond the hunt devoted to preparation, devoted to the plan. When of sound mind, work to complete exhaustion. Maybe mine is not the ideal way to spend energy in Beatus' eyes, but it is energy spent, in large quantities on behalf of my people. My Dirts. And we count too even if we are different.

Sometimes it's more settling to be hungry and engaged in the all-out hunt for food. A hunting brain doesn't cycle so fast, froth the emotions. Thinking, so counterproductive when it detracts from survival. Miles of drop fields strewn with garbage, survival dispersed somewhere within. Scarcely ever, a bag filled with the best, unscathed foods. A charitable plant by a Beatus with a conscience? Or, an anomaly, a mistake? Those in and around The Core know, clearly, don't they? They too are some kind of human. Is it possible that as the *Motum Ducit* grows, it consumes the prefrontal cortex in equal proportion? Maybe it's decidedly human to white-knuckle everything until it is ripped from us, soul be damned.

Pat, Pat, Pat

"Pham, you awake?" William asks, popping his head through my tarpaulin door.

"Yeah, how'd you know?"

"That restless shifting didn't sound like sleep."

"Sorry, I hope it didn't wake you."

"Nah, not me. Can't sleep anyway. Haven't found much in them last few days, starting to keep me wake at this point," he says. "You know when the acid starts creeping up from y'stomach, stings the chest? Well that's where we're at."

Baiting, putting the information out there. Courting serendipity. Bones in his shoulders, humeri are not visible yet, doubtful he's here to beg. When did someone last ask outright? His leak, not a question. No requirements. No obligations. No bad feelings one way or the other.

"You know Will, I have some extra, got lucky yesterday." Shuffle to the bin. From it, a jar of pale green, then a quick shuffle back to him. Goodbye glance to jar, "You mind returning the jar tomorrow?"

"Yeah, yeah of course. Thanks Aphamli, thanks so much man. And thanks from Reanne too," he says, turning, tears pooling on the cusps of his eyelids. "I'll bring yer jar back first thing in the morning." He pulls the tarp, hesitates, looks back sheepish, "Thanks Pham". His face laden with shame, embarrassment. Frustrated enough to scream, hungry enough to eat the jar and its contents, and sad enough for the hanging gardens. The falling tarp reflects the moon's dim glow as William's tarp crinkles, wakes Reanne. What more could a six-year-old want at 2 AM than a few swallows of green shit?

It comes at a cost, but yesterday was full of good fortune. Nine jars now in the bin, the transporting giggles of an ecstatic girl are equitable compensation for the missing tenth. Focus, burn fuel efficiently. Many details to work out.

A blink, her last perhaps, pushes a tear. Did she pass? Can't tell. Can't speak. Can't move. What now? Who's left watching over me? Throat's hot, could use a drink. She's gone, for sure, she's gone. Her eyes, gazing static through me into some far off realm. She bore it, the entirety of it. Stayed with me through thick and thin. The physical, emotional distance. The infidelities. The Collapse. She could have left. Gone to her sister's. Instead, she stayed. For one reason or another she stayed, collecting abuses and gifts in equal measure. What was her final thought as she left this world in pain? Did she know this was coming? She blame me for it? Was she rational enough to see the bigger picture? Do I even care? I should have answers for simple questions, but perception is tricky behind the mask. If there's existence beyond here, reconcile the fragments there, do a better job with the apology game. For decorum's sake at least.

Euphoria rising, scant oxygen in the pipes. Colors, fizzling on the peripheries, closing toward center. Is anything making sense? Does it even matter? Did anything ever matter? Blips on a screen. Sunshine on a face. A memory of stars on a clear night. Seconds, how they tick by in oddly lucid fashion. Helplessness as relaxation, forced comfort. No pain, just this detached reflection. THERE IT IS AGAIN! Instantaneous, a light switch flicking on, back to the *how*. *How* did we get here? The question, an echo folding back onto itself with infinitely decreasing volume. *HOW? WOH, How? Woh, how? woh, how?* Search for it. Pick through the fragments of memory emerging at random, the first falling raindrops, indicative of the impending torrent. Must be something useful here. Tall buildings. Unfriendly faces, wrestling, discussing. Dark shadows passing easily through stoic glasses of water perched on a conference table, the occasional stripe of red, blue, green interspersed. Deluge.

...

We worked in lockstep with the Corp legislators developing the mutually beneficial game show. The Corps were busy pushing their *Science Economy* agenda, that legislative ingenuity designed to subsidize entertainment ventures with even a vague whiff of economic growth potential. On paper, *How Far Will You Go?* was the perfect venture, providing a new flavor of low-cost entertainment for the easily beguiled Irons. The Corps had recently passed legislation legalizing game shows for the "nihilistic entertainment" format on the basis that new show proposals met three criteria: (1) the subscription cost for Irons was nominal, (2) new Platinum jobs were created, and (3) a guaranteed four-month ROI for Diamond investors, *Cha-ching!* And the unspoken, most important, fourth criteria; substantive contributions to reelection coffers for Corps legislators.

HFWYG was a focus-group success ahead of its primetime launch, plucking the basest entertainment desires like so many steely strings. It was clear *HFWYG* featured that critical vicarious appeal Iron viewers required, so much so that several underperforming shows were canceled upon its lauded launch. Revenue forecasts, while difficult to pinpoint precisely, indicated the new game show would provide a return to investors within three episodes. No pilot necessary, full steam to the black ink.

As the returns for *HFWYG* hit unprecedented levels, *Cha-ching!*, Corps at each level of the government reaped the benefits, bolstering election funds to ensure the Citizens, the Religious and the Radical parties were discretely sabotaged many years into the future. Iron viewer demand reached full saturation meriting a tri-weekly broadcast. The magic of a shared, participatory viewing experience! How it's alluring to watch a train crash, but even more fun to compete against others to cause it. As demand peaked, live-recordings were expanded to new cities enabling more Irons around the country to become contestants rather than idle spectators. *Fever Pitch*, the name dayshift Irons gave to the one hour between getting off work and the live *HFWYG* airtime at 9PM on Mondays, Wednesdays and Fridays. Bets taken on whether contestants would be criminally charged, whether deaths would occur, or if property damage estimates would exceed defined thresholds. *HFWYG*-themed bars in The Blocks filled beyond capacity during Fever Pitch as patrons settled in to watch two hours of government-sanctioned anarchy.

Andrea Silva, that woman. Yeah, Andrea Silva, contestant of the year! An immediate inductee into the *HFWYG HALL OF FAME*. The most ambitious contestant in the show's history. How she shook off the substantial legal advise sought prior to air-time. She wanted to make her mark on history, do it her way, do it the way only a consummate psychopath could. How she basked onscreen in the sheer brutality of her actions. The easy smiles, the carefree way she lit fuses. The way she played to, flirted with, the camera. How you could sense the satisfaction she squeezed from each moment in the limelight. All eyes please. Her complete absorption in her work, as though the substantial prize money she stood to win didn't even factor. Andrea Silva. Low on intellect, and not a creative cell in her body. On contingency she invested in strategic play services, *HFWYG* show consultants helping her carve a violent path to the winner's circle. After all the strategic plotting, the final outstanding question was, would Andrea's legal counsel provide adequate defense to avoid permanent lockup, or even execution, after her win? A question considered, but certainly not laid to rest, in the standard, pre-show risk and reward analysis conducted as a service for contestants. The sort of standard *HFWYG* calculus justifying the employment of a small army of judicially-minded Platinums, a contestant service to channel the typical one-third of contestant winnings back to Barristers Inc. *Cha-ching!*

How we insulated ourselves from everything. Watch Inc, as a whole, liability-free, even while providing the detailed action plan to Andrea, helping her seal victory over the less vicious. Responsibility for actions, not ideas. The brilliant corporate structure of Watch Inc, distinguishable and easily parsed layers, an onion, spanning out fibrously from a tender center. If *HFWYG* Consulting is found liable, peel that layer off, throw away the liability. Risk isn't mitigated, it is eliminated outright using the legal cipher crafted by well-funded Corps legislators. Simple and clean.

And how even when everything went completely awry, the legal cushions protected us. The 146 Iron children killed, the hundreds injured, after Andrea's firebombs ripped through the elementary school, cost only a half-day of lost work. Acting gloomy before a panel of "Citizen's Party" legislators for a bout of public shaming. The many cues to listen for, to apply the appropriate heart-felt reactions.

That gritty, militaryesque southern twang, "Listen up guys. When the congressman says 'moral obligation', take a moment to really flatten out your lips, give a long, lost stare down at your testicles. And when he says, 'fiduciary responsibility', don't go searching the stands for a nice piece of tail. Nod. Nod like this, nod approvingly. Pucker your lips a bit and imagine someone slowly driving a meaty fist up your butt hole. And please, when he starts banging on about a corporation's *social contract with society*, keep firm eye contact and tuck your lips up under your teeth. Don't be afraid to wipe gently at an eye or push that center-brow up to the hairline. Transition between these gestures subtly, smoothly, don't dither. Remember, more is less. Now let's go get 'em, hands in everyone.....Go Team!"

An odd theatre of actors on both sides of each question winking and nodding through the script. A Corps-shimmed Citizen's Party receiving praise for taking action against perpetrators, and the grand provider of televised entertainment, forgiven, simply for fielding some inane congressional questions before the public. The beauty of a toothless interrogation, a farcical trial of conscience! The letterhead, forever collateral damage. The poor letterhead and how it suffered when *HFWYG Consultancy* was trashed, quietly reopen under the name *HFWYG Advisory Services* the following day (later to become *HFWYG Professional Services*, then *HFWYG Consultations*, then *HFWYG Planning Services*, then *HFWYG Analytic Services*, and on and on). How the real backlash targeted Ms. Silva, a backlash tempered with an extravagant television spectacle for everyone to enjoy. Two weeks long, watching, and producing, the trial of the year which found Ms. Silva guilty, her crimes resulting in a five-year prison stint and a one-million Credit fine evenly distributed to the victim's families. How impressively Andrea's attorney acted on the national stage, a star was born! Three-and-a-half years later, Andrea walking from prison with 50,000 Credits loaded to her device - the remainder of the original 12 million Credit prize money after fines, consultancy fees and attorney fees. *Cha-ching!*

And how Andrea's exploits further elevated the show's popularity as soon as short memories designated The Archives to solely tell the legacy of the dead children. Those few hold-out demographics turning up in *HFWYG* bars for *Fever Pitch*, anticipating carnage, and hoping to expose themselves or their kiddies to a payout by way of prizewinner fines. *Potential Cha-ching!*

The myriad inexpensive opportunities to unwittingly self-oppress and how the Irons indulged, chipped away at their humanity from the inside out. Provide a platform, compensate the social architects to endorse it, then voilà! Sit back and watch as carnal impulse leaks from every pore. *Cha-ching!* Keep society's muscles limber, the hindbrain hyperactive, on a heavy dose of instinct stimulation. Addict them to subsidized fetters. Corral them to prefer massive consumption over the dopamine-squirt-free mundanity of political climax. How these people from the past called activists used to demand corporate accountability, fair play, a government that worked for them. Instead, rogue consumerzens threatening to blowup some shitty institution of their own while they bark loudly for evermore low-cost entertainment. Cheap, easy and immediate consumption, the great opiate for all. *Cha-ching!*

Irons, human commodities! Commodities enabling the extraction of value from any situation, all situations. A viewer commodity. A contestant commodity. A labor commodity. A client commodity. A voter commodity. A soldier commodity, or rather, an energy commodity. Each new business plan defined clear commodity thresholds required for successful implementation. If the numbers worked, plan enacted, if not, plan scrapped. Numbers, simple and tidy and devoid of the irritatingly mushy human component that complicates even the best plans. Did we discount the humanity of Irons too much? Did we expect to patch a tattered social fabric by increasing distraction, upping the noise? Even if rather loathsome and primitive, Irons still had life in their systems, life suppressed by years of aggressively pursued dopamine squirts thta is. Maybe it was a matter of time before they remembered how to reason. Schedule the lessons learned meeting to ensure the next plan accounts for current missteps. Document. Refine.

The Dirts. How we did it right with the Dirts. Applied a different theory, one tested throughout history. Extreme oppression. Shatter the spirit until even the thought of retaliation isn't tractable. The most obedient human is one who loathes himself more than his oppressor. The plan, how it worked perfectly until that Aphamli Twist asshole stood up and made everyone scratch their head. Blindsided by a tail event, an unaccountable anomaly.

...

He's back, standing overhead, a fistfuls of leather belts in his massive, meaty hands, a drawn face. Staring, waiting. He wipes his brow with the back of his hand. Kneels. Sits. Stares at me. Feet continue thumping, echoing throughout the house. He touches the pool of blood between us. Inspects his fingers, looks away in disgust.

"You know," he glances back at his fingers, wipes them on his shirt, a sloppy child. Searching for his thoughts, "I hate myself," sniffles, "I hate you."

Feet thump overhead, everywhere, as he pauses, searches his lap.

"I hate this fucking world we live in," the goon tells his genitals.

"But more than anything, I hate these feelings of hate... the way they consume me, diminish everything."

A different sort of pounding. Feet running through my house, my head or something else? A heavy, dull sound. Far-off thunder, rolling.

"Do you remember the first question you asked me after I told you we were expecting?" He's waiting, rubbing his nose. If I could move my arms. My legs. He's going emotional now, eyes welling. He's distracted, vulnerable. It's no use. There is no signal between my head and body. Lay here as easy prey.

"You asked me, 'Are you keeping it?' You remember?"

Pounding, from somewhere unknown.

"And when I answered your question, you and your curt follow up. Do you remember what you said?"

Enjoy your moment. You'll still be you after I'm gone. If I could move my arms, I'd rip you to pieces buddy.

"You said, *this is your problem*. Plain and simple, that's what you said and then you walked away. That was, *is*, my daughter. The best thing that has ever happened to me. I didn't understand what you meant at the time and I still don't today. No matter how I parse the words, I can't make sense of it, make sense of you. But it, it doesn't stop there. I can't seem to make sense of anything anymore. What has it all come to anyway? What is this? I can't make sense anymore. Everything has come undone, nothing is recognizable. All we do, all anybody does, is move around with elbows and I can't figure out why, can't make sense of why. Everybody hates everybody. Everybody hunches over their dinner bowl. Everybody glares out from behind heavy brows. Everybody hates. So I hate too, become angrier with hate each day. And why I tell you this, who knows."

He wipes his leathery face with a shirtsleeve, sighs.

"Time passes so quickly, the four of us now. One room and an outhouse, isolated on the far side of the garden, invisible to the physical world. Eight hands, one income, nothing to speak of. Twenty years in your service and growing poorer each day. Not hungry but never full. Not forced but never free. No more. No more."

He wipes his face again, smashing tears into his hair. Staring into space, sighs again. This is a human being? Fuck me!

"The man who attacked your dogs, your wife, Mark, is my brother you know? He's been with us down at the shed for months, hiding out, wondering what's next. A victim of the 33rd. He had a wife and two kids. Two beautiful kids. Ryan and Lindsay. Two months after the 33rd passed, he and his wife were let go. No notice, just dismissed from jobs they'd been at for years. They were able to pay their portion of a shared apartment for about three weeks, then, without options, they packed the car, drove to The Core and found a hidden spot to park in some place called Border Park. The four of them lived in the car for three months. Three months during which he and his wife scavenged for food while searching for jobs. Searched for any kind of work. But, nothing."

Pounding, cheering, in the background. Celebration, his eyes hold steady.

"When the police knocked on the car window, it was early, Mark was out sifting through the trash bins, hoping the early start would net results. Ironically, he told me the best places to find decent trash was the alleyway between Ivory and Juniper Towers. He would stake out the buildings in the evening, watch for catering vans, because he knew if there was a catered function the bins would be full after midnight. As dawn broke, Mark headed back to the car to feed his family. The walk along the concrete drains beneath Route 4 was the most direct, concealed path, he told me, to return to Border Park from Central Core. He scrambled up the embankment from the drain as he entered the northern edge of Border Park. There, under the maple where his car sat for three months, a staked slip of pink paper. One of those ubiquitous pink signs. The final act of decency granted to a demoted Iron after his family is cleansed from society. The language of the notice, terse and memorable as it was, has been repeated incessantly by my brother over the past months as he attempts to come to grip with losing everything."

CAR AND CONTENTS, DESTROYED.
INHABITANTS DISPERSED IN THE PILES.
MARK DELTEPE IS A SOUGHT FUGITIVE.

"His family, all he had left, spread out among the millions of Dhalytes in The Piles. Three grains of sand hidden in plain sight on a beach. Intentionally dispersed as punishment for not self-evacuating. My brother is a human being. One of many human beings served a pink slip."

Pitifully, muttering on. Imbecile. The pounding has diminished, wherever it was coming from. Tingles, rippling from the head down to neck. Words keep pouring from the idiot's hole. Tired, so tired. He say Deltepe? Mommy's maiden name. How consanguineous is the split between Beatus and Sapian? Irrelevant. Distracting.

"With no hope of reconnecting with his family in The Piles and nowhere else to go, Mark wandered underground, traveling by night, sleeping in ditches during the day. Disconnected from everyone, everything. You know, he only stumbled upon me because of the statue at the entrance to your estate, an object I mentioned to him years ago in our sole conversation as grown men. The world's largest gilded Credit symbol. Who could miss that, huh?"

Again quiet, wipes his face. I'm dying but *he* is wilting, the weaker one. Even in his big moment he doesn't know pride. Shameless.

"But you know, it's that hate, the hate I feel which grinds me down the most. When you come to the point where cynicism feels refreshing. When simple anger feels airy and light. When your single hope is to watch the world, and everyone in it, burn to ash and you don't even know why. But what's the point? Why do I even bother?" he says, eyes red.

His chin burrows into his chest, breaths. A hulking, Neanderthal carcass blots out everything. Lying motionless, watching psychosis bloom pathetically in a man. My short sips of breath. His long, slow cathartic ones.

"This. *This* is your moment to reflect. I'll leave you to it. Just know, no matter how much I hate myself, I'm not sorry. Not one bit. Your eyes tell the whole story," knees cracking as he stands.

He looks at the belts in his hand, sighs, tosses them on me. Clicking buckles, no sensation. He steps over her, walks down the hall.

Fainter breath. Slowing heartbeat. He left me, wants me in this state. His wants don't matter. He doesn't matter. A nobody who got lucky. He's an anomaly, an asterisk, a character in a drama nobody bothered to watch. History forgets him long before he stinks.

But he's right. This is *my* time to figure. Thoughts that linger, bits of memory needing to square. This how. One pathetic man's employment gripes don't justify collapse. Where's my fucking how?

Ignorant Irons, ungrateful as they are. Paid to wash and wax 'em, but fucking up my cars. Really, a rhyme? Focus. Where am I? How. Dithering focus. And back. How?

Commodities without reason, without purpose. Human drones, fucking Irons, unplugged from reality, their choice. Don't like it? Do something. No purpose in life, don't like the options? Then make yourself instead of having me make you. Drag your own cross, like us. Miserably, dutifully. Just because I give you handcuffs doesn't require you to clamp them shut. Choice. Free society is based on choice.

And these Dhalytes, their silent complaints taxing the conscience of society's witless, dying young the way the lowest rungs have since the dawn of time. Nothing new. Nothing unusual. Modus operandi de la société. A world of no guarantees.

And her. How about her? How does she fit into circumstance? Another one of life's fragments, another piece of the how. The nebulous accountability of mutually-consenting victims.

Alarms wail, drowning feeble blood thumps in my ears. Vacillating lucidity, increasingly brittle thoughts. It would be nice to hold her hand. Nice to touch the living, anything warm. Jesse. The gardener's name? Or the chef? My commodities, lifestyle cogs. Malfunctioning servants, how is this what money can buy?

Freedom. Freedom and growth. Two universal concepts which in and of themselves are the very foundation required for reaching the upper boundaries of human potential. Pure and simple concepts innately understood by any sentient being as the engine driving ingenuity and sparking creativity. In the abstract, they encapsulate the essence of the human spirit, in the definitive, they are measurements enabling us to quantify civilization's progress.

Pondering those two concepts in my study, that evening before voting on the House floor regarding the fundamental provisions of the *Science Economy* framework. The process of mentally slicing the two concepts as many ways as possible, searching for retorts to my reasoning. Flushing out any epididymal blockages in the neurological plumbing. A sparkling mind is required. By analyzing increasingly complex scenarios, it became obvious our direction was sound. Along with fellow Corps members, we rooted out what was perceived as the fundamental driver, and engineered the intricate matrix of social constructs to sit atop the foundation underpinning the *Science Economy* rationale. Sure, like any legislative decision, it came packaged with collateral damage nasties, however, all big decisions were a balancing act, a process of measuring aggregate positive against insidious negative. That particular politico-business decision spawned massive short-term risk, but long term, it was the best move. The Core's population had swelled exponentially, and using an explicit divide and conquer approach with the underclass was the tidy way to preserve social coherence. One half of the populace to be re-branded, castigated, or, more appropriately, outcasted. The other half of the economic underclass would be the big, ballsy growth engine of the *Science Economy*. And the social strategy carroting the underclass growth engine you ask? A clever package of expanded freedoms aimed at fostering a sense of self-determination among the penniless trapped on the economic ladder's lowest rung. The euphoria of expanded freedoms and the existential bliss of self-determination used to soothe the muscular sting caused by huge increases in human labor required from those freed and awakened souls. Unlocking the human spirit, the reason to expand freedoms! Any productivity increases *discovered* were just fortunate collateral benefit, or so went the messaging prophylactically wrapped around the citizenry's consciousness. Citizens, still nominally accountable for their actions, no longer shackled by archaic laws instructing them how to behave, what to ingest, what relationships to foster, and how best to utilize one's pitifully meager assets. Freedom. Freedom to pursue one's destiny! < *Insert voracious applause here* > Freedom to tap the personal growth potential previously suppressed by years of inane directives, directives crafted and enforced by a ninny state. And the products, oh the sweet products trickling down from the social restructuring - massive economic benefits unleashed for all! Oh the difficulty suppressing the rising Egmont Overture teasing the nerve endings on my swollen psyche. The supple dance of flutes, the relentlessly thrusting violins!

That evening, many years ago, the hallowed swell of patriotism, a call to duty, a spark growing to a flicker then a blaze in my gut. We were on the cusp of significant change, significant social progress. Gone was the nagging sense of obligation to those who, through their innate shortcomings, had become a toll on society's makers. WE were moving on, evolving to the next level, shedding skin to differentiate ourselves, the first generation of Homo beatus to emerge from the primitive Sapians congregating in filthy piles on the city's western edge. The evolution born from the scientific realization that all men are not created equal. Man had split, and for the first time, the queer, volatile haste of biological progression was laid bare for all to witness in real time.

It was about 10 PM. Catapulted to an intellectuophrodisiacal high from parliamentary reflections, a craving lurched. Transporting blood tingles oxygenated heavily nerved extremities. A lightening bolt from cloud nine, luscious thoughts of sweaty intervention piqued, and Michel Addler's name inundating brain cells. Vibrating fingers did their best to follow the directives of an endorphin-soaked brain, to punch a few digits,

"Hello?"

"Michel, it's Zuberi."

"Oh..."

"Can we meet?"

"...hey, uh, now?"

"Yes, if possible."

"Uh. Ok, I guess. Let me check. One second."

His footsteps thumped as he jogged, checking the family's status. Creaking doors, several flights of stairs consumed. A door clicking shut as Michel's voice crackled to life,

"Yeah. I guess I'm free."

"Excellent, I'll be over there in thirty minutes. Usual spot?"

"Yeah, yeah, usual," Michel said.

"Ok, bye."

"Bye."

With a teen's giddiness arcing lasciviously, it was time to freshen up, don a clean shirt, do the obligatory spot check in the mirror. Gray temples, the never-ending debate, wisdom versus youthful virility. That slight sinking feeling for the crows feet stretching to the gray. Daily treatments halted their steady march, but passing time had done its damage. More aggressive treatment required to cock-block the ticking clock. Most troubling, the subtly rounding features, the cartilage failures and the deteriorations in elasticity staking victories in several locations. Once sharp, aquiline lines from bridge to lip were taking a more leisurely, bulbous path. A pair of earlobes, victims of gravity's dangle. Taut ocular borders morphing into lazy apertures, like soft, folded dough. Age piling on its brutal victories. More aggressive treatment to be pursued, however, on that particular evening, there was no time to lament. Plans established, expediency was required as time was of the essence with those sort of assignations.

Walking toward Hudson's bedroom and the ephemeral bubbles of juvenile anxiety gave bounce to steps. Breathe in. Breathe out. Calm control. Maintain a cool levity, friendly but buttoned. Professional! Go somewhere else in the mind. Imagine, a world without any victims. Every snowflake falling pure and white until the chaste sun reclaims it. Sadly, all the world's erections flagging to propriety's tune with no opportunities for a highly skilled debaucher. Ugh, but necessary for composure's sake. Flaccid ambassador.

Hudson's door pushed open, moving quickly and quietly, pausing briefly to peck his cheek before tightening his tuck and escaping down the hall. Going on six, and the thought was, *a wonderful world of opportunity awaits him if we can set the right course for the future. My diamond in the rough, not yet conscious of the fortune buffering him from an honest day's work. Crafted from Promethean loins, augmented with choice attributes, and pushed from the finest flower in the garden. Precious. Pure. A snowflake guaranteed to melt gracefully in the sun's gentle beams instead of being salted into oblivion.*

Left down an adjacent hall, stairs consumed before entering the living room to find the latest signora, that lovely Patrician vessel. Engrossed in a novel covered with a shirtless man whose bronzed chest outsized her own generous allocation. She paused momentarily asking,

"Heading out?"

"Yeah, unfortunately. Michel and the gang want to address a few details ahead of tomorrow's vote. I thought we cleared everything this afternoon, however, some believe there are details needing revision. Most politicians, as you well know, love the glory hole more for its stage appeal than for its outcomes, but I digress..."

"Colorful."

"Right. ...Well, bye, Patricia, see you later."

"Bye," she said, not looking up, the placidity of her face oddly juxtaposed next to the image of striated musculature, thick, ropey veins. Disproportionate cock bulges. My wife, the supposed sexual revolutionary in youth reduced to flicking her fleshy flower with an overly worded literotica on a Wednesday night. *Machinations on how to best hide the meat cylinder, this cavern or that? Ding Dong. Do you mind if I cum in? His generous member erect, pointing the way to heavenly bliss.* It could go on all night, probably did. A sad way to exercise the acquisition of hard-sweated social gain. Hobbies, to her, how they were so abominably working class. Play in the dirt to create something green? Don a pleaty, white skirt and swat at yellow orbs with stringy, bovine bowels? Never...a degradation of the God-given right to physically stagnate. Killing time in the tantric abyss of carnal longing, ah, now that's more like it! Certainly a task for the most incredibly ennui and

Patricia, my sweet Patricia, embraced it with every cell in her body.

"Yes, OK, bye then, bye."

A flaccidly raised hand, no eye break from the text. Stretching the mind's fecundity taut until all possibilities are whittled down to one word-free, conclusive climax. Squirt!

The arduous ride across town, the driver, waking from his nap, lethargically executed the banal tasks of pedal and wheel.

"Could we speed things up Franklin, I'm in a hurry here."

"Sorry sir, just doing my best not to get pulled over. My rushing in the past got me nothing but speeding tickets. One more and I'm on the bench for six months."

"Your rushing earned the accolades of your boss, yes?"

"Yes sir, but I'm no good to you if I'm unable to drive."

"Well there is a fix for that too."

"Sorry sir?"

"Forget it, keep pushing the pace. I'm late."

"Will do sir."

The thought, at the time anyhow, was that once tomorrow's vote took place, trivial concerns of a speeding ticket would become history for Franklin's ilk, and more importantly reduce administrative irritants. Cycling through bum drivers every couple months wasn't saving time or making life easier.

Flush with adrenaline and excitement, thoughts reverted back to Michel. What circumstances may have changed since we spoke? What if he's now unavailable? What if our meeting has been foiled and I'm unaware of it, driving pointlessly toward the bluest of balls? Giving into anxiety, I dialed the phone,

"Hey, it's me, Zuberi."

"Yeah? What's up?"

"I'm in the MRAP, on the way over."

"And?"

"What do you mean and?"

"I mean, why'd you call?"

"I'm concerned on this end. Is everything still a go?"

"Yeah, nothing's changed. I'm here, sitting in the dark with a pair of sparring gloves, waiting. Hurry up, it's getting late, I'm getting tired, and I have school tomorrow."

"Yeah, yeah, yeah, I'm whipping my driver the best I can, be there momentarily."

"See you soon."

"Ok, call me if the situation changes."

"Fine. Hurry up."

"How're we doing up there Franklin?"

"Sorry sir?"

"I said HOW ARE WE DOING UP THERE?"

"Getting close sir, five to ten minutes."

"Jesus Christ, hurry it up!"

Agitation and anxiety, tickly beads of sweat bloomed on my upper lip. That thick musk of deodorant wafting up in steamy plumes from within my shirt, a trigger for more anxiety-tinged sweat. Break the windows to release the tension, get some fresh air? Numb fingers and a expanding, light head attempted to disconnect from my neck, float away. Vision sharpened.

"A couple minutes sir."

Gulping air and running fingernails scalp-wise triggered that little tingle down the spine, opened up a new region of sensation. Shoe laces tightened, the belt buckle loosened a notch. Two. An unnecessary flattening of the shirt against moist skin. Head circles. Shoulder rolls. Jaw muscles stretched limber. The encounter forecasted, the moves anticipated. Oddly, no faces were made out, just vague forms, shapes and their relative movements and memories. Primal instinct dictated thought, dried up any ability to step through a detailed sequence of events. Instead, choosing to focus sharply on outcome's euphoria. Reason seemed irrelevant, distracting, as blunt satiation edged out attempts to understand the variables at play.

"We're here sir."

"Wait down the road a few blocks. I'll call you when the meeting is over."

Across the concrete slabs leading toward 57 Constitution Street, heels echoed off glass structures towering overhead. At that time of night, few pedestrians were out walking. A man and his dog. A couple's arms tangled loosely. The lights of a few passing cars, an MRAP. At the entrance, my card scanned, the door pushed, and the elevator hailed, bound for the 21st floor. Nobody in the lobby. Nobody in the elevator. Silence was broken by my clicking shoes, pant swishes.

The elevator passed through the floors, adrenalized feet circled, fists clenched, lungs huffed. 20. 21. The metal doors retracted revealing the cavernous, dimly lit room covered floor to ceiling in gym mats. Exercise machinery and punching bags, tidied along the room's edges. Out from the elevator, hunched over and guarded, then, the immediate head strike with a hard object, forced my knees to the mat. A blow to the back, another one cracked my skull. Head down, chin tucked to chest, buried between the protection of my shoulders, legs collected in a bundle beneath. In a ball, the blows came rapid fire, lightening into my back, arms and thighs. Relentlessly, jolts continued, me in my abused ball, waiting. After a few minutes, silence. A muted solemnity hung in a cease fire. Two sounds emerged, my moans and his gulps for air.

Stabilized, I put my guard up as eyes continued adjusting to the dim light. A blurry, shadow flashed from left. My hopeful lunge, splayed arms, a clench secured. A lion's iron jaws lock, its heavy body drains life from the prey forced to carry it. His little body squirmed, lashed out, but the lion smothered it. Weak thumps slapped at my sides, legs, a couple shots to my head. Survival grunts whittled down to pathetic whimpers. A weight advantage disarmed the quickly diminishing attack. Prey tenderized, wallops to the chest, the stomach, the legs. Loosened up and worn out. He struggled for a few more minutes before his arms were folded neatly to his body, his torso squeezed, recuperative air robbed. He fell limp. Grip adjusted, two spindly wrists in one hand and a neck controlled with the other. He was finished, it was time to revel in bruised victory, pain pulsated everywhere. Blood and sweat from my cheeks to his. Eyes fully adjusted to the light, Michel's figure came into beautiful focus. The smoothness of the supple, hairless skin on his arms and back. His flush, upward-facing cheek. Proudly preserved whiskers sprouted awkwardly from his chin. Eyes cast to the floor. A pig tied up, resigned to slaughter. The libidinous joy of forced acquiescence. This boy just shy of majority and lacking enough testosterone to fully qualify for entry into man's pernicious world. Precious. Subdued. A pretty little snowflake in the cold, salty dark.

Rolled onto his stomach, it was my turn. That was the arrangement. A full-contact sparring partner comes at a cost. If he is contained, he is had.

Sweat glistened on his nape, salt for a marauding tongue. His parents were asleep on the 24th. The excitement of taking prey without concern caused excited hands to jitter, me fumbling with his belt, the buckle pressed between his waist and a sweat soaked gym mat. He breathed hard like a fish out of water, neck crooked at a submissive angle, eyes vacant. His panicked attempts at a last moment escape, futilely funny. Tenderize the back, the head. The audible rapture of moans and whimpers. The calm of inevitability washed over. And thus began the story of a half-foot of engorged tissue swimming ecstatically in Perineum's filthy neighbor, so Humbert Humbert might have said.

...

Today. Years since the *Science Economy's* launch, passage of the 32nd amendment, and the frequent spars with Michel. Adjusting the tie's knot, a dapper man smiles back. If Michel saw me now, perhaps he'd lower his guard? Wisdom and virility hitting their peak simultaneously in the ninth decade, a technological tip of the hat. But Michel is passé, merely the first name in the obsession spanning scores. He couldn't hold a candle to the colts in today's stable. Even the Dirts nicked by Franklin are stunning after thoroughly washed and loosened up with a snort of The Pine. But, *nya!* lusty thoughts are errant on a day like this, a day for immersion in the peoples' business! The business of our great nation! Two hours until the stage. Two hours before subsidy announcements for the silly Irons, playing savior yet again.

As predicted by some Corps members, the recently implemented 33rd created ripples of unrest in The Blocks. *Eh*, nothing organized, but outcries, recurring instances of violence, tagged with spray-painted "33". Hints of discontent. Working through the final draft of the 33rd Amendment, it didn't seem possible for society's lowest rung, being so socially disintegrated, to view notions of brotherhood and family as more than quaint, outdated. Isn't an overworked hyper-consumer mentally saturated beyond the point of being concerned for the disaffected, or even realizing his own antipathy? Isn't he too engrossed in completing the day's tasks and more concerned with getting home quick to channel remaining energy into reaping consumer payoff?

We'd pushed so much capital into the damn entertainment subsidies that the idea of Irons spending precious free time bucking social norms seemed odd, wasteful even. Why engage in a protest-of-one when everyone you know is playing the latest release from **SensaGames** - *Children: Find, Rape and Kill!*, or watching *HFWYG's latest episode*? My stupid calculations were off. No big deal, time to adjust, restore calm.

Care was taken in crafting the 33rd, right? Direction articulated, yet tone tempered, so as not to scare folks with the wail of train horns coming to carry the constitutionally deprecated to concentration camps:

Citizens finding themselves without work for greater than three months are effectively in a work default status. If a work default status is not corrected within an additional three month time period, the citizen has, by his own actions, willfully neglected his social responsibility to reenter the workforce, thereby indicating motivation and ambition levels commensurate with the Homo sapian classification. Ipso facto, citizens classified as such are subject to the terms and conditions of the preceding amendment without recourse.

Blight, growing concern in The Core. Ever-improving technology required fewer hands to produce a quickly decreasing range of consumer goods. Penniless Irons plopping tents on street corners, under bridges, in parks. Not always welcomed in The Piles, they clogged up The Core, even migrated along roads into the Bunker's outer sections. *Ugh.* Cleanliness and order waned, caused the legislative stir. A solution was needed and fellow members of the Social Balancing Committee explored the possibilities rather diligently, right? Sheltering was viewed as a bandage, regardless, housing subsidies for society's takers didn't have a single vote among the Corps. Expanding production to merely employ a labor glut? No, no, no, silly... would erode corporate profits, and again, would find no support among the 90% majority Corps legislators. So, leverage an existing paradigm to underpin the 33rd Amendment, an efficient option! "Social pruning" the most reasonable method to dissolve the clot of homelessness! Anyway, here we are.

So, today's challenge. To find the right mix of words to separate the wheat from the chaff with an air of congenial finality. No, more direct Zuberi. To placate extant Irons with a pall of goodwill, albeit resigned for many. A careful tongue-dance no doubt, some are raw (don't be blind to that), fearful from witnessing the outcasting of neighbors, friends, and family members. But everything in life is a cost-benefit analysis, and if a difficult-to-swallow change is delivered wrapped in a succulent carrot, then acceptance of misfortune is more palatable! And boy do we have a carrot in store for those who toe the line! A fully subsidized technological gadget fresh from the labs more than a decade before its initially projected launch! Stabilization, the ultimate goal. Cut the dead weight, but retain the vital human engine necessary to further advance prosperity at the top. Piece of cake.

And all of the complements accompanying this latest subsidy, a bevy of expanded freedoms launching Irons into the blissful realm of self-actualization. Sweet Maslow nectar! Remove the shackles of an overreaching government, enable people to achieve their full potential. Eliminate that annoying appendage restriction on gambling! Implement the right-to-choose post-birth! Retribution rights for all! Eliminate the age of consent! Create a sense of individual empowerment, or distraction, depending on one's perspective of course, while stabilizing society's grand march forward. Cake.

One hour and fifty minutes until show time. Must run over these lines once more. This speech must smoke the hive.

When you awake from a dream, many threads of memory linger, each nagging for the recollection of the ephemeral details from the previous few unconscious minutes. The contours of a face, the trajectory of flight or perhaps the raw animality of sexual encounter. When you awake from sleep without dreams, there is a silence, an absence, a sort of suspended ambiance. In a dreamless wakening, in those first few conscious seconds, you consider what's immediate: an aching neck, sweat beads rolling down the backs of your legs, that bitter, salivary paste coating the tongue. The dreamless waking experience is an inventory of state as opposed to a projection of what could have been if the dream were prolonged. Thoughts. They flip in the cold of morning after a night tossing and turning behind the car's steering wheel. An aching neck, a numb butt, a sting in the small of my back radiating out.

Good morning Bryson.

Saying it doesn't make it so. Dashboard screams 4:45 AM. Exactly forty-five minutes to report to work. Hardly enough time to run upstairs, shower, eat and hop back in the car. Me, pawing at the door handle from a critical viewpoint outside my body. Suspended. Motorized by unknown forces, or perhaps, just an involuntary need for motion when of a conscious state. Work is due, I'm due there. That is what I do. Work is what people do. I'll go to work. I'll buy food. I'll eat food. Then, sleep. I'll do this over and over. I'm alive, 120/80 at 65 BPM. The process of living life. Why complain? I have a roof. I'm not hungry. I'm not sick. Body is capable. Mind is functioning. Happiness is a choice made. Morning thoughts, gossamery at best.

A shutting car door echoes, grip reaffirmed on my bag. Walk. The parking level is peppered with people hustling to cars, from cars, under dim yellow light. The to-cars clean and fresh, smell of MorningZing. Fellow from-cars, disheveled and bleary, stale like me. A morning alive. The irregular metronomy of clicking shoes on concrete. 824b and 831c start their engines. 836e, 821d and 818a reverse from their spots. Sleep deprived faces of two men and three women pass me, long shadows distorting their faces. Hurry, closing elevator. Inside, hold breath, avoid The Pine, preserve beloved reality. What's more insulting than feeling content against your will? Alone and quiet, silhouettes streak by, feet press into the floor. My body divides the people on my level, narrow cinderblock corridor, a tunnel to infinite nowhere. A black hole sitting at the end of a shallow tube of lights flickering to death. A deep inhalation of unmedicated air on my level, musty and stale. Threadbare carpet, wet, dank and sour. The musky, fecal odor of neglected dogs. An olfactory stew of functional poverty. Direction is predetermined by the location of my apartment door, the trick is advancing toward it. Rational thought implores a leap through the prisonesque hall window, blissful flight for thirty-some floors. Irrationality pleads self-preservation.

Bryson, you need to report to work in forty minutes.

A small plane, painted aeons ago and a dull brass knob, dented and askew. There's only one logical method to unlock my apartment door, insert key. There's only one logical method to open the door, turn knob till latch bolt clears strike plate. There's only one rational way to move past Corinne's sprawled carcass blocking passage to the kitchenette where caffeine awaits, step over her.

Plastic, faux-wood veneers curling off swollen wafer-board boxes. Cabinets. Latex hematomas bulging from the walls. Paint. The snag and snap back of laminate countertop edges as you brush by. Moisture's cumulative degradation of shoddy construction. The yellowed plastic of an ancient coffee maker. Press the brew button, hot water trickles, but she doesn't stir. Motionless. A depression in the drywall near her head indicates a fall, but isn't that too presumptuous? Her left arm is oddly contorted beneath her torso, a single red pump clings to the toes of her right foot. Those pumps, same pair, the pointy heel of one having recently explored my back's musculature, splitting its taut red striae as the heel's velocity slowed upon impact. *Beep. Beep. Beep. Beep.* Fetch cup. Bryson, coffee time.

Cheap coffee, a vague reminder of the beverage adored during artificially flush college years. A grayish liquid of synthetic pungency, a cheap delivery system for the first dose of chemical motivation. Nothing elegant like The Pine, just traditional, blunt stimulation. Fingers curl through the mug's handle. Along a path of muscle memory ingrained long ago, cup glides to mouth. In the hallway, she's still lying there, peacefully inert. She's partially dressed, not for work, but in a set of evening leathers. Evanescent wisps of hair simulation lay blinking colorfully across her neck and a single dangly earring, a glowing orb, drapes across the perfectly blushed cheek of her forever smiling face.

Kneeling, more clues emerge. Plunged into her head, below her eyebrow, a plastic syringe, the needle of which exits further north on her forehead. A pool of burnt crimson clotting amid the sparse, trampled tufts of filthy Berber. Some sort of crude piercing, the syringe appears to have pushed through the skin on her forehead after she fell. Toxin? Something else? The coffee won't go down, unbearably bitter, back into the mug. After swirling it a moment, the strands of saliva circling into the vortex, it splashes on her face. Wakey, wakey, eggs and... Nothing. I don't hate her, right? I don't. It's simpler than that. I don't care. Her presence no longer registers. Doesn't matter. The coffee was not worth drinking. They belong in a separate world together, strange axiom of pairing. Or, is it the carnal pleasure of taking a shit? Pleasure and indifference, one-in-the-same when love is so far gone.

Here on the couch, it's wooden frame pressing my hamstrings, hands folded, eyes straight ahead. The many questions want to come pouring out. But, shouldn't these next few steps focus on squashing those questions? Searching for, hoping for and wanting, nothing? Absolutely nothing.

Bryson, if you don't leave for work in one minute you will be late.

On the table are various prosthetic genitalia in a wide array of colors, shapes and sizes. Pushed aside, the dried remnants of many meals. On the screen are the muted images of a man attempting to squirt fire from his urethra in the direction of a pig hanging lanced on a spit for a beguiled audience. Noise. All of it, noise. The oily, fart-laden fabric of the couch, foul but oddly homey. No, utterly foul. Back to hall. Back to the floor, next to her. Lie down, face up, on the filthy carpet patch. Back perfectly flat. Eyes to ceiling, watching the comfortable repetition of monotony. A white plane.

Bryson? Brrrrrrrrryyyyyyyysssssssssoonnnmmzzzzz......

Quiet inches one breath at a time. Cold floor fades, becomes unnoticeable. A relaxed back articulates the surface pressing from behind. Focused breathing, soon forgotten. A beating heart, the last remaining sound. A muffled thump soft in my ears. Splotches of gray, white and black fizzle and morph across the ceiling, the minute shades of an imperfect white separating then shapeshifting into vaguely identifiable images. What appears to be a flower becomes a fist. Interlocking hands, a knot in a rope. A heart to a spade. And her big, bright eyes morph to communion wafers spinning violently, causing the tiny crucifixes at center to freeze, spin backwards stroboscopically.

...

She was lying on the couch belly down, completely naked, the lower half of her legs pointing skyward. Two fleshy, inverted pendulums counterswinging. The odd dichotomy of orgasm's moans; how otherworldly they are from the mouth of someone you adore, how grating from someone loathed. He was face up on the floor, naked, dripping with sweat, recovering. Peter his name, if memory serves, though they all started looking and sounding the same. From the front door to the kitchenette for a drink, buttons loosened on my work shirt, settling in for the customary freak show. With a jolt, her head popped up from the couch, the elbow of her telephoned arm denting its fabric, "Yes, hello?"

A brief pause.

"Right, Ok. Yes, ID is 294-2483-6474," she said to the person on the line.

"Yes, that's me."

"Well, I'm calling to report an adultery."

"Yes."

"Yes."

"Yes, I know."

"Well, you see, well, it was awful. I, I just, well. I didn't know how to control it," she sniffled, cleared her throat.

"I know."

"Yes."

"Ok, I'll do my best," she said wiping an eye, lips quivering illegitimately slow.

"You see, he came over for a quick visit to wish me a Happy Birthday, and, one thing led to another," she said, subtle victim voice discernable from the emphasis on *he*.

The conversation continued for several minutes, words such as 'good man', 'poor husband' and 'didn't deserve this' scattered amid the one-sided dialogue. Truly impressive though was her ability to completely disembody from the neck up for the purpose of the conversation. From the neck down, she was a separate entity, servicing a recovering Paul still sweating and coughing on the floor, her delicate, spindly fingers choking his waning erection.

As her tears began flowing at an annoying rate, Patrick brushed her hand aside, stood, walked to the kitchenette. He grabbed a drink from my refrigerator, looked at me, shrugged, said '*hey*.' What to do but reply in kind, Corinne in the background,

"Fi-ive Credits?" she asked, sniffling through tears.

"And twenty lashes?"

"Oh Ohhh Kay," she said as Pavel returned to the couch, his bare asshole grinding my favorite spot on the couch.

"And that cleans the slate?"

"I see, Ok, let me get it."

"Ok, I just sent it. Confirmed?"

She said her goodbyes, curtain call of the mouth, her highly retouched face an odd mélange of mutually exclusive emotions, colorfully confusing. Her Atonement calls were becoming increasingly frequent causing a noticeable dent in the meager finances. In all probability, Peter most likely dialed 8-1-1 upon arriving home. They all do. Beyond scrutiny, perhaps he was less the actor and more the epicurean of personal chastisement. To each his own. She, though, happily fed off the energy created by openly confiding faults, to strangers no less. It was the opportunity to star in her own reality show even if only for a tiny, costly, and perfectly indifferent audience. And as the inevitable sobs of redemption boiled inside her, saline leaking from her eyes staining cheeks black, it was clear that the consequence of forgiveness was more concrete than the froth of vice. The bank account was five Credits reduced and nobody cared about her fifteen minutes of fame. The price one pays for being poor and self-indulgent, money gone.

...

The shapes on the ceiling, ceased. All is still. No sound. No sound apart from my beating heart. Outside the kitchenette window, the sun falls, casting long shadows in the hall, a small splash of dark yellow on the ceiling above. She is still splayed out at my feet. The pool of blood has spread slightly, moving toward me. Propped on elbows, observing her is like being strapped to a chair in an odd theatre of autocannibalism. Self-deconstruction one nibble at a time. But, it's noise. Noise to ignore. Noise without sound. No sound whatsoever. Back to the floor, eyes to the white abyss hovering above. A silent return to the ever pressing search for that something. Hard. Logical. Deterministic.

Dark. Dark and stagnant. The two overarching attributes of a night spent in The Piles. No electricity. No running water. No heat. Constant shuffling of bodies on plastic sheeting, a crunchy noise. Phlegmy coughs and screechy wails, part of the unsettled dissonance droning through the night. Night after night, lying awake, pondering what is, all that was and all that won't be. Sariya doing the same. Both of us, backs to the ground, eyes peering anxiously through a hazy plastic window facing a star-spangled sky. At some point, we release hands, recommence the nightly ritual of faking sleep. She may roll over a bit. I'll adjust the lump of rags supporting my head. All the while, arrhythmic breathing outs the liar in us both.

And so, tonight. Here. Thinking, awake with millions. What comes next? After we pass, judgment. Unable to speak, our legacies take shape from the actions and words that most impacted those left behind. Beyond our control and cognition, we become something larger than life, shadowy caricatures of our fleshy selves. Placed into crude buckets of 'Good', 'Bad', 'Compassionate', 'Brutal', 'Honest', 'Corrupt', 'Defiant', 'Obedient'. Probably shouldn't matter, but it's difficult not to wonder about the buckets. It's not an ego thing, is it? Hopefully this life's work is remembered as something more catalytic than 'Honest' or 'Conscientious'. The milquetoast buckets. That nagging desire to echo beyond yourself, be something bigger than life. A single relationship, honed over time, and a collection of impossible objects lying in wait in a beat-up suitcase. Aphamli. An opportunity, a singular reason for optimism, or perhaps, another failure for the future. Who's to say.

Diminished coughing these last few hours, no gut strength remains. Instead, shallower breathing, sweats, chills down my spine. Fingertips tingling. A dull pressure at center pushes out with greater affect, each breath more anemic, more painful. Something consumptive lives inside and it's eating through resolve. It's not fear, but regret, clouding over. A regret perhaps unwarranted, but a regret all the same. Possessing little and with nothing to gain, material comfort lies in the hope that meager resources were used well. Regret. Did the real opportunity slip through my fingers while I was busy pitying myself? Failure, a constant companion.

Bloody mucus, slippery and cold. Close eyes and focus on short, cadent breathes. An unknowable urge to cry, to purge, and the longer abstained the less rational it seems. Shame for the subliminal tenacity of self-pitying thoughts. Ok fine, there are the tears, now, strain uncomfortably to resist the manly cover-up cough. Be a complete human, embrace all emotions. Eyes, the corners leak, beads through sideburns, pooling in the ear's cartilage before overflowing, gliding napeward. The wet path, pricked with cold air, almost visual. Clear throat, quietly, quick as possible before thick fluid coats cavities. Suffocation. Do an exercise. A diversion. Anything. Where do we stand? Account for things. Yes, exercise the mind.

Aphamli. Aphamli Twist, my lone student, my reincarnation. Ambitious, idealistic, consumed by prickly angst. Lessons done and dusted. His awakening is complete, yet it's unclear whether he will collapse or spark. Sariya. Sariya, foundation of life. She will find a way to move on without me. Life will be easier without me, more of her energy to Maven and Valerie. The girls. Victims of a cruel life, raised with both hands tied, begging for mercy at gunpoint. Aphamli's potential, their single reason for optimism. Me. John Spencer Voyes. Broken man. No capacity to fight anymore. If ever. Consumed by anger. Hatred. Remorse. Sadness. Fear. Crippled by years of humiliating inaction, allay a guilty conscious by proselytizing, recruiting. Hoping, childlike, for resonation. John Spencer Voyes, forever that guy standing out of reach, one foot in the shadows, never himself at risk. A guy you meet multiple times, can't quite remember his name, let alone his face. Big ideas, no guts to push them. Such is the quick-to-fade memory left behind. Whoa is me, embarrassing.

Open again, blurry stars shine through beads of pooling saline. Pinpoints of light stretched wide, shining bright across the field of vision. They blend into one another, slowly becoming one orb of light suspended above. Orb hovers, tepidly, begins to vacillate gently in a pool of black. Begins to fade. The orb steadies, begins to shrink, a shallow breath rips through ear-drums. Fading, the orb looses brilliancy, shudders as it dims. Light continues to fade until there is nothing left glowing in the black.

The ups and downs. Life, coming in waves, the most cognizant moments on the happy crest or amid the chaos tumbling underwater. The sharpness of anticipation. Even in the worst times there's solace in knowing another cycle begins, it's a matter of holding your breath long enough to surface. That crutch developed when uncle's hand wandered selfishly. Crutch used while Janine coughed through her last breath? Used when the bank reclaimed the house? While falling asleep on the church's slab floor? When we added our section onto the growing expanse of tidy garbage in The Piles? And now, tuck the crutch deep into the armpit again, right? Hold it. *Hold it.*

While stroking his cooling, limp hand, the enemy hovers. Palpable. He's there. Forever trying to wedge into attempts at emotional asphyxia, a stalker, waiting for the right opportunity to attack. Waiting for vulnerability's muffled bleat. *Hold it, steady.* Those childhood years spent developing a fluency in prostration, conditioned to acquiescence to His control. *Hold it.* Another hardship. Mr. Ethereal, fabricated from the motives of evil men, attempting to weave into the goodbyes, my goodbyes. My chance to disconnect with grace, with the sobering strength of solitude. *Breathe now, but don't waiver.* The comfortable lie of omniscience, the overwhelming, dewy-eyed solace it promises to bring. *Steady now.* Needing to break down, but not wanting to break. *Steady.* And this force, it wants nothing less than to guide my feelings, my thoughts, my emotions. *Steady.* Holding back the ocean with a single plate of glass while the swimming creatures swimming laugh in my face. Aquatic caricatures of sorrow mocking sentiment, making it feel cheap and lazy. Go somewhere else. Escape. Girls need you. There's too much to do. Is that sweat on my back? Did I close the bin? Did we collect the water today? Did I fix that leak? Is that shortness of breath? Should I swallow? Should I swallow? Should I swallow? Should I swallow? Swallowing is bad. Swallowing is attempting to push the emotional reset button, but in its slow labor, time stretches uncomfortably. A heavy swallow only underscores the mounting tension, further articulates the enormous physical presence of a moment beyond control. Swallow.

They fall down. It's happening, happening exactly how it shouldn't. Nothing holds back the ocean, the glass cracks as tears trickle down his stoic face in blurry madness. An instant heat radiates out, draws back in. Falling, but the brain hasn't signaled the body, so everything hangs like the final note of a song.

> *"The Lord is my shepherd; I shall not want.*
> *He maketh me to lie down in green pastures: he leadeth me*
> *beside the still waters.*
> *He restoreth my soul: he leadeth me in the paths of righteousness*
> *for his name's sake."*

Something akin to touching wood or rewashing clean hands until infinity frowns. Beyond control.

> *"Yea, though I walk through the valley of the shadow of death,*
> *I will fear no evil; for thou art with me; thy rod and thy staff*
> *they comfort me.*
> *Thou preparest a table before me in the presence of mine enemies:*
> *thou anointest my head with oil; my cup runneth over.*
> *Surely goodness and mercy shall follow me all the days of my*
> *life: and I will dwell in the house of the Lord for ever."*

Those many years, his constant pushing. Never giving up. All the little things done to ease pain. Deliberate, gentle intonation. The coiling of fingers. Eyes held in kind attention beyond the precipice of understanding. But, gone. Valerie, Maven without him. There's no strength in a weary neck, so, face down to his. Blackness and warmth. Steady breaths create moisture on a cooling forehead. His clammy head at odds with a world he didn't want to fight. Sinuses, their contents running out in parallel. Forced focus on single, unnamed point in space-time. Discomfort to exhaustion. Exhaustion to the sublime realm of incognizance. Existence merely by the indisputable fact of physicality, haunting the periphery of thought.

The elasticity of time skewing perception. Snot and tears finding home on a shirtsleeve. Minutes become hours, then seconds, and back again. The girls still asleep on the far corner of the mat, the stars still performing their nightly circle. At a glance, John's mouth ostensibly gaped in mid-thought. A silly hope he'll say something profound, shake death's stupor. Collect his face for a kiss, lay it back on the mat again. His lost face. The prescience of the next ten, fifteen, twenty years. A perpetual straw grab, a search for something concrete to stand upon. Nothing comes to mind, nothing solid. *Goddamn you John, why?* Damn you God and the guilt from which you are woven. Nothing but the austere core, that steely cord running through me, will provide sustenance, connect the past to the future. No amount of knee-bruising worship will save us from this socially-mandated purgatory, thinking otherwise is a head in a hole or a hole in the head, whichever comes first. Next steps, uberpractical. A bootstrap life. Whatever's required to deliver two vestal souls from innocence. There is no control. No haunting salvation. Beads of sweat, the stains left behind, are survival's markers. The End. Valerie will receive a painful life lesson over a scant breakfast this morning while Maven watches with a toddler's curious oblivion. We'll talk about how Grampa's gone. That stupid fucking story about angel's carrying Grampa's voice and mind to heaven where they will remain until the angels reunite us with him. Propagating lies is unconscionable, a child's first break with trust, but more torturous is the truth. The lies, oh how they make us whole, give us hope until the capacity for reason blooms. Removing the shackles of sentiment from a child too early is like polishing an apple with sandpaper. Even in the face of fruitless efforts, attempts are important, aren't they?

Upon John's head again, hot against cool. Life passing its last wave of energy to death. Behind closed eyes, searching for that road to walk, the road allowing you to purge everything that ever mattered from your mind. The sign for it is up ahead glowing maniacally, but it remains forever beyond reach. In the distance, the quiet hum of garbage trucks circling, The Pile's lullaby.

The first thread of light illuminates the canopy's tip, dissolving night and making the tarpaulin space feel larger. John's head, a lead weight in my arms. Cramps burning all over. Neighbors awake in the morning reprise. Feet scuffle plastic sheeting. Flatulence and coughs. Sorting, shifting, digging through bags. Muffled whispers in irritable tones. John's greasy hair clumped into rows extending back from his forehead where my fingers must have raked for hours. A chilly morning, drops of condensation randomly fall to the floor from plastic overhead. Lingering hope of miscalculation, the potential for bad dreams of intense lucidity. But his body lays silent, unrecognizable, oblivious to the space it occupies. Her eyes appear, fighting off the last clench of sleep,

"Gamorning Gramma."

"Goodmorning sweetheart. How did you sleep?"

"Fine."

"That's good dear."

"I'm hungry Gramma."

"I know sweetheart. Give Gramma a minute and I'll make some breakfast, okay?"

"Can I have bread?"

"Maybe sweetheart, maybe. Let Gramma see what we have." Careless words, automatic, ignorant of reality.

John's head lowered gently to the floor, Valerie given the *shuush* eyes so as not to disturb him. John, motionless, an oversized puppet. Succumbing to morning fatigue, she collapses next to him, throws an arm over his dead thigh.

The bin's cover removed and a cloud of fruit flies flitter up, float along the canopy's surface searching for escape. They give in to futility, perch on the clear plastic, wait. Dry, scratchy eyes and a loose, sleepless head. In the bin, half a rotten apple balled in brown paper. A plastic container nearly full of used cooking oil. A handful of sugar cubes. A half dozen glass bottles containing pastes and gravies in a range of grays and browns, one holding last night's poultry and rice flavored mash. Habit chooses the oldest bottle, the one with the rare hint of strawberry. Civility's rhythm maintained through banal rituals; reach for a plate and place a lump of strawberry-laced garbage on it, a single sugar cube to its side. Swat laggard flies, reseal bin, knee-walk past a sleeping Maven to Valerie and John. Valerie blinks lethargically, lips part, her eyes assess the plate.

"I'm sorry sweetheart, there is no bread right now. Maybe we will find some today."

Poised to whimper, instead, she exhales deeply and pushes herself up, grinds her fist into a sleepy eye.

"We do have some strawberry, and, as a special treat, a sugar square. Doesn't that sound good?"

"That's Ok Gramma," she says reassuringly, "we can eat bread later."

"That's a good girl, here you go."

She processes the sticky lump, pokes a finger into it, tastes. A sleepy indifference washes over her face as she grabs her spoon to tackle the day's first chore.

"Is it Ok honey?"

"Yes Gramma." Monotone, reprimand's manufactured response.

"Why don't you come sit on Gramma's lap sweetheart."

Clumsily, she rises to her knees, walks to my lap leaving John lying quiet on the mat. She plunks in my lap, balances her plate between chin and outstretched arm. She chews silently as Maven's eyes pop open, her waking confusion dissolving into a reconnection with the known world. More people stir in adjacent tents and the rituals resume. Alden's urine splashes tinny against a bedpan on the left. Gertrude's signature coughing fit crackles phlegmatically from eight tents away. The Claxton children argue mercilessly with their parents to the right. Familiar morning sounds and John's new indifference to them. What was formerly his critical squint, gently dissecting the cacophony of sounds, now his solemn repose. Crawling across the mat, Maven flops her head down on my thigh.

"Why is Grampa still asleep?" Valerie asks.

"We'll discuss that after breakfast."

"Is he sick?"

"Eat now sweetheart, we'll talk later."

The polonaise starts of its own accord, stymieing questions, as hands work gently through Maven's wispy hair. Eyes closed, a catatonia-induced daydream of floating, looking down on the morning with bird's eyes. An odd configuration of cells, in each a creeping progression of tattered bodies pissing in cans, picking teeth, and folding bedding to my mental Chopin. Little mitochondria, ribbony golgi, tiny lysosomes lurch reluctantly within their membrane, executing functions autonomously. A crude symphony of action. And our cell, struggling to maintain time, the components move limply in the plasmic goo. A silent nucleus. Sputtering mitochondria. A flagging structure about to implode under the pressure of a million competing cells pressing in. The music continues, view expands, centered on the blackening dot of our cell amid the larger organism. The expanse of The Piles comes into view. Arterial roads leading east to The Core. Music surges as exurbs take shape, meticulously patterned as if designed from space. Beyond lies the coast, water kissing the shore. Zooming out further, swirling white clouds hover pattern-less over patches of blue and green, the circular perfection of Earth. Light years away we sit with our yellow companion, a mere twinkle in a black ocean. Finally, an indistinguishable fleck nestled among hazy bands of circling light suspended in time, insignificant and spinning infinitely, nauseously.

"Gramma?"

Piano ceases. Valerie's extended plate fizzles into focus.

"I'm done."

"Good girl."

Shuffle binward with her plate, wipe it and fetch Maven's breakfast.

Last night's flavorless paste chosen for Maven's naïve taste buds, flavored ones reserved for a fussier Valerie. Sitting up, she immediately rakes fingers through her ration.

"Gramma?"

"Yes dear."

"Can we wake Grampa now?"

"In a minute sweetheart."

There is no time left, no point to forestall inevitability. Grief is irrelevant, a complicating factor. Everything's remediable . A cut is washed and bound. A bruise is protected. Sadness is forgotten. People disappear. Tidy resolution.

A cold, strawberry smear to my face, "Gramma did you hurt yourself?"

Clarity. The galaxy spins slowly back into focus, halts. Our black cell sits in stark contrast to its surroundings, suspended.

"No sweetheart, it's my allergies acting up, you know how Gramma gets sniffly this time of year. Come, sit on my lap."

She crawls into the pocket of my crossed legs nestling her head beneath my chin, faces John.

"I have to tell you something about Grampa, something sad." We rock, slowly back and forth, chin burrowing into her hair, Maven rapt in the easy textures of breakfast.

"Grampa's not sleeping right now sweetheart."

"Is he metatating?"

"No dear. You know how Grampa has been sick lately?"

"Yes."

"Well, last night while you and your sister where asleep, Grampa's sickness got really bad and his body couldn't fight it anymore."

There is no God. There is no peace. Salvation isn't real. Death is the remedy. Dumb, cathartic mantras. Hey, look at that dead body lying there!

"So Grampa's sickness won the fight?"

"Yes, yes sweetheart, Grampa's sickness won the fight and because of that Grampa's body died."

"Is that why he doesn't want to wake up?"

"Well, yes. Yes, that's correct dear. You're awfully smart, you know?"

"What if we make lots of noise? I can play kitchen, you always say that's loud."

Maven's breakfast detours onto the mat, wet slapping noise amid giggles, coos.

Wiping the hair from her forehead, "Even if we shout as loud as we can, Grampa won't wake up, ever again. Grampa's body has died sweetheart."

"How will he go on our walk today?"

"Well honey, you won't be able to go on a walk with Grampa. But, that is Ok. In many ways, Grampa is still very much alive."

Silence. Rocking together while she attempts to line things up. Murmurs of conversations pierced with cries waft in the audible ether between us and the rest of the world, John lies. Billions of neurons lighting up, on fire, squirting juices across the synapses searching for a way to relate. A brilliant organic computer running through infinite binaries, calculating everything within proximity. Birds, bugs, a fading sun, a new moon, garbage trucks, bad smells, new neighbors, stillness, quiet.

"I don't understand Gramma."

She shifts, jerks, as she comes unstuck from our conversation with a frustrated whimper.

"Well, you see, Grampa's body is only part of him. The other, more important parts of Grampa, will always be right here with us. The lessons Grampa taught you and everything Grampa did with you lives in your memory. Every time you talk about Grampa and every time you practice the lessons he taught keeps him here with you, in your mind. Your memory keeps Grampa alive and in your heart."

"But I want to hold Grampa's hand. I like holding his hand."

"You may do that sweetheart, but this time, when you hold his hand, you need to tell him goodbye. Ok? Isn't that what we do when someone leaves? We say goodbye until we see them again."

She approaches John with caution, sits down beside him, working fingers into his hand. She stares at his face, waiting, then leans over and kisses him on the cheek. There is no sadness, no consternation, just a little mind overclocking on a fuzzy notion of mortality. The disappointment, frustration as one marvels at a completed puzzle, a lone piece missing. One piece missing to complete the picture. Holding his hand,

"Grampa is cold."

"I know sweetie. Let's get him a blanket."

Amid a pile of musty sheets lies Valerie's favorite blanket, the one flecked with pink carnations.

"Here sweetheart, let's put this over Grampa."

We drape the sheet over him, tuck the ends beneath his body. She places a hand on his chest absentmindedly.

"We shouldn't cover his face Gramma. It might stuffocate him."

"Remember sweetheart, Grampa isn't using this body anymore. Now he is in our hearts and minds, he doesn't need to breath anymore. He's free to roam around inside your mind, my mind, and Maven's mind. Grandpa's free."

We play the game as the day progresses. Valerie continually rooting John into the physical world, me pushing him into the realm of our minds.

At times she's giddy with the idea of John floating inside of her, but dithers frequently back to the missing puzzle piece.

In the evening cool, preparations are made, assistance sought. Jim Claxton and Alden carry John's wrapped body the half mile to The Piles' outskirts, breaking frequently for rest. At the road's edge, a space is cleared amid the bank of debris, his body placed face up on the splintered macadam. Awkward condolences, goodbye hugs. Squatting in a field a few dozen feet from the road's edge, watching, waiting. Sun disappears, a low drone hums ominously from the distance. The humming increases, headlights arc over the horizon glaring down on us. In a minute, the massive trucks are upon John, their giant spinning brushes raking the edge of the roadway. An armored truck, #429, approaches John and a barrage of whirling plastic tines lash, then consume his body. The street where his body laid is damp, shimmers in the moonlight. #429 crests the hill heading toward the pit it reports to.

Walking home, lamps highlight confused emotions on Valerie's tired face. Her thoughts? *Grandpa must be floating around like a tiny angel, visiting us all. Grandpa, tired from flight, alights on the ground. An angry, screaming truck swallows his body with the rest of the trash littering the ground. Is Grandpa garbage?*

The pressure, to ease suffering, confusion. Fairy tales and comfortable lies. Valerie given the God piece missing from her puzzle, unimaginable stories told as we tread ironically through the detritus of a million wasted lives. Something of a complete picture. Her broad, peaceful smile and Maven's warm drool on my neck. Things to cling to.

"Do you think ambition adds more value to society than intellect?" he asked one evening as we sat on the crumbling pavement, overlooking my former soccer field.

"I don't know what society means."

"Come on Pham. The whole population of walking, talking humans as a homogeneous group, living and interacting among one another, and bound by the simple concept that everyone is constructed in the same form and are all driven by the same basic set of needs and wants."

"In this scenario, when did I eat last?"

"For this scenario, eating is irrelevant. Abstract it away."

"Eating is never irrelevant, especially when working through your damn scenarios."

"Fine then, answer the question with the baggage."

A cramping stomach amid attempts to be a voluble little prodigy. It must have been about three days since my last meal, maybe four. The fog of irritation. Listlessness. Distraction. But for him, my best, push through the hollow feeling.

"No. They are equally valuable and to the same degree. A strong intellect helps me to identify and associate patterns, catalog attributes, reason my way through alternatives, and learn from failures and successes helping me to continually refine my hunting process, hopefully generate better results. Ambition helps me rise from my bed regardless of headaches, the diarrhea, the swollen hands and feet, the utter lack of energy. To remain on my feet for hours at a time until food is found."

"Reasonable answer, however if you're unable to abstract away food, eliminate yourself from your response."

Like many times before, the desire to grab hold of his Adam's apple, rip it from his veiny neck. But that was the pissed Neanderthal, the hungry animal rejecting mental work because of unmet primary needs. Sitting motionless, methodically disassociating the angst triggered by his pressing. To carefully separate the antagonist from brewing anger. He was oddly patient, calm amid a teen's frustrating slog toward temperance. Self-righteous huffs. Petty, indignant posturing. A goofy, cracking voice. Strange whiskers poking from pimply chin in constant need of fingering. Racing thoughts of blissful perversion. Enduring starvation like a fucking man. And then, the next step in our exchange,

"Does ambition even hold value if it's not guided by reason?"

"Is the intellect productive without a motivational spur?" he replied.

"Why is everything measured in terms of value or productivity?" thoughts spoken in frustration.

"What's the point otherwise Pham? Humans exist to survive, to procreate. As we evolved over millions of years and developed a sharper understanding of our condition, we had no choice but to optimize our existence, refine our capabilities as a means of survival. Do you want to spend your limited energy on fruitless effort? Can you survive on knowledge?"

"No, but, at some point, we moved past the animals, past kill or be killed. Beyond the survival of the fittest. Didn't we?"

"That's debatable Pham. You see, along the evolutionary process, some saw fit to define a new animal. Surviving is a noble aspiration for us lesser animals, but thriving excessively, lavishly and at the expense of others is the aspiration of the highest animals, those endowed with the capacity to properly cultivate a sense of malice. Kill or be killed, version 2.0" he replied, smirking.

"This doesn't even make any sense. I mean, what the hell's the social benefit of malice?"

"Population control is a motivating factor. Survival would be another. I guess it depends on the relative prosperity of the person answering the question. But, back to the original question, ambition or intellect, which is it going to be Pham?"

"I'll keep my first answer. They are equally valuable if your so-called society is to amount to anything."

A heavy exhale, Mr. Voyes responded, "Perhaps you don't see the same picture I see. For me, the bigger question has always been *why is there a need to separate the two when considering humans?*"

"Which humans?" I asked.

...

Time.

Again, it slips. Focus, stop walking through fragments of past conversations. The direction is known, is clear. The past has been used as needed. Focus. Review, keep shaping the plan else all the conversations were pointless, for naught.

The basics, again. Go over the damn basics again. Repetition. From everything gleaned, the distance from here to The Core's center is roughly forty miles. Ninety-eight percent of the route is paved and mostly flat to allow passage for the trash trucks. Roughly ten miles beyond The Archives it's time to change, scrap my identity, prepare to blend in. That leaves about twenty-five to The Core's center. Within a few miles of The Core, ready the lines, my back-story. Chip needs to be planted well in advance to allow for healing, two or three weeks. And the alcohol, don't forget the alcohol. Must be clean and tidy upon entry to The Core to support my identity, so, no pushing the pace. Walk measured. Say an average of fifteen minutes per mile. Slow and steady. Total trip should take ten hours, maybe. Allot additional time to find the venue, wherever it is. Suitcase will be heavy for the first fifteen miles, rest often, keep fresh. Ditch the case well in advance of the DMZ, wherever it happens to be. Head up, always head up.

Food, the never-ending concern. What if I'm hungry, without any food leading up to the departure? Journey could be impossible. Emergency measures may be necessary. May need to violate the one rule everyone in The Piles lives and dies by, no stealing. There is only one shot at this, must be prepared. Others may have to unwittingly sacrifice for the greater good. Cross that bridge then. Mattison's usually gone for the afternoon on alternating days. Avery is a dead sleeper. William now *owes* me, may not attack me if caught. Volskev's away for an hour before sunrise in the mornings.

Rain. Something as simple as rain could complicate, or rather, delegitimize my second story. The plastic poncho must be tested to ensure waterproof. Must arrive at the Town Hall appearing clean and respectable among the Beatus. If it doesn't rain this week, rig a test at the water hole somehow.

Robbers. The roving groups of criminal Dirts several miles beyond The Piles are a concern as they constantly pick strays clean of possessions. A suitcase is bait. They will have blades, stones. I will have something more potent but it's a bluff, can't be spent on them. A lie and a poker face are my defense.

Walking through The Core, the other side. Never been there, have no map, know nothing of its geography. Keeping relaxed will be important while navigating. Are there paths to walk on? Are there checkpoints or gates? Detection systems? So many details about the mechanics of daily life are unknown from the scant scraps of literature scattered in the drop fields. Murky mental images of concentric circles with opulent towers at center is the map. Loose contingencies strung together to account for myriad situations. Remaining relaxed and flexible is critical.

And what happens once there? No way of knowing at this point. John always said it would be clear when I should act. When the time's right. What sort of plan is that? So much confidence. Too much confidence. His faithful protégé, groomed and indoctrinated. Or his little drone, oiled and primed. All the same. Aim for the chest, he said, fire three quickly. Squeeze, squeeze, squeeze. Best chance for a hit. Is it possible to fire three before they react? **Latency (a time interval between the cause and the effect of some physical change in the system being observed. Latency is physically a consequence of the limited velocity with which any physical interaction can propagate)**.

Several days since the last look inside. Too much time has passed since the items were pondered, the application of each, visualized. The plan, rehearse often to keep thoughts fresh, vivid, centered in consciousness. Muscle memory is repetition realized. From behind the ragged pile of blankets, a mouse darts, shoots under the tarp into William's cell before there's a chance to lunge at it. Never mind. The case. Sitting on the mat, the tattered nylon case stares back. Years of dirt grinded into faded blue fabric, a fabric rough and brittle. Thumbing the clasp, push open the clamshell, an impeccably organized, clean interior. Two disposable razors. A tiny bottle of shaving oil. A phial of cologne. Deodorant. Two bars of soap. A pint of rum. A shiny pair of ersatz leather shoes. A pristine, brand-new gray suit wrapped in clear plastic. A shockingly white oxford. A solid red tie. An Iron tag and chip. The nickel glint of a .357 peeking from behind the loose folds of a red handkerchief.

"Practice."

The word slips, reluctantly. The biggest concern, no real practice. Held it a million times. These motions, walked through over and over. Disassembled, cleaned, reassembled. Every nook relentlessly inspected. Its ribbed, vented barrel. Its smooth locking cylinder. Its expertly machined frame: edges precise, sharp, a testament to its quality. Prominent hammer, a visual underscore of its explosive potential. Lubricated with scavenged oils over the years, smells vaguely reminiscent of something edible, yet industrial. Cold to the touch regardless of the air. There's a regal quality about it, it looks at me with a well masked contempt, discernable only by its staunch, unwavering physical presence. Why does it feel like the more I manipulate it, the more it seems to manipulate me?

Mr. Voyes patiently fielding the millions of questions about what to expect. The sensation of recoil. The smell of discharge. The best way to grip it when pulling the trigger. Hold it frequently to know every minute contour, unite with it. Make it an extension of self to dissolve fear and apprehension.

But how does it feel? It hardly exists. It's mostly imaginary. It only feels semi-real when fully dissected, its parts scattered, vulnerable.

Pulling the trigger, the one elusive experience. Three cartridges in the cylinder, one with the primer pressed sideways into the shell, likely a dud. Not enough to take a single practice shot. A miracle, the three cartridges, let alone an actual gun. A mixture of luck and dogged perseverance making it possible for the gun to exist in The Piles. And, through the tumult, he never used it. On himself or anyone else. Temperance. Another miracle.

Coughing fit in the distance and a renewed focus on this hand squeezing burled wood grips. The man in the distance choking violently and dozens of bodies crinkling on plastic sheeting in response. A dry, clapping fart a couple decibels above the chokes. Sounds die in unison, again, gun into focus. Stay focused. Repetition and muscle memory.

But, Renaldo. Forever sidelined, watching me, waiting to see what I'll do next. His dripping face, a bloody stick in my hand and the tears coming down after processing the brutality unleashed on a friend. A goddamn handful of crackers, who even spotted it first? A reaction so violent and thoughtless, pangs of hunger could hardly be at fault. To bludgeon a friend's face. It was there, looming, something ominous, charged. An energy passing through me leaving an oblivious child wondering what happened. The nothingness from beyond, whispering into my ear. And his face. Swelling with infection, his mother relieving the pressure by puncturing tiny holes in his cheeks and forehead. His screams enveloped our wing in The Piles. Lying on the ground, in the dark, crimson heat radiating from Mr. Patel's angry face, the piercing shrieks of my best friend sentencing me to another night of guilt. Awaking the following morning to Mr. Patel's terse instructions of final apology. Renaldo's parents, busy, preparing to take their son's body to the roadside. Dazed, no response granted to my muted, tearful babbling as they hoisted his body, carried him down the narrow hall toward the fuzzy yellow exit. Violence sworn off that day, long ago. A promise of vigilance against the impulses that encourage violence How to reconcile with this sweaty grip on hope? His bloody face then, my hand on a gun now.

Will I hesitate? Will I crumble? Will fear lock my joints? Never-ending questions. But that was years ago, different circumstances. Reaction, not planned. Yet, the use of violence, something conditioned against for many years. Meditate. Meditate on the motions. The situations. The sounds. Smells. Adrenaline squirting like raw pops of crystal clear motion. Build neurological pathways for action, billions of sprouting dendrites carrying electric signals to the nerves, to the trigger finger.

Close the case, push it under the blankets. Concealed. Lying, back to the ground, gun on chest, index finger across trigger guard. Metal rising and falling with each breath, eyes closed, begin the process. Images take shape, the fast-forward blooming of flowers. The Piles. Sunlight. A murky waterhole. Faint odors of oil and this plant called **Lavender (a flowering plant in the family Lamiaceae, native to the western Mediterranean, primarily the Pyrenees and other mountains in northern Spain)** as the bar foams. The tug and rip of whiskers being sliced at the skin for the first time. Cologne's pungency. Pearlescent teeth. Walk. Walk. Walk. Walk. The bite of alcohol on my tongue. Questions. Interrogation. Walk. Walk. Walk. Walk. Faces. Lots of faces. A crowd. Sparse images. An open space with no details. A white void. Here come the trees, plopping themselves into the ground.

Here comes a stage, a podium, falling from the blue sky. Oh, sky, there it is. People, figures, milling about and quickly growing in numbers. Dense, no room to move. And now a target, situated on stage, a plump bull's-eye-of-a-face yet blurry, vague. Loudspeakers crackle. Everything hangs, actors hold positions, wait for direction. Then a gun. Fingers wrapped around it. Pressure. Pressure. Fate? Destiny? My control or someone else's? John posthumously pulling the strings? Angry God washing everything away? Moral mandates. Oh right, God. The eyes in the sky watching over the flock. Force or a farce? That article, oh yeah. Strange. *The Scientific Discovery of the Millennium*. The odd comedy of it all.

The images evaporate, focus lost again. God derails the train! Mystique demanding consideration. Glinting, winking, as it's placed back into its case. A final flash through compressed time. Shifting across dirty sheets, the stack of tattered books piled in the corner. The taller stack, third book from bottom, folded and placed at center. An anemic beam of moonlight shining through the roof, insufficient. Crawl over to the diode, touch the wires to illuminate the expansive sheet of the Tribune. At top, the image of an airplane and a beautiful half-nude smiling, waving.

THE SCIENTIFIC DISCOVERY OF THE MILLENNIUM!!!

GOD DOES NOT EXIST. In what is clearly the most important scientific discovery in recorded history, a team of scientists have proved, with absolute certainty, that no greater power beyond mankind exists, or has ever existed, in the Universe. Not only does this discovery provide answers to questions long plaguing mankind since the dawn of ~~creation~~ formation, but it also provides insights into how social systems may benefit from natural realities. The future of scientific discovery has never looked so promising, so utterly illuminating.

"CHANCE WAS ON OUR SIDE"

While conducting experiments on trash samples in a remote section of the drop fields recently sprayed with anti-biological agents, prominent scientist and television personality Dr. Fred Bhoyle became a witness to the most fundamental force in the Universe, now being referred to colloquially as *formation*. Out on a research venture, Dr. Bhoyle was performing spectra analysis on dirt samples when, some fifty feet in front of him, a disturbance. Initially, nothing out of the ordinary, just a charming little dust devil dancing about. The agitation though continued for a few moments until a rather sizeable vortex took shape spitting dirt and trash out from its center. The whirlwind persisted for a minute or so, gaining strength and beginning to consume larger debris from points nearby in the drop fields. Within a couple minutes, the whirlwind strengthened considerably causing Dr. Bhoyle to seek refuge behind the burnt out hull of a car, protection against random chunks of flying debris.

Crouched behind the hull, Dr. Bhoyle watched the disturbance grow into a formidable F3 tornado (wind speed analysis still pending) violently sucking every scrap of debris within a two hundred foot radius. Dr. Bhoyle continued his retreat from the funnel, placing himself at a safe, observable distance from the event. The churning continued, and, as Dr. Bhoyle noted, "The most amazing aspect of the tornado was its complete focus on cyclonic motion with zero deviation from its point of origin. To my knowledge, a tornado with this sort of stayed activity knows no precedence."

Translation? The tornado stood perfectly still, spinning on an axis seemingly anchored to the ground rather than roaming about as is typical with tornados.

For five minutes the tornado churned, collecting every speck of debris within its suctioning range, even claiming Dr. Bhoyle's new felt mortarboard directly from atop his head. Eventually the winds ceased spinning and the typical calm of the drop fields resumed. Gradually the area, previously obfuscated by debris and violent winds, cleared and Dr. Bhoyle saw the most amazingly impossible object sitting gloriously in the spot where, no more than five minutes earlier, existed nothing but a sprawling pile of trash. A brand new jet airplane painted in a flawless powder blue, not a hairline scratch visible. As Dr. Bhoyle approached the majestic aircraft, stunned silent, an even more impossible situation unfolded. Descending from the fuselage of the plane, a beautiful brunette, clothed in nothing more than a white satin shawl. When Dr. Bhoyle's voice returned he questioned the woman, learning she was entirely unaware of who she was, where she was or where she came from. It was at that point Dr. Bhoyle began snapping photos of the woman and the plane and subsequently called every scientist he knew over the course of his long and prestigious career.

The team of scientists wasted no time searching for the origins of the airplane and the woman (whom the scientists named Victoria Salvador). Long into the night, the scientists conducted tests on both subjects searching for clues, evidence. In the pastels of morning, the lab tests concluded. Victoria, who by all accounts appeared in her mid-thirties, was less than twenty-four hours old as verified by extensive analysis of her orthopantomographies and posteroanterior chest x-rays. Being thorough, the scientists ran a DNA match of Victoria's DNA against every living and dead person, finding zero plausible matches or relatives. The final piece of Victoria's puzzle was inserted when scientists verified that the particular section of the drop fields where she was discovered was sprayed by the anti-biological drones that morning. Soil tests after her arrival revealed that absolutely no biological matter existed within a five mile radius of the patch of ground where the plane sat.

The airplane too, provided a slew of evidence pointing to its age. Upon opening the cabin doors, a potent new-plane odor pricked the scientists' noses. Tread analysis of the landing gear revealed absolutely no scuffs. And each cabin seat was still sealed in its protective plastic bag as if recently delivered from the factory. Based on this evidence, experts concluded the plane was precisely twenty two-hours and thirty-three minutes old. Industry analysis was also conducted on the airplane revealing that no corporation or individual aeronautic engineer was responsible for its unique design or build.

With no existing DNA ties to the living or dead, an age clearly inconsistent with Victoria's visual appearance, and proof that no biological components (not a trace of a single amino acid!) were present at the time of formation, the scientists were able, for the first time, to prove the feasibility of abiogenesis, establishing the fact that a higher being is not required to instantiate human existence. Rather, the first humans were formed by ultra low probability events mashing together the needed chemicals to spawn life independent of a preconceived design. Sorry

God! Additionally, by establishing the precise age of the airplane, and proving that it wasn't produced by any person or corporation, the scientists were able to definitively prove the previously elusive complementary hypotheses of aengineerigenesis and aconstructogenesis. Immediately following the discovery, engineers set out to search for a way to deterministically replicate the process of aengineerigenesis in order to free up more of their time to learn how to feel rather than to spend all of their time thinking. What an amazing world we live in!

As the intensive study wrapped and the scientists meandered about, pondering the existential, we approached a bleary-eyed Dr. Bhoyle and asked him for a few comments on the day's events, "The probability of spontaneous human creation from a pile of trash has long been estimated at 1-in-10^{40000}. The probability of a large, complex piece of modern machinery spontaneously creating itself from a pile of trash has also been estimated at roughly 1-in-10^{40000}. Combine these two events and we are witnessing probabilities that are, well, smaller than the ambition of a Dhalyte! I say this tongue-in-cheek of course, but, being precise, it is critical to point out that these are very, *very* minute probabilities indeed. At this point, all there is left to say is that chance was on our side for this discovery."

Insanity. My initial assumption was that the article came from the paper's Humor section, no consideration given beyond its apparent comic value. But, weeks later, that scientific journal found buried beneath a pile of shredded tires, the exhaustive detail printed about that *momentous* day. Do people actually believe this? What is reality? What is faith? What is the purpose of science? Why does the world seems so upside down? Who is after what? False discovery? False news? Isolated only a few dozen miles from the other type of humans, but a constant struggle to understand anything about them. God, complexity on a mind-bending scale. The subject of thousands of years of intellectual thought. A reality or not. God. The ultimate cross-section of philosophy, science, faith, history, religion, morality. Some sort of unknown force of origin. What is the reason for a tidy, bullshit dismissal of its entirety? Who stands to gain what and why?

Pulling the wires, the diode fades, the room returns to the bluish grey of night. Into the book goes the article to lay dormant a while until the next attempt to plumb the unknowable. Crinkles of plastic, a hard bed, the aura of a higher power pressing in. If there's something there, does it care about my plan? Will it exert influence? Appeal to intellect and Providence simultaneously, a smart hedge? Hey, Pham…What Would John Do?

Up.
Down.
Up.
Down.
Then, Muhammad.
Up.
Down.
Up.
Down.
Both animated.

On all fours, crawling in slow motion echo. Cold floor. Red kids. Everything's leaky. Throw a hand to her bodiless head, it falls away with a thud, Magdalene's eyes pop open, she jerks. Her eyes focus, she stares. Parted, motionless lips sedate.

"Honey, you hurt?"

Muhammad's sobs, a tinge of hope. Fumbling at Magdalene's lashed wrists, pry a heavy knot.

"Honey, can you hear me?"

A thousand fingers scramble to loosen the knot, Magdalene's hands fall limp to the floor. Scooping her up, Judy's head rolls away. Then Muhammad. Pinched face, stochastic whimpers. Magdalene catches Judy's vacant stare, shrieks, heart drops, Muhammad goes silent.

"Don't look honey. We're leaving."

She slaps Judy's face with horror, Muhammad's cadent whimpers, fingers tearing his knot. Wiggling free, Muhammad clenches, buries head in my chest, Magdalene's hysterics. Autopilot, smother them with arms, lift, limp to elevator. Prickles, memories of legs. Another tattered flag in the hall, push kids into elevator. Little bodies, sticky and quivering. The scent and shine of stainless panels. Rush to car, start it, slam into reverse. Whining engine, launched upward into the waning daylight. Drive, drive away from Bunker. A figure disturbing shadows on the edge of the bunker's vent stack. It ducks low, out of sight. Press accelerator to gate III.

Catatonic sniffles break the car's silence. Magdalene and Muhammad motionless, eyes bleary, minutes from sleep as we barrel to police headquarters deep in The Bunkers. Thirty minute drive at high speed? The acrid flavor of vomit. Reach for stale remnants of morning coffee sitting cold on console. Swish it around, uncontrollable chokes, keep those images suppressed. My lovely Judy. Butchered. Tears bubble, run down, soak undershirt's neckband. Stare ahead, blink vigorously, maintain rhythmic breathing. Foster calm, be the adult. Things like composure, rationality, measurement. Adult behavior.

Traffic. Limited to the infrequent passing MRAP this far in The Bunkers. Periodic clumps of filthy blankets, crude shelters on shoulders. The occasional crouch and hide of a dissident attempting concealment. Hands, eyes, locked defensively. Widely dispersed and subterranean, Diamond residents this far out ARE their own police department. Their own grocery store. Utility company. Self-contained cities underground, each serving a family, members countable on one hand. No Platinums here. Few even on The Bunker's cheap western edge. Judy's dream, the out-of-reach lifestyle. A lifestyle not fully disconnected, requiring access to nominal public services out east. Fucking long drive through the only extant orchards. 360 degrees of halcyon affluence. She loves this drive. Loved. "Natural opulence," I think she said. Tears, again. Hot eyes. God? A few minutes and we're there, piece together what's next. Children, shellacked head to toe in brownish red, slumped over one another, sleeping. Jesus.

"Get yourself together Kaysen."

Police station in the distance, mash accelerator, run through the tape. Into the parking lot, all three cruisers at base, a full house, this odd fear stabbing. From the car, children asleep in the back, run sloppy to the entrance, rip at door. Inquisitive eyes.

"My wife, she's, she's dead...they..."

"Sir, come in, please."

"…they killed her…and my kids, my kids, they…they cut her fucking head off!"

"Sir, come in, tell us what happened."

"…*Oh God*, they…*Oh Jesus Christ, they, Oh God!*"

We're all wearing them, huddled together, hair still damp and growing cold. Thoughts drift, shake stupor, try to focus on one at a time. They don't know what to do or say. They sob one minute, fight the other, cling to me momentarily then whine for home. They are hungry. Thirsty. Tired. Bored. Aren't thirsty. No longer hungry. Tired. An outward facing schizophrenia, mine churning horribly within. Her immediate reminder washed off, replaced with uncomfortable police jogging suits stinking of cellophane, cheap synthetic fabrics overexposed to the sun. Muhammad and Magdalene, two dark blue blobs, as are the three children sitting adjacent. Their father, clad in blue, relentlessly attempting eye contact. Why did I come here? Why am I here? Why does a police outpost employing three cops have so many goddamn jogging suits? Tangential. He wants to talk more, he's shifting, rotating his head to capture my eyes with his. That thick bead of caulk squirted sloppily along the floor's edge, pasta dangling limp from the edge of a pot.

"So, you said you live along the perimeter of The Bunkers right, near the first zone?" he asks.

"Yeah, inside zone one."

My Judy. Was there pain? Dried blood staring at me, embedded in cuticle frowns. Stinging eyes.

"Come here Muhammad, come here."

"And you said you arrived home around five, right?"

"Yeah, sometime around five."

Muhammad puts his head in my lap. Magdalene follows.

"I don't know if you heard me, but my name is Roger, Roger Townsend."

"I'm Kaysen. McMrrMurty…" Firecrackers, tiny lumps of sour esophageal debris. "*Ehhem*, sorry. Kaysen McMurty."

"I guess we are sort-of neighbors. I'm up the road from you, ten minutes or so, zone two."

Wait, why are they wearing jogging suits? I could go for a run. Why are the lights in this room so fucking bright? The thick scent of The Pine, tongue tastes greenish. White. White tile walls, white benches, white light. Harsh white, blending corners and edges into walls. Enclosed in an empty white bubble. Echoes reverberating off one another.

"Yeah. Close."

"It's just, that, I wh… I spoke to her before leaving Morten Street, and, and she was fine."

He won't shut the hell up. Don't want to talk. Can't talk. I don't want to talk dammit.

"She didn't indicate anything unusual."

Too tired to talk. I don't want to talk. Morten?

"Sounded normal."

"You said Morten…"

"Yes, Morten. My office is at Morten Street."

"…you work at Salvation Inc?"

"Yeah, as I said, I'm the Vice President of HR. You an employee?"

A merging. Emerging. Blue blobs, Salvation, despondency. Emerging emergency.

"ARE YOU?"

"Yeah, was. I was a regional director. Atonement Centers."

His knees catch elbows and fingers dig through his hair, nails scrape his scalp. Large eyes freeze on me. That falling feeling.

"You know what's going on, right?" he asks. "The attacks along the southern rim of The Bunkers?"

Ringing ears muffle his voice, his mouth keeps going, increases in speed. In aperture. He levitates and floats over. What, gravity's broken now? His face ballooning, swelling red.

"…NNNo, I…no, I just found her dead." My voice returns from across the room, someone else's. "Dead. I came home and she was completely dead."

"*This is it, it's happening.* Attacks against Salvation Inc execs everywhere. In The Core and in The Bunkers. Ely Powers, sorry, the CFO, was impaled right on Morten, hours ago. Quorum members and their families, attacked too."

The CFO was a plump man, a gelatinous man, right? Lumpy yellow blobs of adipose dangling, melting, from a fence post or a pot rack.

"Wha, what the…*why* the hell did I come here?" he asks, knees piston up down.

He inches closer, face beginning to shake, vibrate. Rapid, vibrating motion. Seconds skipped over, then repeated. Very close, his lips brush my ear. Personal space is broken too?

"*I don't think we can trust the police.*" Whispers through clenched teeth. "*The thirty-third.*"

Heart jolts, lingering fear crystallizing into something indefinable. Substance with no meaning. The big, vibrating blue blob moves away, pulls his two smaller blobs to his lap, stops vibrating. Objects become crisp, sharply contrasted. A fading out then a quick, nauseating return. No subtleties. This or that. Figures teasing shadows around my home, Hans? A deputy? Where's my security detail? Why was nobody in the house?

"What the hell am I doing here!" he asks. He digs at his scalp again, aggressive knees, looks at me irritated. I didn't pot rack your wife.

"I'm heading back to my place in The Core while the police begin their, *thing*," he declares assuredly, stands. Walking to the door, he calls the lead officer. In walks a sinewy man of forty, clean shaven, blue tinted jaw line jutting out. Zero adipose.

"Officer, rather than stay here, I'm going to my apartment in The Core. It is highly secure, safer and more comfortable for my children." Unflinching executive orders.

"That's not a good idea Mr. Townsend. You are safer here, besides, additional reinforcements are heading here from The Core along with investigators to work your case. You and your children are safe and we can set up cots and private amenities for the evening." The officer's voice, flat, hollow. Lacks intonation, lacks that nuance of woeful pleading known to a voice meant to comfort victims.

Townsend presses, "I understand, but my children are traumatized, need the comfort of home. Plus, my MRAP is highly secure, my apartment is a fortress."

"So was your Bunker," the officer says. Tiny, barely there, but it's there! Certain of it. Hardly perceptible, but, the corner of his mouth pulled back slightly. It pulled back. It did! His squinting eyes, they smiled. His eyes smiled and this sour shit's coming up my throat. His crow's foot sharpened, it did.

Unbroken eyes, Townsend asks, "Am I a suspect?"

"No sir, not at this point. Procedurally, we prefer to keep tabs on victims and suspects until we have a basic understanding of the events that transpired."

Fishing in his pocket, "Here are my contact details. If I am needed for anything I am immediately available, day or night. I'm happy to return as necessary. Kids, let's go, NOW." Townsend shakes one, lifts the other, makes for the door. A second officer stands blocking, reluctantly steps aside after a prolonged stare with Townsend. Cramps and a hollow head. Townsend's heels click faintly, a punching heart, he turns to me. Me! Time is broken, not moving in the way in which things that are not broken are supposed to move. *Huh?*

"How are we doing over here?" he asks, the same flat tone, checking the clock, squinting at me, assessing.

Anger in the squint! This, this oddly lucid, blinking calculus. Downy heads in warm lap, code running a billion lines per second.

99.9% of the police force is comprised of Irons, with a mere handful of Diamonds sitting atop them setting mission, writing checks. The police force, unspoken, is an organization meant to serve and protect the Irons as each Diamond and many Platinums have the means to employ private security. The few police posts in The Bunkers are ceremonial since there are no Irons to police in The Bunkers. The populist anger arising from the recent passage of the 33rd Amendment, reducing the force to a nominally protective, angry, band of Irons. Years of socially constructed pilfering at the hands of my employer and others. One plausible outcome. I'm a target.

Judy's wet eyes, dry mouth for them, "I, my…my kids are a wreck, sir, you understand? This…is hard. I'm sorry, I'm, so sorry."

"They're safe here," he says pursing lips, cocking his head. "We can help." A distant voice, unburdened by emotion.

"I know, but they don't understand. This is too much. They need something familiar, family. I have, I have a place. My brother, their cousins. It's best. For them. I'm so sorry, you understand, don't you? You have kids right, you understand? I'm sorry. I'm so, so sorry." Lightheaded, dizzy.

"You sure I can't convince you to stay? Never know what you'll find out there."

"No, I think it's best really," rubbing soft heads awake.

"Perhaps we could offer an escort. Safe passage to your brother's?"

"No, thank you though, but my car is very secure. Drive isn't too far." Pull Magdalene to chest, usher Muhammad to door. Eyes maul us, judging, weighing, assessing. Attention oscillating between us, the clock. Throat clenched, sour and narrowing. Brace. Brace for the walk by them, past them. The exit, nearly to the car. An audience watches. An angry mob contemplates. Townsend calls,

"Say, business must be good, huh?"

"I'm sorry?"

"I said business's good, yeah? Ringing phones all day long?"

Tasers and billy clubs. Bony fists and contusions. Methodology. Sanctioned vengeance

"I've never known of a Platinum with a spot in The Bunkers." Corner of his mouth pulls taut, revealing a little white glint. Erect hairs. Door handle missed, face into glass. Steady, push door, backpedal and drag kids into the night. Key fumbling, jerk engine to life, squeal into the black bound for wherever. A nonexistent brother. A home that is no longer. Into the future, a convoy of police cruisers rip by on the opposite lane. Accelerator to the floor once again.

"...but let's get to the main reason why I'm here before you today. Without further ado, it is with great pleasure that I present to you an amazing, fully subsidized technology that will greatly enhance every citizens' ability to communicate, and to fully enjoy all the wonderful entertainment options available in the marketplace. Ladies and gentlemen, introducing -"

"Excuse me, Master Ortiz?"

In a perfect world, anyone who interrupts would face summary execution. In a perfect world. "*Hhhhhhhhhh*, what it is?"

"I'm very sorry to bother you Master but we've found a few candidates who may fit your requirements."

"Fine. Give me five then send in the first."

"Yes Master Ortiz. Is there anything else I can do for you?"

"Yes, leave. Pull the door behind you."

"Yes Master, sorry."

Reviewing the speech will have to wait, vetting requires full attention. At his core, he is intelligent. He must be articulate but in a manner digestible to an absolute idiot. A countenance of respectability without ambition is preferable. Most importantly, he must have charisma gently suppressed under the weight of a nagging modesty, the sort of charm that oozes credibility. Of course a boon if he flaunts a 25 inch waist, 29 inch chest, baby-smooth light brown skin and an openness to suggestive discussion.

Tap water flows cool into hands, filling to the palm's edge. A quick splash to the face, the last opportunity to freshen before makeup arrives. Patting off the excess water, the towel's softness, reminiscent of that night, some thirty years ago, standing in front of the mirror in my quarters at the Assembly. Exhausted, fighting the late night battles to bend wills, clear paths and bolster support with the aim of arriving here, at this point in time. Not perfect yet, but getting closer.

...

The reddish hues of mahogany were the first traces of light to hit my eyes after sucking warm, moist air through the towel pulled down across my face. Blunt pressure on the top of my head steadily grew as the wood paneling held me from tipping over. Wanting sleep, craving sleep but not yet satisfied with the progress made, so, committed to fighting on. Droplets patted from chin, towel tossed, a long walk down the hall. Wood heels clapped the marble as the indistinct chatter of hordes grew as did the stately paneled doors upon approach. Doors pushed open to a flurry of activity, a mixture of stale odors from overworked bodies and spoiled food. Distinct in the ocean of chaotic activity were the four solid colors, yellow, red, blue and silver, of opposing political viewpoint peppering the hall.

We had been at it for weeks. My fellow Corps and I held a simple majority and with it, a mandate from *The People* to do whatever was necessary to pull the economy from the depths of the Super Depression, caused officially, by rampant speculation in little bottles of gas. A timely tragedy for us, as the previous year was spent revamping our party's structure, including full integration with the biggest players in each industry. Ready to compete with the other political parties, our two-point platform was clear. First, vastly expanded technological capability in the consumer space. And second, the complete corporatization of government to eliminate bureaucratic waste once and for all. An expansive program of subsidies to the entertainment industry was key to stimulate both platform points. The stated party goal, to bump every other party out of existence. A simple plan, but it took time to forcibly shift party allegiances by injecting our own personnel into the opposition. Slowly infiltrating, and, in time, shifting voting patterns of the opposition to subsume a majority of their seats into ours.

The debates were vigorous. The Citizens Party with their yellow banners pushed for expanded education, subsidized healthcare, workers' rights and investment in experimental revitalization of The Wastelands. The Religious Party, members adorned in bright red ties, attempted to align policy with the accepted principles and behaviors as decreed by the Quorum of Religious Institutions. And The Radical Party, with their ubiquitous blue armbands, pressed for free psychostimulants for all Feral Rock Pigeons, an all out ban on the production of sharp objects, and legalization of late third-trimester abortion.

Among the three opposition parties, the only real competitor was The Citizens as the other two parties constantly garbled the benefits of their boutique issues, alienating all but their ardent base. Citizens had a viable platform diametrically opposed to Corps values, which constituted a real threat if not handled properly. Holding 29% of the voting population, Citizens controlled a solid base, a base with growth potential.

Back in my seat, listening to the windy drone of an exhausted man jawing about society's obligation to mitigate the self-inflicted psychological damage caused by neurotic birds, it dawned on me. It was a moment of clarity that pierced the harebrained argument in motion. A simple exchange, an agreement among fellow elected officials. The typical horse-trading between politicians, nothing more. Just a pause, a momentary alliance, then back to the swords. Healthcare was their baby, their must-have. The Citizens viewed it as a right and an obligation within an advanced society. The man at the podium continued but his volume faded, echoed, leaving behind the odd visual of a grown man acting out the silent plight of psychotic birds. As his head bobbed forward and back, arms stitched to his sides, strutting with his hands tucked in his armpits, I knew I had arrived at something, an idea, a path forward. In that moment, the idea of nationalized healthcare looked completely different, a method for customer retention in fact, perhaps a component of a broader consumer loyalty program. Something to flesh out in future meetings. With that perspective quickly crystallizing, the urgency for a huddle was clear. It was time to get down to serious business.

In a back corner of the hall, six of us, three Corps and three Citizens brokered the deal to tally the 90% necessary to automatically enact the landmark legislation. A big win for Citizens, but a monumental win for Corps. Each citizen would now have access to GoverMed, and, to help stimulate economic activity, the government would begin subsidizing both industrial production and retail pricing of products and services labeled as *consumer entertainment*. Heralded as rare bipartisan legislation, the law advanced quickly through budgeting, lubricated by a shift in alliances and an adroit cultivation of new allies within the Radicals and the Religious. Several weeks of back and forth but ultimately we prevailed, acquired a threshold of votes for an opaque provision granting priority funding of all new federal revenues to entertainment subsidies. Iacta alea est, *The People* were ours, we were *The People*. The linchpin for the Corps entire strategy was in place, marking the advent of our beautifully utopian corporatocracy, and establishing the foundation for the corporate apparatus to grow and expand. For our allies-of-convenience, the only concessions were a relatively inconsequential bit of funding for Pigeon Ritalin and a nationwide ban on masturbation from 10 PM Mondays through 3:45 PM Wednesdays.

...

Towel falls limp across the bar, snowy white and pure. And there I am, eyes connecting to themselves across the glass, stomach flutters. "Thank God I'm not a shy man, else the eye contact would be blushingly intolerable." Wanton ripples, starting at the head, working down through the chest, tingling to the extremities. My world on my terms. Swelling. The tingling fizzles out, but memory remains. Of course it's going to bulge, there's no stopping it. Unzip then. Inhale to suck him in, to pull him out. In the mirror he looks back at me, in my hand he grows. "Tamed them, haven't we?" A careful stroke, squeeze, to push the blood through. An assistant finger down the back, slip beneath the waist. A pinch, a...whispers knocking from across the room,

"Master Ortiz?" her muffled voice bounces off the closed door, "Are you ready?"

No time. There's never any time. Zipping up, "Yes, send him in."

Behind the cracking door emerges a head of chestnut fuzz, a spindly pair of arms. As he moves sheepishly across the room to the spot-lit seat, he smiles, flashing a deliciously innocent crooked white.

"Sit down please."

Dressed cleanly, he carries a shoulder bag, and is clearly intimidated by me. His glancing eye contact struggles for grip; he's overly conscious about where to place his hands. They eventually fall folded into his lap, working one-another. He settles, eyeballing the fruit bowl on the coffee table with complete awe.

"Do you know why you are here?" Ground him into the floor with eye contact.

"Yes sir. I've been selected as a Corps intern."

"Not exactly son. You have been prescreened as a candidate for the position because of some basic attributes identified by my staff. You are here, before me, to *interview* for the position. We are looking to select several bright, young men to groom into future party leaders, and, your prescreening indicates you *may* be a good fit. At this point in the process, I'd like to know more about you, so please, tell me about yourself. Start with the basic demographics, then sell *me* on *you*. *Why* should I be interested in the young man seated before me?

"Well sir,"

"No, no, that won't do. Call me Zuberi, or Beri if you please."

"Uh Ok, I will. So my name is Francisco Alder and I'm 16 years old. I live in Block N section 957 subsection 112 with my mom, two step dads, three baby sisters, one Brother, four lodgers and one infirmed closet dweller."

"I'm sorry, *infirmed closet dweller*?"

"Yes, he is a sick old man who pays one fiftieth of the rent to sleep folded in the lower half of the closet. His legs don't work, they fold conveniently beneath him. For his rent he gets one bed pan change per day and one meal."

"I see. Very enterprising, your family. And your brother. What's your brother's name, how old is he?"

"He's not my biological brother, that's his name, Brother. I think he's nineteen. He stays in the room with the four other lodgers. I don't know any of their names."

"Continue on then."

"I am in grade 7.5, and was promoted to the electronics stream last year. I was thinking about majoring in Microchip Manufacturing in college. Right now, after school, I work part time as a runner in the Palette Distro."

"Ahh, the BSMM! The degree of the consummate celibate, the lust of eunuchs worldwide!"

"Actually, Unix is no longer compatible with the prevailing 128-bit architecture of ninth generation systems."

Christ, one can never figure out what these pizza-faced-bundles-of-lust are talking about. Never mind. "Well now, is that a fact?"

"Yes."

"Certainly a trove of the most useful facts young man. Right, well anyway. Tell me, have you any hobbies beyond your love of computational pedantry?"

"Yes, I'm a Moderator in two SensaGame Forums."

"Shocking. And which two game forums might you moderate Mr. Alder?"

"On Mondays I moderate *Going Postal* and on Thursdays I moderate *Beastreality - Find Em, Fuck Em, and... Flea*?"

"I see. And what do you enjoy about being a Moderator?"

"Well, I guess I enjoy putting down the trolls, helping to keep the conversation going. I also like showing people tricks, you know, to improve their gaming skills."

"*Umhmm*. And these trolls, how do they make you feel? Put me inside your...brain."

"Annoyed, I think, more than anything. I don't understand why they want to disrupt the Forum. I wish I could kick them out entirely, full censorship. Unfortunately, as Mods, we can only edit and guide conversation, not kick people out. You need admin permissions to boot people."

"But shouldn't these people speak their minds as well? This is a free country is it not?"

"Sure, I guess, but in their own place, I think. The forums are not about them, they are about the gamers. Most people come there for answers, not to be attacked. The trolls are distracting, and they make it more difficult for everyone. They should be banned."

"That's an inflexible way of seeing opposition. Without a touch of frictional dissent, how can we ensure we're adequately stimulating the corpus of our fine democracy?"

"*Umm*, I'm not sure I understand your question. I guess it's just frustrating, dealing with the trolls. They make it hard."

"Indeed they do, but let's move on. So, tell me, what else do you do in your free time? Music? Toys? ...Girls? ...Animals? ...Boys? Or are these far too much ...noise with the potential to disrupt your asexual ...joys? Pardon the lyricism; I'm constantly stewing in banal legalese with few outlets."

A silence washes over him. The little nurp squirms slightly in his seat, a precocious prepube, aware of the real question lurking behind the words but ill-equipped to handle it gracefully. Momma's boy perhaps, or maybe too full of a zit-popping wonkiness brought on by a bits and bytes childhood. What happened to beautiful 16 of yesteryear? Loose clothes, tan bodies, and skunky ganja reminders of blurred perception (nay, diminished guard!) wafting from swollen, kissed lips.

"Um, well, *huh huh*, I mean I don't have much free time. With school, work, and being a Mod and all. I listen to music sometimes. I like the jingles about snack foods and cars the most."

"Ok, I think I understand where you are coming from. Looks as though you keep quite *busy* with your many activities, so let's get on with it shall we?"

"*Uhm*, Ok."

"You know, something interests me, tugs at the mind really. By your admission you are most interested in technology, chips nonetheless, yet you agreed to explore a position in politics by interviewing with me today. So tell me Francisco why would a young man, with such high marks in technology studies and an interest in pursuing the supremely neutered BSMM, have any interest in governance? Governance, politics, diplomacy ...these are the fertile ground for the raucously connotative to breed and flourish. A place where will doesn't compete with influence and influence is money's currency. Nuanced, a sleight-of hand-business, hardly scientific. This is the crucible where deities are forged, not the place where a meek shepherd of binaries could survive, right? But hold-on, maybe I'm being too figurative, let's go more to the point, get literal. Policy and microchips don't exactly intersect do they?"

"I, I think they do. The government's always giving free tech gadgets to citizens so there are lots of ties between microchips and politics. My teachers tell me I have an aptitude for engineering and software, talents that make me useful for technology companies. Instead of working directly for a technology company, I could help by reviewing new technologies and suggest which devices are best for people. Maybe a tech advisor or an interface designer...some, someone to help the government choose or maybe design useful devices for citizens."

"Is that what you believe? That government provides technologies that are *useful* for people?" Time to dig out the virginal roots, spritz them with vinegar. Listening to this bullcrap makes me want to coathanger even the gorgeous, nascent lambs.

"Yes. I think modern technology helps make peoples' lives better. It gives them opportunities to relax and communicate with others."

"So again, how exactly can you provide value to The Corps? I'm struggling. And be succinct this time. Say it in as few words as possible."

"*Uhhmm.* By..., by helping to find devices most useful for Irons to use."

"And *why* do you want to do that? Again, succinct. Make it tighter for me."

"Because I could work in a technology job but also help my country."

"Is that your goal here, *help* your country?"

"Yes, I think that's a good goal."

"What, are you kidding me? You view yourself as some sort of patriot?"

"*Ummm*, yeah, I think."

"Care to share with me why you *really* want to work for The Corps?"

Again, he's fidgety, sweaty. The smooth flesh of his cheeks slowly flush red as he scrapes at his lower lip with his teeth. Oh those lips! Eyes running from contact. He'll get there. Takes some youngsters time to flower. But when they do...

"I think it would be fascinating to see how the government works on the inside."

"Honestly, I'm not impressed you little shit."

"I hear The Bunkers are nice."

"Oh OK, there we go little buddy. *Warm.*"

"This is only my second trip to The Core. The rest of my life, my entire life, I've been stuck in The Blocks."

"*Warmer* you silly taint. Keep going if you dare."

"Our little apartment is cramped, it's hard to breathe."

Inspecting the floor, passing his eyes over the fruit bowl. He creeps tepidly to the edge, afraid the palisade will crumble beneath his swelling bravery. Big, ballsy boy?

"*Go on.*"

"I tried an apple once and I liked it. I liked it a lot."

121

"STOP. FUCKING. WITH. ME."

A huff and consternation defined, "I want to get rich and leave The Blocks and the miserable damn people rotting in that horrible shithole."

"Bravo young man, bravo! That wasn't so hard now, was it?"

Seething, how delicious! His flaming eyes squinting through a moist, rising heat. Hungry, and so expressive under mild provocation! This shitty, nerdboy could be useful. Sexually an infant, which is decidedly unfortunate. However, intellectually, clearly above par. Deep awareness with a sense of caution. His goofy speech needs a heavy polish. But, his intelligence and passion, attributes to steal from the opposition! We can nurture these traits into the ever-important charisma. *Eh*, not fit for today's task but certainly cut from the right fabric, worthy of inclusion in the Libro d'Oro.

"Ok baby Brutus, why should I give your ass a shot?"

And thus begins the best part of interviews, at least the interviews which serendipitously move in this direction. Once the candidate comes to the realization that exposing the taboo, vitriolic truths embedded deep in his heart net a positive response, the wheels spin wildly. Instantaneously, he flips through a million responses to the question, his organic microchip parsing sentences, sorting the perfect mixture of a few syllables to generate the most brutally pointed response. And for my gush alone! The speedy maturation of a limp blow-up doll under massively pressurized air.

"Because I have no limits. Mind, body or spirit. There is nothing I won't do."

Oooooooo! Ladies and gentlemen, a round of applause please for our future dear leader, Mr. Francisco Alder!

"Well Francisco, you may have an opportunity to test that assertion yet." Standing, flatten the protruding pants, "As you know, I'm a busy man. I need to return to my speech preparation. You're advised to pay full attention to what I say today. Today's speech is a basic exercise in how to use the carrot as a crop; it must leave a sweet taste in the horse's mouth. Run along now, you will hear from my associates soon. And boy, this is but a game, don't you ever forget that. Welcome."

He smiles, walks differently, juvenile swagger, on exit.

Slamming metal echoes in the hall, a population concluding the daily routine. Chickens coming home to roost after a long, hard day. Time for the workaday nodes to decompress, connect. The sense of sound must be back on now. Sounds coming in layers and waves.

Bryson, you have fifteen missed calls, eleven messages. Shall I play your messages?

Oh, right, her.

A day of work missed. Will they check on me? Labor was missing. Something was certainly left undone. Maybe a knock on my door? Perhaps the quiet and tidy process of a name deleted from a work schedule. Replace one warm widget for another. A different body standing on the same black rubber 3' x 3' anti-fatigue industrial work mat. Different body, same script, collecting the same compensation. Modular efficiency. Pluggable commodities inserted into the proper location at the proper time to ensure maximum profit.

Bryson?

The irrelevance of differentiation for the inputs, the utter obsession with it for the outputs. The sense of contentment extorted by the constant nag of inadequacy. Forever two steps behind in the race to be the most current, the most fashionable, the most informed person. A race where the top speed is infinite. A race with no discernable track. A race where crossing some line is the only objective, whatever the means. And there it is! An instant meaning transcending its physical matter. Something stark, concrete. It's there, contrasted against the white ceiling just outside the bathroom. A perfect, curious little circle. A dark green blob no larger than a shirt button sitting, aged in an ocean of white. Years now since it took up residence there, but the memory hasn't faded. Its memory, an icon for what was, what is, and what probably always will be.

...

She burst through the door, wailing and doubled over, holding her stomach with one hand, clearing a path with the other. "Out of the way I can't hold it!"

Sidestepping just before she rocketed past, into the bathroom. Cabinets banging, glass vials chinking and shattering as she scrambled madly through the contents.

"Where's my insert! Where the hell is my insert!"

In her wake, "Hold on baby, I saw one on the sink earlier!"

"Hurry, hurry! I can't hold it!"

Racing to the kitchenette, I retrieved the thin rubber insert from the dish rack.

"Hurry Bryson, HURRY!"

"Coming!"

In that moment, how ridiculous her interests seemed, but she was into it, I was into her, and several of her friends had managed to turn a surprisingly solid profit. She was beautiful then; natural curves, haunting eyes, perfect skin. Married a year at that point and still enveloped in a connubial bliss where her idiosyncrasies sparked wonder, adoration. If this was how she wanted to spend her free time, who was I to judge? *Hobbies, as well as speculations, have a tendency to run the gamut* was the justification at the time.

Her pants around her ankles, face strained crimson, she stood there, crouched over. Holding her stomach with one hand, her other pressed into her butt hole. Running from the kitchen, the black insert extended as far as my arm would reach, she stretched her arm, ready to receive the tiny baton in our relay race to catch the invisible, transient and potentially lucrative investment. A slow motion sprint against the clock and unstoppable human biology.

Deftly, she received the insert with one hand while her other lifted a glass vial toward it, plunging one end of the insert into the vial's mouth. While making the connection, she twisted sideways, moving the rig toward her awaiting anus, bulging under the pressure of a million gaseous particles in search of escape. As the insert penetrated Corinne she howled, and a noise similiar to a deflating balloon rang out. Only, instead of a tidy capture of the initial flatulence, *the cream*, the pressure was too great causing the immediate release of all three states of matter accumulated from several meals. She shit herself in such grand fashion that the nearby walls and floor were coated, along with one little button-sized splotch of brown-green clinging fast to the ceiling outside the bathroom.

On her knees sobbing, she cried out, holding her beautiful face amid an aroma so potent that most would salivate and dream of cash while a tiny minority would race to the toilet to orally evacuate the bread from the basket. And me, standing in the lonely chasm of a social dichotomy, confused, but wanting to be a good husband. Wanting desperately to salivate, for her.

"I'm sorry, oh God, I'm sorry!" she began, struggling for composure. "You, seeing me like this. And nothing, nothing to show for it, oh! Oh God. OH GOD!" She bawled. It continued for hours. Me, doing my best to console her through the ineffective filter of my shirt sleeve, her, kneeling in her mess, too embarrassed to stand and face what happened.

Quite a few years since *The Great Gas Bubble* was in the process of growing to proportions unseen in previous speculative manias. The practice, its origins in extreme smuggery, was thought to have galvanized in the more avant-garde communities along the east coast. Quickly, the practice of sharing one's wind in intimate social settings spread to large parties where specific odors developed favor among socialites with highly developed olfactories. When the trend was published before the scroll, it spread further and soon even the barely bourgeois began fostering unusual relationships with their sphincters. Before long, what once was an embarrassing public occurrence turned into emphatic proclamations of "I dealt it!" followed by the subsequent scramble of opportunists hoping to catch a fortuitous whiff of an intriguing new scent. Shortly thereafter, the first attempt to monetize flatulence emerged after a chemist ingested a handcrafted array of oligosaccharides producing what his literary friends dubbed "the most redolent bouquet of wind known to mankind". The first transaction was completed when a highly respected Flatusommelier paid the chemist's asking price for the jarred gas.

An explosion from there as everyone began collecting gases. Ball jars and Tupperware with sticky labels describing the sealed aromas, itemizing the originating foods. Soon, cottage industries popped up serving unmet needs for professional collection, archiving, measuring and labeling. Companies specializing in tempered glass storage vials, tapered no-leak rubber collection stems, and digital labels measuring and displaying precise chemical contents and proportions in real-time. Specialized food manufacturers engineered products designed for enhanced flatulence production. At the high end of the investment food chain were the exotic Brassica derivatives laced with synthesized fructooligosaccharides capable of producing the most odorous, sought after, and highly valuable gases. And it progressed further. Foods were infused with additives to regulate peristaltic movement, ensuring consistent flow and a stable collection process, in addition to supplements providing increased control over puborectalis muscle. The entire gas-related industry boomed as citizen-speculators worked countless angles in search of greater profits. Noise, deafening noise.

As the bubble hit its peak, prices for the rarest gases hit the stratosphere. Wasn't unusual for the well-heeled speculator to pay several times the average annual salary for a standard five-cubic-inch vial of wind. Even mid-grade wind sold for breathtaking sums with an average speculator forking over several weeks of pay to purchase a desirable vial. Those lacking self-control sniffed, consuming their investment and going bust in no time. Those with a mind for making money, rode price increases until the market teetered on the brink of collapse. Corinne, of the latter group, focused intently on building her portfolio, building for the future. Like any serious wind investor, she used every square inch of the apartment to store product. Every closet, every shelf, every drawer neatly filled with glass vials, stacked one upon the other, tidy scrolling digital banners affixed to each, quantifying the contents with reassuring mathematical precision.

Her ardent claims of a twofold investment strategy. First, create in-house the best possible gas based on careful research and a deep understanding of diet, supplementation and best practices for collection and storage. Second, obsessively scour the markets for under priced assets based on deep knowledge of industry trends, fashion trends, and socio-cultural drivers. She read the critiques of every prominent Sniffer, analyzed infinite technical pricing charts, and even sought the eternal wisdom of Guru Pādanā when facing big investment decisions. She religiously tracked daily price moves of each wind class and scoured analysts' reports for hints of emerging consensus. She did her research. She put in the time. But in the end, like the rest, what remained was odorous apartment full of glass jars, an empty bank account, uncomfortable eye contact and a million unanswered questions.

An unbearable relationship strain. In her eyes, the market was coming back, it was just a matter of time. Life hung, immobile with a jittery hope of recovery. Week after week, eyes fixed to the financial news, waiting for the uptick. As one famous Sniffer after another disappeared and gas-related businesses dried up, inevitability sank in. Bouts of depression interspersed with flits of mania further dislodged her from reality. When she finally realized it was time to cast off the chains, discard the vials and equipment, remorse fomented odd theories implicating me as the antagonist. I enjoyed watching her suffer. I tampered with the vials, decreasing purity and causing devaluation. My gas, never captured or appraised, could have made us rich if I wasn't so prudish. My lack of involvement, either as a producer or as an investor, undermined the industry as a whole, increased systemic volatility. My refusal to capture resulted in a large intestine of compressed gas of such immense density causing a gravitational disruption (albeit, and admittedly quite miniscule) thereby increasing Earth's orbital eccentricity to 0.017 resulting in a slightly longer winter which subsequently resulted in a shorter peak investment cycle causing a pricing jitter in the wind market which lead to a panic of selling that cascaded into a market crash. Logic tortured into fetal, thumb-sucking submission.

The irrelevance of logic, of sensible dialog. Instead, doing my best to absorb the vitriol, hoping it would leave her, neutralize in me. Hoping that once the anger and pain left her system, the woman I married would return. Hoping that the clichéd healing time would pass quickly. However, before the acid stopped leaching, it was clear that hope was a failed enterprise. In need of cultivation was a sense of acceptance, a more productive view of life. Something internal needed to act as the great neutralizer of the external world. A little volume knob inside me, to view the screaming madness in the sanctity of complete silence. Unaffected. Unaffecting.

Working on it, this religion of self-change. Day after day, learning how to become me, the real me, the me that had been shoveled under by the distractions and conventions shaping life's narrow, acceptable footpath of modernity. At first, a focus on concrete ways to dig out of the hole. I decided that for any situation beyond control, the resulting outcome was deemed unimportant. Like when she insisted on prostitution as a way to earn extra cash to recover from the investment losses. She had my input, she knew my opinion, but when she began serving clients on the couch, my eyes saw nothing but two sweaty bodies locked in congress. Or like the time when she stabbed me in the back with a pair of scissors for simply leaving the toilet seat up. That dull pity I felt for her as the doctor stitched the gash shut. Or when I found the metal bin on the fire escape, its smoldering contents comprising the remains of my personal possessions, set alight in a rage. A simple process; carefully revise my association with each object and identify specifically why each one was unnecessary for happiness. Then, step forward into life's next phase whatever it may be.

...

Here and now. The passage of many more years, the search for me extending well beyond her. Success and happiness are the rewards for flaw- less execution of tightly bound goals, the parameters of which, exist entirely within my control. Eating breakfast in precisely three minutes. Clipping fingernails into mathematically precise, 180 degree arcs. Brushing teeth in exactly 300, two-and-one-half-inch strokes. Many, many more. Happi- ness and joy harvested from a tiny domain ruled with tyrannical control. A domain protected from the chaos of the outside world - a world providing no nourishment, just gimmicks. Entertainment options; an underscore to social decline, symbolic of social disease. Each new reality show, obnoxious fashion trend, and demoralizing game was a chain of distractions hanging from everyone's neck. The constant low drone of bald-faced talking heads in the media reinforcing the social script, useless and evanescent. Every conversation, riddled with the inane dialectic shrapnel borne of a society imploding amid is own ignorance and misdirection. The sole escape is an internal retreat into a massive chair facing the neatly organized control panel of this orchestrated existence. All the levers and knobs required to fine-tune my emotional wellbeing.

But even a retreat from the noise isn't enough. Lately, even the obligatory processes of maintaining life weighs. A paycheck, a reminder of a yoke. A meal, a reminder of a pang. A glass of water, a reminder of the body's constant demands. All these chores, these distractions, keeping me from the mission of harvesting the unexplored fragments of consciousness before they wither on the vine. Every motivation, analyzed. Every ambition, analyzed. Every attachment, analyzed. Everything questioned a thousand times over from every imaginable angle. Self discovery is now life.

Silence, an overwhelming presence in the room. The odd lack of pitches. No voices. Sound, perhaps forever muted. Room, filled with the fuzz of cotton. Ears, eyes, in my mouth. Darkness. Eyes open, yes, my eyes are indeed open. Time, marked by an increasing putridity and little else.

She must have some relevance, some impact. And that voice. Remember her voice? Impossibly steely and soft at once. Sweetly firm. Control, yet vulnerability. Intoxicating complexity, a Siren clouding judgment. There was something of the *how* in her. The situation and the tangle it brought about. She's part of the *how*. Somehow.

...

It was a typical day at the office. A few calls, a read of the exchanges, a quiet day of personal affairs. How the five X-14 nuclear jumbo jump jets in production had recently opened for preorders, mine secured on full payment, ensuring a substantial cut to the commute by fall. Helipad in The Core to Bunker helipad in ten heavily fortified, luxurious minutes. Absolutely state-of-the-art; variable-flavored infinity pool, creeping bentgrass putting greens manicured with cuticle scissors, painite-encrusted toilet seats, 20-star restaurant with etched rhodium-paneled dining room adorned with platinum filigreed moldings. Those classy customizations giving it personality; floor tiles of polished ivory, leather recliners made from the hides of the last white rhinos, and rugs of luxurious white Bengal. Everything meticulously maintained by a 200-person cleaning crew of five-year-old test tube tikes. Those dexterous digits, petite and nimble enough to reach into the tiniest nooks, working on rotating 24-hour shifts. Twelve hundred tons of aircraft perfection. 10,000 square feet of commuter-craft. Sublimed by the thought of swimming passion fruit laps at 30,000 feet, how that strange desire crept in. A need to feel the evening air, a charitable plaza promenade among the emulous commoners.

Riding the elevator down from 238, eying the sprawling western landscape, the patchwork of colors marking The Piles' eastern edge flattened upon descent. A geometry of brown's shitty shades with flecks of blue, yellow and red interspersed. Occasional winks of reflected sun jumping off metal. The sprawl stretched for miles, rising and falling in perfect articulation of the land's contour. A grotesque agglomeration of trash and bodies. Along its border, smoldering hills reached for the sky, rising smoke dissipated into the brownish-yellow haze that hung over The Piles giving stench a dimension of visibility. Disgusting, but, isolated, definitively bound and capable of being constantly surveilled. Behind The Piles, like a huge charcoal canvass stretching earth to sky, sprawled The Wastelands and their ominous nothingness. Along the horizon they extended beyond The Piles, the canvas stretched, without break, beyond the elevator's view, giving strange credibility to Homer's flat earth. In a descending moment, invisible. The Piles fully flattened, visually compressed into a squinting footnote on the horizon. In the foreground of The Piles, immediately after the iridescent sheen of the ionizing Membrane, a stately cluster of glass buildings punctured the sky denoting civilization's demarcation. The Archives. The buildings stood, solemn, shadowy fingers stretching toward The Core as each day clocked-out. Snickering fingers pointing at the silly masses hammering away their days in the grinding monotony of manual labor. Warm-blooded machines finding sustenance in artificial reality and catharsis in the shared bedlam of constantly manufactured crisis. Simple people with simple lives and simple ambitions. Beautiful little laborers. My lucrative consumer commodities.

My feet hit the plaza, skin felt the rush of balmy May air, the first notes of summer delivered on a heavy, warm breeze. How, as with all previous excursions among the proletariat, their eyes darted feverishly as Irons and Platinums alike stole glances while my feet consumed the plaza's red bricks. The penalty of stature, the jealous, beady eyes constantly pecking, agitating your peripheral vision to insanity. Funny though, how upon eye contact, the lesser man always recoils, his eyes darting to an adjacent phantom or that smart hat not resting upon your head. One of the many social dances revealing a person's fabric. Platinums, but more often Irons, and their inability to establish and maintain eyes, a DNA flaw? If the flaw was remedied, would competition increase here in the rarefied air? If geneticists added a touch more cytosine, took away a speck of thymine from an Iron's eye contact gene, would that inch him toward perfection? Initiate the shift from slothy indecisiveness to concerted action. From primitive desires to refinement, sophistication. Could progress waterfall from one simple gene augmentation? How scientific inquiry could benefit greatly from such broad, unorthodox approaches to thought. Lament the deficit of time!

The stroll along the plaza toward Rashomon Park at the far edge, people glowing enviously at my enigma, the distant, unattainable light of stars! Stepping down into the manicured square park to relax a moment, absorbed in Spring's surging warmth. Sitting adjacent, a cleanly dressed man and woman rapt in discussion. A dozen manicured maples lined the park's perimeter on three edges, a western vista peering through a treeless fourth. Narrow, concentric bands of ever-smaller squares encased the gaudy geometry of an art deco fountain at center, a smirking aesthetic atavist to simpler times. Chunky blocks of square benches. Repeating zigzag motifs of grass. Chevrons of pansies. Fountain. Nauseatingly periodic. The park jutted over an escarpment on a concrete foundation facing the park's tree-less west, overlooking The Archives. Huge phalli of stiffs, glass and metal, stood silent, rigid. Without context beyond their soaring vulgarity, one could be conned into thinking the buildings represent the scale of achievement, the grandiosity of an indomitable enterprise. But, the absurdity of reality. Lacking space inside the Membrane, mountains of otherwise useful capital was plowed into vertical graveyards causing people to compete on how they adorned the nearly and dearly departed. Oh, the great irony! Few actually worthy of commemoration after interment as indicated by the sparse hand-ful of yearly mourners to The Archives.

Sitting there, looking between the two rows of maples at The Archives, how I couldn't help but overhear the conversation in progress, this man and this woman, sitting next to one another but talking as if on the phone, miles apart.

"So when was the new exhibit launched?" asked the man, crisply articulated syllables outing his Platinum status.

"Last Thursday I believe," she said, alternating her attention between him and her Palette. "Marion knows people who work at Death Inc, they were telling her about it. The grand idea is to attract a younger market of mourners to The Archives to boost ad revenue and to up-sell social media clauses on life insurance policies."

"Wait, they run advertisements there now?"

"Oh yeah, all over the place. Rolled them out at the end of last year. The Virtual Archives run ads now as well, look," she said, pivoting her device.

"Humph, nice placement. Yes, yes indeed, I *would* like to purchase some moisturizing lotion after gawking at grandma's pruny husk. Anyway, what's the nature of the new exhibit?" the man asked.

"Quite simple. Do you remember that spoof on Prattle a few years back when Gorge Profunde streamed herself cutting off her big toe and how it magically grew back a few seconds later?"

"Yeah, I remember. She said something about how appendage regeneration was one of the amazing, little-known side effects of inhaling The Pine. Video went viral, people in The Blocks started lobbing off toes to see it for themselves. Morons. Classic celebrity hoax."

"Ha! Yep, that's the one. Well, anyway, a critical mass of Irons who cut off toes have since croaked and now they're holding an exhibit titled *Toetally Gone - A Retrospective* in The Archives spotlighting the human impacts of viral events."

"Hold it, lots of Irons died from cutting off toes?"

"No, not exactly. Well, I'm sure a few did from gangrene or whatever, but most died of other non-related incidents. But that's aside, the idea of the exhibit is to showcase the power of ideas in a highly connected world and, more importantly, to generate some green shoot revenue for Death Inc."

"Sounds, I want to say, compelling?"

"Right? But who knows. Infrastructure's already in place, maybe Death can snag some voyeur revenue."

"You planning to visit?" the man asked his device.

Silence.

"That's what I thought. Back to the drawing board boys. Time to find a better way to hit those GDP targets."

"Anyway. Did you hear the latest on the Atonement Centers?" she asked, a smile in her voice.

"Hmm, maybe not, what's new?"

"Turns out over 50% have shuttered due to huge decreases in call volume."

"No kidding? Is the fad on the iron lung?"

"The Centers have been around for years, hardly a fad."

"Wait, wait, wait, don't tell me *you* are a customer?"

Silence.

"Ha! The mighty Miss Preslin calling up to sobbingly inform a perfect stranger she bitch-slapped her maid for not putting lemon in her tea. Oh, and furthermore, forking over Credits for this bewildering service. Unreal."

"Characterizing me as a customer is a little hyperbolic, but I'm not ashamed to admit, I've called from time to time, for the pure intrigue of it. To try to figure what it's all about."

"So that's what it's about, these Centers, a creeping fascination? I assumed it was some sort of religious vestige dangling from mankind's coccyx," the man said.

"Look, who knows why the Irons seem so reliant on the Atonement Centers, I'm not confident they know why they do most of what they do. Far as I'm concerned it's a cheap mode of entertainment, a laugh when I'm feeling bored and puerile. On top of that, it's a sort of social experiment, a peering into another world so to speak...a rough anthropological study. I don't know, boredom's known to spawn funny warts so don't act so damn superior."

"Fine, fine, do as you please, though I've got to be honest. I can say that even in my most juvenile moments, I've never felt the need to phone a stranger for the sole purpose of baring my ass."

"Ahh, bullshit, you just don't get it. It's role-playing, it's like an investigation of sorts. Something I do probably a few times a year for the pure intrigue. Not your thing, fine, but don't parade your ignorance of something around like it's a of badge of honor."

"Ignorance? You mean avoidance. Very purposeful at that."

"Intentional ignorance, something you shouldn't boast about so loudly."

They dissolved into uncomfortable laughter and grew quiet, focused on their devices. Conversation lulled. My curiosity piqued.

Leaning to the woman, "I'm sorry to interrupt you, however, while sitting here enjoying this lovely breeze, I couldn't help but overhear you mention advertising in the same breath as The Archives. Did I hear correctly? Are they now advertising in The Archives?"

As if fondled by a salivating lecher, the woman recoiled, glared and said, "THEY. ARE." Eyelids choking sclera, she burned a hole through me, vitriol in a channeled stare. Like a switch, she shifted, from chatty conversationalist to pissed-off aggressor. Clearly Platinum's ambitious upper echelon, the type forever dialed in to competition, blood dripping preemptively from the ladder's rungs. Equally as clear that she didn't realize the overwhelming rank of her inquisitive interlocutor.

"Again, sorry to interrupt Miss, I was just caught off-guard when you mentioned a mode of advertising unknown to me. You see, I'm in broadcasting and, well frankly, experimental modes of advertising, well, they intrigue me."

Acidic eyes, words milled, she squinting hatefully. Yikes, so much hostility! Her companion didn't look up from his device, engrossed in anything except unsolicited conversation. "Wonderful, now take your new insights and piss off." Blunt, tasteless aggression! What were we feeding this lot?

"Again, apologies for taking up your precious time. A departing thought; perhaps for your next Atonement call you could beg forgiveness for berating a complete stranger? Meretriciously basking in the spiritual guidance of those for whom you've nothing but disdain? *Hmmm.* Your warts are beyond odd, princess, DNA defects most likely. Thick, apish fragments stuck to your genetic code, sad really, though oddly amusing to watch your kind embrace their shit-pitching urges. Have a pleasant evening." Her little guypal bit his chuckle, bing! Resonation. Beat down the silly fools attempting to posture from below. She got it, it sunk it. How her eyes, breaking contact and softening into realization, absorbed the luxurious sheen of my vicuna-platinum weave suit, the God-like sparkle of purple taaffeite buttons. How wealth is a beautifully unspoken insult in-and-of itself. How it rains down derision on the hapless nobodies responsible for its creation who sit pathetically beyond its attainment. If only I had the gall to walk around with my net worth printing in huge, blinking letters upon my shirt!

Swallowing, her eyebrows migrated north, lower lip sprinted for warmer climes. Miss Preslin's distant eyes fixed on my shoulder, then something on the bench, the ground before us. Leaning forward to reclaim her face, I slowly scanned her from toe to top with the assessor's eye.

"Kitty cat got your tongue doll baby?"

She rose, tapped her impotent companion, who consequently neglected to pay the full laugh earned. Two nobodies.

Invigorated, the mild evening air stirred as the massive glass sarcophagi twinkled the dying sun in a maple tree frame. Those Archives. An opportunity unexplored? Perhaps these giants should be investigated, a bit of due diligence? An opportunity to promote the fringe shows drawing insufficient audience figures? If nothing else, an opportunity to establish a specific list of items for the Corps to defund.

"Roger that?"

The irritating pause. Silly monkeys scrambling in vain.

"Yes, yes sir?"

"I want to visit The Archives. Pick me up in ten at Rashomon Park. Bring eight guards and ensure the MRAP is stocked with hors d'oeuvres and wine."

"Sir, I don't think I can gather the guards, food and wine and get to you in ten minutes. Is fifteen Ok?"

"Not Ok, make it five."

"Ok sir, sorry, hurrying along now. Bye."

The sun continued falling and soon it was choked out behind the charcoal canvas, casting a red-orange glow across the cloudless sky overhead. The soothing hum of nearby traffic drowned out the incessant tweets of an obnoxious bird. Heavy feet, the dull smack of cheap resin on concrete in broken cadence on the plaza. A lamppost buzzed to life as the others launched a faint glow, caught fire and twinkled among the fluttering maple leaves. A strong westerly gust and that omnipresent, yet subtle, smoky odor filled the park. The acrid, lingering sting of ancient creosote burnt anew on wind from The Piles.

Twelve minutes later, tires chirped on the plaza behind me. Emerging hastily from the MRAP was the moist embodiment of personal service. How Roger that's face, a collection of forgetfully bland features, overtime, morphed his most frequently used reply into his namesake.

"You're late, I said five minutes. No excuses but I do want a tulip of Pinot in my hand immediately."

"Roger that."

"And Roger that, a little hustle for a change would be nice."

Out of the plaza and onto the street toward the ramp leading to the main west-bound arterial. A colorful spread accompanied a perspiring chiller reading "48". Drippy carrot stick into mouth and a quick swivel to face rear where one guard knelt among the rest, drawing plans into a gloved palm. Watching through the smoked glass, helmeted heads periodically bounced up and down in rapid agreement, while the occasional leathered finger pointed to an invisible structure hoisted before them. Along the wall behind the guards sat stoic rows of various-calibered machinery, for targets near or far, clumped or dispersed, skinned in cutis or steel. Ventilated this and tritiumed that, banana-shaped magazines and eyes powerful enough to make an owl drool. Security, Bang! Bang! motherfucker.

The impenetrable capsule tore down the road, Roger that, the driver and three additional guards warming the MRAP's front bench. While my fingers worked around the colorful hors d'oeuvres tray, the land flatten as we left The Core's boundary, passing through an industrial wasteland. Massive corrugated steel warehouses sitting among a never-ending network of dirt roads stretching to the charcoal on both sides of the highway. A flurry of single purpose trucks moved in concert; sweepers, trash trucks, movers, towers, lifters, pullers. Mile after mile until the landscape flattened completely, a single band of black highway narrowing to the shadowy giants in the distance. Warehouses gave way to clumps of switchgrass orbing across desolate dirt, and in that moment, the realization I had never been that far along the western highway before. *Hmph.* Several miles more and the blackening remnants of the orange sky cast silent darkness on the landscape. Clumps of grass turned to shadowy, streaking blobs. A fog rolled in, obscuring the tops of the silhouetted towers. The MRAP's lights illuminated a wide swath of road and terrain as the tires ate the last few miles on approach to The Archives. Along the outer edge of the headlight shine blinked the image of human clusters, frozen images lingering after the visual. A chill down the spine and gloved hands pointed aggressively. A sip of the Pinot as heads switched into automatic contingency-check mode.

We pulled into the parking lot, a forgotten stretch of broken blacktop peppered with fuzzy yellow spheres of lamplight suspended in the fog. Lampposts slalomed, we arrived next to the canopy entrance of the nearest tower. Roger that's voice crackled to life overhead,

"Please stay in the MRAP Mr. Nelling. The security team will establish a perimeter, signal, then we may exit."

The goons spiraled out, weapons scowling at the dark staring in on us. Creeping humanoids shelled in armor, crouching, arching, cautiously walking their muzzles into the dark. The door clicked opened, the night air rushed in, and Roger that looked unsettled as he glanced at his Palette. Oddly quiet, no sound of life beyond the audiovisual dampening of a thick fog and the gritty sound of tactical boots scraping macadam.

"Ok, let's get in quickly, yes?" Roger that said.

The tower's facade disappeared confidently into the cloud cover. The yellow fog beyond the guards, the palpable unknown, time crouching in wait, heaving heart and fingertip tingles. The Piles, a couple miles further down the highway, but their hints scattered around the parking lot. A makeshift knapsack of woven plastic bags sat lumpy and frayed, leaning against a canopy pole beyond the sweepers' reach. Crude containers of yellowed plastic and gnarled aluminum mixed with fragments of filthy cloth and weather-worn plastic bags. How the increased pungency of creosote, the bite of ammonia, coated the tongue. Back underneath the canopy and onward to the door, Roger that in tow. Credentials approached the entrance causing the hollow reverb of retreating bolts, massive sliding steel doors.

Inside, a universe of tiny lights flickered into existence, revealing a cavernous lobby with no discernable ceiling. A massive, diminishing space. Paneled in a repeating pattern of stainless steel tiles, the cold sterility of a morgue. Minimalist and over-lit with nothing more than a few steel, wall-hung benches, signage for toilets, and a few dozen silent, human-sized screens. On each screen, a single glowing directive: *Begin!* The guards and driver planted upon benches while Roger that skittered around me, a lonely, stray dog. Echoes heaved and diminished on approach to a screen. *Begin!* dissolved into three options:

PERSON

EXHIBIT

STORE

Recalling earlier eavesdrops, *"Exhibit!"*

Immediately a tiny, comically archaic clock icon flashed in the upper corner, 'loading' winking rapidly below it. Soon, a rising wave of electronic noise screamed forth, the swirling image of a face steadied, hinting a woman. Abstract, the face blended into the white background leaving a fleshy pair of shiny red lips and massive black-lined azure eyes floating in white.

"Roger that, what the fuck is that?"

"It's Cherry Pop Pop sir."

"Cherry what?"

"Cherry Pop Pop sir. Listen Inc's highest grossing Newpop sensation. This is her #1 hit, *Meathole.*"

Then it hit me. Cherry Pop Pop, Listen's hot new star! Those discussions with Listen's CEO about the new manufacturing process and its greatly reduced production costs. The grand ad campaign to push more fauxmeat into Iron hands. The Cherry Pop Pop brand, carefully crafted over the last few years, the face of synthesized protein. Listen finally cornering her into a multi-year contract locking her legacy to the artistic expression of dried meat analogue.

Then the beat dropped,

> *Put the meat, Slide the meat, Put the meat in a hole!*
> *Put the meat, Slide the meat, Put the meat in the hole!*
> *Put the meat, Slide the meat, Put the meat in Your hole!*

Brown shafts of meat substitute danced phallically around the screen before dissolving into a still of *Meat 'N' Go's* shelf-ready, Newart packaging system. Image faded, music ceased and a range of sepulchral exhibits were listed.

Food fellatio lingering, fingers scrolled through the exhibits, pausing at,

.

.

.

MEDICAL OOPSIES – PROGRESS THROUGH MISTAKES

VACANT EYES – THE FAITHFULLY BLIND

GASSED OUT – IMPACTS OF THE SUPER DEPRESSION

FOR LOVE OF COUNTRY – KEEPING YOUR HEAD ON THE BATTLEFIELD

STICK EM UP! - CRIMES OF ODDITY

LOOK MA, NO HANDS! – ACCIDENTS AT WORK

TOETALLY GONE – A RETROSPECTIVE *(**NEW!**)*

JERKING IT – AN ONANIST'S NIGHTMARES

.

.

.

"Accidents at Work, *hmmph*, you see this Roger that? Interesting stuff huh?"

"Yes sir, fascinating indeed."

The stories had dribbled out between meetings, the boys shooting the breeze, tossing around anecdotes, random bits of nonsense. This schlub getting a leg stuck in the metal grinder. That schlub losing a finger in the package stamper. Some moron who forget to set the overflow valve, boiled to death in a huge spray of cooking lube. Sometimes mundane, often hilarious, the stories always lifted moods during long, exhausting negotiations. Advertising due diligence *and* a few new funny stories to share with the board next week. Time well spent.

"Accidents at Work please!"

The screen flashed and colorful dance lights rained down to a reprise of Cherry Pop Pop's latest achievement.

"Please follow the green path behind you and thanks for visiting The Archives!"

Put the meat, Slide the meat, Put the meat in a hole!

Glowing green floor tiles led to the far wall where my grinning face projected huge.

"Ok! Let's get a move on! Roger that, run to the MRAP, grab me a Pinot and meet me at the exhibit!"

Put the meat, Slide the meat, Put the meat in the hole!

"Roger that."
"What?"
"*Umm*, I said 'Roger that' sir."
"Oh... Hah! Roger that, you silly son-of-a-bitch, you kill me!"

Put the meat, Slide the meat, Put the meat in Your hole!

Led by Roger that, the troops pooled to the entrance as I followed the green path to my smiling face. On approached, my face sucked upward, the sliding door giving way to a narrow corridor and a bank of six elevators. Projected on the doors of one elevator, my face. Enhanced, improvements in pore size and skin texture attributed to a simulated treatment of STAPHERIFIC!, the leader in facial refinement kits.

Create a better you today!

At the elevator, my better face split apart as the doors opened to a shiny capsule waiting to take me to the 300th – frustratingly higher than any level in The Core. Immediately, the ubiquitous hissing noise common to enclosed public spaces in The Core, the sickly sweet odor of The Pine permeated. Asphyxia to protect brain cells.

On 300 gasping for air, the green path pointed me toward another version of my face, this one hugged in self-morphing smarthair, the absolute bled-out-edge in conceptual coiffure.

Don't wait! Decorate your pate at SpaLicious today!

Face dissolved into a BOGO voucher for a cherry mint high colonic from SpaLicious, an offer bypassed to the exhibit of metal containers beyond. The pods, accurate to descriptions heard over time. Each pod a few feet wide, a glass front, heavy lighting bearing down on each body, a couple large buttons embedded in the glass and a thick band of digital screen bordering each facade. Uniformity down each long line of pods with the exception of the personalized screen circling each. Intricate floral scenes on some. Others with race cars zipping around the band on a virtual track. The vast majority black, forgotten. How one, seemingly hacked, had a few clever stanzas of urinal poetry circling in thick, red marker font,

I met a woman in The Piles and this is what she said
"Your eyes will float up into space if I give you head"
And then I asked her "how is that?" and this is what she told
"I suck for crumbs of bread and I'm but ten years old"

The red letters careened around the band like race cars, banking a hard 90 degrees at each turn, a race to the punch line. Next to the defaced pod, that hand. A wrinkly, mummified hand sitting lonely atop a wooden stool, the crimson-brown severed end, eternal beef jerky. Approaching the pod, the text on the glass illuminated, explaining Jim's demise,

Here sit the remains of Jim Alvin MacKenzie. Sixteen and a half months ago while operating a pipe cutter, Jim glanced over at a friend to answer a question and in doing so, shifted his body left causing his wrist to come in contact with the cutter's blade. Jim's hand was immediately detached from his body. Dutifully, Jim collected his hand and went to find his supervisor to request medical attention. Unfortunately, Jim's day continued its downward spiral when Jim slipped on a footpath next to a vat of molten steel, falling into the liquid metal. Fortunately for Jim's legacy, his hand was spared the fate of his body and fell outside the vat. We welcome Jim Alvin MacKenzie's hand as the 108th inductee into the Accidents at Work exhibit.

Jim's details faded, glass blacked over, then that funny ad from the voice of a exceptionally chipper man,

> *Do you struggle to effectively multitask throughout the day?*
> *Do you find yourself wishing you had just one extra hand?*
> *Well, TongueTied is the answer for you!*
> *With just a few minutes of training, you can convert your tongue*
> *into a purpose-driven appendage!*
> **TONGUETIED ~ PROSTHETICS FOR TONGUES. PROSTHETICS FOR LIFE.**

Tongue rolled in mouth, thoughts percolated.

"*Hmph*, clearly an Iron product."

"They do work quite well sir."

Startled by a rejoining Roger that holding an extended flute, "I'm sorry, they?"

"TongueTied prosthetics, they work well sir."

"Oh. Oh right. *Hmmm*, a little skeptical myself. Dare I ask what you use it for?"

"Well, sir I own several attachments. The one I use most often is the tiny flesh-like hand. It works quite well inside tight spaces or for manipulating small objects. I use it to pull splinters, wash the inside of baby food jars, anything that is difficult for a normal sized hand to reach. In fact, last week I discovered lice on my son's head, and, wouldn't you know, the clever prosthetic worked wonders picking the tiny buggers off the little guy's head. Honestly sir, you're looking at something close to a million uses with that gadget."

Nausea. "Roger that, honestly, that's disgusting. Completely foul. Please, inform me the next time you're harvesting bugs off heads with your tongue and I'll call in your replacement until you're properly irradiated."

"Oh. Oh Ok sir, sorry," said Roger that, his face a deep ruby. "You know sir, the hand gets washed like any other hand."

"Good enough Roger that, leave it there."

"Yes sir. Sorry sir."

Research continued along the exhibit's rows of pods. A double amputee and an ad for an escort service rendered in the absolute epitome of Newart. How meticulously designed the escort was, radiating God-like perfection and proportion, rousing the intended boner. And then a woman missing the digits on her right foot accompanied by an ad for orthopedic shoes. Scalped by an auger and genuine cowboy hats at 50% off. Good ads, lots of customer immediacy and huge potential for intimacy, though lacking tight personalization for my purchasing habits. How the ad selection algorithm probably looped neurotically on my credentials, unable to retrieve Diamond demographics stored inaccessibly in secured databases, reverting instead to known parameters to generate generic ads. Hard-on waned, the escort's image supplanted with an endless array of useless nubs and the ubiquity of surprise forever stamped on the faces of the dearly departed.

Weary of gawking, "Well Roger that, think I'm done here, got what I need. Take this, poke the troops and ready the MRAP."

"Yes sir," Roger that said with a bow.

Trailing Roger that, the walls made their final plea to engage my currency. Pills for a firmer butt. Cutaneal implants to automatically neutralize propionic and isovaleric acids. Creams to kill superfluous hair follicles. An exercise regimen to increase penis girth. Supplements to increase pheromone production and disseminative range. A barrage of ads shot from a machine computationally stretching itself to relate. Sensors collecting data, crunching it, spitting out over-calculated relevancy. As I increased my pace, the words sped up accordingly. Ads, catching and adjusting to my pupil's moving signature, maintained continuity between walls, the ceiling, the floor. Three-hundred and sixty degrees of seamless advertising perfection. Pervasive audio, decibel-steady, kept the messaging alive. Exhilarating! Boarding the capsule to go down, ads continued unabated. Injections to reduce sebaceous gland secretion. Lotions to dissolve adipocytes in the hypodermis. Patches to increase mitochondrial density. Sensors to monitor caloric balance, elasticity, height, pigmentation, bacterium levels, synaptic activity. Capsule dropped, stomach fluttered. Testosterone, estrogen, progesterone, dopamine, serotonin, adrenaline. How my hands grew moist and the pressure, how it increased in the cavities above my eyes. A tongue dry in excess of the Pinot. Tight chest. That strange deflated sensation never experienced before. A pile of cash lost on a sure bet. That little band of fat circling my waistline, a rolling ocean of sloppy, pathetic gluttony.

"Roger that."

"Yes Mr. Nelling?"

"Throw away the rest of that damn Pinot. It's disagreeing with me."

"Roger that."

Flipping through Palette contacts, in search of my attorney.

"Someone's going to pay for this shit."

An ad indicating my height was below average, a problem resolved with minor surgery.

102

101

Halitotic breath detected, the byproduct of above-average oral bacterial levels. A massive product line of sprays, gels, pills, gums, lozenges, injections, and rinses to zap those revolting mouth bugs that are causing people to hold their breath in your presence.

100

Trace smears of fecal matter detected on an imperfectly wiped anus, blooming faintly, but detectable. Odors of stale shit managing to waft beyond undergarment's permeable bounds. A wiping solution guaranteed to reduce post-wipe bacteria to defect levels in the 8.50 sigma range (Mr. Nelling, that's merely .000001 bacterium present for every one million wipes of the ass).

99

RRRRRRRRRIIIIIIIIIINNNNNNNNNG

RRRRRRRRRIIIIIIIIIINNNNNNNNNG

"Hello?"

"Jim, it's Alain, got a minute?"

"Hi Alain, certainly, what's going on? Why are you breathing so hard? You Ok?"

"No, uh, Jim, I think I have a problem here. Wait, hold on."

Bowels churned angrily. A film of cool sweat stretched across a forehead. Mouth coated with the sticky, overworked smegma of defunct, ineffectual, broken or otherwise useless salivary glands in need of fixing, I thought.

61

60

59

Mr. Nelling it appears the proportions of your face are not in line with the

Golden ratio ranking your attractiveness in the lowest decile of the entire population.

"Jim, yeah hi, I think I drank some bad wine. I want to file a suit against, against, against *uhhhh*, whoever makes this fucking shit!"

23

22

Mr. Nelling, you don't have to live with those sagging earlobes, and to be honest, they make you look a little twatty. There is a simple solution.

21

"Now slowdown Alain, obviously Beverage Inc is the manufacturer. Tell me the subsidiary listed on the bottle and I'll get the suit filed accurately."

DING!

Elevator doors separated to the silent corridor and a yawning paramilitary.

"Alain, are you there? ...You there Nelling?"

Jog, run!, from the elevator bank to the main hall. Dozens of black screens, silence. Walking to the middle of the hall, the patter of boots moved discretely on concrete, the susurration of pant legs.

"Alain?"

The heat in my collar dissipated. Chest loosened. The pressure in my head, released.

"ALAIN?"

"Yes, sorry Jim."

"Alain, is everything Ok?"

"Yeah, yeah Jim, I'm going to have to call you back, bye."

"Goodbye Ala-"

"Roger that!"

"Yes sir?"

"Let's move out."

Air freshened considerably as ominous pressure lifted, stars twinkled on the periphery. The wine? The hors d'oeuvres? Lunch perhaps? Who knew, who cared. Get out, leave.

Progressing toward the exit, the guards triangled ahead of me, Roger that tethered tightly to my left. Hands dried as spirits lifted, a moist collar cooled evaporatively. Things felt more crisp. How I almost apologized to Roger that for the harsh rebuke, but, as it would only ring awkward, instead giving him a hearty backslap, a drunken smile. In reply, that forgettable hole in his face smiled as we marched to the exit, unlikely soldiers, side-by-side.

At the exit, the point man signaled his team, flung the door open. The yellow spilled into the lobby as barrels rushed out, stabbing the night. Sauntering with growing relief into a calm evening. The fog had lifted completely, a cool, easterly breeze danced with my tie. Roger that opened my door and then a guard screamed,

"DIRT! DIRT! DIRT!"

A three guard scrum surrounded a shadow tracing the building's edge.

"GET THE FUCK IN THE LIGHT OR WE'LL SHOOT!"

Stepping gingerly into the yellow, a woman draped in dirty, loose garments walked forward showing empty hands, beggar-style.

"WHO IS WITH YOU!"

Response quiet, beyond earshot.

"ONE AND TWO CLEAR THE NEAR EDGE. FOUR AND FIVE CLEAR THE FAR. THE REST SET THE PERIMETER."

The 'all clears' trickled in while the woman's arms were gathered, kindling behind her back. The light cast harsh shadows across her face and she appeared distorted, simian. She jerked and grunted, searched for a position to reduce pressure on her clenched arms, the light playing off her face. A macaque. A gargoyle. Mohini. She shapeshifted through a cast of characters. How that chilly intrigue compelled me to take a closer look at my first outcast, first Dhalyte.

"Hold up guys, I want a word with her."

"Sir-"

"Not now Roger that..."

Guards pooled around her, created a buffer between us. On approach, she lifted her face to the light and the shadows receded, smoothing her features. Grunts became groans. Her wet eyes played endearingly off the light. How I accidentally swallowed hard in that untimely moment, stupid, reactive self-incrimination. The dampness of my collar. Her gaunt face, holding a few threads of shadow, the odd dither of emotions; pathos, seduction, then back again. Her lips moved to speak, she hesitated, winced sharply, hung her head.

"Loosen your grip guard."

Exhaling recuperatively, her eyes settled back on mine, speaking volumes ahead of her pale, cracked lips. Soil streaks on her brow. The clumps of matted hair defying gravity didn't discount the fact that she was staggeringly attractive. A timeless beauty peering out from behind age's common marks. Captured, a lashed dog, but clenching to dignity in the face of fear and degradation. How our eyes locked in the moment, each waiting for the other to break first. Not a cold stare, not an aggressive one, but the sort of stare that seeks to answer a single, pointed question, 'what *is* your next move?' How the world beyond our stare dissolved, disappeared.

"What's your name?"

She continued to stare, her eyes growing distant before snapping back into focus. She blinked, moistened her lips, claimed a few seconds as decidedly hers before answering.

"Ava. Ava Singh. Would you kindly ask these men to loosen their grip?"

How it pierced the moment, shredded expectations. Bound as she was, her voice unaware of constraint, demanded full attention of all within audible reach. How her eyes locked back onto mine, and that warm timbre of her voice settled, left me dumbstruck, self-aware and embarrassed. Honey-eyed overtones danced sweetly around a thick, low chord of gentle authority. Something to marvel at, something even, to respect. The impossibility of those tones emerging from a disheveled, wayfaring beauty. How it suddenly became impossible to breathe. How.

The police don't pursue. Move fast regardless Kaysen. Miles from the station, but nothing calms down apart from the children who find sleep once again. Heart pounds viciously even without immediate danger. A head discarding thoughts as quickly as they crop up, nothing stays in focus more than a couple seconds at a time. Nothing slows down, a redlining brain. The car's power reserves at nearly zero, 30 miles at most remaining? Atop everything else, that constant looping, four-second intervals. Judy. The Core's distance in excess of the reserves. House isn't an option. Step one, breathe, hold it together. Step two, drive, straight amid the nothingness to somewhere. Step three, help? God, you do exist, right? Zany human contrivances, *hmph*, life. Making a living and such. Feeling stupid to ask, but....are you mad at me? Did I fuck up? Did I? Silly, keep moving Kaysen.

Bolting down the road, scramble for the device, time to weigh options. Vague hominids, appear tiny, grow fast, close!, flashing bright in the car's pale yellow bath before disappearing. Judy's sister. We spoke, once, some twenty years ago? That long? No, too awkward. Fredrick? Deputy of ten years but no longer professionally obligated. He didn't care for me, tolerated me. No, shelf that idea. Richard? Mentor from Salvation, years ago, seemed a decent person. Hold it, he sits on the Quorum now yeah? Promoted last year, won't answer my call. Bill? Saif? Marco? Been too many years, wouldn't know how to begin things. Rohini it is.

Dialing Judy's sister, focus, does she have children? What might be their names? Her husband spoke of Slavic roots way back, right? Why is this in my head? Why do these thoughts swirl so violently? Vladislav if it is a boy, maybe Kazimir. But what if it's a girl? Maybe Morana or possibly

Borislava. Fuck, is Borislava even a name? Oh Judy, my Judy.

"Hi this is Rohini."

"Rohini hi, this is yo-"

"I'm sorry I can't come to the phone right now, leave a message."

No rings, screened. Fuck.

Fine, Frederick.

Riiiinnnnng, Riiinnnnng, Riiinnnnng

"This is Frederick, leave me a message please."

Fuck, screened again.

Saif. Saif it is.

Chirp, Chirp. I'm sorry, the person you are trying to reach is deceased. For next of kin, say 'next', otherwise, please hang up and call a living person. Chirp, Chirp.

"This is pointless."

"What daddy?" asks Magdalene.

"Nothing honey, please go back to sleep, everything's Ok."

Broken yellow lines blinking in the headlights. Streak. Streak. Streak. Wheels hum. Cousins, I have cousins I've yet to meet. Sense of obligation, right? Even if we've never spoken, never met? Who are they? Where are they?

"Show Kaysen McMurty, blood lines exclusively."

Device shows a messy tree stretching across the country.

"Proximity sort. Filter 30 miles or less."

"One result."

"Speak result."

"Sariya Ribeaux. Zero miles from your location. Whereabouts and contact information unknown. Sariya Ribeaux is your cousin and the daughter of Luke Ribeaux. Luke Ribeaux was married to your mother's sister, Sadie Micah Ribeaux nee Deltepe."

Shit, no good.

"Filter by 40 miles or less."

"One result."

Oozing sweat, itchy skin. Judy flashes. Reserves at 25. Magdalene shifts. Streak, streak, streak blips through an inky night.

"Filter by 50 miles or less."

"One result."

"Filter by 60 miles or less."

"Fourteen results."

"Speak second."

"Bryson Julhar Acenes. Sixty-eight point four miles from your location. Last known address is Block C, Section 84, Subsection 38, Unit 827. Bryson Julhar Acenes is the son of Emanuel Acenes. Emanuel Acenes is the son of your father's sister, Michele Acenes nee McMurty. **NOTE**, Bryson Julhar Acenes has been deceased for five years.

"Removed deceased results."

"Two results."

"Speak second."

"Mark Deltepe. Seventy-two point one miles from your location. Last known address is Block Q, Section 102, Subsection 35, Unit 529. Mark Deltepe is your cousin and the son of your mother's sister Sadie Micah Ribeaux nee Deltepe."

"Call Mark Deltepe."

Riiiinnnnng, Riiinnnnng, Riiiinnnnng, Riiiinnnnng, Riiinnnnng, Riiinnnnng, Riiiinnnnng, Riiinnnnng, Riiinnnnng, Riiiinnnnng, Riiinnnnng, Riiinnnnng

Seventy-two miles. Car won't get us halfway there.

Riiiinnnnng, Riiinnnnng, Riiinnnnng, Riiiinnnnng, Riiinnnnng, Riiinnnnng, Riiiinnnnng

Please, pick up. Please.

Riiiinnnnng, Riiinnnnng, Riiinnnnng, Riiiinnnnng

"End call."

What now? Drive and try this Mark Deltepe again in a few minutes. Try Rohini again.

Pitch black, no lights visible in any direction, a typical Bunker night. Everyone's underground, hermetically sealed security for the evening. Safely protected in warm, subterranean palaces. She loved nights, said she felt invisible, pure soul.

Call Rohini again. Nothing.

Call Mark again. Nothing.

Repeat. Nothing.

Reserves, 15.

Panic, sweat itching. Frederick. Saif, no Saif is dead. Marco, who's Marco again? Nothing. God? Any input? Nothing. Rohini, Rohini, Rohini,

Rohini. Her phone no longer answers. Absolutely nothing. Itchy arms, itchy head. Trickles down the small of my back, into the crack, itchy. Streak. Streak. Streak. God, can we work out a deal?

Reserves at 12. In the distance two points of light leap from the horizon. Two more. More. A cluster of lights in the distance, floating in the black. Lights growing quickly. Five. Now ten. Perhaps fifteen cars grouped together, approaching. An expanding halo of light encasing the caravan, bleeding into the darkness. Butterflies. Nerves. Fear. Relief. Sadness. Confusion. Confusion and anxiety. God, we need to make a deal. Little white spots bubbling at the eye corners. Chest tight, hollow, but tight. Reserves, 11.

Light cluster approaches, decelerate Kaysen, get a look. A shaky inhale. Compression slows car as opposing headlights flash rapidly, alerting. My headlights consume a couple more streaks before creeping up the point car's hood, illuminating the windshield and a group of men dangling from open windows brandishing clubs, blades, ropes, poles. Pound accelerator! Go, Go, Go! Muffled screams seep through closed windows. Caravan's last cars screech one-eighties in the rearview, shine white through the car, projectiles plink off windows, waking children.

"Daddy?"

A million angry red dots hang in the rearview mirror, contemplating. Push the accelerator through the floorboard.

"Daddy, what's going on?"

Still red. Arch back, press harder. Straight line, toe to chin. God, we need to make a deal.

"It's Ok sweetheart, you rest. We'll be there soon."

"Where?"

The red fades, shrinks. No additional white.

"Your cousin's house, hun, now go back to sleep."

"Daddy, what's a kuzzhun?"

"Just sleep sweetheart, let daddy drive."

No red. No white. Reserves, 8. Remote nothingness. God, I'm yours, whatever you want. Whatever you need.

"Call Rohini."

Nothing.

"Call Frederick."

"Your call has been declined."

"Call Mark."

Riiiinnnnng, Riiinnnnng, Riiinnnnng, Riiinnnnng, Riiinnnnng, Riiinnnnng, Riiiinnnnng, Riiinnnnng, Riiinnnnng, Riiiinnnnng, Riiinnnnng, Riiinnnnng

"End Call."

Reserves at 6. Get off the road Kaysen, not safe. Banking to shoulder, headlights illuminate a dense orchard enclosed in a high fence. Along the shoulder, creeping slowly, in search of anything. Lumps of rags *kadunk, kadunk* under tire. Shadows move ominously. Ahead, at the terminus of the headlight haze, a forest of umber, then black trees. They grow, taller, darker, promising. On approach the orchard fence veers away from the road and tall trees sit bare against the road's wide shoulder. Slow now, scan for an opening, a gap. Solemn trunks stand side by side, a thick copse meanders between. Reserves, 5. Tree, tree, tree, tree. Tires crunch gravel, the shoulder drops slowly from the road. A narrow path cuts through an opening in the thicket. Veering off the road's edge onto the depressed shoulder, car thumps, undercarriage scrapes the crumbling edge. Car bounces unevenly, bobbing rearview heads, settles onto a grass patch lying ahead of a dirt path littered with ancient trash.

"Where are we?"

"We're taking a break sweetheart, just relax and we'll be there soon."

"Where?"

"Magdalene."

Dirt path smoothes out between two large trees, limbs scraping the doors. Branches slap, leaves flatten against the windows as headlights stretch down the path. Rolling slowly, wide eyes in the rearview, the persistent scraping inside. Reserves at 4, the path stretches beyond infinity. Power down to a world gone pitch black, steering wheel disappears. Doors are locked. Are the doors locked? Yes, the doors are locked. Triple check. Yep, locked. The doors are locked. Fine, lock them again. Lock the doors again Kaysen. Locked.

"Daddy?"

"Yes Magdalene."

"Why are we stopping here?"

"Daddy's tired, needs to rest a while hun."

"I'm scared."

"Don't be sweetheart, everything's Ok. Sleep now and we will begin again shortly."

"To the kuzzhun?"

"Yes sweetheart."

Time to think, figure something.

Fishing under the seat, hand bumps it, the penknife, the catchall emergency tool. Into pocket. *Weile, Weile, Waile!* God, we need to start talking about another deal.

Staring ahead, blackness breathes, grows closer, then steps back. Closer, then back. Suffocating then liberating. Back to front, front to back, then back again. Anxiety then confusion. Is this confusion? No, I'm clear in the head, push through accumulated stress. This is normal. This is how normal feels. Yellow dashes still streak, still maintain some sort of tempo. Just stress. Who wouldn't be stressed?

"Daddy?"

"Daddy?"

Whimpers. Tears. From far off, then from much closer. A distance commonly referred to as the back seat. Crying, they are scared. Breathe, to slow time down. Time don't want to slow down. Time don't like to slow time. Time is of its own brain. We need to make a deal. We should talk.

"Daaaaaadddy? **Daaaadddy, I'm scared. What are we doing!"**

Confirmed. I know this, I just thought it not three seconds ago! Christ. Scared, all scared. But what is this? What is fear anyway? Fear, when the options run dry. Fear, when every path looks the same, is the same. Fear, an invention of the mind. A silly clotting of thoughts. Slow the thoughts down, breathe. Ignore the wood's eyes. This is called stress and it fucking sucks.

"It's Ok Magdalene, Muhammad. A short rest." Words from far off, a monotone, disembodied voice. Annoying and bland. Sweating ceased, why's everything damp? Her tears. Tears running, but no sting, eyes not hot. No light, no blur. No tears? No idea. This is called stress.

"Daddy, will you hold my hand?"

To the back seat, two wet hands clench it maniacally. Fear's moisture. Fear's fickle fluid dynamics. Stress oozes, weird stuff that stress is.

Sniffles and whimpers from the abyss edge out nauseously spinning thoughts. Fear, that point when the streaks decide they will never go away. Where did focus go? My device and a call log, a list of names. Blur, yes, tears. Dear self, your mouth is gaping, you should close it. Tears are a normal response. That is what you do when you discover that your mouth was hanging open and yourself didn't happen to notice it. I mean myself. I mean I. I didn't notice it. Stress is normal. Eighty-one calls. Zero results. Head back, eyes shut, tears jump from flashing micro-ridges. Perspective. Breathe. Sniffle. Streak. Sniffle. Streak. Sniffle. Streak. I really think we need to make a deal. It's important to breathe in order to slow time down to its actual pace in reality's space. Perspective.

"Why don't you kids crawl up front."

They scramble like crumbs of dirt. Dirty crumbs. They scramble like Dirts to a crumb, how does that saying go again? Settling into the pocket of the front seat, huddled together. Gripping my arm to the shoulder. Four hands, five hands, six hands. Lots of random hands slapping at my arm. Fear, when silence muffles all sound. The screaming aural fuzz of a soundproof room. Don't forget to breathe, time depends on it.

Sitting, wet. Dripping. Pools of sweat. Oceans of sweat. Stick heads above water to breathe. Oozing stress. These metronomic breathes. Reclining, those spindly arms fall away. Judy, Salvation, Iron, blood, police, headlights, home, gardener, streak, streak, streak, Rohini, knife, pots and pans, Atonement, blue blobs, plastic, Townsend, 33. No, slow down. Mark, Quorum, God, sacrifice, Atonement, God, sins, Atonement, obedience, God, sacrifice, God, Atonement, God, sins, God. God. Hey God, remember me? Swirling, the swirls, each word swirls. Nothing roots in an ocean of sweat. Vortices. There is no such thing as a direction. Ideas are those fibrous tangles of lint you pick from between your toes at the end of the workday. Nothing gels apart from a call to sleep from tired limbs. Hello, and thank you for calling. This is your limbs speaking, we'd like to request a few hours of sleep. Oceans of limbs, slapping and breathing. No, don't slap, slow down. Sink, immersion. Sink and breathe. Breathe in water little fishy. Across the gills and over the hills, we wait for thrills while God chills. God, *huh*, you silly 'ol bastard. We are one into the other, you and I. I can't escape you, but you can't escape me either. Breathe in the water. Sink. Let's sink together. Breathe in the oceans of sweat. Sink deeper. Breathe in the oceans of limbs.

Sink deeper. Breathe in life everlasting. Sinking, sunk. Wheeling. Thinking, thunk. Dealing. Stinking, stunk. Feeling. Chinking, chunk. Reeling. A, E, I, O, U and sometimes why? Limbs sway in the breeze, eyes blink in front of vacant minds.

"Who the hell are you!?"

"Really? You couldn't tell by the smoke, *O Fortuna* whispering ominously in the background?"

"Smoke? What smoke? I can't see a damn thing, it's pitch black in here. Something's strange though. It's like…"

Bang!, Bang!, Bang!, Click, Click

"Anything?"

"Huh? Oh, no, nothing. It's like I can…I can *feel* you or something. This isn't right. Something's off. This sensation. It's a twisted sensation, as though you're pasted all over my skin, sticky and resinous."

Rustle, Rustle, Click, Click

"How's that, see me now?"

"No, I only see my Palette."

"Good enough. Do you see the goddamn smoke yet or not?"

"No… sh--should I?"

"Not sure. The machine could be bust. Let's continue on, (*BANG!, BANG!, BANG!*) …but please, assume the smoke is there billowing around you…all mysterious and shit, yeah?"

"Oh, Ok. Why are you here?"

"I was about to ask *you* the same question."

"I see. I think I get it."

"Do you?"

"Have I been bad?"

"*Hmmm,* well would you look at that, he is a clever one! You know, I'm not entirely sure, what d'you think?"

"Are you messing with me? Is this a joke? I'm lost."

"Lost huh, my absolute favorite kind! No, to be honest, I'm not aware of your status. I've been busy lately and haven't had time to review your file. Catch me up if you would 'ol buddy."

"Oh, uh, Ok. Well, I think it's fair to say that I'm not the worst, but, well, what I'm trying to say is that I'm sorry either way."

"So solemn, look at *you*! Not exactly your M.O. from what I remember, *hmmm*? I'm sorry, forget it. You were saying?"

"Yes, well, I have sinned, but, I couldn't be the worst, I know there are worse than me, I've been in their company."

"Ah, the 'ol '*his* knife was duller' defense. Look, slicing a man's head off nets the same result regardless of the weapon's whet. As such, compassion therein amounts to splitting hairs, and, with a razor sharp knife mind you."

"I didn't kill anyone! You've got this all wrong. There were no knives involved whatsoever, as God is my witness!"

"Is he now?"

"Huh?"

"Oh you're so precious, just look at you! Now, don't forget, sometimes we use analogies to enhance our comprehension of a particular situation. Drawing parallels help us to better understand each other, wouldn't you say?"

"I don't know, I'm so confused."

"Let's move on. You were saying you are a sinner, blah, blah, blah, but not among the worst yada, yada. Ok, pick it back up."

"I sinned, I sinned! I did! But, I have a good heart. I am a good man. I'm a father, a damned good one. I'm a faithful husband! And Jesus, yes Jesus! I love Jesus!"

"If I had a nickel..."

"Well what then, how does this go? Are you going to punish me?"

"Whoa, whoa, whoa! Jumping right into the deep end, huh? Slow it down my friend. Don't forget, it's the flippant banter that makes dialog interesting! Remember, somebody may actually be forced to read this nonsense."

"Well, are you?"

"....*Humph*, you disappoint me. But, seeing as you have fee will, or at least the paradox of it, I will indulge your blithe bulldozing of my simple request for pleasantries. That being said, let's at least try to steal a few moments with the intellect... *My* motivation for this visit was about collecting respect, you know, a couple smooches of the ring, the standard *'knock, knock, time to pray muthafucka'* sort-of-stuff. *However*, it appears *your* motivation in calling me here is about something far different. Hell, your briny brow, it's thick, silvery beads, scream penitence! So, I propose, for your kind consideration of course, that we find an amicable solution to knock off both birds with a single stone's throw. Whattaya say to that? Please, don't answer. Now, tell me, how bad are these sins of yours? And please, don't spare any details! It's in the details we discover the slippery little personified spirit of evil, my arch-nemesis and ruler of fallen angels, el Diablo! Also, bear in mind that I've seen some horrid shit in my tenure, so I'm not easily impressed."

"I've profited handily from others' pain."

"FUCKING YAWN! You and billions more. What else you got my dour little fiend?"

"I've peddled lies and fabrications to intentionally lead people astray."

"You and me both my friend, it's called leverage, and it's a bitch of a responsibility. Good luck *not* abusing it! But, I'm going to be honest with you, you're wasting medamn time thus far."

"I worked for an enterprise that scientifically erased your existence and, in your place, set up a mechanism to hook people, like addicts, on a simplistic form of telephony repentance to generate massive profits for an elite handful of people."

"Ouch, that's gonna leave a beastly mark! Oh, and, apologies for the lame innuendo. I'd say you upped the ante with that maneuver."

"I know. Is it too late to say I'm sorry?"

"As much as I love tearful, self-flagellations, I'm afraid it's going to take a fair bit more than that my friend. So, pray tell ....btw, why the hell was 'pray tell' dropped from the common vernacular anyhow??..., how long were you involved with this organization?"

"My entire career."

"*Ewwww*, that's going to cost you."

"But I didn't start the enterprise, the Quorum of Religious Institutions did. They are the ones who funded the science against you. They decided to cut you out of the new business plan. They are the ones who developed the for-profit Atonement scheme, popularized it and carefully guided it into the social phenomenon it became."

"Leaving you to profit by lazily administering the scheme? Seems a slothy way to break commandments. *Hmmm.*"

"Forgive me... please!"

"My deputies do the forgiving, me, I'm old school muthafucka."

"Weile, Weile, Waile?"

"Exactly. I'm confident you knew where this was headed. Oh, and, cut me a goat in half too, I love that bloody shit!"

"Really?"

"Nope, just messing with you. Tots'll do."

"Are there no other options? Certainly we can find less violent ways to atone? Why do the innocents have to be entangled in this?"

"Look, if you were me, how much into negotiating would you be? *Hmm?* Besides, I've little interest in dissecting slippery notions of innocence with my toys."

"Oh God, but I'm afraid. I'm so afraid!"

"Fear, the most painfully boring gray blob on the emotional palette. It's amazing how much you people let it control you! I tell you what, you've dialed me on a good day. So, if you can't bear the Weile, Weile, Waile, what else you got? And bear in mind, casually suggesting remediation that doesn't fully respect my stature is, well, unwise."

"*La, la, la....laddy freakin dah, the silence goes up till the sheep go bahhhh!*"

"Unfortunately, nothing comes to mind."

"*Bahhh, Bahhhh!* As is so often the case. Not to worry, you are a man of integrity, no doubt you'll settle your debts with the house. While this has been most delightful, I must run to my next house call, the flock's a mess you know? I'll leave you with my favorite exit music!"

"There was an old woman and she lived in the woods, Weile,
Weile, Waile.
There was an old woman and she lived in the woods, down by
the river Saile."

Blurry and cold. Quiet. Rubbing eyes, shift about in a moist seat, an aching back shoots pain to my neck, the temples. Salty crust on lips, a hollow stomach, the bumpy skin on a raw, plucked chicken. Hangover of sorts. The beep. A beep opened my eyes? A dull gleam of dark blue light filters through a black canopy overhead. Why my steering wheel? Where am I? ...PANIC!... Police. A cluster of headlights. Hidden road. Reserves at 4. Judy's legs dangling limp from pothooks. Her mutilated body, pools of blood, rivers of blood. Severed head on Magdalene's lap. Pupils halved, staring unconsciously behind limp eyelids. Mouth agape, frozen. Red scarf around her neck. Kids drenched in her blood. Officer, my, my wife was butchered, and my kids, *my kids!* Waking at a thousand miles per second. *Oh God, what has happened?*

"*Oh Judy.*" Awareness trickles, this strange hand wipes my face. Blurry and cold.

Stirring. Two unsettled bodies, shifting. Heavy exhales. The sound arriving from far off, no, from the back seat, no, right beside me, no inside me, no right beside me. Two little bodies encased in blue, ready to go running, away from you.

Beep. Same fucking beep again.

Moaning, eyes gnarled by clenched fists, two bodies writhe against one another. Two white slits. Four. A few tears. More. I am dad, dad is I. This is where Kaysen says something profound. These two are my children. They watched somebody slaughter their mother yesterday. Holy shit, look how incredibly cognizant I am! I am dad, dad is I!

"Daddy, I'm cold," says Magdalene.

"Daddy, I'm hungry," says Muhammad.

Stupor. I think that's the word.

Electric adrenaline! A huge punch from inside my chest. "They're coming!" Did I say that out loud?

"Daddy?"

Blood rushes. Over-oxygenation. That fear. Metal implements burrowing deeply into doughy flesh, slow motion, no resistance whatsoever. Scalding knife through butter. Cauterization.

Beep.

Focus. Pocket. Fishing in my pocket, brush against the penknife. Reach over, set a numb hand on Magdalene's head. Check it out, I am dad!

"It's Ok honey. It's Ok." This strange buzzing noise, my voice. The drone of an electric razor pointlessly reciprocating on a bathroom sink down the hall. A low, steady vibration, the cosmic noise of the universe. Alien chatter.

Focus. Device, missed calls. Nothing. Somewhere inside a mushy, meat casing, this thing called a bladder. Shiny, smooth muscle spiraling around, tiny buttholes of muscle permitting and denying access. Excretions, extraction of metabolic by-products. A meaty sac that fills with pungent lemonade, jets into the porcelain doughnut through a narrow tube of epithelium.

Dark blue flecks above lighten and the green of a million leaves emerge, camouflage. Silent black giants keep vigil, perfectly still, ominous. Eyes, they're looking in. Whimpers and sniffles.

"Call Rohini."

Nothing.

"Call Frederick."

"Your call has been blocked."

"Call Mark."

Riiiinnnnng, Riiinnnnng, Riiinnnnng, Riiiinnnnng, Riiinnnnng

"End Call."

Fear, a boring emotion piqued when the world decides not to take your call. Wet, when the bladder and urethra grow bored, decide to disregard the parasympathetic screams from within, just for shits 'n giggles. Piss.

"Daddy I'm thirsty."

"Me too," says Muhammad, sniffling, moaning.

Sad, my boy marooned on planet mirth.

"Kids, patience."

A faint, rapid popping noise. Firecrackers in the distance. Neuron bombs. These vibratory stimulations called tingles, tiny electric charges trotting epidermally along the fingertips finding a juicy path through the many synapses en route to the sensory cortex. Meaty sacs all around!

"Call Mark."

Riiiinnnnng, Riiinnnnng, Riiinnnnng, Riiiinnnnng

"End Call."

Loud packing noise! Shattered quiet and a violently throbbing hand. Pump (blood pumps?). Pump (blood pumps?). Whimpers grow to wails, five fingers searing, pulsating. It appears that Kaysen's hand attempted to punch through the dashboard!

Human emotion, that thing requiring me to return this throbbing hand to Magdalene's head, to gently touch Muhammad's face with the other. Thumb stroke a teary cheek. They clinch then scramble to my lap. My lap. Dad's lap. I am dad, his lap is mine. Shuddering balls of flesh. Morning breath stink mixing hot and moist with young hair. That muted, slightly powdery scent of kiddy sebum carried on heat radiating from charged little heads. Close, but really fucking far away.

Huddled together as the rising sun shoots a thousand thin beams through holes in the camouflage canopy. The eyes are looking in, inward at us. Faces buried, their moans overlay darting thoughts. Dew twinkles on the hood. God smiles. Juvenile bodies grow warmer. God raises an eyebrow. Wild-eyed men charge. God points a finger. Shame. A bendy river carries sweet water through the forest and God fizzles away, dissipating too slowly. A dog fart in a room crowded with uneasy, disassociating eyes. Spot, licking his red shooter and laughing maniacally under the bed.

"The car is conspicuous, we need to move. We can go find water, kids, then walk to your cousin's house."

Beep. Fuck a beep.

"Don't shut your door! I'll come around and do it."

Scan the area. Place door gently against the side of the car, press slowly until it...*click*. The kid's side, they slide out. Quietly press the door shut, *click*. Scan the woods. They are looking in, but I can't see them. Ephemeral dog farts.

"Let's go." Cold silence and lethargy.

Walking the dirt road, Muhammad on one hand, Magdalene the other, eyes on the bend ahead. Constant surveillance back to the shrinking car, the disappearing road behind it. Dither between two threats. The eyes, pressing in. Walking hurriedly, sweat returns, morning's cool, prickly skin. Stumbling in the rut of an ancient tire, silent and brisk. Step, step, step. An occasional bird outing our presence. Footfalls pound dirt and yellow light squeezes through leaf gaps overhead. Behind, the car ducks behind the trees. Forward, the bend hangs on each step. Step, step, step. Two sweaty hands and muted thumps. Chirps, faint pops, the gravity of a smoky aura all overlapping one another.

The numb of over-stimulation. Head wanders like a stray cat. A normal day? Is this a new normal day? What about the old normal days? What is normal? I should go to work. Why am I walking in the woods? Kaysen, why are you wandering in the woods? There is work undone, people will wonder where I am, people need me. To calculate the monthly P&L. Thirty new Irons needed in center AC79. Must fire ten nascent Dirts in AC48. New desks for AC67. Quorum wants an 8% increase in atonements by next year. Implement new game plan. The Quorum, the slickest of the slick. Faceless. Adaptive. Driven. Pervasive.

...

It struggled for years under the duress of flimsy operational financials, The Quorum, instead of reinvesting in its enterprise, it siphoned profits, to prop up the corpulent lifestyles of its few dozen eminences. The Quorum, leaning over irrelevance's brink, was a minimally cohesive group of religious leaders struggling to provide a range of products and services under dozens of names, relying predominately on the charity of an ever-shrinking base of devotees for survival. Chartered initially to consolidate quickly diminishing political power, the heads of the world's organized religions established The Quorum and began the process of religio-integration. However it was clear, even to a neophyte fresh out of Divinity clerking for The Quorum, that a year after integration, the prospect of collapse was very real.

Even as they united, the leadership of The Quorum struggled to execute the top lines of its charter. Political power continued to wane and victories in the Legislature, nominal at best, were mere tokens given by the Corps leaders for its participation in votes, of much larger consequence favoring Corp positions. Economically, The Quorum struggled for survival and failed to keep up with shifting tastes. Devotees and their goodwill continued to die off. Products designed to engage youngsters; *Tickle-Me-Jesus*, *What-Would-Muhammad-Do?* slap bracelets, and *Stretch Mahakali* with her twenty rubbery limbs, flopped. Imbecilic oversight of the snack food product lines, bacon-flavored halal crisps, crabby knish crackers, and beef-filled panipuri bites, isolated even the blindest of the faithful. It was apparent, very few people were interested in God, his various incarnations or the few acres he white-knuckled in The Blocks. The Quorum's disparate business models needed revitalization, if not consolidation. Science Economy Fever was spreading widely, and members of The Quorum weren't immune to a re-branding, a revitalization of their venerable institution. A year or two after the 32nd passed, The Quorum decided to kill God to stimulate revenue growth and to save religion from its steady march to the catacombs.

Beep.

With Consult Inc's direction, The Quorum, and its affiliated enterprises, initiated a major restructuring. The first order of business was to establish the detailed, science-based proof substantiating God as a long-believed farce. The Quorum scraped the mite box to its grainy wood bottom to buy a new, unmarked airplane, to grease the palms of notable scientists and to pay for the breathtaking cosmetic overhaul performed on a Dhalyte woman snatched from The Piles. God vanished with his stale cadre of products and services. Gone were the confounding inverse pyramid schemes aimed at compounding donations at the individual level, the anal-chastity belts protecting the vigilant against would-be attackers, *GAY-AWAY* supposito-ries and the do-it-yourself exorcist kit. Each new product and service was carefully designed, placed under The Quorum's operational direction, and amalgamated under a single new brand name, Salvation Inc, including the extremely lucrative Atonement service.

Atonements, to be the foundational revenue source for Salvation Inc. The Quorum, under the tutelage of senior partners at Consult Inc, realized

165

that in the absence of God, people, not only in need of repentance services but also emotional or spiritual healing, would find themselves without a mechanism to absolve guilt, to dampen grief or to mitigate existential anxiety. Since the dawn of time God and his many earth-bound representatives were responsible for providing the bulk of these services. In his absence, a massive revenue gap would open, creating a glaring opportunity to sell services to a core constituent. To reach desired revenue targets though, customers outside the core constituency would also need to engage. Advertisements to these more cautious sheep however, focused less on a flimsy, new-age sense of spirituality meant to replace God. Instead, these Irons were sold on the scientific benefits of telephony-self-abasement with a psychotropic adjunct of course. In a sense, a sort of "Godspace" was created inside the customer's head. Enter Project ACUltra. The newly partitioned Godspace was nurtured over time by repeated and escalated interactions with Salvation Inc associates, associates driven to establish a marketing channel directly into the amygdala of every man, woman and child.

Reinforcing the atonements, was an array of companion products and services directing people back to atonements, over time, creating cycles of repeat business enabling Salvation Inc to build deep profiles for each customer. Frequent caller programs, discounted drug incentives, implantable sin-detector modules, grief-meters, and a host of purchasable auxiliaries were crafted to channel both customer data and dialog back to the Salvation's Atonement Centers. Subliminal messaging nodes retrofitted at Pine sprayer locations, celebrity endorsements, and fully socialized data to spur customer competition for ever higher levels of health and spirituality rounded out the marketing plan.

Me! Kaysen McMurty, a rising star in the organization. Assigned to head operations for one of the first Atonement Centers. A job overseeing many dozens of centers in no time. Year after year, ever-more demanding revenue targets, call volume targets, Iron wage cuts and real estate cuts were announced. Impossible strategies for Markov-based callbots to handle completely unpredictable phone dialog. Genetically-modified African Greys fitted with voice box modulators to replace underperforming Irons that, after twelve highly caffeinated energy drinks themselves, sounded only slightly more cogent than unmodified African Greys. Sodium chloride swapped for sodium biphosphate in the cafeteria salt shakers and toilet paper in employee bathrooms impregnated with copious amounts of epinephrine. Twelve headsets and twenty-four call lines issued to each call agent, agents who were fitted into stackable *comfortcubes* allowing precisely 45 efficient cubic feet of workspace per agent. The never-ending search, and annihilation of, operational waste. The never-ending search for operational expansion opportunities. The ever-new acronym denoting a revolutionary strategy meant to rethink the operation, top to bottom. The ever-new acronym referencing the research substantiating the fact that last week's new revolutionary strategy didn't live up to theory, and was subsequently being deprecated in favor of a chart shaped like a fish that explained an even newer strategy for rethinking the operation going forward. Whatever it took to tweak, modify, enhance, and expand. There was never enough. Doubled revenues deemed lazy. Tripled? Still short of the mark. Staff perpetually perceived as bloated. Operating budgets halved even as revenues skyrocketed. The Quorum, a constant, dark pressure bearing down, never satisfied. It's Diamond membership, hidden behind a volley of multi-faceted electronic directives; staid voices with minor tonal fluctuations giving audible decoration to the subtlety of a veiled threat. Threats to bear as the typical coercions of a driven executive class, nothing more, nothing particularly insidious, just BAU. Normal job stress, with obvious industry-specific nuance, that any man experiences and subsequently mitigates with the time-honored traditions of cast iron plate dances and extramarital indiscretions. Paid well? Yep! Never hurting, always standing tall amid the upper echelon of Platinums, providing well beyond family needs. And always, as a matter of prudent Darwinomics, the occasional financial bungles were properly managed, the negative impacts quickly trickling down for the poorest to swallow in the form of unannounced rate increases, pay cuts. Good management of the top and bottom enabling personal buoyancy in the space between.

I must go to work. Thinking, reflecting, won't increase revenue.

Beep.

The device demands attention. Two percent battery remaining. My precious Palette, diligently instructive. Bobbing, lost in a sea of undirected thought without it. Path, one foot, two, and several plumes of dust. Walking, hand in hand with trust. Walking toward salvation, hoping for redemption. A Quorum. The Quorum. Who is The Quorum? Daddy said they're demi-gods, saviors of our way of life. Maybe just reluctant providers, tight trickledowners? The world doesn't see them, but feels their fibrillation flowing through. Millions swindingly served, manipulated into free participation of a consumable service by a few sneering oligarchs seeking eternal wealth. To stake every last piece of earth in a crusade for currency. It's a choice for everyone to make. The fibber and fibbee, both willing participants in the atonement narrative. Fear, waking up in the morning and buttoning a shirt, tying a tie. Stupid, recurrent fear. A hunched-over, hairy-legged sit upon the foot of the morning's unmade bed, anxiety's tears drying to the sound of the daily affirmations. *I'm safe, I'm happy!* Self-deprecating laughter for no one to witness. Shake it off, go to work.

"Daddy, I'm hungry," a child says.

So were they.

"*Beep,*" notifies a device.

How may I serve you?

"*Chirp, Chirp,*" alerts a bird.

Hey, asshole bird. Will you please stop telling them our location?

The bend, the bend again. At any moment, the bend could attack. Something's changing, smoke. A heavy, black smoke billowing out, enveloping the path ahead, blocking view of the bend. Fear, when fate's visibility is obfuscated. Sparks shoot from the smoke, rain down on a lone bush sitting quiet amid scattered rocks at the path's edge. A low howl of rushing wind the little bush afire, dancing for the obnoxious birds. Burning bush.

"To the River, Onward Ye Shall March! The path is no good," says the flaming bush.

Confusion, waking up and realizing you actually haven't. Is that the sort of statement requiring acknowledgement? Can a bush bear witness to a nod? Am I communicating with plant life now?

"We'll get food at your cousin's house dear, watch out for the bush."

"What bush Daddy?"

Kaysen, did you just nod to a bush? Did it nod back? Walk on. Into the thicket we go, away from burning bushes, the unknown of the bend. In search of water, the place where debts are settled and the spirit is revived. Where fear is washed away. Rebirth.

Beep. Kaysen, your Palette is now shutting down.

Looking on with wide eyes, waiting. That time of day when we sit on the mat together, open the bin, plate up. They stare at me, sitting crossed legged, expectant. Maven with her constantly outstretched finger pointing randomly at things, explaining the world in tangle of overlapping syllables. Valerie, with her huge brown eyes and whisper-thin hair launching from both sides of her head. The trick, to stay away from the bin when it's empty, ignore it as it stares at us from across the room. Hunger's silly mirage. The bin doesn't exist. Stop thinking about it. It's best to ignore misfortune's subtle nag. Woe is not me. Distractions. Diversions. A redirection of energy and focus. Pangs go in cycles. Keep active as cramps peak, knots twist and wrench. Water helps. Enough of it drowns pangs temporarily, trick them into a confused, parallel state.

"Valerie, here, drink this."

"I don't want to, I'm not tursty."

"Go on now, do as Gramma says."

She tips the cup reluctantly, glares at me while sipping. Droplets cling to peach fuzz, she fastidiously collects them with her lower lip, passes the cup back with elbowing eyes.

"Good girl. Maven, sweetie, let's have a drink."

Cup to cracked little lips. Trust embodied, bending eagerly to whatever's impressed upon her, dipping her head backwards into my hand, mouth gaped submissively. Baby bird. She drinks and her eyes search mine, looking for cues, hints, directives. A child's keen sense of the subtle expression, my smile eliciting hers, then, fading together. She continues on and on, ready to drink the ocean if required, until her head is returned upright.

Inherent connections in humans, hardwired in the womb. An innate desire to complete another's sentences, to empathize, to nurse. She smiles again as the water drowns wrenching muscles, calms her belly. Return smiles twofold, *I feel you little girl*. Eye contact won't break. With a thousand words she doesn't possess she says she feels better. Playful eyebrows trying new positions to illicit a response, baby's first litmus.

Yesterday, nothing. Nothing found in the two days prior. Three days without food, one day for them. A full revolution without sustenance. Headaches and irritability. Discomfort and fatigue. Worry. Grinding, relentless worry without a moment's rest. Intensely carnal, a worry constantly capable of rooting out vulnerability's softest spot, second to second, then looping infinite, unspeakable catastrophe upon it. Limbs, thin and angular, skitter about with abandon, unaware of their possible, if not probable, calamitous trajectory. Neurons waiting for fuel, receiving nothing, then going dark as the body conserves energy for the pump and bellows. The hope of a new cell extinguished before possibility germinates. A creeping, vaguely understood notion of abandonment in a child's subconscious. A sense of deprivation delivered with something akin to intent. Why else wouldn't you ease my pangs? You are the responsible party here, you realize that right? How was your childhood? Did your joints ever hurt? Did your gums bleed? Guilt, the one emotion oozing from each action taken, brutally present. Feet swollen and gnarled from endless hunting. Hands lacerated and stiff from ripping open bags, sifting through another world's refuse, searching for their beautifully discarded, our chance at life. Give us this day our daily slime. Valerie and Maven's chance. The Claxton's, saviors, no doubt growing weary of the extra burden placed on them. And the guilt. It's the guilt. Oh they're forever saying how they can't risk feeding the girls, how it exposes them to the possibility of loss. The awkward sterility of the words chosen, *possibility of loss*, and the sullen break in eye contact. But their hearts are visible. Sitting with them in their moments of anguish, seeing what happens to good souls as the body wastes away. How they can only broaden their view under duress, breathe what's left of themselves into others in the hope that the energy will return from the cosmos and grant them one more chance to be. As one. All that is fucked up in the world can't balance without a measure of opposition. It would be forced to consume itself into oblivion unable to bear distinction or identification, let alone a name, without some counterbalancing goodness. But goodness and survival share a common need and a common enemy. Both march toward the light, alternatively whipped and coddled by the same thread of guilt that ties us to the darkest part of our being. The guilt you smile through at the door of your neighbor all the while knowing it's your fault that life's on tilt and everyone's abstaining. Goodness and charity are not analogous, they are partners of circumstance so long as survival isn't a question. Jesus Christ, thanks for The Claxtons and the dissolution of guilt. Your time on the timber was well spent.

These thoughts, these flailing, overly self-indulgent thoughts. Poor me, woe! Woe is me! No. Practicality. It comes down to practicality. Existence hinges on practicality. There's no scrap of food found elsewhere. Calories will not appear if I manage to enlighten my perspective, theirs or anyone else's. Practicality. There must be a skill associated with hunting I've yet to acquire, on what, my twelfth day now as sole provider? Twelve days nosing through trash, a hungry rat. Twelve days watching an overhead drop land closer to another, luckier, or more skilled, hunter. Twelve days since John found peace. Twelve nights without sleep and twelve nights of picking cuticles into twenty irritated, red smiles. If not for The Claxton's, The Mallory's, where would we be? Three of us in the sun, one barely walking, searching, burning calories without having found their replacement. Few reserves stored, skin marching close to bone. That's practicality. The distance between hunger and starvation marked by the quantity of digestible tissues separating the two realities.

"Tell me Valerie, how was your morning at The Claxton's?"

"Fiiiiiine."

"Fine? Alright, well, what did you do this morning?"

"Plaaaayyy."

"Go on dear." Stubborn Valerie, always working things to her terms, dropping a single bread crumb at a time. A path of breadcrumbs growing stale where cheerful primrose should flourish. "Tell Gramma what you were playing."

"Blazzel."

"Well that sounds like a fun game. How do you play Blazzel?"

"I can't tell you Gramma, only kids can play Blazzel!" A defiant tone protecting sacred ground from the unwanted interest of grazing authority.

"Ok sweetie, but I'm not asking to play, I'm curious how *you* play the game."

Thoughtful consideration, she tucks her lips, bends her eyebrows down then a smile cracks her charade and she runs with it.

"Well Gramma, Blazzel is a *new* game Alli learned from her older brother," she says, proud of an association with someone who consorts with big kids. "All you have to do is get a bunch of rocks and everybody sits in a line. One person has to play leader and it is always Alli because she never shares and because she said that she is the one who showed us the game and because she has the most dolls and I think someday Alli might get Blazzeled if she doesn't share."

"I see honey. Did you ask Alli if you could take a turn as leader?"

"Yes, everybody asks but she never shares, she just says they are her dolls and she is the one who told us how to play Blazzel and she is going to play leader and that's that and don't ask about it again."

"Well then, how do you girls play Blazzel?"

"I'm telling you Gramma! After everybody sits in a line, Alli walks in front with one of her dolls and sits it up against the wall. She usually starts with Allison, the prettiest doll, the one her dad found last week sitting under the best goddamn chair he's ever seen. Then she runs away and yells *POOR!* and everybody races with a rock to Allison and the first person to feed Allison a rock wins."

"Well that sounds like a nice game. Have you ever won?"

"Mmmhmm, I won a hundret times yesterday."

"Well, it seems to me that the person who wins should be the next leader. Perhaps you could suggest this to Alli?"

An idea relished, aroused fingers spin pigtails.

"But sweetheart, why is the game called Blazzel?"

"Oh that's because sometimes Allison puts Tamas or Shaytan or Ahriman against the wall. Then she runs away and yells *RICH!* and everybody jumps up screams *BLAZZEL!* and throws their rocks at Tamas and whoever hits him first wiiiiiiiiiins!"

Wins ejects breathy and light, accompanied by a celebratory pirouette that falls to the floor in a jumble of giggles.

"Valerie, honey, do you think that is a nice game?"

"Yes, *of course Gramma*, it's everybody's faaaavorite game to play!" she says squirming ecstatically.

"I see. But isn't it wrong to throw rocks at people?"

"We're not throwing rocks at people *Gramma* aren't you listening? We are throwing rocks at Tamas. I told you, Tamas is a doll, one of Alli's dolls. Alli has many dolls but she doesn't share. Alli never shares Gramma."

"I see dear. But, Tamas represents a person right?"

"No Gramma, Tamas is a doll, I told you already! Tamas is Alli's doll."

"I understand honey. I know you are not throwing rocks at people, I know. That is not something my little girl would do. I know you know better. What I'm saying is the doll *represents* a person in the real world."

"Gramma, what does represents mean?"

"Represents means you wish the doll, Tamas, was in fact, a person whom you do not like, and that you throw the rocks at that person you don't like because you want to hurt them."

"Gramma, Tamas is a doll. I don't want to hurt anybody. Tamas isn't a represents, he is a doll. He's not a person."

"I see sweetie. I guess what I'm trying to say is that not everyone who is rich is necessarily bad, and it's not right to place everyone who is rich into the same category."

"Gramma?"

"Yes dear?"

"What does rich mean?"

"Oh honey. Come here on Gramma's lap."

She rolls on the floor to her knees, pops up and throws her arms roughly around my neck. She twirls, a flurry of stabbing elbows and knees, until she settles in my lap facing outward. Stray hairs from her head tickle my nose. Squeeze.

"I love you sweetheart."

"I love you Gramma!"

"So, rich. Rich means that a person has lots of money and lots of stuff."

"You mean like Mr. Claxton?"

"Well, not exactly honey."

"But he has five chairs *and* two mattresses in his cell."

"Yes, sweetheart, Mr. Claxton is very fortunate. Those things certainly make life more comfortable. But he is not rich."

"You mean like Mr. Parsons? He has twenty-nine hats! He showed us and even let me try one on."

"No, Mr. Parson's hats are very nice, but I wouldn't say he's rich."

"Then who is a rich?"

"Well honey, nobody you know. Nobody that lives near us. All of the rich people live on the other side. You know how we've talked about the other side before, right?"

"Yes, I know. People on the other side look like us but they are more lucky than we are."

"Well, yes, but I think the word you are looking for is fortunate. The people on the other side are more fortunate than us."

"Does that mean they are rich?"

"Well, no, not exactly honey. It just means they have more than we do. More than Mr. Claxton does. But it is true, some people on the other side are rich."

"Gramma?"

"Yes dear?"

"Grampa said people on the other side are cunts."

"I know dear, but do you also remember Grampa telling you you're not supposed to use that word?"

"Yes, I remember."

"It's a naughty word. Something pretty little girls shouldn't say. What Grampa was trying to say, in a less than eloquent manner, was that *some* people on the other side are bad people. These bad people frustrated your Grampa, that is why he called them bad names. But it is wrong, we shouldn't call people bad names."

"Gramma?"

"Yes, dear?"

"Are rich people cunts?"

"*Valerie!*"

"I'm sorry Gramma. I mean, are rich people bad people?"

"I suppose some are sweetheart. But there are bad people who are not rich as well. Being rich doesn't necessarily mean a person behaves badly, but it increases the probability that they do."

"Gramma?"

"Yes dear?"

"What is probablyity?"

"It means as a person gets more stuff, there is a greater chance that they behave badly because they have more chances *to* behave badly. Do you understand?"

"No."

"Well, imagine for a minute you are rich, that you can have whatever you want, when you want it by simply snapping your fingers."

"Like sugar cubes?"

"Yes, like sugar cubes. Sugar cubes are a good example."

Her fingers launch into rapid fire clicking, a crazy, faraway look in her eyes.

"That's right sweetheart. So all those clicks and then, all the sugar cubes that come after. Now, since you are rich, you can keep snapping those fingers and getting as many sugar cubes as you want for as long as you want."

"Gramma, I'm never going to stop snapping my fingers."

"That's right honey, because you don't have to right? Each time you snap, you receive another sugar cube. Now imagine you snap your fingers a million times, and you eat every single sugar cube. What do you think will happen."

"I would ickspload?"

"Well you might honey, but more likely, you'd have a terrible tummy ache for eating too much sugar. You see the simple fact that you had the choice to consume unlimited amounts of sugar gave possibility to a poor decision. You could eat some of the sugar then save some for later or share some of the sugar with your sister and your friends."

"Maybe, but I wouldn't share any with Alli."

"Well, that's your choice sweetheart. But my point is, if you are rich, you have the option to make more decisions, and, with that option, an increased *probability* that you will sometimes make bad decisions. It is these bad decisions that frustrated Grampa, and the reason why he said some people on the other side are bad."

"Cunts."

"Valerie, what did I say? Do not use that word anymore, do you understand?"

"Yes Gramma. But Gramma, Grampa didn't say that some people on the other side are cun-, I mean bad, he said that all people on the other side are bad."

"Yes dear, I know. But again, your Grampa was frustrated, upset by circumstance, so he would mistakenly label everyone as bad."

"Gramma?"

"Yes dear?"

"Do you know anyone on the other side?"

"Well, I did, when I was younger. Well before you were born."

"Are they good people?"

"Well yes, yes they were good people. We enjoyed good times together. Dinner parties, birthday parties, cookouts. Your mom loved inviting neighborhood kids for sleepovers."

"Why don't you see them anymore?"

The topic is too complex for a four-year-old. Time to shut it down. A lethal dose of God and lies sweetheart, that's what Gramma can afford at this time.

"Well honey, time's have changed and people get busy and well, you will understand when you are a grownup."

She sits in silence, milling through my response, trying to will herself into adulthood, scratching a dirty fingernail along the edge of her rock. Focused on her rock, her lips pucker and relax, pucker and relax, her thinker's tick. A shriek from Maven shakes Valerie from thought and she shifts on the mat, plastic crunching beneath spindly legs.

"Do you think they might invite us for a dinner party?"

"Anything is possible sweetheart, now let's hurry back to the Claxton's so Gramma can return to work. Hurry now, grab Maven's hand, let's go."

Crunching across the cool floor to our shoes. Maven grabs hers diligently, raising them above her head in celebration. Valerie, increasingly quiet and introspective, lumbers to hers, plucks the laces then halts.

"Gramma, can I come to work with you?"

"No sweetheart, not this time. It's dangerous there and not a safe place for children. Besides, I thought you enjoyed playing with the Claxtons?"

"I do sometimes but I told you Alli doesn't share and she always wants to do things her way. Mrs. Claxton says she has a hard head but I touched it and it feels the same as mine so I don't know what to do."

She unwittingly reciprocates my burgeoning smile, and we progress into staccato chuckles. Clenching the sides of her head, pigtails through spread fingers, a kiss to her forehead.

"You let Alli know your head is just as hard as hers and you'll show her if necessary."

Wincing, "Gramma, your breath is stinky!" a disgusted smile behind a pinched nose.

Clutching pigtail handlebars, "Won't you give Gramma's sad, stinky mouth a kiss?"

Hesitation before puckering sharply, pecking my cheek indiscriminately.

"Good girl. I love you."

"I love you too Gramma."

Valerie drops to the floor, ties her shoes, while Maven continues celebrating hers.

"Come here Maven dear, let's get your shoes back on your feet."

Grinning hard and playfully lunging, chomping her teeth at me, Maven slams her shoes to my hands, giggles.

"Gramma, will Grampa find me a new dress to wear to the dinner party?"

Heart jump, as if the casual mention of him by a four year old will deliver his apparition through the tarpaulin door. Reality punches back with equal force, but that childish, naive sensation washes over; a covert glance to the door delivers superstition's deadpan outcomes.

"Valerie, sweetie, now remember what we've said about Grampa? Can you show me where Grampa stays now?"

She points sullenly, almost sarcastically, to her chest, "I know, I know. I just thought that if we went to a dinner party, he would want to come."

"I understand sweetheart, and he would want to come, only that he can't come with us, at least not in person. Remember though, he is always with us in our hearts and minds, Ok?"

"I know," she says in singsongy dejection.

Maven, fascinated with my ring, digs at it while overly tight shoes are wedged onto her feet.

"Tell you what, when Gramma gets home from work tonight, we will play Crazy Chair, sound like fun?"

"Yaaaaaay!" Valerie brightens, does her best grand jeté, while Maven, blindsided by the excitement, claps with reactive vigor.

"Ok, we ready?"

Grabbing the bag of jars and pushing the tarp aside, Valerie navigates the musty, dim corridor of patch-worked trash while Maven squirms in the crook of my arm.

"Watch the puddles sweetheart."

"I know," she says, hopping around the shimmering splotches.

The corridor, the most somber aspect of The Piles. Damp, chilly, dark and ureic. Sparse light trickling through its immensity from the few portals to the outside world; a dot, like a candle flame, in the distance struggling to shed light on those living in the bowels of the tent city. The acerbic mammalian stench of thousands of unkempt people living atop one another. The must of a perpetually wet environment. The utter lack of an echo as every hertz of sound is immediately absorbed by the swollen, damp layers of trash feigning privacy. Surreal in a hauntingly real way. Each blink, a snapshot to the past. Bucolic green fields, wrap-around porch, a garden bursting with uncontrollable vitality. Wide plank wood floors and a gentle shade of yellow warming the home's heart. Eyes open to a dark, wet cavern of malnutrition. Eyes close to the blinding white of a down comforter drying in the lemon beams of late afternoon sun.

PAT PAT PAT

The Claxton's tarp door rustles, stabilizes.

Funny, these little games of normalcy we play with each other, an etiquette evolved for poverty. Of course there isn't a doubt in the world Jane heard every word spoken between me and Valerie. What, about eight feet apart from each other and divided by millimeters of worn plastic, damp cardboard? Not possible she didn't hear us shuffling on the mats, putting on our shoes and pushing aside our tarp to pat on hers. Yet, as she pushes the tarp aside, she, in the most honest and forthright manner, acts surprised at our presence. A favor to return. The collectively cultivated illusion of privacy.

"Oh, hey there!"

"Hey!"

Wanting something so bad you will the necessary conditions, lie to yourself to maintain sanity, then believe those lies over anything rational. Games we play. After a degrading, nightlong squabble between Jane and Marby, the type of argument that colorfully elaborates previously unspoken, and painfully intimate shortcomings, Jane patted our tarp, apologized red-faced for the disturbance. Flashing back, hard to remember though. Did I hear a quarrel or perhaps just experience an unsettling dream? The elasticity of recollection. Perhaps my memory is flawed to the extent that her morning visit, and specifically her apology for the argument, was merely a self-deprecating mechanism to blunt her breach of etiquette, to disrupt the potency of her socially unacceptable request. We need salt! She, promising God to repay threefold, wanted to borrow salt, a concern about Alli's spasms and vomiting. Concerns about hyponatremia. Or so memory says. Maybe the squabble was between John and I and Jane's salt request was merely a method for sharing sympathetic eyes. Nothing in plain sight is transparent when life is a series of coping mechanisms.

"Hi Jane," touching her hand, a cutaneous transfer of gratitude for her help.

She accepts with a warm smile, nodding away the need for sentiment.

"Hi kids, Alli was waiting for you to come back!"

Ditching shoes, Valerie heads for Alli.

"Staying in or heading out?"

"Oh I reckon we'll stay in for a while, perhaps conjure up some *new* games to play," she says, winking.

"Yeah, wow. Well, kids certainly are perceptive."

"See, You, In, Tea, huh? I struggled to hold that laugh in, ha! It was nice to hear John's voice again. He knew how to apply the right words didn't he?" she says, smiling.

"He did and damned if he wouldn't have relished the chance to teach these kids more obscenities. But anyway, on to it. Ok then Maven, let's pull these back off your piggies."

"How are you managing?"

"Hanging in there, trying to get my feet wet, figure out this whole hunting thing."

"Yeah, yeah. I know it took Marby some time to nail down a technique. He claims he constantly refines it as he notices changes in drop patterns, bag shapes and such. I guess there's a science to it, though I know nothing about it."

Perhaps she really doesn't know how to hunt. It is possible Marby hasn't discussed his strategy with her. Why would he, isn't that his responsibility? Wasn't it Johns? But it seems strange for her not to know the basics about the one activity that means life or death. If she did know, there's only a slight possibility she would share the knowledge. The danger of new competition constantly looms. Inedible charity is the glue of social interaction whereas spirited competition is a relic fit for an era when the stakes weren't so high. And John, why couldn't he step out of himself for a moment, realize the magnitude of the skill he possessed, teach it? Sadly, his academic aloofness leaching into the more critical aspects of life. But the blame lies with me, not the rest of the world. Why do I ask the most important questions in life after their answers become critical?

"It's not a problem, just a matter of time," avoiding her eyes. Pity always stings. You smell like shit, your body is eating itself and you can't care for those who depend on you, yet the pity still stings. She knows this. Everyone knows this and keeps certain eye contact to an absolute minimum.

"You know.... Marby, he uh, he had a very good uh, you know. Wait, hold on a second," she says as she turns and walks across her cell, kneels in the far corner next to a stack of blankets. Glass knocks together, my stomach wrenches as a vague mind catches up to her intentions. Shuffling back across the frayed fragments of jute, she slips a cool glass bottle into my hand, pushes the small of my back, whispers,

"Ok, don't you worry about Valerie and Maven, they're in good hands. Best of luck out there today. I think you are about to hit your stride. Bye now."

Ushered beyond her tarp, time to only say,

"Oh, um, thank you, see you kids later Ok?"

And the tarp falls with a rigid crinkle.

Conceal the bottle, steal down the corridor, dodge puddles shimmering vaguely in the dark. Three inches long, equal in girth, energy for the whole day. Gut burns prickly, a hollow knot of fire, does that make sense? But why did she do it? Do I look particularly gaunt? Ill? Is she fearful of a

181

more permanent burden guilted upon her family? Hard to imagine neighbors would allow two innocents to perish alone. Unspoken protocol basically guilts the adjacent into guardianship. The twisting, the sting of acids in the back of my throat. Dodging puddles quickly down the lane. Yield to the sunblinded march of oncoming silhouettes, brown tones pound the ground as outside light gets closer. Undisturbed puddles of milky taupe freckle the heavily tamped earth, shadows of lumbering passersby whisking overtop. The sibilance of loose, dangling plastics disturbed and the rise and fall of tones from transient conversations. Emerging from the corridor, a fulgent sunbeam bears down. Weave through the slowly sharpening clots of muddy children playing, the seniors in huddled lament, the men repairing plastic sheeting. Walk briskly. Beyond the reaching fingers of newly added cells. Jogging. Beyond the isolated tent clumps of the misanthropic and into a clearing, a clearing leading to the drop fields beyond. Running. Among the spindly saplings hoping for a chance to grow tall before hacked into kindling. A patch of packed dirt, quiet, no one in sight. Jittery hands rip the bottle from my bag. Suck out the contents, whatever they are, tongue dislodging gelatinous globs from edges. Something brownish-orange, reminiscent of earthy carrots. Paste slides down between gasps, blood pumping through head, heart hammering bone. A few cursory chops for each successive mouthful, unnecessary, the masticatory habit of eating. Accumulating, the paste larger than my stomach, leaden and misplaced. Fingering out the remaining bits clinging to the bottle's bottom, swallow them and eye the bend for anyone approaching. Lick residual smears from the bottle's rim, miniscule amounts, maybe a gram? A gram of carbohydrates is roughly four calories. A body at rest needs fifty calories an hour to sustain. Four calories is three minutes. Three minutes of life. Three minutes to breath. Why do I know this? Why do I know anything? Memory's opacity.

Empty. The bottle, exchanged for the jar of cloudy water sloshing in my bag. Delayed satiation washes over narcotically. Rippling gurgles of relaxing tension, the repetitive buzzing of a process in action, instantaneous sedation. The water rinses the paste's bitter, metallic tinge from my tongue. Sensations bend warmer, softer. Easy thoughts emerge while perched on a solitary tuft of crabgrass poking from the earth. Free time. A three-minute reverie. Bliss. Maven squatting forward with her oversized toddler-head, balance overcorrected, causing a heavy wobble, a fall, and a look of surprise. Valerie lecturing yet another four-year-old on the virtues of taking turns. John fouling his pants, blaming the scent on my inability to properly diaper Maven only to be caught by Valerie scrubbing 'poopy undies' in the middle of the night. Moments of calm. Anxious faces heading for the drop fields, dirty feet through plumed dirt. The irresponsibility of relaxation, the wastefulness. Three irretrievable minutes gone forever. Shame. Stand and walk.

The muffled clink of empty jars in my bag while passing through the narrow void between the sprawl of tents and the sprawl of trash. Veiny networks of narrow dirt paths lead up a knoll into the drop fields. The stench bears down. Acrid decay at first, then, a soup of indistinguishable odors, the fetid odors one eliminates or avoids as a matter of hygiene. The empty jars of reminder slap over and over on a march up the hill. *Clink. Clink. Clink.* Upon the crest, the overwhelming size of the drop fields. The sprawl, endless miles, a wavy landscape flecked with every tone of every color imaginable. Insignificant figures, ants among the mounds. Bent, erect, bent, erect. Incessant repetition. A hard sun, ducking intermittently behind roving clouds and the patches of shadow marauding on the ground. Quiet repulsion, silent nausea.

A big toe worms through a shoe hole upon descent into the fields. Pressure on tired knees, raw feet pounding. Nobody hunting nearby, area looks picked over, scrambled. Scanning, no desirable black domes indicative of unopened bags. Hunt begins. Walking. Step gingerly on chosen points of relative cleanliness, free of liquids, tiny platforms of cardboard, plastic, a chunk of broken flakeboard. One toehold to the next. The first mishap, the second. Shoes, sinking deeper with each step, unknown juices dampen, saturate worn fabric. Wet. Lubricated toes glide slimy against one another. The careful search for toeholds resolves into the steady, indiscriminate march toward anything resembling a black dome. Squishing and sucking. The rancid steam of a warm day. A pea green ooze flashes, sitting shaded in a white cardboard nest below the windblown frays of a torn black bag. Upon closer inspection, the green material appears rotten. Foamy white bubbles cling to the ooze's perimeter, caution. It appears passed over by another, press on without a sniff test. Eyes closed. Remember when maggots were considered repulsive? That summer when the neighbor's dog died in the cornfield. Rasputin right? The Elroys, constantly losing an animal. Stepping blind into the bloated corpse and the gush of fluids squirting up my leg. Mobile rice. Panic! Grab the hose! Soap, disinfectant, bleach, wire brush, whatever. A rush of cold, crystal water and a fluffy white lather sitting on emerald blades. Problem solved. Inside to wash hands, grab an apple, reflect at the table. Laugh off the day's drama with disgusted lips.

Eyes to the wavy bands of steam rising blurry against a backdrop of endless trash. Walk on. An incline, unsteady, slippery, hand to the ground, both hands to the ground. A knee to the ground. Both knees to the ground in search of stability. Stable, not sliding. Hands compromised though, be careful. Steady and walk on.

The sound overhead, could it be? Growing in volume, high pitch whistles from one direction, reprising in a slightly different tone from the opposite direction. The pitch of the whistle drops. It is, one's arriving! The sound's nearly overhead! The sky, in this moment, all that matters. The world above and suspended bounty. Fuck all else, fuck that cloud, let the sun burn out, clean hands or not, please let the bags land on my head. Every one of them. Drop a mountain on me. The sound grows. It's growing. Nearly upon me. The volume increases, the pitch drops, a rumble of exhaust. Where is it? From an envelope of clouds it emerges, like a Phoenix on a half-hourly rebirth, shiny with promise. A glistening fire-red underbelly, the roar of burning fuel and a gush of air from whirring turbines. Nearly overhead, it's opening up, it's actually opening up above me! Doors sliding apart, a gaping mouth directly next to the shockingly yellow scrawl of "Sanitation Inc" jumping off the fire-red underbelly. Creeping. NO! NOOO! Banking left, a full ninety degrees. Straightening on a path heading away from me above the expanse of drop fields narrowing to the horizon. NOOO! Beyond reach, it continues, the gush of air dissipating and the sound of exhaust muffling, fading. And then it happens. The first payload bubbles out, falls down. A black dot, followed by another. Another. Another. Another. Another. Another…..The tail of the huge bird and a series of periods, a continuous ellipsis, leashing the bird to the ground. It continues to shrink and the ellipsis becomes more and more faint till all that's visible is a feeble gray line extending from a red blot in the sky. Gone. In its wake, a flurry of figures in the distance, energized ants, scrambling to paydirt. Hundreds of bags.

Thousands perhaps. A bounty of immeasurable proportions, gone. Sinking sensation. Toes work deeper into the muck. Or maybe that's hunger or perhaps being close, but not close enough. Sinking. All three. Keep walking.

A pattern, there must be a pattern. Why haven't I identified it yet? There must be a pattern. It follows a clear path upon each entry. How are the paths related in time? Sometimes a border drop, sometimes up the middle, sometimes a stalled dump, occasionally a curve in and back out. The sun peeks from behind the clouds, blisteringly hot. A piece of fabric from my bag, a makeshift scarf. Steam rises putridly. There is a pattern, must be a pattern. Decipherable with enough observation, enough time. God damn it John. Walk on.

Across the mushy mounds one step at a time, eyes fixed to the ground, scanning for the covetous black domes. Sweat tickling cheek. A jagged pile of painted wood, broken fragments of furniture. Fabricate into something useful? Perhaps, into the bag. String, a twinkling chard of mirror, the rare pair of children's shoes heavily worn but not beyond use. Into the bag. The glare of glass, a plate or container of some sort, useful maybe. Push aside a matted clump of wet hair, the crumbling remnants of an ancient makeup collection, a frame. A wooden picture frame, teal paint rubbed off over time, "Grandma" carved in gaudy high relief across the bottom, a font screaming of wily coyotes and ACME anvils. Inside, a picture sharply contrasted against the juvenile frame. Behind a cracked pane of glass, a stately-looking women, steel-gray hair pulled into a bun, overlapping layers of black chiffon draped elegantly across her shoulders. Dangling over the delicate clavicle protrusion, a silver necklace with a series of staggered pearls, graceful and understated. Piercing eyes analyzing the photographer's moves, and the crow's feet of critique as her partial squint sets her skin into a position known for years. Her faint smile suggests strain, something left undone, nagging her in the moment. Wistful perhaps. Why am I wasting time? Through her coaxed smile she maintains an air of confidence, appears steadfast and decisive, arriving at this point in her life cognizant of the path walked. Need to keep walking. Her smile, not pride but not humility in those eyes, serenity. A serenity betrayed though, by hesitant lips. This picture, her record now imprinted on posterity's forgetful mind alone. Who would throw away this marker of history? Who would toss grandma? Grandma. She stares at me, returned.

Her familiarity, her chin's sharpness, cheekbones set high about the eyes, a jaw line flaring out defiantly. Can I afford a couple minutes rest?

...

'Her smile, intractably wry, a fixture on her face, some kind of preempt to the cynically rooted jokes she knew were being crafted at any point in time against her. Intelligent, the barometer in the room everyone visually consulted before responding in conversation. Highly skeptical, not as a device to cast doubt, but more a tool to tease out the fragments of truth sitting buried in the motivations of others. She strove to see the best in people even if she had to wait an eternity for her sliver of proof. Fearless on her best days, precarious on her worst.' That's what was written in blue on the back of the black and white photo dug from the bottom of the box labeled *Memories*. Five odd sentences, author unknown. Five sentences, a collection of mostly backhanded compliments, withering a legacy in tidy summation. Why? The photo, snapped in her graying fifties, represented Ava Ortiz as I remember her. Not as a born Singh or any of the trial surnames of her twenties, thirties and forties. To me, Auntie Ava, Auntie A.

Sitting there, flattening down the photo's worn, fuzzy corners, its frame discarded to free more room in the box for priceless items. The box, initially designed to hold a pair of black velvet pumps, bulged under the pressure of wedged stacks of photos painstakingly selected for survival from a vast, treasured and meticulously organized collection. As I stared through the faded blue ink, searching for the author, Ingrid scooted across the blankets for a closer look at the photo being studied.

Ingrid must have been about fourteen when we were sitting on the Church's floor, John off hunting anxiously for a job after being fired from the University the previous year. Unbelievable. Twenty years, like yesterday.

"Who is that, mom?"

"Really? You don't know who this is? I never told you?"

"No, not a clue. And why does everyone in old black and white photos look so serious?"

"Well Griddy, this photo isn't exactly old, it's only *meant* to look as though it's from a long time ago. This photo was taken about thirty years ago."

186

"Thirty years is a pretty long time for some, mom," she said, smiling. "Ok, so, who is it?"

"This is a picture of my Auntie A, or if you like, your great-great-Auntie A."

"She still alive?"

"No, sweetheart, she's not, she died quite a few years ago. If memory serves, she died the year after I stayed with her in the city."

"The city? You mean The Core? Mom, people call it The Core nowadays. See, told you thirty years is a long time!"

She leaned in closer, getting a good look at Auntie A's face. "How'd she die?"

"Well, Auntie A was, ...well, troubled. As you can see, she was a beautiful woman, and smart, terribly smart, but, she struggled with mental illness for many years. Can you believe she is in her fifties in this photo?"

"I can believe it, look how gray her hair is!"

"Well right, but, ...oh, you're too young to gauge these things. *Anyhow*, she struggled with the disease for many years, well before I was born. Sometimes people would say she was perfectly fine, acting normal, other times she wouldn't leave home for weeks at a time, shutting herself off from the world. I remember, so clearly, all the endless, snarky names the grownups called Auntie A, in her absence, of course. 'Looney Tunes Ava' and 'Vanishing Ava' and 'Ava, Ava, Quite Contrary', new ones popped up often, and as a child is prone to do, I'd run around asking everyone what 'contrary' or 'lamentographer' or 'melancholinista' meant. Everyone thought they had a clever tongue. After a while, with the collection of new words swirling in my head, I came to view my aunt, mind you I had not met her yet, as an enigma, a walking, talking riddle. Over time, she was verbally deconstructed into a quasi-human being to the extent she existed as a figment of my imagination rather than a relative. A cartoon morphing in my young mind. I remember I was so apprehensive about staying with her the summer my dad, your Grandpa, fell ill. I truly thought that if I didn't eat my peas she would make me hand-deliver them to some malnourished child starving in the Orient."

"So how long did you stay with her?"

"About four months, while your Grandpa was in hospital fighting cancer."

"So, how was it?"

"You know, in a word, life-changing. Guess that's two words huh? Transformative. Anyway, I know it sounds hyperbolic considering I was, what, seven or eight at the time. But those few months left an impression on me, indelible enough to recall with a strange clarity even today. As I quickly learned, Auntie A was a dynamic, often abrasive, person. When she was *on*, she was a force of nature, attacking life with zeal, engaged with debates, challenging adversaries and often in an aggressive way. I learned later in life she was very passionate about politics, and, being a politician's wife, thought it her moral obligation to influence the direction of policy by engaging her husband and his powerful associates. So, she would argue, relentlessly as I was told, her beliefs, her ideals. Unfortunately, her offensive posture remained after the suits left for the evening when the only people present were a few yawning family members stirring coffee. It seems she rubbed people the wrong way, and, I assume that's why people took shots at her behind her back when she became vulnerable, depressive."

"What was she fighting for? I mean, what did she believe so strongly in?"

"And you know, that's the question, right there. I asked it for the longest time. It bothered me that I couldn't make sense why she was so passionate, so inclined to argue. Of course as a child overhearing adult conversations, I understood little of what was being said, so my attention was usually fleeting, disjointed. I do remember though, at times, watching Auntie A, her hands cutting through the air, her voice trilling above the baritones. I remember, watching her, focusing intently on those lips, those pencil-thin lips, taut rubber bands ready to snap in her adversary's face. But the words, the words always appeared to me, as if they took physical shape upon leaving her mouth, as little knots. Tangles of meaning bound too tightly for me to unravel. I even remember telling her once that she talked in knots. I called them her word knots. Auntie A's word knots. And I remember, she laughed at this, said something about how the knowledge difference between a child and an adult was only a few thousand knots and growing narrower by the day. And then, after summer, after your Grandpa died, the family broke apart, it utterly disintegrated and I ended up at the orphanage as I know you've heard a million times before. Apart from a single visit from an uncle, I think I was about twenty at the time, I never saw or spoke to a family member again.

And that visit, in that one visit, I learned the few bits I know about my family today; dad's cancer, my brother's disappearance, and some of the scattered facts about Auntie A among other things. So looking back, without having the vocabulary, the knowledge to follow the conversation, it was her tone, the potency of her presence that struck me so profoundly. She was fearless, unflinching present in the moment. I remember her force, her passion, the way she comported herself even when surrounded by intimidating men. She didn't back down, never wilted or left the room when discussions became heated. She would charge forward confident in herself, not giving an inch. It was like watching a rambunctious Chihuahua spinning wildly inside a circle of growling wolves. Something unique."

"So then you don't know her politics, or any of what she believed in?"

"No. Well, not the details anyhow. Oh I have a broad idea from the stuff my uncle told, but, by and large, no. For me though, Auntie A's memory is bigger than politics. Through all these years, across all my experiences in life, Auntie A's voice stayed with me, in the back of my mind, a tiny point of light refusing to dim. Her aura, her presence. Something intangible about her haunts me. Of all the things she said to me that summer in our many kitchen table chats, there is one sentence, a single sentence, I remember word for word with absolute precision. Just one. It has stuck with me through the years, burnt in my head, constantly buffing my own cynical edges. One sentence. I can even remember the way she gravely flattened out her voice, her words thickly underscored, and stared into my eyes to brand the words on my brain; *'Sariya, it is important for you to know that, deep down inside, all people are the same, more-or-less good, at the core'*. And in that moment, I remember, I felt oddly brushed aside by Auntie A. Betrayed. Her words seemed to clash so violently with her actions that I thought she was placating me, the dumb kid, with a simple lie. That I was not worth her time, that she didn't care to help me with the knots. I started realizing why everyone talked about her behind her back. She was quirky. People thought she was a loony, a fake. It wasn't until my uncle visited me years later, gave me some background on Auntie A, that I was able to start untangling the threads of love and hate in her passion. It wasn't until I had a little more context, a little more adult understanding that I was able to appreciate the importance of her words."

"But I don't get it mom, I thought you said she was depressed? How could she be so energetic, so... recalcitrant, if she was so sad, so down-and-out? It doesn't make sense. Wouldn't she be withdrawn, detached?"

"Well Grid, for starters, the fact that you know the word recalcitrant brings a smile to my face. Clever young lady. But as for Auntie A, you see, she wasn't exclusively depressed, she was bipolar, she would go through these wild up, down cycles. Most days I stayed with her, she was full of energy. When depressed though, she morphed into a shadow of herself. She moved slowly, despondently through the house, not bothering to dress, spending most of the time locked in her room. On those days, alone in the high-rise with her, I would sit outside her bedroom, ear pressed to the door, listening to her muffled heaves, building a narrative for the other side of the door. When she would finally emerge, red eyed and puffy faced, she looked bewitched, as though she was trying to remember how to remember. When asked questions, she would reply, minutes later in a hurried manner as if making up for the slow response, in a rambling drone that sounded similar to the announcements I made to my stuffed animals through the paper towel core. It was in those moments that everybody's snide remarks about Auntie A would creep back into my head."

And we sat there, my beautiful, blossoming Ingrid, on that cold hard Church floor shining light into the past's dark corners, digging for those serendipitous clues of self-identity. The past to explain the present, the present to whisper the future.

"You still haven't told me how she died."

"Right, ...right, I haven't. So as I said, these depressive waves, unpredictable as they were, would shift her demeanor rapidly, sometimes in the course of a day. Furthermore, it was no secret that her marriage, like each one prior, was tumultuous, as she attempted to impress her ideals on a reluctant, power-hungry husband. Of course these things were unknown to me as a child, but as my uncle told it they caused her intense emotional strain, triggering her depression. She refused all medication, said it flattened her out too much, made her 'lifeless', according to uncle. Unmedicated, she was susceptible to the whims of her wobbling psyche.

Now, Auntie A practiced the majority of her activism online; she was something of a lightning rod in social reform communities. Uncle told me that prior to her death she was actively involved in the famous *Peeple v. The*

People case, leveraging her network to galvanize support for the respondent. As the story goes, in a 5 - 4 decision, *Peeple* prevailed, much to Auntie A's horror, prompting her troubled response. So as the story goes, in protest of the decision Auntie A went shopping. She bought thousands of little wooden blocks, black markers, a jerry can, a pack of matches, and gasoline. She returned to her apartment, spent hours writing WIDGET on the face of each wooden block, stacked the blocks in her office, completely filling the space. She then doused the stacks of wood with the gasoline and logged onto her regularly scheduled Wednesday afternoon discussion room. As the discussion started and members began lamenting the court's decision, Auntie A asked to speak. Auntie A backed up from her webcam so that her entire body was visible amid the widget blocks, wrote the word WIDGET in black across her shirt, said 'It is seldom that liberty of any kind is lost all at once', poured the rest of the gasoline over her head then lit a match. Motionless, immolating with the widgets."

"She set herself on fire?"

"Yes, Grid, she did. It's awful I know, but you must understand that Auntie A was troubled honey, and well, maybe she thought she ran out of options."

"What was so important about that case?"

"Well, lots, in fact. It changed how people acquire and retain power at the highest levels of government. It also changed the motivations behind why people seek power. Actually, it upended the entire power structure if that makes any sense. Ahh, clearly we need to dig deeper in your Civics lessons, you probably should understand the details by now. Know what? Wait. I have something that might help you understand. It's rather obscure, necessarily so, but well, let's see what you make of it."

The shoebox labeled *Remainders*, the bit of newsprint with the faded yellow circle.

"The day after the decision, somebody anonymously submitted this to the Obituaries, and surprisingly enough it slipped by the editors and the paper printed it. Here, read what's circled in yellow."

"The People. **OBITUARY. Everytown** - *The People* passed away today at the highest court in the land, wide-eyed with

shock as they were, unable to believe they were capable of bearing witness to their own demise. They were a good lot, these *People*, however, the strong winds of change clearly favor those with pockets deep enough to alter the direction it blows. With an artfully crafted tapestry of esoteric legalese bullshit, the petitioner's counsel adroitly shaped society's future by winning provisions that automatically assign all extant constitutional rights to any recognizable *persona ficta* so long as a 'warm-body surrogate' is designated to directly represent said *persona ficta* in the capacity as a natural person, specifically to establish three attributes: age, citizenship and residency. Unfortunately, The People will not be missed because, sadly, there are no survivors."

She blinked a few times, handed it back quietly looking again at Auntie A's picture.

"Don't worry sweetheart, we'll get to it. It'll make sense."

"The uncle you mentioned, the one who visited you after the family fell apart, was that Auntie A's husband?"

"Oh, no, no, no Grid. That was my actual uncle, your grandpa's brother. Auntie A's husband was my grandmother's brother. I only saw him a few nights when I stayed with Auntie A. Suffice it to say, Uncle Beri was a very, well let's say controversial person. A man who evoked strong opinions in people. To be honest, I don't know what came of him, where he ended up."

"Do you have a photo of him?"

"No, you know, I don't. And you know what? I don't remember what he looked like. His face has been fully wiped from my mind. He's a vague, featureless memory."

...

An all-out, crazed effort. Two men scrambling feverishly over mounds of trash, contraption in hand, chasing a low-flying pigeon, itself searching for a morsel of food. A long plastic tube slashing through the air, propelling by centrifugal force, gnarly chunks of scrap metal. Impact. A bird flapping helplessly on the ground. Saliva, loose memories of fried chicken. The ingenuity, sheer necessity of using every part of the buffalo. Picture frame falls to the ground, glass shatters. The woman stares back, unaffected by her return to moist refuse, the matted tangle of hair, broken compacts. Hard eyes cut through the broken glass, attempting to hold mine. No. Pivot, return to the hunt.

They stand there, solemnly, far in the distance across the short side of the hunting pitch. They throw daggers of sun into tired eyes each time a glance is cast to high. Towering glass mountains, gateway to another time. The Archives. They don't offer the modest charity of shade, instead only blunt reminders of the consequences of prolonged hunting failures. Some relatives interred there? Who knows. Enough room to empty half of The Piles, enough electricity to serve the whole of it. Instead, an incomplete catalog of what has been at the expense of what could be. A brutal disconnect and the screaming silence lingering in the space between. Hunt, focus, the hunt. Scan for black domes, pick through remote possibilities. Caloric tick tocks.

"You're on in forty minutes Your Highness, oh and I apologize, but I've been told to change the tie you're wearing."

Shitbag. Always telling me what to do, who the fuck does he think I am? What a treat to squish this particular one into a powdery fine nothingness. Is it the way he speaks? The way his voice squirrels away at the end of each sentence, in an odd, skittery, panicked way? Like his voice is scared of his vile, blackhead-speckled nose so it attempts to run from it at every chance.

"What did you call me?"

"Sssorry Your Highness?" shitbag says.

"My name, what did you call me?"

"Your Highness, I called you 'Your Highness', Your Highness."

The beautifully reactive vibration of nerves. Meaty barometers, love it!

"Yeah, that's what I thought. From now on, you will refer to me as Caesar, with a big 'ol capital C. Think you can do that?"

"Sorry Highness?"

"No wait, God! I want you to call me God. When you need to ask, or, as is more often in your case, *tell* me what to do, you will call me God, as in, 'God, will you please engage in this pointless charade for me?' Clear?"

"Ah, yes, yes Your Highness."

"Highness?"

"I mean, yes, yes God."

"Very well then. Proceed."

"Right, Highness, I mean God. Sorry, sorry! As I was saying, we need to change your tie to one that is paisley with Corp silver. We have promoted paisley as the pattern of reason on Palettes for the past two months and your tie needs to align with the strategy, God."

He hung *God* out there at the end with a short pause both times. Is he mocking my new title? Is he fucking with me?

"Fine, whatever asinine tricks you want to employ, please feel free to use my body as your canvass you flapping donkey twat."

"Ok, God. James will arrive momentarily with your tie."

He did it again! Hung it out at the end, sarcasm, his squirrelly voice tucking its tail and running away with my title in a bloated cheek.

"Fine, tell that peckerwood to knock first."

"Of course, God."

Shitbag! Again! He *is* fucking with me!

"Say My Name?" Sidle close, hook around him, belly to belly. An exhalative jet of musky lunch truffles targeted directly to his polka dot snout.

"Sorry?" Gulps.

"My name, SAY IT."

"God?"

"Yes, louder. It's not a question dipshit."

"GOD."

"Go on."

"GOD!"

Inky black pupils slung beneath an instant forehead sheen. Curious odors blooming from the squeak of a poorly controlled sphincter. Lesson learned.

"Good, now get out of here and don't ever fuck with me again."

So many years and still can't tell the difference between Irons and Platinums. Certainly not for a lack of trying. Francisco, yeah, he was cherry, a Diamond in Iron clothing. The other two candidates, what *were* their names? Dipshit 1? Dipshit 2? Both lifted from the same mold as the poorly cast Platinum handlers lurching indecisively around this enterprise. Mushy, unsure, jittery. Synapses a klick wide at best. Take this James schmuck, and that straight line one could draw from his lower lip to his clavicle. Are you joking? He's to put my tie on? What the hell does a turtleneck know about a tie? The crap to tolerate. That other shitbag, Mr. Paisley. Both hopeless.

What was it Dipshit 1 said when pressed, 'Uh, huh? I don't understand. Huh? I just don't understand. What? I don't think I'm feeling well. I don't understand. Huh? I think I'm going to be sick!' Ha! The look on his face as he lunged from his chair, ran for the door. Priceless. And Dipshit 2, what's more classic than 'because I will do well by you, sir.' Seventeen years old and probably still wakes up with wet boners and illusions of success provided he works hard, makes good choices. Sad. A waste of my time, really, but funny as well. Sad, horny, naive; a bittersweet cocktail to swallow. Enough. Focus. Need to rehearse. Thirty-five minutes till show time.

Ahem, "...but let's get to the main reason why I'm here before you today. Without further ado, it is with great pleasure that I present to you an amazing, *fully* subsidized technology that will greatly enhance every citizens' ability to communicate, and to fully enjoy all the wonderful entertainment options available in the marketplace. Ladies and gentlemen, introducing -"

Knock, Knock, Knock

"WHAT THE FUCK!"

"Dad?"

"Hudson? Hudson, my boy! Come in, come in, come in, come in, come in, come IN!"

"I catch you at a bad time?"

"Good God no! What brings you here my boy, fruit of my generous loins!"

A thing of beauty. Twenty-eight-year-old CEO of Barristers Inc. Hotshot attorney-whipper, barrel-chested Lord of the Sophists. Oh, how the chicken skin draws in, secures, the family jewels in its protective hug, keeping them warm and safe. Infinite possibilities.

"Just in the neighborhood and thought I'd stop in, wish you well on your big announcement today."

"Who are you kidding? Come over here and give your father a hug!"

The tip of his nose nearly touches his future reflection on approach. Same boxy jaw, an identical pair of eyes, a familiar smell even, and the same pair of swinging bull balls bowing his gait outward. One-hundred percent *Beatus,* maybe something beyond, built from the best stuff on earth. Ah, the joy of the time-traveling mirror. To crawl into his body, take the reigns of youth once again. To hump this world dry.

"So tell me, what are the donkeys over at *Barristers* working on today?"

"Well, the big push at the moment is an evaluation of the cost-effective-ness of cleaning up and reclaiming some of The Wastelands. Several industries are interested in expanding operations, provided of course, there's a clear return, so a joint-venture may be in the works should the money pan out."

"Cleanup The Wastelands? What the hell for? Why throw good money after bad?"

"Well, there is concern the old studies used data that wasn't scrubbed, *clean*, if you will. I suggested that we cleanup the data, take a fresh look, but one of the engineers said we have SOAP issues. So, now I'm working my industrial connections to get my hands on a thousand tons of suds while the engineers investigate the possibility of collecting new data."

"Sounds like a waste of time, money and soap. I imagine you could get a better return on investment by reanimating the Philosophy, Anthropology, Dance and Music Departments at Education Inc and push courses to clueless Irons, bored Platinums. Come to think of it, know what you could do? You could stage an all-star cast from *HFWYG* cycling through as professors. Stream it exclusively on Palettes, incentivize classroom disruptions, call the series *Bully*. Imagine that, a lecture on Kantian Perpetual Peace cut short by a classroom brawl, brilliant! *Hrmm*, may need to write up a proposal, send it to Alain. Anyway, why the need for more space anyhow?"

"Several reasons. Victuals Inc wants to expand it sewage harvesting facilities, Electronics Inc needs a new factory, Healthcare Inc wants to expand their new patient conveyor-belt system, and the list goes on. The beast must grow!"

"Indeed it does, but I don't get it. The Membrane works efficiently and at a low cost shared by all. Plus, there's plenty of room inside the Membrane if everyone would agree to take the obvious next step in sociological evolution."

"You mean doze?"

"Of course I mean doze. How many years has it been discussed in private circles? Huh? And all that ever comes of those discussions are concerns about some Dhalyte Spring. It will never happen, mark my word. Bump the Dhalytes into The Wastelands, doze The Piles, resurface, rebuild. Badda bing Badda boom! Let the Dirts take it, the unending, charred expanse of it. Instead of throwing money into impossible cleanup projects, focus the money on directly satiating the consumer base; faster communication towers, new shows, complete neural integration of devices. Hell, have the engineers develop a new sense, or something, anything, to stimulate new marketable opportunities. You know that's it, that's it right there! A new sense. Another dimension of perception, stimulable with new gadgetry. Let's see…the ability to sense… cowards! No, wait…fear! That's it, the ability to sense fear! A little protuberance that sits right here, in the middle of the forehead like an auxiliary nose, capable of detecting and translating whatever human secretions are emitted when a man locks up, frozen with fear. Call it, …hell, call it the fearometer! No no no, we can do better. Call it the phobiameter, no, phobometer…..NO!, phobosceptor! Yeah! The phobosceptor! Hold it, I'm onto something here. Wouldn't it be amazing if you could, instantaneously, generate an exhaustive list of a person's most deep-seated fears and leverage them in the moment, in real-time! Imagine the opportunity for highly individualized marketing campaigns, I'm talking GDP through the stratosphere. There, right there's some perpetual growth for the beast! Work longer and harder only to buy more shit to keep your deep-seated fears at bay! The circle of money! Velocity baby! Or better yet, imagine how exciting a debate would be if both parties wore phobosceptors! Under that sort of duress, only a true man could rise to the top, a man born supreme among the rest, a…….., a…….., a Homo Virtus! Holy shit, I think I just discovered a new human! Get Bhoyle on the horn immediately!"

"Wow! Really, wow Dad! I've told you before, your mind is far too scientific to waste on politics."

"Yes, yes son you are probably correct, but you must understand, the id cannot be fed on numbers alone! Hold on, give me a second, one second."

"Note to Palette"

"**Palette ready.**"

"First note, fear sensor called the phobosceptor, second note, *Bully* series featuring *HFWYG* stars teaching, end Note."

"**Notes saved.**"

"Toss me that towel would you son, I just broke a sweat."

The towel glides soft across my face, the thought of sniffing out a man's hippopotomonstrosesquipedaliophobia before deftly dismissing his policy proposal as a cynical "floccinaucinihilipilification of the truth" in a critical debate. Tears of anguish stream down his pathetic face, salty-sweet victory! Black-purple shadows, Hudson's handsome face eases back into perfect focus.

"So, anyway, think it will work?" Hudson inquires.

"What, the phobosceptor?"

"No, I'm sure that will work. I mean the subsidy today, do you think it will calm the herd?"

"Oh, right, I nearly lost myself! Science, it just carries me away at times. Work? Of course it will work, when have the subsidies failed us? These dog turds will eat it up. How does that saying go? The busier I am the less I do?"

"Scientist, Politician, and Philosopher. Dad, you set the bar too high!"

"Don't worry son, it's in you, most certainly it's in you. Give it time to blossom. With age comes wisdom, with wisdom comes titles and titles wield the remarkable ability to self-generate even more wisdom and more titles! Eventually, authority by virtue of authority alone!"

He's working through it. There's no need to have concern for this young man. His occasional ripples of confusion, merely a poker play. A ploy to reel in the vulnerable for an easy meal. Look at the way his eyes glass over. He plays possum with a method actor's emotional precision! This old fan won't fall for it though, no way Huddy my boy!

"*Uh*, so I ran into mom last week?"

"I'm sorry, *mom*?"

"Patricia?"

Those expectant eyes! Hudson, my boy, I must have known a hundred Patricia's in my lifetime, let's not pay these games!

"Patricia Cheung?" he says, "Patricia Cheung, *your* ex-wife, *my* mother?"

"Oh! Oh right, right, yes. But I thought you knew I assigned them numbers? I thought we discussed this recently?"

"Numbers? I don't recall anything about numbers. Assigned who numbers? Does this have anything to do with the goddamn soap? Did those stupid-ass engineers also start bitching to you about the soap I ordered?"

"Soap? What? No, nothing to do with soap whatsoever. *Hmmm*, guess I must have imagined it, although I could have sworn. Anyhow, about the numbers, I'll catch you up. You see, for the past few years I've endured constant haunting by one of the earliest ones, Belinda Mayford, number two to be precise. She would call and call and call and call and call. Fuck! I'd set up a block and she'd tear it down. I'd set a call filter and she would scramble her origins. I'd gate with an auto answer to detect her voice signature and she'd use preceding conduits. Well, I finally established a technologically impenetrable barrier, but she went old school on me, started worming through actual people to get to me until presto! One day the crazy beast waltzed into my office, started making deranged financial demands beyond the nuptially-oriented contract, caused quite a stir. So, that afternoon I established the *EX Number Policy* organization-wide. Pictures of each EX along with a unique identifying number for each were distributed along with a rule never to use anything other than the prefacing word 'Number' along with the respective spouse's actual number when referring to each. I must say, things have been much quieter since, no name mix-ups, a 100 percent blocking rate! So, to the point, your mother, should be referred to as Number 4 going forward please."

"Oh Ok, smart. I religiously number my undershirts just to be on the safe side."

"Hudson, focus, far too tangential. You were saying about Number 4?"

"Yeah, so, I must say mom was quite a wreck. She spotted me walking on Rand Street, took up my arm and started asking why I hadn't returned her calls. Unsolicited, she said she was on the verge of being booted from her shared spot in The Blocks, shameless huh?"

"Yeah quite. If I recall correctly, Number 4 was a brazen one, forever felt she deserved something on merit alone and always managed to put her hand out with a puppy-dog alacrity. And so you did....what?"

"What could I do? I was trapped. I waved her some Credits, gave her a fake priority gateway to me, apologized for having to run off to an emergency meeting but begged her to reach out to me ASAP, public congeniality being so critically important for men of our stature."

"Smart boy, always thinking on his feet! Since we're on the topic, have you heard from that sister of yours?"

"What sister?"

"Oh, right, my mistake. I meant to say brother, busy day son, busy day, you'll have to bear with me!"

"What brother?"

"Oh, never mind. Must be Number 5. Well anyway, what's on the docket next at *Barristers*?"

"Ah, more of the usual churn, nothing too out of the ordinary on the horizon. Victuals Inc is suing Sanitation Inc for unreasonable market encroachment. Sanitation filed a counterclaim alleging anti-competitive practices. Victuals filed a double counter seeking an injunction against Sanitation, a service company mind you, for all non-service sales. Countering that injunction, Sanitation filed a triple based on the inherent illegitimacy of a 'poo-peddler' requesting the court to issue directives. To that, Victuals filed a quadruple positing dual claims of slander and corporate douchebaggery of the highest order, namely, name calling."

"Oh fascinating, I didn't realize there were quadruple counterclaims now."

"Yeah, precedent was established yesterday, so we filed the quadruple this morning. These so called daisy chain suits are all the rage at the firm because they permit us to bill a single attorney hour multiple times based on work done on associated counters at the tail end of the chain. We are hoping to break the company-wide record this year by billing a single attorney's 18 hour work day for more than 1,200 hours. With daily overtime rates and special case billing that is quite a nice chunk 'o change!"

"Brilliant! Is a quintuple expected?"

"Oh absolutely. We're already working on pre-discovery for a quintuple counter theory we're basing on the notion of qualified privilege. Specifically that 'poo-peddler' was written in the original filing in a spirit meant to express a term of endearment, substantiated by utmost love the authoring attorney felt when typing out the words 'poo-peddler' in the court filing. Turns out we possess a video clip clearly showing the attorney's effusive affection when typing out the court filing."

"Sounds reasonable."

"Yep. And you know, the most interesting thing about this case is that one of our two regulatory attorneys is out of commission at the moment with a pretty nasty groin injury, leaving us with a single regulatory attorney, Futakuchi Usotsuki to argue both sides of the case."

"Oh really? How to avoid conflicts of interest?"

"Simple. Our engineers devised a solution quite recently, under my direction of course."

"Of course! Intriguing, do tell."

"Well, without bothering the details too much, we called the solution *Operation Daisy Chain*. We started by assigning Mr. Usotsuki a second office on the opposite side of the building labeled **Defendant** and changed the name of his first office to **Plaintiff**. Next, we embedded a real-time thought-stream digitizer in the base of his neck and attached a pair of electrodes to his scrotum. Now, when Usotsuki enters the office in the morning, the output of his thought-stream begins constantly running through a natural language decoder, then through what we've dubbed the CF, or *CognitiveFirewall*. It is essential to note that his Pallete's GPS transponder is constantly sending the CF his location details second to second. As is the case, the CF is also constantly aware if Usotsuki's thoughts are on behalf of the plaintiff or the defendant, so if the CF happens to identify a situation where Usotsuki is located in say his **Plaintiff** office and his thought stream is identified as on behalf of the defendant, or vice-versa, then Mr. Usotsuki will receive a substantial jolt from the electrodes attached to his scrotum reminding him to focus on the client he is supposed to represent at any given time."

"Efficient, effective and, dare say, creative. Quite impressive!"

"Yeah, you should have seen our pilot, Mr. Menteur Esq., when he deposed a witness for the plaintiff in the wrong office before we updated the CF with the capability of handling double counter claims, it was classic! He danced and howled like a man on fire! The video was featured as the introduction for last month's board, you really should have attended."

"Well, that is the last time I miss a Hudson Ortiz boardroom production, mark my word."

"You know Dad, I don't want to brag, but I was responsible for the design of the electrodes used in *Operation Daisy Chain*."

"*No shit*? Mr. Industrial Designer *eh*?"

"Yep. Instead of using a set of rusty old alligator clips, I created a little mesh bag of metal into which we slip the attorney's scrotum. The increased surface area allows for better transfer of electricity, and a more natural, comfortable fit for the attorney."

"See, what did I *just* tell you? Business Titan, Scientist *and* Inventor. It *is* in you! Son, do you know how proud I am of you?"

The struggle to hold back tears. They want to leak, underscore the words... *cough, cough.* This is emotion!

"Aw Dad, you're too kind, too easy with the praise."

"No. No son, look at me, this is serious. LOOK at me goddammit!"

His eyes, the conflicted, bashfully uncertain eyes of a young executive, straining to hold steady to receive their due.

"There is no sense, no point in false labels. Not in a society built so unapologetically on the merits of man. Remember that."

He absorbs it, in his own time, gracefully, a man raking in the chips after a pure bluff. A bluff to make the other punters at the table look stupid, irrelevant.

"Thanks Dad."

Knock, Knock, Knock

"God, this is your thirty-minute warning. On in thirty."

Shitbag again, interrupting precious time with my family!

"Get out!"

"Yes God."

"Where were we son? Ah yes, daisy chains and laughs. So tell me, when this *Victuals v. Sanitation* suit ramps up, should I expect a knock on my door?"

"Probably, so, get your coin-flipping finger ready for action, unless of course you prefer *Victuals* or *Sanitation*."

"My boy, I've no money or interest in either, so it's all the same. Wait, you know...second thought, I want to be involved in this Wasteland cleanup thing you mentioned, make certain my voice is heard in the matter. Let's meet tomorrow, say, after lunch in your office to discuss our moves."

"Of course Dad."

"Atta boy. Alright now, I should scan this speech before I go on. You planning to stay around until the end?"

"I wouldn't miss it for the world."

"Beautiful."

"Ok Dad, I..."

"Oh, Hudson, before you go, I almost forgot, I thought of a new one..."

"Wonderful! These always make my day, hit it!"

"What is the difference between a cat and a lawyer?"

And they're off, those wheels! How quickly they spin in such a young, vibrant mind! So fast, in fact, they seem to wield influence over the health of his stomach. That look on his face, a sickly green typically reserved for spinning carousels, dizzying heights.

"*Umm*, I want to say the fur?"

"*Uuuummmmm*, no. A good guess for sure, an entirely logical answer and I can see how you arrived at it. However, the punch line for this particular joke is 'You can only kill a lawyer once'."

"Oh, ha! Classic Dad! I couldn't agree more, I've always disliked cats and their stubborn inherdability!"

For the life of me, can't imagine where he was going with that fur answer. Probably something to do with the soap. His mind, working in mysterious ways. Brilliant ways.

"Alright then, I'm off!"

"Ok son, pull that door behind you please. Need to keep the vermin out."

Door opens. The silhouette of a perfect man framed in a white jamb. Door closes. Almost. Door is almost closed. Anticipation. Door is still almost closed. Fucking door. Dumbass door. Stupid me, my mistake. He was told to pull the door, not shut the door. Sharp minds require precision in order to act with precision. My soft, aging mind cannot keep the pace. Oh Huddy, you could consume the earth!

But back to immediate matters, must get this pitch in my head. Wait, no…actually, this is wrong. This is all wrong! Holy Shit! I need my ambassador. The ambassador should be leading the charge, *duh*! I need a nice warm body who speaks in the proper tones. This speech needs to resonate, must resonate. How could I be so obtuse? AHHH!

"Help! I need help in here! Help! HELP! NOW!"

"Yes my lord, what do you need?"

Who the hell is this? Never even seen her before. What's that shit on her head? Oh, hair.

"Who the hell are you?"

"I'm Rachel my lord, one of your assistants."

"Are you new here?"

"No my lord, I've been on your team for five years."

"Oh. Well, what's the password then?"

"My lord, I'm not aware of any password."

"Ok, good, neither am I. What's the update on our Iron ambassador, any more candidates to interview?"

"We are scouring the crowd for potentials right now. Twenty people are on it."

"Put another twenty on it."

"My lord, we don't have twenty extra people at this point."

"Then tell everyone to double their speed. No, triple their speed. No, they won't be accurate...two and a half times the current speed."

"Yes my lord, I will send the message. *Umm*, my lord?"

"What."

"I regret to inform you, it's time for makeup. You go on in twenty-five."

"Makeup? Do you think there is something wrong with my face, something to cover up? You know what, forget it, don't answer. The day's accumulated ingratiation is starting to chap my butt hole. I'm going to need you to call me God going forward."

"As oppose to 'my lord'?"

"No, in addition to."

"Yes, my Lord God. IMA will arrive momentarily."

"Shut that door all the way until it closes and the latch audibly clicks."

Ok, breathe. Can't suffer another strain, not right now. Focus. Focus on today's message. Happiness. Happiness my Iron friends! My Iron constituents, my customers! You are the voice of the land, the reason for this glorious nation. Rejoice and indulge in the newly expanded feast of digital recreation. We are here to serve YOU! Makeup. No. Makeup. No! My beloved customerituents! Makeup. NO! I will not choke-out the makeup guy. I will not choke-out the makeup guy. I **will not** choke-out the makeup guy.

Knock, Knock, Knock

"Almighty God of Gods and Master of the Universe it is I your humble slave and eternal waste-of-space punching bag, the Insufferable Makeup Asshole. However unworthy, will you kindly grant me permission to enter these hallowed quarters?"

"One minute shit-for-brains."

I **will not** choke-out the makeup guy. I **will not** choke-out the makeup guy. I **will not** choke-out the makeup guy. I **will not** choke-out the makeup guy.

"Enter."

Good. He's crawling like a dog, head down per protocol, naked apart from his recently issued fuzzy pink undergarment. Fits him well, actually.

"Permission to stand."

"Granted peckerwood."

We are off to a good start here. The thick black letters, *HOPELESS!*, written neatly across the smooth, bony canvass of his chest. The exclamation point not a requirement but an appreciated embellishment nonetheless. Normally this much skin gives rise. Weird.

"Permission to begin."

Escape, just step away. If his orbital breaks another finger he must die, and that's unwanted paperwork. Plain and simple. Escape. Escape into the good, the successes, the victories! **Exopost-postmodern Capitalism:** *A journey into the process of building capital, exclusively by amalgamating going concerns.* A reasonable title for the DIY book, right? Yes, something along those lines. Makeup Asshole is wearing a lot of his own product, the black eye covered over impressively with a coat of new skin. Appears as if he could benefit from a highly targeted weight-loss plan – about a half a pound of edema to shed from the left side of his face. Swollen flesh. Something freakishly androgynous about this man-stick. Loves mom, hates dad all at once. No, loves dad hates mom with reservation. No. Hates and loves his mom and dad simultaneously with the barrel of a gun clenched reluctantly between the fluorescent teeth of a crying Oedipus. Walk steady on three legs old man, don't choke-out IMA.

Exhale.

"You may begin."

Eyes closed. Breathe in. Breathe out. In. Out. Go there, let's start on that outline big guy. No choking, not today. Progeny will need to know, will *want* to know how to roll their own, especially the entrepreneurs. What were the milestones, the substantial steps taken to pull this massive enterprise off? List it out. Put it down in order. Slap a clever acronym on it. Make it memorable, accessible. Single words, verbs, always verbs. Action-oriented!

Step one. Step one is about shaping the playing field, creating the conditions for success. Of utmost importance, make the rules to ensure success. Laws for all to abide. End discrimination by extending civil rights to persona ficta! (wink!) Amendments to account for the realities of a modern society! Targeted funding to promote strategic industry! It is imperative to craft the laws that advance society. Craft, C!

Let's see, step two, step two, step two...what is step two? Well, think. People, other people, how do they engage? The like minds, you must corral similar minds, play in harmony on the freshly shaped playing field. Scratch a few backs, have your back scratched, favors, alliances, infiltrate then saturate opposing political parties. Create a unified purpose, a charter of sorts, to guide everyone. It's all about organization. Organize, O!

Stop touching my eye, stop touching my eye, stop touching my eye! Choke, punch, choke, punch, choke! The brushing, the repetitive brushing, like the eyelid is being thinned with eight-hundred grit. Flimsy little turd, attacking it over and over again. Escape, save the wad of paper, avoid the paper!

"Easy on the eye!"

Back to it.

Ok, after the party is organized, what comes next? Or rather, what came next? Hoards of people, the utter superfluousness of human bodies clogging up the works, sucking down the resources! Separate the wheat from the chaff, divide and conquer the masses! Reclass, recast, and nudge them out extra fast! *Ooooo,* a rhyme! Nudge, N!

Ok, so that's craft, organize, nudge. We're getting there, we're making some real progress here! All positive, good vibes, good energy. CON.

"I will hurt you."

"I'm sorry Almighty God of Gods, I will remove my filthy, worthless hands from you very, very soon."

And now, step four. You must know your market, know your constituents. What do they want? What do you know they want that *they* don't even know they want! Establish the economy, a science-based economy producing products and services of the highest quality. People as the marginal inputs into the great machinery! Know the market, create the market. Establish, no, set the market! Set, S!

This book will be written by tomorrow evening at this rate! Onto step five. Now, with an economic engine serving up low cost digital everything, you must build an associated fan base. Create product pull rather than push! Develop raving fans who define their happiness, their very existence through imbibing chaotic, gadgetable entertainment. Fans are wonderful, but unifying them is better, more potent! People talking about the same things, craving the same things, needing the same things. Each reinforcing the others' emotionally driven needs, reinforcing one anothers' pursuit of dosage-based contentment. Connect them, then channel and control discussion accordingly. Unify the raving fan base. Unify, U!

But the costs, there are always costs! Labor and materials must be controlled, must be shrunk to the bare minimum. Ultimately, this is business! Tighten the wages, cut out the fat. Reuse the waste, inject the scientific process into every aspect of life to squeeze every penny out of every opportunity. Step six is all about minimizing costs! Minimize, M!

What's left? The complexities, the divisions, the stupid dances industry and government must perform to create the illusion of a competitive marketplace. Ditch it! Eliminate it all! The hassle and cost of checks, balances, separations, redundant providers of the same products and services. Shitcan all of it. Step seven, eliminate, E!

There it is! A seven step process for building capital. A DIY guide, a how-to for shaping society to your benefit, my gift to the future. Create, Organize, Nudge, Set, Unify, Minimize, Eliminate! CONSUME!

ALARM! ALARM! My eye, my eye, my fucking eye!

"My Eye Dammit, You Son of a Bitch!"

THUD! He collapses, grabs a squirting contusion, squirms on the floor in his fuzzy, pink thong. His new skin's gonna need a retouch.

"Jackass. Take this, get the hell out."

The fluttering wad of bills smacks on his oozing, writhing head. Easier to throw a pittance to a fool than listen to his grumblings. My throbbing hand - A Memoir. A semi-nude lying on the floor covered in blood and banknotes.

"Come on, get up, get out. Gimme that tie, I'll handle it."

On his knees, silent and dripping, he wipes juicy red hands on pink fuzz. Winces. Scrambling to collect the bills while eyeing me peripherally, he hurries to the door. A trail of red dots in his wake as she bends a cautious head around the door.

"My Lord God, I have someone here you'll want to speak with."

"Count to one hundred outside, loudly so I can hear. Then let him in."

The scent of her neck, human as human can be. Skin and nothing more. Nothing contaminating her perfection. Intimacy predicated on austerity. Subtle hints of secretions blooming on her surface, her immutable aromatic signature, beautiful, singular and pure. And she stays. No discord between body and mind, united they lie exactly where they want to be. Her eyes, relaxed in the moment, calmly exist for no other reason than to observe her objects of choice. When she needs to laugh, she laughs. When she needs to cry, she cries. But maybe more than anything else, it's the fact that she needs me to want her and I need her to want me. And we do this nakedly, trusting each other without reservation, without memory. Without knowing what malice was ever supposed to mean.

But she comes from another state, another realm. She occupies the space between waking hours, then fizzles away as the dawn of reality shreds the night. No amount of will has ever convinced her to crossover so we play this game each night. Fifteen years of nights, her fragrance still drops the heart when the dream's memory rings just so. Recognition.

No sound. The faculty has quit or is being suppressed by something beyond control. All noises, stopped. There is no static, no fuzz. No cotton. Occasional misperceptions of sound quickly followed by memory fragments collating and labeling themselves: *Priscilla's bark, Paul's gasping breath, Patrick's nonchalant hello.* Muscle control has withered and the consciously transmitted signals to an arm, a leg, are returned with the memory of a *busy signal*. Limbs are still connected and they press against the floor, though not mine to manipulate. The white abyss above grows, expands beyond the apartment walls, to infinity in all directions. A vast movie screen, no beginning or end. Me and a puffy woman with a needle sticking out of her head stare upward, wait for the show to begin. The olfactory still churns, fetid wafts of decomposition give way to a crippling odor pressing leaden on the chest. A startling *Corinne Mayford-Acenes scream* launches the movie reel into motion, the show begins. Opening credits from Movies Inc give advanced thanks to Agnosia, Narcissism, Bloodlust, Avarice. Bold, black letters scroll across the white abyss.

Progress: A Theme in Three Acts

Act 1: Food

A grainy, black and white image of an apple tree emerges. Jerky frames, the illusion of a vibrating tree. A frumpy chap in overalls leads an equally frumpy, rag-clad boy to the tree, picks him an apple. Boy takes a bite, looks back at the apple, finds a worm wiggly from the bite. He frowns, cries, throws apple to the ground. Man hangs head in shame. Scene fades to the white abyss.

The second scene blooms in infinitely high definition, an endless palette of colors embellishes the wastewater treatment plant in view. A superimposed schematic reveals a subterranean pipeline leading to a massive, shiny building labeled Victuals Inc. The words "efficient", "reusable" and "cost-effective" appear in smiley green font and travel along as if moving inside the pipe. At the terminus, a white coat army in a clean room pour over an ocean of glass tubes while polished machinery dumps barrels labeled "detergent" and "dye" into the vats collecting the watery excrement fed from the pipe. A complex array of machinery; injectors, formers, fillers, boilers, bakers, cutters, baggers, canners, and sealers process the sludge and deposit a single, neatly wrapped, apple-shaped *Nibblerette*. Next frame, a boy celebrates his *Nibblerette* atop a unicorn, the duo racing toward a smiling sun. Obligatory rainbow bowties the scene. Screen fades back to white. Final image, no accompanying visuals. Billions of souls, sewn together asshole-to-mouth around the Earth like the rings of Saturn, their eyes staring in wonder at the Gods below eating apples picked fresh from halcyon orchards. The abyss returns.

The screen comes to life again.

Act 2: Warfare

Muted greens and browns of a smoke hung battlefield contrast the blue sky above. An explosion here, one over there. Raw bodies ejecting from the blasts. A pale soldier lies on his back, scrambling to scoop his entrails back into an eviscerated cavity. Battlefield falls quiet, smoke disappears, revealing a filthy roughneck in a plastic hat manning a pumpjack. Abyss returns.

In fades a military barracks, whirls of razor wire enclose nondescript, windowless cinder block buildings. The scene focuses on a single building, zooms to, then ghosts through the closed door revealing a cavernous room. Rows of plush lounge chairs, each facing a large monitor, inhabited by bored, feet-propped teens. Joysticks in hand. Row upon row of dry, red eyes staring blankly at a screens saturated with geographic coordinates, positional hash marks, wind speed, elevation, closure rate, rocket count, bank angle. An esoteric jumble of green pixels overlaid on the black and white activities of ant-sized people. Cross hairs marauding the screens hold steady once evil incarnate has been found: evil ants circling around, each of them 80 fuzzy pixels of pure nefariousness. Massive clouds of smoke poof into existence. Target splattered. Enemy vaporized. Terrorist annihilated. Abyss returns.

A flurry of dust particles flicker, the reel begins again.

Act 3: Onanism

Doubled over and sweating profusely, he aims for the toilet the moment his fleeting brain and shaky limbs are consumed by euphoria. Time quickly slows to a crawl and a comically large magnifying glass hovers over the milky squirt at just the right moment, just before it plunges into the bowl. Seen are a million crying faces, horrified tadpoles, staring down their imminent watery grave. Away moves the magnifying glass, a plash is followed by a toilet flushed callously with a foot. Once again, the idleness of the abyss clears the images, an infinite white plane.

A fresh scene emerges, the same sweaty man with the magnified squirt takes shape. This time, as the squirt plunges toward the bowl, a plastic cup shrouded in divinity's bright white light, captures the squirt before the plash. Up in the corner, a image of Mrs. Magnifislurp dressed in angel's wings, winks, gives a thumbs up. Next scene shows the man walking to a building marked "Mortuary". He inserts his cup and a few bills into the sidewalk kiosk, the machine spits a receipt. A massive ticking clock superimposed over the scene dissipates, the same man returns to the kiosk. He punches in numbers and the kiosk ejects a large box comprised of millions of honeycomb cells. He proceeds to The Archives to deposit the box. The final scene fades to white on a cartoonish image of muted tadpoles resting peacefully in tiny cells, Charon's toll resting upon their eyes.

Blank again, the abyss hangs white. Chest goes up, down. Up. Down. Presses against the lead. And now she takes the screen as she always wanted to, the needle protruding from her bloated face, coffee still dripping from her nose. She stares straight ahead, right at me, right into my eyes. Behind her, in the distance, they clump together, all of them. Millions upon millions of them. A crush of salivating people, clambering atop one another. A massive volcano of bodies struggling to reach the rungs of a single ladder stretching up through the clouds. And Corinne, she keeps staring forward, lips flat, a blank look on her face. In one slow movement of her arm, she holds it up for me to see. A huge, sparkling glass of the purest water imaginable and there, refracting through it, the writhing, colorful television fuzz of clambering madness. No. Close eyes to recall the scent of *her* neck. No.

I will not acknowledge the existence of pain.

It came in the form of bright orange pamphlets, some balled up and soaking in the putrid garbage juices, others shredded into dozens of tiny pieces. Many of them bore angry scribbles, frustrated messages in bottles addressed to the abyss. "Fuck You!!!" scratched across one. "Not For Sale" across another. "Done." in thick black marker on another. And many, many more. For a month or longer the bright orange pamphlets flashed from within each new plastic bag torn open during the hunt until finally, their sheer ubiquity made me think, wonder.

The message, a jubilant font dancing across the orange paper, read like an invitation to a party. *May 1: Unwrap with Us!* The most *amazing gadget ever* promised, free of charge, along with the chance of being selected to attend the event in person at Town Hall. *Enter to win your chance to unwrap with us, live and in person!* Billed as the event of the decade, *a remarkable achievement combining the best technology with the best in government policy. Freedom for the people at a cost that would make the founders blush, FREE!* Clearly this was a landmark event, a solid chance the powers-that-be would present to bathe in the limelight. Thinking, alone in my cell. Leaders would want to capitalize on this much goodwill. This is a sign, The Sign. As good a sign to be expected.

"Aphamli, you have twenty one days to finish preparations." A pact with myself.

Three weeks ago, now, sore feet pound the pavement. Some twenty miles into the journey under a starless night sky in the black space between The Archives and The Core. Alvin Tan's identification chip still itching between my knuckles, behind a pink scar. The outcasts among the outcasted, the most wretched of all. Dirts camped along the road miles back, their stench still wafting periodically, carried on easterly winds. A humid, penetrating odor of biological disintegration. The most vulnerable, rotting, camped on the roadside, lacking comprehension of state and rejected by other Dirts for that very reason. Each step, closer to something, anything. Mentally unstable. Oh wonderful humanity, you never cease in the splinter of differences, you never fail to delineate one from another. Power not in numbers, power in the gerrymander. Sore feet. Find your likeness by subtracting your differences, conquer, then repeat. That smell. The smell of defeat, of human suffering, lingering from the road behind, with each step.

Each step inching closer to nothingness, deeper into the black. The edge of the road doesn't exist, there is no space beyond it. Time and anxiety persist, amplifying one another uncomfortably. Choosing to die is not a choice. It is an impression left behind by circumstance, an impression too tangible to ignore, too abstract to regard, but perfect for measuring peripherally against a ticking clock. Ticks like steps. *Choosing* to live, the ass-end of the slug, is a bland inspiration manufactured from a series of pretty lies. Killing logic to save faith. Why couldn't she keep her lies to herself? Inspiration, like fire, feeding to build momentum else it suffocates and dies.

...

"Does it hurt Mom?"

"No Pham, it doesn't hurt much. Maybe a little prickly in my toes, but nothing more."

"But Mom, you don't have toes."

And she smiled in her delirium as the phantoms danced, tricking her. Her eyes taking eternities to blink. Mr. Patel, warming to his new role by splaying fingers around my shoulder, looked on quiet. Her severed limbs a haunting presence in the corner of the cell, black to the knees. Necrosis.

"Aphamli, I need you to listen to me."

"I'm listening Mom."

"You know your father loved you wholeheartedly, right?"

"I know that Mom."

"And you know he loved you like a biological son, even more, since he made the conscious choice to accept you as his son."

"I know that Mom."

"Good boy Pham, you've always been Mommy's good boy. I know

you are hurt. I know you are heartbroken about his death. It weighs on us all. Everyone misses him immensely."

The tears, how they wouldn't stop tickling my face. Errant flies.

"It's important to have a father, a man you can trust. A man who will protect you," she said, her voice breathy, strained.

An owning clench on my shoulder, a million words conveyed instantaneously by a fingertip flex. A clash of foreshadowing thoughts fighting for prominence. Empty plates. Angry faces. Directives. Sweat. Heat. Shivers. Cold. Pain. What am *I* to Mr. Patel?

"And as your father loved you, Mr. Patel has agreed to love you in equal measure in exchange for the right to live in our cell with us. He made the conscious choice to accept this proposal. Do you understand what I am saying?"

Mr. Patel, silent. A huge breathing object in the room, expanding with each second, pushing me and mom into a tiny corner of the room, our voices pressed into a concealable whisper.

"Mom?"

"Yes dear."

"Are you going to die?"

She smiled. The contented smile she gave, the one always followed by praise for something good done.

"Pham I am in rough shape, clearly. But what I have in me is much bigger than what's visible. There is a strength inside me growing, carrying me along, helping me. And my choice, the choice *I* have made, is to stay. To stay here with you. To stay by your side. To watch you grow tall. That is *my* choice."

Hours later, Mr. Patel carried her and her legs to the road's edge. In his wake, me, trying to figure out what *choice* meant. First time hearing the word. Mom's limp hand dangled, slapped Mr. Patel's thigh, but reality didn't exist because of the haze created by that word. A piece of the puzzle was missing, and natural responses were stymied because of it. Too shy to ask my Dad's hunting buddy to define it, so, walk in silence. The thoughts, the wondering if there would be anything to eat that night. Wondering if there was a possibility, ridiculous as it may seem, that Mom and Dad were just extremely tired. The haze.

...

Today, in the now, walking further up that same road. *Choice* never seemed so meaningless. A gibberish entry in Mr. Patel's dictionary. Choice. The liberty and power to receive that which is afforded. The right to act the script.

A faint glow rises from the road ahead, projecting from behind some sort of structure. Time to change. Time to magically morph into the higher species.

"Wait, wait, wait, backup here, let me get this straight. A law passed, on moral grounds mind you, that all coital-free ejaculate was to be placed under a microscope, and, each individual sperm therein, separated into its own little burial chamber?"

"Yes, that's correct."

"Well what about the unused sperm resulting from conception attempts?"

"Deemed acceptable collateral damage. A necessity for preventing population collapse."

"Smart. So, who was responsible for writing the law?"

"I don't know *who* specifically. The Quorum doesn't have a name or a face. My responsibilities were limited to setting up the depositories, facilitating the transactions."

"And people paid you for this service?"

"No, not me. Salvation Inc."

"How much?"

"Between five and ten Credits for the funeral services. Price was dependant upon next of kin's sperm count."

"What exactly did the mourner get for the money?"

"Piece of mind, mostly. The knowledge that their potentials were recognized as individuals and buried as such. Respectfully and with dignity."

"What amazes me, is you say this with an impeccably straight face. It's nothing if not impressive."

"What can I say, it was a solemn business."

"Yes. Yes that much is obvious. But tell me, why wouldn't people simply discard it, save the few Credits? I sense I'm missing something here. And you said this was enacted after I was killed off right?"

"Not to be overly pedantic, but you weren't killed, you were recalled. Determined incongruent with science. Some Bavarian syphilitic with a lip-squirrel already killed you a few hundred years prior. The Quorum only took the next logical step, cleanse you from memory. But wait, hold-on here. You're all-knowing, you tell me why people do what they do. The comfort of habits, norms? The love of discernable patterns? A precise ordering of nucleotides? Maybe these factors and more. Seems most people play their hand attempting to avoid as much pain as possible. Pain, of course, subject to the perception gap between people."

"Funny enough, I've never really understood the fallout of this 'free will' thing. I've always been more comfortable with the infallibility of my physics, the precision with which the clever bits of my universe dance in such a perfectly calculable manner."

"Probably because free will is a hoax. Absurd inputs will give you absurd outputs. What rational person chooses pain over comfort? Faith, subsequently, is a chore a sane person performs with a plastic smile or a meaty frown, everything else is masochism. But none of this matters anymore because you don't exist, never did."

"Clearly. Well it looks as though my work is cut out for me, you being one of many with unsettled debts."

"One of many. But staying on topic here, is there no leniency granted for exploiting *your* loopholes, playing into the hoax? I mean, certainly we knew the faithful were manipulable, and of course we whipped the horse as hard as we could, but I think our only sin is enterprise and I don't recall seeing enterprise written on your stone tablets."

"It's not so much that your implications are accusative, which they are (God sneered), or that your tone is impetuous, which it is, rather, it's that you don't seem to understand the simple truth at play here. **I am the power and nothing else matters.** But, to be precise, and you can call this indulgence if it makes you feel any better, enterprise did replace me and *that* transgression was clearly etched on the first stone, wasn't it?"

"It was, My Lord."

"I prefer *The Almighty*."

"Yes, Almighty God."

"Atta boy, sing it with me now! *There was an old woman and she lived in the woods, weile weile waile.*"

"I haven't sung that song since Dad died."

"Eh, lighten up. Living is monotony, dying is rebirth! *There was an old woman and she lived in the woods, down by the river Saile.*"

Shivers, again. Bird calls and some blurry light creeping from behind the rheum of morning. Numb arms, two vibrating balls of flesh sucking the life from them. And the birds again, the betraying birds. Fear, where have you gone? On cue, the rising whimpers, soon followed by…

"Daddy, I'm so thirsty."

"Yes, that's why we are going to the river."

"Daddy, I'm so hungry."

"Yes, that's why we are going to your cousin's house."

"Daddy, who is she?"

"Daddy?"

"DADDY?"

"DADDY?"

"What! What!"

...

"WHAT?!! WHAT?!! WHAT DO YOU WANT KAYSEN? D'YOU KNOW HOW MUCH STRESS I'M UNDER? D'YOU HAVE ANY FUCKING CLUE? DO YOU? ANSWER ME GODDAMMIT!"

His face, so close, a scream so forceful, droplets of spittle sprinkled my face. Something of a money problem. There was always a money problem.

Fighting tears, "you can have all the money in my piggybank," found its way from my tiny, dry mouth.

And he laughed, he laughed before swinging, then some kind of indictment, something about ignorance, stupidity, my hopelessness. Typical stuff. Another swing. No laughs. Grunts. Again. Mom's face peering from

221

behind the wall, watching. Watching the domestic with wide, frozen eyes. No tears from me, from her. Scriptures. Oh yeah, the scriptures.

"Proverbs 29:15! The rod and reproof give wisdom, but a child left to himself brings shame to his mother!"

The impact of a baseball bat on a back makes little noise apart from the rush of breath it ejects. *Umph*. A man unburdened with the casuistries inherent in ancient text. Rather, find a single quote and put every ounce of force behind it.

"Proverbs 23:13! Do not withhold discipline from a child; if you strike him with a rod, he will not die!"

Umph.

"Proverbs 22:15! Foolishness is bound in the heart of a child; but the rod of correction shall drive it far from him!"

Umph.

...

"Daddy?"

"Daddy?"

"Daddy?"

"WHAT?!"

"How far is the water Daddy?"

Peals of thunder, this shaking underfoot. Trumpets. A falling star and these flying human heads with huge, glinting teeth. More trumpets, cacophonously brassy.

"Revelations 22:1, dear...the angel showed me the river of the water of life, as clear as crystal, flowing from the throne of God and of the Lamb down the middle of the great street of the city."

"Daddy?"

"Magdalene, Muhammad? We need to get up and keep walking. Walk to the river. That is where we can begin again."

Standing, they wait, looking down. Down. Down, at me. What the hell are they looking at? What do they want from me? A forest comes into focus. Triangular pines. Thick columns. A broken network of lines. The forest appears as yesterday's, it's chilly canopy, damp and dense. Tingles:

fingertips, feet, scalp. Fear. A zillion crazy bubbles racing to the top of a soda bottle after the cap has been wrenched off.

"Let's kids, let's walk kids, we need to keep moving kids."

Pushing aside branches, kicking through brush, whipping limbs smart. A spiderweb tickles cheek. Fear sounds like twigs snapping from behind.

"It's time to pick at the pace, we need to move keeping, keep moving. We need to move."

Pushing through the brush, scrapes and pokes. Pressure from behind, closing in. God, are you there? He doesn't pick up. On another call? There's much work to do, he'll be busy for a while. My own devices, to my own devices. To my own reason.

"Come kids, quicker. Keep looking forward. Move, keep, move."

"Daddy?"

"Daddy?"

"Daddy?"

"What? What do you want Magdalene?"

"Who is she?"

"Never mind Magdalene, it's nothing, a burning bush, a thirsty mirage, an apparition. Forward Magdalene, keep moving forward. Your brother. Move. Catch up to your brother now, move, move, move."

Children scramble, pushing away brush, picking through the dense growth. Looking back, she's there. She sobs, pursues quietly. Dirty, a mangy girl Magdalene-size but gaunt. Sentinel? From here or beyond? Pursuit. Always pursued or in pursuit of something. Never a sedentary mind. Perpetual calculation. No break. Racing brain cycles. Whittled down to a buzzing core, shaped for reactions, sprints. Capable of pushing and pulling, not threading or weaving. Blunt motions. Wanting begets pushing begets anger begets more pushing begets more anger begets pulling begets anger begets more pulling begets more wanting. And she pursues in attempt to reach us. Prostrate until a zebibah stains your forehead. Lie until truth is gone. Politic until the mind goes numb. Push, push, push. Shop until you're mortgaged into perpetuity. Reason yourself into a tiny hole. Fuck until maximum apathy. Push, push, push. Compete until you hate everyone. Slave until you collapse. Stab until the last drop of blood leaks from the corpse. Kill until all of humanity expires. Run, run, run. Run until lungs explode. She pursues. Unexplodable lungs.

"Kids, we need to run. Run, it's time to run!"

Ground pounds, the thunder of hooves. Running, keep running. Life as running. Life is running. Run from better judgment, appease a merciless boss. Run from an ideal life, appease a demanding wife. Run from dreams, appease a violent old man. Run from fears, protect a subservient old woman. Run from memory, forget the unhappiness. Run from God, find myself. Run until lungs explode. Run until death.

No.

No more running.

Not today.

I will not run.

Square shoulders to the task at hand.

"Kids!" The sting of lungs attempting to exit the body.

"We don't need to...run... anymore."

"There. There is... the water."

How time ceased to exist until his voice, ingratiatingly timid, pierced the moment.

"Uh sir, uh, what now?"

"Roger that, I need you to shut it up, now. For at least a couple hours. In fact, set your timer for two hours. Make it two and a half. You know the rule, not a peep till the beep."

The epileptic jerk of a head in approval. A damp collar. Cool night air. Many eyes wrapped in balaclavas surrounding two wrapped in dirt. How two filthy eyes could hold sway over reason.

"Ava, that.. that's a lovely name."

Those silent stares. Something like seduction. Something like angst. A sprinkling of shock. Difficult to pinpoint exactly, but a stare with gravity.

"What brings you out here this evening?"

A little squint, like she was trying to decipher the contours of my face, read the back flips going on inside my head. Sparks!

"Could you ask your guards to return my hands to me? I'm no threat to you or anyone else."

"Yes, yes of course. Guys, let her go."

"But sir..."

"Do it!"

Assessing her arms, she rubbed them gently, let them fall to her side, before reconnecting with my eyes. The looks, the unblinking stare. Snaps of electricity arcing between our eyes, the age-old dance of physical attraction. She could feel it. I felt it. Something closer to seduction, less like angst.

"Are you uh, are you from around here?"

That squint again, how she struggled to absorb the full picture, the complexity of someone like me staring back at her. A bat in a bird's nest.

"I live in The Piles with the other Dhalytes. Is that not obvious?"

And that voice, as it twisted the air around it to the breaking point, a wrenching type of power. The ability to create vacuums.

"I'm sorry, I didn't mean to come off as blind or stupid. I see the physical differences between you and I. Honestly, I was aiming for deference."

"To what end? What do you owe me?"

"It's not a matter of debt, really. Just the usual decencies of encounter."

"And I guess that is where decency ends? With the formalities of an unfortunate encounter?"

"I would hardly call this unfortunate, and again, I apologize for a completely inappropriate response on account of my guards. They are paid to react, not consider."

"Fine. Am I free to go?"

don'tlethergodon'tlethergodon'tlethergodon'tlethergo

"Absolutely, this is a free country and I am entirely at fault for harassing you with my security paranoia. Before you go though, do you mind if I ask you a question?"

"I am powerless to stop your mouth."

"Then I'll speak, and you decide if the question is worthy of a response. Fair?"

No reply. A million shades of playing hard-to-get, her lack of response being the faintest shade, but a shade none-the-less.

"Would it be too much if I asked what brought you out here this evening?"

Immediately engaging the question, she milled. She wasn't obligated to stay. She wasn't required to answer. She could have immediately walked. But she didn't.

"Starvation."

"I'm sorry?"

"Starvation. A condition of not consuming enough food to adequately sustain life."

"I'm sorry. That is difficult to hear."

"And difficult to endure."

"But why The Archives? What's here?"

"In the daylight, you would see the land fall-away over there beyond that tree, at the western edge of The Archives. The land descends into the drop fields. In the off-chance you do not know what the drop fields are, they are your garbage pit and my smorgasbord."

"Oh, I see. I'm sorry for your struggles. They must be troublesome, difficult, I mean."

"Why should you feel sorry, you didn't personally bring about my situation?"

"No, but clearly we are separated by circumstance, and I, as a friend once suggested, was lucky enough to fall on the cozy side of history. Of course I didn't plot to bring about your misfortune, but the sorrow remains."

"If only sorrows were calorically dense, then we could both feel better."

Could have been seduction. Could have been angst. Could have been about anything challenging a hazy mind. Memory being so difficult to reconstruct.

"You know, it's this system, and how wrong it can be sometimes. This cold, unfeeling machinery doesn't possess human intuition, human brilliance. These algorithms don't see through human eyes nor do they understand how to process the many subtleties required to achieve a sense of compassion. These damn machines! And, in the immensity of it all, as you well know, individuals get lost in the shuffle. These mistakes, they are a shame, a shame for which we all bear responsibility."

"A shame?"

Seduction definitely, but with a trace of confusion, the two emotions wrestled on her face. The sort of conflict expected when thrown into unexpected situations. Empathy.

"Yes, shame. A horrible, terrible shame. How can we, as people, create more perfect social systems, self-healing systems, or better yet, error-free systems? Man's intrinsic fallacy almost seems to preempt efforts."

"Millions of people starving to death is beyond shameful."

"Agreed. Yes. It's impossible to argue that, especially in this moment."

How that imagined vision of her -- salted hair draped over evening silk, hands polished into delicacy and adorned with stones, the scent of jasmine -- wouldn't leave my mind. How pursuit became much more than gamesmanship. How it was surprisingly easy to interpret confused seduction as horniness. For the millionth time, note to self.

"But why get tangled in semantics? Who does that serve?"

"To be honest, I'm not interested in questions. I'm interested in surviving. Feeding my grandchildren. Feeding myself. Goodbye now."

Her voice. The authority in it. The strength. Her filthy toenails outlined with dirt, a musty heap of rags dangling from her coat rack frame. Hands gnarled from doing god-knows-what. Every bit of perfectly remediable.

"Wait! A woman of action, another clear sign of the system's flaws, it's inability to evaluate people, to properly..."

"DIRT! DIRT! DIRT!"

From the shadows, a diminutive Dhalyte emerged. Running. Wailing.

"FREEZE OR WE'LL SHOOT!"

"NO! SHE'S WITH ME!" Ava screamed, lunging toward the bouncing ball of rags.

"Guys! GUYS! Back off!"

Muzzles retreated as Ava tearfully collapsed upon the child.

"She's my granddaughter! She's a child!"

Cupping the little face, Ava examined the grimy child, kissed its disgusting forehead. In a polluted embrace they sat, Ava comforting the child, petting clots of hair, the guard's rifles keeping vigil over them.

"Lower your weapons. Women are no harm to us! And back up, everybody back up. Go make some perimeters over there or something."

The guards in retreat, "You're Ok? Again I'm sorry for this, this whole ...disturbance."

The child nuzzled into Ava, hiding her face. A momentary irritant, but a necessary hurdle to arrive at our next point. In retrospect, how it would have been nice if this interruption shook me to reason, snapped the stupor. Time-sapping complexities, humiliation, could have been avoided. How Pothos can be the worst sort of antagonist. Stupid little fucker.

"Can I help in any way?"

"*Pfff*," and she shook her head, rolled her eyes. Somehow even her rejection enticed, made inadequacy feel refreshing, a sort of rebirth. How she knew what she was doing! Seductress. They sat, embraced, as the child's shudders whittled to stability, their rags at home in the dirt, tears rinsing trails down the girl's sullen cheeks.

"Do you have any water?"

"Yes! Yes I do! Roger that, water, now! Lots of it. Bring it all! And wine, bring the wine. Lots of it! Grab the Grand Cru, Cote de Nuits!"

"I think you'll appreciate this wine, the complexity of the vintage is perfectly mind-bending. You see, the vintner developed this grafting technique to attach intravenous drips to the rootstocks of his crop. He drips these special serums during veraison to achieve, what I think you will agree, are flavor *miracles*."

"I haven't eaten in over a week. I doubt I could keep alcohol down."

"Push yourself, really, you must try it. I'm not overselling this, honestly. At least a taste. ROGER THAT, LAST WEEK GODDAMMIT!"

Clearing hair from the girl's face, Ava tucked the tangled clumps behind an ear, the girl looked up at me. Indistinct and dull, the girl looked glazed, governed by a pouty, unappealing manner. A doughy, featureless face. A kiddy face. Needy, expectant.

"Janice."

"I'm sorry?"

"Her name is Janice."

"Oh, right. Hi, hi there little Janice, my name is Alain. Uh, so do, uh, do you, d'you like water?"

How the urchin-interruption continued to drain oxygen from the moment, stalling the flirty banter. Ava's eyes continued their strain, teasing out the previously inaccessible elements in me. How I worked to lighten the mood, applied frequent smiles, was the 'friendly'. Externalizing the me.

"Janice hasn't eaten in several days. She's normally quite sweet when she's not starving."

"Oh right, yes, of course! You both are probably hungry. ROGER THAT, BRING THE FOOD TOO...ALL OF IT! AND SOMETHING TO SIT ON! PRONTO!"

How hungry looked shockingly similar to horny. Seductress! Goddamn my poor interpretation skills. Goddamn her mixed signals.

Huffing and drippy, Roger that pounced through the rising dust, arms loaded, handing water to Ava, setting up my chair, side table and ottoman. On the table he placed the evening's stale hors d'oeuvres, wine, and glasses. The filthy girl attacked the water, running the majority down her neck like a pig. Ava daintily sipped over, and, over and over again as I watched, perched on the chair's edge, a thirsty spectator on a cultural bender. And over, and over.

"Here, here, have some of the cheese, the fruit. It's from my farm. All of it's top-quality nosh."

"Thank you. Thank you very much."

"Roger that, stop hovering, you're making them nervous. Just look! In fact, go help the guards with the perimeter."

They chewed, my mind wandered. The many courtshippy questions wanting to ooze from a smitten mind. Memories of ill-timed boners. Pimples. A breaking voice. Is she married? How long has she lived in The Piles? Does she have any diseases? How attached to this child is she? Ah shit, she's not an orphan, is she? How sometimes it is so difficult to get answers for the most pressing concerns. Threading frayed twine through the needle's eye, back and forth until insanity screams.

"So uh, did your husband die?"

Chewing, "Well, *ahem*, to answer your question, no, I've uh, I never married. It's one of those milestones, a steady relationship that is, which didn't pan out for me."

"I'll leave it there. I'm sorry for intruding."

"No need to be sorry. It's certainly a *reasonable* question. So, how about you? How long has your wife been dead?"

"*Hah*! Ok, I get it. Oh, I don't know, about five, ten minutes max."

Her eyes back on me. A hazy film of seduction, subtle, but present. Regardless, even as she tore into the food, those eyes fixated on me, as my overture hung in the air.

"Sorry, that was too forward. Suffice it to say, relationships are, well, extremely complicated."

"I understand."

"How do you find the food?"

And then it happened, no warning whatsoever. One minute, stoic as a marble column. Then, in an instant, a sobbing mess, perfectly out of control, but a dewy-eyed mistress nonetheless. Girl in her lap broke too, a simple reaction. How regaining composure takes some people a long time.

An irritatingly long time.

"I'm, ...I'm sorry. I'm at a loss. I don't mean to breakdown. This is not who I am. I don't know what to say. The food is difficult to comprehend. I don't know what else to say. I don't. Thank you. Thank you very much."

"Yes, well, yes. You're most welcome. And honestly, I really don't mean to impose, but you should try a sip of the wine. A taste now that you've eaten?"

"Sure, I'll try it."

She took the glass and wiped the tears from her eyes, muddy streaks to her temple's hairline. Euphoric eyes rolling back into her head as the wine touched down. The paralyzing effects of 80,000 Credits a sip.

"Pretty shocking, huh? Huh? Was I right? You'll continue trying to sort it out days from now I assure you."

"What can I say? It's amazing. I haven't tasted wine in, decades."

A few more sips, each one larger. Empty glass.

"Here, have more."

"Thanks."

"So how long *have* you resided out this way?"

"I guess it must be going on about twenty years now, give or take. That's when our situation ...changed. Options ran out."

"Our? She couldn't be more than seven."

"Janice."

"Yes, Janice. She couldn't be more than about seven, right? Maybe eight?"

"Janice is my son's daughter."

"Son?"

"Yes, my son Gerard. My baby boy. He passed away several years ago."

Fuck. "I'm sorry to hear that...then the saying is true? A mother's heart is always inside her children?"

"With."

"Sorry?"

"With her children. But I understand what you're saying. It's true. It's quite true."

"These years have been hard on you, yes?"

"It's never easy being invisible. For me or anyone."

"Well, you're not invisible now."

"Sure, yeah, I guess in a way. It's surreal. It's impossibly surreal. In one moment, I'm thankful for the encounter. In another, I'm scared to death of this situation. Of you. Of everything. And beyond that, I have no idea why I'm even telling you this, why I didn't up and leave the second you said you meant me no harm. I have a strong imagination, but this never registered. Never played these events in my head."

"I'm not perfect, but I was being honest when I said that... that I mean you no harm."

"Oddly enough, I believe you, though I haven't a clue why. No clue. Nothing makes sense. Things haven't lined up for so long though."

And then, the tricky one. For me, the elephant in the room. How trying to craft a reasonable question pertaining to the relative cleanliness of a stranger's genitals is like trying to belch with dignity. You will fail, and miserably.

"May I ask...are you...are you in any pain? In need of any medical attention?"

"No, not that I'm aware of. It's a rather strange question."

"Sorry, just thought I could help. Are you sure, because I can arrange to have you tested."

"Tested?"

"Yes tested, you know, evaluated. Thoroughly scanned by a medical professional to remedy any health problems, or any other concerns rather, you may have."

"Apart from being underfed, I reckon we are both in fair health."

How the math worked out well enough. Well enough to begin closing the deal. The forbidden fruit is, annoyingly, the sweetest. Nagging hindsight.

"I want to help, if possible."

"I understand."

"No, I mean, I want to see about helping to change, change your circumstances. And Jamie. Jamie too."

"Janice."

"Yes of course, Janice too."

"And you offered. Thank you for that. But I believe we are as fit as our condition allows."

"I don't think I'm being clear so I'll speak plainly. I want to take you from The Piles. Remove you from your lifestyle, change your condition.

Help you begin again."

Those eyes, how they changed. How they seemed less self-assured. No less sultry, no less analytical, but wavering. Searching rather than scrutinizing. Running the numbers but caught on an ill-registered figure.

"I don't understand. Why?"

That voice. The same strength of authority, but laced with subtly collapsing undertones. The undertones like a thousand muscle fibers flittering on an impala's quivering body squeezed between the lion's jaws.

"I don't have a clear answer for you, I don't. This is unexpected for me too. My plan was to come to The Archives to learn a thing or two about, *pffft*, well, ...a new advertising strategy if we're all being honest here. Now, it appears, my focus has ...changed."

"This doesn't make sense. None of this makes any sense."

"What can I say? Not everything in life does. In fact, more often than not, little does. Maybe serendipity's a real thing."

"But I have nothing to give. Nothing I will give."

"That's just as well. I don't have expectations, only an interest in testing an idea of progress. *Hmmph*, imagine that, a trip to learn about advertising morphs into a trip to test charity. How's that for making sense?"

"What you are proposing is beyond charity. Here. This food. This wine. This is charity. But a whole new life? It sounds more like a commitment, like sponsorship. And sponsorship, it, well. It grows roots. Creates connections. Connections imply obligations, duty."

"I don't want to mince words here. I'm extremely wealthy. I have numerous places throughout The Core I rarely use, some never. Charity is certainly relative, relative to one's perspective. From my perspective, helping you to reestablish hardly impacts my financial world. Won't even blip my financial radar screen. I'm not proposing a quid pro quo. This isn't a sort of mechanism to establish a *connection*, however you define the word. I don't want anything from you and I don't need anything from you. This is a simple gesture you may refuse of your own volition, although I hope you don't. My personal interest in the matter is built upon your previous comments, something, perhaps, to do with the 'shame' you mention. Maybe there is a better path as yet unclear. Options, I feel, ideas, are becoming more apparent. I don't even know if that makes sense."

"I can't wrap my head around your interest in charity, this is way too much. I'm not blind to the ways of the world, how grossly unusual this gesture is. How could I, or rather, why would I expose myself, my grand-daughter, to such risk?"

"That's entirely fair, and who could question your doubt? What's left to say? I'm stuck in a strange moment too, wondering for the first time, if there is a chance to find a different way. A better path. I'm a businessman not a philanthropist. This is all new to me, the concept of 'giving' without quantifying the fiscal return. But, maybe there is an opportunity to rethink the way some systems work. It's worth exploring, analyzing. Perfection certainly isn't possible, but trying is."

"And the way you look at me? The lascivious comment about your wife?"

"Lascivious? No, I think that's rather presumptuous. Inappropriately playful is more fair. But you don't know me well enough to put the comments in perspective and I should know better. Either way, I apologize. Men have been plagued with poor judgment since Adam."

"And that is what I am afraid of."

"My poor judgment?"

"Not exactly."

"Then what?"

"Motivations. Your motivations are what concern me, and my obvious position of weakness. This is far too candid. Nothing makes sense. This doesn't make any sense whatsoever. What the hell is going on? I think it's time for me to leave."

"No, wait, wait, wait...look, we could dance around this idea until morning. You've never been able to trust anyone?"

"Yes, I have, but it is easier to trust someone of similar circumstance. Someone who sweats the same existence."

"I can't change who we are at present, so what do you propose?"

"What can I propose? You have all the power. Trust is always questionable when disparity exists. I'm completely exposed to your whims, now in this moment, but much more if I let you help. This is all too candid. Why are you even here?"

"I told you why I'm here. Why do you make it sound as though I'm a predator, a opportunist."

"Your words, not mine. I'm pointing out a reality. My life, my grand-daughter's, hangs on this moment. For you, well, maybe you will have forgotten this encounter by next week."

"Not a chance."

Sitting amid the impasse, how she continued to collapse. Time was not on her side, clear thinking not on mine.

"Alright then, I have an idea, a thought anyhow. What, in your mind, is the root of power, the driving force behind it's creation, it's use? Put it this way, what is essential for power to even exist, its point of origin?"

"That's easy enough," Ava said. "Personality. Without question, per-sonality. All of life's decisions trickled down from personality."

"Personality? Perhaps you didn't hear the question?"

"Yes, personality. I understand the question. Without a particular type of personality, power can't root. Once established, it then requires a certain type of personality to want to expand power, to broaden reach. After it's accumulated, an even more specific type of personality is required to abuse power, to harm people at will. It then takes an even more specific personality type to enjoy inflicting pain, or conversely, to feel remorse about it. And so on."

"Ok, but I'm already wealthy and powerful, so doesn't that presume that my personality is disposed toward power?"

"Yes, without a doubt. But, it is an ever-narrowing range of person-alities that ultimately abuse power in the worst ways. I've always thought it's possible for people to wield power without abusing it, even if history tends to disagree."

"Ok, so how can I possibly disarm? How can I shed power to put us on equal footing? What exactly does it take to earn your trust? I can't physically discard my personality or give it to you for safekeeping or audit."

"No, you can't, this is true. Ok then, now I have an idea. A simple thing you can do. You could start showing some empathy by permitting your assistant to speak again."

"Roger that?"

"Yes, I believe that was his name."

"What will that prove?"

"Little, but it's a step in the right direction."

"Roger that! Get over here! Ok, k, k, k, stop nodding like a fool, listen to me. Turn off your timer, you may speak again."

"Roger that. What do you need sir?"

"Ava, the floor is yours."

"You could apologize for calling him a fool."

"What? Why? I always call him that."

"It's true, he always does."

"Not that he'll tell you honestly, but I seriously doubt he wants you to degrade him. Demanding respect, for him, is a conflict of interest with grave financial impact."

"I'm sure he'd tell me this himself if it were a problem."

"I'm quite happy being your fool, sir."

"You could be right, but chances are you're wrong. This is another one of those personality things."

"Ok, fine. Roger that, I'm sorry for calling you a fool. *Whew*, Ava, I must say, this is oddly cathartic. Let's keep going, what's next?"

"You could ask Rajathit if his feet hurt."

"Ok, I'm not sure what we are doing here but, Roger that, Do. Your. Feet. Hurt?"

"Uh, sorry sir?"

"Simple question Roger that, do your feet hurt? *Snap, snap*. Don't look at her, answer me. How 'bout them 'lil piggies eh, any pain? Them doggies singin' the blues?"

"Uhh, no more than normal, sir?"

"Ava, Roger that's feet are tip-top. Where do we go from here?"

"Alain,"

How the sound of my name rolling off her tongue for the first time sent shivers down my spine. The tiny ripples under my skin extending out to each finger, each toe, Alain junior. Hindsight, you silly prick you.

"You know as well as I that Rajathit won't express his grievances to you. Everyone's feet hurt after a day's work, wouldn't you agree?"

"Roger that, I need your complete honesty here, Do Your Feet Hurt? Roger that, stop looking at her, I'm the one asking the question. Want the timer again?"

"You could offer to show your kindness. You could offer to massage his feet."

"Sorry?"

"You could offer to massage Rajathit's feet in a show of kind appreciate for all he does for you, day in and day out."

How the thought of massaging another man's hooves was the ultimate boner-crusher. A scalding coat hanger jabbed down into a star-gazing urethra. Libido aborted.

"Not a chance. How does degrading me equalize a power imbalance, or more importantly, establish trust between you and I going forward?"

"It's not degradation, it's humility. It's compassion, and quite nominal at that. How many times has he massaged your feet?"

"My feet are not Roger that's responsibility. Goddammit Anna takes care of them."

"You claimed you don't like getting trapped in semantics. Rajathit's feet are fine for showcasing your personality."

"This screams of sabotage more than anything else. But, I'm game. LISTEN UP, EVERYONE! Turn your back to me, squat down, close your eyes, and bury your head in your crotch. No moving, talking or interacting with your device for the next five minutes. Roger that, you too. Ava, I must say you *are* intriguing, you are one *fascinating* woman. If not for that though, I wonder where we'd be right now. Ok Roger that, may I massage your painfully disgusting feet?"

"Iragea oodnndt baaataakkk oooo whodeefffr."

"Roger that, pluck your head from your crotch, I can't hear a word you're saying."

"I said, I'd rather you didn't sir, but thank you kindly for the offer."

"Rajathit gladly accepts your offer," she said.

"Fine, take off your shoes."

"Sir?"

"Your shoes, off with them."

"You *could* help him with his shoes."

"*Hhhh.* Gimme your foot Roger that, and put your head back down."

How when your penis shrinks, you can feel those little circles of flesh stack upon one another, the foreskin consuming the head like a ravenous hyena. Choad fully consumed by the moment. His shoe untied, a stink leaked from the cheap, faux-leather upper. A foul, moist sock. Five crooked brazil nuts, each overly-tufted with a toupee of pubic black. At the point of no return, how I dug in, drilled angry thumbs into the tender arch of his foot until he winced, knowingly. Message sent. Message acknowledged.

"Ok, I've thoroughly fondled my employee's foot making him and me uncomfortable in the process. Are you sufficiently comfortable with my personality now?"

"No, but this is progress."

"Ok then, how else do you want to debase me on this fair-weather evening?"

"You could kiss his foot, really put your heart on display. The foot-kiss being the gold standard of history's most beneficent."

Flatly, "I'm not going to kiss his foot, and this is getting ridiculous. Do you realize that this man's tongue, on a normal day, plucks bugs off his kids' heads? Where do you suppose that finds his foot? Forget it, game over. No chance. I guess I'm some kind of evil son-of-a-bitch because I place a premium on a fungus-free mouth."

"If you are not willing to entertain such a simple request, how could I possibly begin to trust you with my life? My granddaughter's life? I'm not labeling you evil, I'm trying to prove to myself that I'm not making a huge mistake. That I'm not throwing myself and my granddaughter to the wolves."

"Sure, you know, I get it. Talking nicely to the help, something we should all strive for right? Massaging your employee's foot? Weird, but Ok, I see it. A symbolic gesture perhaps, a sign of a man's ability to, as you say, show humility. It's all reasonable. Kissing your employee's foot though is nothing more than debasement. It's not going to happen. My guards and I will just leave. I'm sorry to bother you. If this is the criteria, perhaps I'm just not fit for philanthropy."

"Then I trust you."

"Sorry?"

"I trust you, nominally though, but it's the best we could hope for."

"Okayyyyy, what's changed? What's going on here? Roger that, head back to your crotch. This is not for you. In fact, you're done here. Grab your foul footwear, wait in the MRAP."

"Nothing changed, I have the very basic assurances I need."

"Care to explain?"

"It's little, I'll admit, but about the most I can expect given circumstances and now my gamble begins. You, when pushed beyond your comfort zone, bristled, but eventually became flexible. You showed a willingness to understand, an ability to relent. When pushed further, beyond what's reasonable, you didn't bother to bristle, you simply refused on principle. If you were to yield to my unreasonable demands, it would indicate that your worldview implies that abuses, however minor, are acceptable given the circumstances, for expediency's sake. With that mentality, it's rational to assume you're capable of taking similar liberties if the tables were turned."

"I've got to be honest here, you've nailed down nothing."

"Is that a warning?"

"Warning? What are you taking about? Warning what? Good God! I'm just skeptical that this Freudian foot test is capable of displaying my personality, that's it!"

"Ok, what then? How would you describe yourself? What makes you you?"

"Alright then, here, me in a nutshell. I'm hungry. OK, not hungry like you, sorry, but hungry for the best the world offers. A failed marriage, no children, no hobbies, no real pursuits beyond my work. I work to accomplish. I work to conquer. I work to amass as much material as is humanly possible. That is the goal. That is the brutally honest truth about me, like it or not. My life's focus has been acquisition. But you've tipped me off, got me thinking something new, and I want to experience something new. I want to step outside of myself. I want to try opening my eyes. And that, I think, is where I'm finding you and little Jackie..."

"Janice."

"...yes, Janice fit in. I'm painfully one dimensional, that fact is not lost on me. But, helping you may allow me to change that. Find some perspective, some balance, in life."

"And when we want out of your life?"

"You walk away."

The looks. Back and forth. Both of us clawing away at the facade, time pressing in. Still sobering from the experience in The Archives, but still trapped in my head. Fed recently, but still trapped in her hunger. Situational suicides, funny gambles.

"And so our lives are in your hands. You discovered us, serendipitously as you say, in our moment of greatest need. Our cards, reluctantly tossed upon the table. We are yours."

"It's a strange way to thank someone for helping, right?"

"At this point, I'd love nothing more than appearing horribly rude."

"Well then, if you are ready, my MRAP awaits. Shall we?"

As she climbed aboard, a cagey Roger that whispered, "Sir, I truly hope I'm not out-of-line, but are we really taking them with us?"

"Roger that, the foot massage is over. Set your timer to tomorrow."

How as we drove, and The Pine continued to wear off, the dirt around her nails became more visible, the sunspots on her hands more pronounced, bloated freckles. How in the airtight MRAP the scent of decay swirled with the raw sexuality of untreated armpits, triggering an oddly reluctant lust. How her stoic confidence remained but seduction seemed appropriately absent amid her high-alert posture. Wide-eyed, her granddaughter petted the seat leather, poked quietly at the windows, floorboards, the light bars with awe. Speeding along the road at night, we sat in silence as advertising in The Archives was rejected as impractical, a waste of money.

Their heads piston up and down in the front seat as the driver veers off the highway onto a dirt road snaking through a vast complex of metal buildings. The massive security truck skids to a stop.

"I'll just be a second, then we'll get you to The Core, queer."

He slams the door, runs into a building. The driver turns, extends a hand,

"Luke."

"Uh, I'm sorry?"

"Name's Luke."

"Oh, Alvin. Well, you know."

"Yeah, yeah, *Aaaaalvin*. Should call you faceplant with all those surgeries. I've seen people with lots of work, but, you? You win. Look nothing like your former self there buddy."

"I guess it becomes an addiction, like everything else."

"Yeah, well, me? I'd rather push my Credits into barbs, salts, maybe some ludes, or shit, even some good sleeping pills. Better to disconnect than cut up your face. My opinion."

Luke, do you want me to reorder your SLEEPEZE pills?

"What's the rate?"

Two Credits for a one-month supply.

Wincing, "Yeah, g'ahead, put it through."

"To each his own." The innocuousness of my words reverberating.

Digging into my coccyx, the hammer. Pain, a pulsing heart beat.

"Sorry if we was overly aggressive with you back there. N'er know what sort a shit a Dhalyte might pull. Gotta stand ready, y'know?"

"Yeah, I understand."

"This last week, one of them fuckers tried to slip through the DMZ, claimed his hand was hacked off in a fight a month earlier, hadn't got his new implant yet. 'Magine that! This bony asshole, waiving his nub in my partner's face, and I'm figurin' to blow his damn head off, tossem in the flats."

Laughter (the experience or manifestation of mirth, amusement, scorn or joy). This is funny, so, laugh.

"Heh, heh. Stupid Dirt."

The subtle wince on his face, it doesn't go away. Is he playing with me? Did he notice my fading pink scar? Is this defense?

"Your friends are pricks huh? Leave you out there like that? 'At's taking the joke too far you ask me."

"Some people don't know when to stop."

"You know missing a day of work docks three, right?"

"I know the rules."

"Yeah, well, anyone put me in that position, I'd dump them out in the flats."

"We'll see what happens when I get back in town," I offer.

The buzz of activity. The myriad trucks, constantly in motion. Into one corrugated metal building. Out of another. On the left. On the right. Swooping in overhead. A wild symphony of motion, organized chaos.

"Feeling alright? Y'look somewhat green."

"I'm fine. Dehydrated perhaps. A little fuzzy in the head still."

"Here, take a swig of this. Keep those pretty lips off it though."

Luke, did you know that new SuperNutraWater is twenty times more hydrating than water and costs only two percent more? It is available at all STOPIN stores in 32, 48 and 64 ounce bottles.

Again, that voice. Female. Everywhere and nowhere at once.

"Thanks for the drink."

"No problem. You said graduation party huh?" he asks.

"Yeah, this guy I know. Probably should've been on my guard."

"You're lucky it wasn't family. Shit, you could've been dropped dead center in The Piles, torn to pieces by those dogs, *heh, heh.*"

"What family?"

"There you go."

The soft glow of dawn begins its sharpening, dewdrops cling to the windows, occasionally succumb to gravity. The pointless tears of a child, perspiring bodies laboring under the sun, a waking glance through the dewy canopy after a sleepless night. Hydrodynamics for the poor. Irrelevant.

"So what's your reservation number?" he asks.

"Reservation number?"

"Yeah, what is it? You under 10,000? I heard if you're under 10k you pickup the first day."

"Maybe I'm a little out of it, what with sleeping on the roadside all night, but what reservation number are you referring to?"

"Ha, good one. Seriously, what number're you? Pick ups start the day after unwrapping this time, y'know?"

"Oh, yeah. Yeah right. My number's up there. Don't remember exactly. I'll be waiting a while."

"Sucks for you. Me, I got a 25k, second-day pickup. My partner though, he pulled an 825. Can you fucking believe it? 825. Not only that, he *won* tickets to the Unwrapping. Damn joke. Lucky for you else you'd be hiking hung-over right now.

Luck (the chance happening of fortunate or adverse events; fortune). The first time the word has been used to describe my circumstances. Strange sensation. An airy body. Nimble. Tensile.

You know, if he don't go, he gotta wait a full month for pickup."

"Ouch." What the hell is this guy talking about?

"Yeah, ouch's right. Who'd want to sit in a black hole that long? Ok, here he is, finally, Mr. eight-two-five."

Jogging to the truck, the man whose gun barrel recently explored my tonsils. A large, white cone on a handle hoisted triumphantly in the air.

"S'that, Nate?" he asks his buddy.

"This, for the blind, is a fucking bullhorn."

"Yeah, I can see. Why'd we come here for it?"

"Cause I'm gonna express myself at volume, Luke."

"There's your ticket to the hoosegow."

"Fine either way, I need the vacation. So, fuck it, my voice'll be heard."

Turning to me, "What you say to that *Princess*?"

My ally, the bigot. My ally, the abuser. My ally, running perpendicular to my life.

"To each his own."

"Ahgh, fuck you sweetheart and your bullshit. If it's not something you plow into y'ass I guess you're not interested."

Nate, did you know that RectaLube not only lubricates but also stimulates nerve endings prior to intercourse?

"Uh, not queer, no thanks."

The sad irony of it all. If dad could see me now. Or John. John sees this. If there is one thing he negotiated in the hereafter it's the rights to witness the future. My future. And his hand is on the gun, puppeting me along. Dear John, please cock the hammer. Your Princess needs relief. The road inclines slightly and the hammer routs. Metal buildings flash by. Machinery darts purposefully, algorithms executing tasks for civilized people. One appears stuck in a narrow pass spinning tires, jammed in the narrow space between two metal buildings. Constipated. Irrelevant. Must keep present. Must focus.

"So, an eviction huh?" Luke asks Nate.

"Yeah, was this real squirrelly guy. Could never get a straight answer outta the fucker. Lived 'cross the hall from me. I'd run into him from time to time, 'ave some weird small talk about the trash day changing or the latest release. Never a smile on his face. His chick was a piece though. Don't know how he managed that."

"Really?"

"Aw yeah. They must of been an arrangement, you know, a f'nancial thing. Must of been, 'cause she always had dudes coming in out."

The task of rationing attention. Listen to their conversation, but only digest that which is critical. Plow the excess mental capacity into the future's probabilities. What is going to happen next?

"Yeah?"

"Oh yeah."

"And you?"

"Naw man, wasn't her type or something. She'd smile, give up the chitchat, but not the pussy."

My occupation? No, my job. My job? I am a programmer. I write code, the easy stuff. Simple drivers for small machines and whatnot.

"Alright, but anyway, the eviction?"

"Yeah, so like I's saying. I hear this banging on a door, his door, like someone's hell-bent on breaking the shit down. So I open m'door, watch these uniforms bust his door in, all angry like they're gonna kill everybody in the joint. Lead uniform's screaming 'Eviction! Eviction!' at the top of his lungs, you know, as they do."

"Seen that."

"Of course. But, anyway, right then is when the smell came pouring out of this dude's place, and you can't imagine man. I mean, something hadn't smelled right on my hall for several days, a rotten, shitty smell, but this! This was fucking unreal, something I'd never smelled before. Can't even describe it man. Made my eyes water, no bullshit."

"Shit man, that's nasty."

"Right? But, you don't know the half. Anyway, few minutes later, maybe fifteen or so, they start coming out. Guess they weren't expecting what they found, cause the body came through the door but it wasn't in one of those bag things, you know, what're they called?"

"You mean a body bag, dipshit?"

"Yeah, yeah body bag, asshole. So this squirrelly guy, his feet come sticking out the door. Then his legs. The rest of him. Two uniforms, one at each end, are hauling him on some table, like a coffee table. Guy's laying there, all skinny and whatnot. Then his head. His head come through the door and I notice. Most everything looked pretty normal."

The dayshift, usually. Today is a dayshift day. Yeah, I'm going to be late. Don't know, going to plead for leniency I guess. No, beg for mercy. No, kiss some ass. Don't know, gonna need to kiss some ass. Beg or something. What else can I do?

"Except?"

"'Cept his face. And that smile. Not the sit-for-the-ID-sort-of-smile, all plasticky and shit, but this genuine, happy kind of smile. His eyes, open, had all those lines coming out of them, like they was smiling too. Never seen a man s'happy. And that was that. That's the biggest smile I ever seen, last smile I seen. Some weird shit too. Never saw a smile on a dead man. Didn't know it's possible."

"Alright then, how long ago?"

"Man, that was some five, six years ago, maybe longer I dunno."

"And there it is, you know, that's what I'm saying. People don't smile no more. Least you 'member last time you saw one, I mean a *real* one. Not the sort that come with a shank hiding behind it. I can't even remember the last time I saw one. A *real* one."

No need to go home. I keep a clean shirt, a toiletry bag, at my terminal. You know, for late nights. Have to be an idiot not to be prepared. Rather, dipshit. Dipshit is better. They like cussing. Have to be a dipshit not to be prepared. A motherfuckin' dipshit.

Nate?

"Yeah, what is it?"

I've noticed your razor burn hasn't gone away since you tried the hydrolyzed collagen DermoRepair lotion.

"Yeah, neck's been burning bad lately."

Again, unprompted. An aural specter floating about.

Well, I wanted to let you know that tomorrow we are launching a new line of Magic Razors that can solve your problem. Magic Razors leverage a new technology, where purpose-driven serums are microscopically impregnated in the razor's edge to minimize pain while shaving and to repair and nourish hair and skin.

"Yeah?"

Yes Nate, Magic Razors are quite fantastic. The ten-blade Magic system is an advanced facial treatment in a single disposable unit. The first blade, in addition to cutting, cleanses the skin with a gentle ammonium lauryl sulfate. The second blade, while also cutting, delivers an antiseptic to the skin inhibiting microorganism growth. The third blade cuts and delivers lidocaine to reduce burn. The fourth cuts and delivers a follicle sedative to inhibit hair growth. The fifth cuts and delivers catalase to neutralize hydrogen peroxide, reducing gray. The sixth cuts and delivers a customizable mixture of eumelanin and pheomelanin precursors, boosting color. The seventh cuts and delivers a stimulate to the sebaceous prompting secretions to protect the hair shaft naturally. The eighth cuts and applies more lidocaine. The ninth cuts and introduces an enzyme to dissolve the puck of hair below the skin's surface, for ultimate smoothness. Finally, the tenth blade doesn't cut, rather it subcutaneously delivers a heated keratin-wax polymer, cauterizing the cut-end of the hair shaft to minimize future splitting. The whole system leaves the face smooth, toned, treated without a trace of razor burn.

"At sounds, well, uh. Luke, you get all that?"

"Uh, yeah man, sounds pretty incredible. Should be a big help with that fucked-up face a yers."

Yeah of course. All programmers must be clean shaven. I have a razor in my toiletry bag too. Why th'hell are so concerned about my grooming? And you call me Princess. No, too aggressive. They don't care much about me, won't ask. Should be prepared though. Probabilities. Yeah, I've got razors in my bag. Like I said, gotta be prepared.

"Yeah, yeah, bet it would be, smartass. How much it cost?"

During our promotional period, a three-pack of Magic Razors is gently priced at two and a half Credits, only five percent more expensive than your current Monster Blade and thirty percent more effective.

"Two and a half Credits and thirty percent more effective? That, at's amazing, I mean, how can that much innovashun be so damn cheap? How they do it? How much money I've got left this month?"

You have ten Credits remaining Nate.

"Damn, money's tight. Tell me, how can I *not* buy that though? Hell, there's melon in it, and them sulfates. I mean Luke, when was the last time you ate melon let alone put it on your face for, what'd she say, smoothness?"

"You know I can't afford melon Nate, so why ask man?"

Nate, shall I place an order for you?

"Yeah. Yeah, put it through."

Happy to. Luke, would you like to take advantage of this opportunity? These razors will work wonders for those gray chin hairs, that dry, rough skin on your cheek bones.

"Yeah, go ahead. Sounds too good, too cheap, to pass up. Maybe I'll cut out breakfast this week."

No, don't need new razors. Can't afford them anyhow. My old ones work fine.

Alvin, would you like to join Luke and Nate on this deal as well? If everyone orders, I can offer a three percent group discount.

"Uhh, no, can't. I uh, I don't have the money for them right now."

"Man, are you for real?" Nate's eyes burn into me. "You're an odd fucker, know that? Luke, who does that shit? Messes up a group discount? Odd fucker. Why are we giving him a ride again?"

Alvin, I'm unable to pull your bank details. Sorry, group offer denied.

"Odd, broke fucker more like it," Nate clarifies.

Wanting to respond, wanting to say something. To tell them how little

Pham's not odd, he's lazy. Perhaps measurably slow if you unravel the genes down to their permed ends. Though, none of this is my fault. It's nature's inequitable allocation of traits. This is natural. To reassure them that this is not their fault either. They're good Samaritans giving a ride to some fool. To reassure them this is not God's fault either. Of course he loves all his children equally. Really though, this desire to morph. Become what they want me to be. Become what I want me to be. Become what mom wants me to be. Become what Mr. Patel wants me to be. Become what John wants me to be. Become what everyone needs Pham to be. That little voice inside your head that validates every motivation, every thought. A checkmark in a little box indicating completion. A single, clear accomplishment. Something singular. A white-hot heat. Simple and predictable. Remember when John said focus is the easiest state to achieve? All you need to do is subtract everything. Don't discriminate, don't think. Don't choose or process. Those functions are calculated in advance. Subtract. Thoughts minus emotions equal focus. Focus. Subtract. Yeah, of course I'm hungry. I'll make it to lunch though. No big deal. I work with this guy who lives pretty close to me, owes me a favor. I'll bum a ride home. It's not your concern, hell, you guys got me this far.

He continues, "Must be dirt in the blood. Don't forget to smile at your eviction. Odd fucker."

Oh, by the way, Luke, your girlfriend's birthday is next week. Shall I order the same bouquet as last year?

"Shit, forgot about that, you're right. Yeah, yeah, guess so. Do I have enough Credits?"

Yes you do.

"Ok, yeah, fine. Put it through. Nate, where're we at anyway?"

"Whatcha mean?"

"We're talking 'bout something."

"Smiling Luke. We're talking about smiling. You're saying how you can't remember the last time you saw a *real one*."

"Right. Right, right, right, right. So what gives? What happened? I can't picture it, but I remember smiling as a kid. Or I think I can. I think I can remember smiling as a kid, laughing."

"Shit, welcome to the adult world Lukey boy. Somebody walks around with a big smile on they face in they libel to get popped in the mouth. I could care less about smiling. But, I'll tell something man. I'll tell you what gets me. What gets me is the tension. The feeling that everyone 'round you's about to blow. Like everybody's vibrating or something. And you can feel the heat coming off a them, know all the needles are bouncing off the red-line. It's exhausting to be on guard all the time, all clenched up. Vibrating. Ready to burst."

Subtract. No, s'fine, I'll walk. It's up around, no. It's just up 'round th'corner. Extrosoft or something like that. Be all cool-like. I don't know all these damn corporate names. 'Course it's not the main office, a branch location. Thanks for the ride.

"Fine, I'll give you that. S'not that I want people to walk around with a goddamn smile on they face, it's just that when talking, when *interacting* with people, there's no happiness, ever. There's none. Shit, fuck happiness, there's no goodwill whatsoever. There's anger. A constant anger. And you feel it, staring back at you, waiting for an opportunity. Waiting for the right moment. A fight constantly on the verge of breakin' out. Do you know what the fuck I'm sayin'?"

"News flash Luke, peoples' agitated. Pissed off. Government acts like they doing favors, then hits you with penalties if you don't toe some bullshit line. Meanwhile, the whole institution and every asshole in it's corrupt, living fat off my money. And these slack-assholes, that squirrelly fucker, suck the system dry, hiding-out till evicted. And shit, we got our little Princess right here, clearly abusing the system, stealing more surgeries than he's allotted."

Alvin, The Surgery Store is offering 95% off all post-quota surgeries next week! A spectacular opportunity to sharpen up those sloping shoulders of yours!

Subtract. No. Add. Let me ask a question. Ever dined on trash? The kind so putrid that, when you spot the maggots crawling in it, you hold your breath and chew quick, knowing you are fortunate to be consuming fresh, living protein? There's a reason to smile, a real one.

"How d'you know that squirrelly guy's a slacker? How d'you know how many surgeries *he's* had? How do we know anything?"

"Yeah, well, got this drinking buddy, never seen him wear the same outfit twice. Never. How's he afford that? Same salary as me. Scamming something no doubt. Shit's disorganized and corrupt at every level. Officials need to do they job, the job they were elected to do. If the system ran better, we wouldn't need to work s'hard to make ends meet. Less waste, more for everybody else."

Nate, The T Shirt Warehouse is having a 50% off sale on Thursday.

"Shit, government's givin' us the Palette free this time. Free. And tell me, how many shows and games you watch a month Luke? And how much that cost ya? You know, maybe if Security Inc paid us a better wage, you could afford that day off, another new pair of shoes."

Luke, The Shoe Emporium is having a two-for-one special next Wednesday on those boots you've been talking so much about lately.

"And we just got a step increase. What, we supposed to get a raise every couple months Nate?"

"I got no problem with that."

"Yeah, then watch the company go to shit. What about your raise then? E'rbody's gotta *earn* their living man."

Add. You're so angry, yet you have it all. But, mind you, those tonal flitters betray the tough words. When the angst goes up and the volume goes down, there's nothing left but a soul standing alone on a crumbling bridge. No movement and no direction. And sure as gravity, when your feet break through, that voice will mute altogether as you leave it levitating in the past. What is it? What makes you so scared? What do you fear?

"Look, the company's doing fine. The executives, well, they're all loaded beyond belief,"

Luke, The Watering Hole is having a Happy Hour promotion tonight, one Credit off all well drinks from 8pm to 11pm. Get loaded tonight!

"living the life, living in their happy, carefree Bunker paradise. Productivity? Profits? Shit, higher than they've 'er been. How congested is the sky at night? Planes are nearly bumping into one another. Course the government's corrupt, but it's the only voice we got. The only power 'at's supposed to care about our interests," Nate says.

"You're full of it you know? Some corrupt politician doesn't care about your interests or mine. And even if they did, which they don't, they not doing shit about it. So either way, if they give a shit or not, they still accountable to us. They still gotta act for us. Making sure the country runs right s'not the job of the man who runs a security company and deposits to my bank account. If the government's broken, they need to fix it. Clean shit up."

"You talk as if it's easy or something, 'just clean it up'. Where you begin?"

"With the cheaters, get 'em out," Luke says.

"I don't know man, seems hopeless. The two of us, in the same exact position, don't even see things the same way. Same information, two different views on what's wrong. Everything seems so unclear, like you're standing in a room with a million doors and you got no idea what's behind a single one of them. Don't even know what *could be* behind a single one of them. And so you test a few knobs but they're locked. And if you try to make sense of life, everything unravels further, more doors appear. That's it, you know? At's why people are pissed off. Nobody knows what's what. Nobody can make sense of anything. All we know is that every year shit's tighter, and it's tougher to breathe. It's that anxiety man. When you're dead tired at the end of the day, but still waking up in the night in the middle of an incomplete thought. A thought you race to figure out before you fall back asleep. But you know you won't be able to. And you'll wake up with that same thought bouncing around in you head. A constant feeling of being lost. That something's missing. Meaning can't be defined, shit, it's indefinable. Something's not sitting right and it's messing with your damn head. But you can't figure it out, and know you probably never will no matter how hard you try. No matter what you do. And everybody feels it, or you know damn well everybody feels it even if they keep they mouth shut. You see it in they face, no, you can see it missing from they face. I mean, I already asked you... like shit, when was the last time you saw someone smile?"

Add. What is this loss you lurch around? You circle it, a vulture afraid to drop. Why can't you state your fear? Does the thought of mentioning it cause pain? Or, is it so obvious that there is no point wasting energy by saying it aloud?

"Shit, I know what your saying even if you got a fagotty way of putting it. Everything presses in. Everything, everyone acts harder than they should. And it's always there. There's never a break to catch your breath. To be at peace. There's no stop, and..."

"...you can't remember the start of it all. It just is and you push through it. Every day. Angry but trying to act like you don't give a shit cause it's easier. You know, when you stub your damn toe and you take a deep breath, wait for the throbbing to stop. But no more. Shit man, I said it, I'm going to make my voice heard. Make some demands. Whoever they are, they'll hear me. Me and my bullhorn, screaming out demands. I'll be a one man riot, I don't care. I'll be heard, and if not heard, well fuck it, at least I'll scream."

Silence. Neither of them talk. Staring out respective windows, watching the landscape change as we incline toward The Core. Metal buildings gone. Massive roads merge into us from high, from low, many angles at once. Everything aligns, points neatly to the cluster of towers ahead, glistening in the morning sun. Silence grows thick, awkward. Add. Fear, how it motivates and suppresses simultaneously.

"So, what are your demands?" spoken from this tiny, reserved voice. Ephemeral.

"I told you man, improve shit. Eliminate the cheaters. Those abusing the system. Get rid of the waste. Clean shit up, I don't know."

Add. Why can't you say it? Why can't anyone say it? It sits there in plain site, yet everyone ignores it, moves around it as if it's a Leper. Like if you get too close to it you might meet your end.

"And?"

"And don't penalize people for not showing up to some fucking Unwrapping. Why the hell would I *want* to participate?"

Again, congratulations on winning a spot for the Unwrapping Nate! As a reminder, you are in row twenty-four, seat 128b. Traffic is clear and your expected arrival time is twenty-five minutes before check in. Stop by any 24-Hour AmphetamOctane juice stand for 25% off any 24 ounce or larger drink.

Again the silence. Uncomfortable shifting. Heads doing impressive calisthenics just to avoid eye contact, clearly wanting to break through the windows and float away.

"And?"

"And, hell, more subsidies."

"More subsidies? Such as?"

"Shit, I don't know, you tell me. What other sort of technology they working on? Give us more."

Nate, the next Unwrapping event is prescheduled for the beginning of Q4.

Silence. Ahead, the towers grow. Traffic thickens. Silent again, she's working out the right pitch as we cruise down the road.

"Anything else?" Luke quietly asks nobody in particular, eyes out the window.

"Housing. Guaranteed housing. No possibility of eviction, ever," Nate's voice registers just above the engine's hum, the tone of an abused child.

"I thought you're the first to celebrate a Dhalyte's being snuffed out?"

"Yep, 'til the day I die man, till the day I die," subservience whispers.

And it returns. Our best friend, the silence. It sits between them, looking at Luke, then at Nate. Waiting patiently, resolutely, for someone to respond. Beside me, a face, in another car, inching ahead. Talking to himself or perhaps something personified in the aether. Eyes forward, no expression. Autopilot mouth. Add. Getting warmer, perhaps one of you could cross that bridge. But you have to walk. You have to keep moving.

"It's the system, you know? The system's so big, and mistakes, well. They happen. I don't wanna be a mistake. You? If you're an Iron, you should be able to prove you're an Iron, with a badge or something. A credential in case the system makes a mistake. Then you'd have some proof of your guarantee. Of your position in the system."

Nate, Positions Sexploration Cafe is offering a couples promotion next week and free entry to the Latex Lounge for thirty minutes. Slip and Slide On Us!

Add. I am the fear. Your fear. Being me, in my social position, is to realize that everything's lost. Being me is to know that security's gone. Being me is to know that hope never was. Being me is a burial years before you die. How do you know you are not exactly like me? One and the same. Aphamli Twist's long lost brother.

"You want them to measure it then?"

"I don't know. Yeah. Maybe."

"What if your Motum Ducit turns out to be on the small side? What then?"

"I'll worry about me, you worry about you."

"Well I for one don't want the government measuring my brain, invading my privacy."

Luke, your next patrol begins in 25 minutes. You need to leave for Storage

Facility 839C in two minutes for a timely arrival.

"I thought you were all for the government."

"No man, not at all. But I trust the elected slightly more than the hired. But whatever, I'm happy to see them all dumped, dumped out in the "

"Oh! let me guess, tough guy, the flats?"

"Yeah, dump 'em in the flats. Dump 'em all in the flats. Makes no difference to me."

Quiet again as we navigate concrete channels, little pathways efficiently channeling traffic into position. Ubiquitous faces, mouthing incessantly inside cramped boxes moving forward. Add. The many fallen Irons, upon arrival in The Piles, with their indignation, their bewilderment. Then their sob stories. Nothing changes. Everything stays the same. It's only after reality sets in that you know it's real. It's only after the bridge breaks that we start the impossible walk through thin air. Each newly minted Dhalyte, the same should-have-done-it-this-way story.

"Pull over there Luke, there's a break I can walk through."

"Fine."

"Well, be seeing you next year when our shifts cross again."

"Yeah, if you're not still in jail."

"Or if you're still considered an Iron."

"Fuck you."

"Don't get pissed at me, get pissed at science."

The crowd, an ocean of people stretching from the truck. People milling about, aloof but tense, however that's possible. Individuals shouldering, elbowing their way through the crowd. The act of not seeing, just bumping through. Lips pursed. A million brows defying gravity. Nate disappears, becomes numerical among the surreal tide of Irons.

"Thanks for the ride."

Twisting in his seat, he looks at me, rather, looks toward me. Something bitter in his mouth. He presses a couple fingertips against his temple, winces. Intentionally or so it seems.

"Yeah, well, like I said y'got lucky, you all drunk and wandering around out there. Lucky we found you. Where you go from here?"

"I'm up around the corner. I can walk."

"I wasn't offering door delivery, just curious. Where you work?"

"Extrosoft. One of the branches."

"Extrosoft? Never heard of it. Well, maybe I have. All sounds about the same. I don't know. What you do there?" he asks, again wincing, his apparent tick.

"Machine code, low level stuff. Drivers and whatnot."

"I see. Tell me something."

"K, what is it?"

"I did you a favor," temple press, wince, "do me one."

"Yeah sure, if I can."

"Tell me. How many surgeries you had anyway? Nate right?"

The bridge wants nothing but to break. Some mysterious force in the universe manages to keep it suspended on thin threads of misplaced hope.

"I don't know man, sort of lost count."

"Of course you have some idea though, right?"

"Everything becomes a blur with time. An addiction. Addictions are funny in that way, they have no memory."

"Yeah, guess so. I think I know what you mean. Anyway, push it shut, I gotta get going."

"One thing I can say though, Nate's not right. I haven't cheated. I don't know how I'd go about it even if I wanted to."

"At's what I thought. That prick's paranoid. Thinks everyone's trying to take something from him. Anyway, good luck begging to the bossman."

"Thanks for the ride."

Can he still hear the sound of his own voice? Can any of us?

"So long Princess," he says, wincing.

Awake? It's possible. Or is this the famous white light shining on man's expiration date? The great, silent therapist in the sky unrolling the carpet for me? There's a sort of tangible space around, although no method, no compulsion, to explore it. These gradations of color, discernable boundaries, describable as shapes. Gone is the lead. Gone is any sense of linearity. Gone is the ability to identify and collate markers of time, apart from the occasional wink of a passing day. Above all else, clarity. A clarity within, a snowball rolling downhill. A clarity, indescribable, but becoming easier and easier to sense, to feel. I will not acknowledge pain.

Eyes closed. The abyss, the infinite screen. Not white. Not black. Nonexistent. The absence of color and space, rather, the absence of the thought of color or space. Does this make sense? Of course it does. This is it! This is the realm. This is where seeds are planted. The place for roots to set foundation in untainted soil. A place for the want of nothing, clarity of vision. Goodbye *Baby Makeover*. Goodbye *Unanesthetized Surgery*. Goodbye *Inbreeding Roulette*. Goodbye *Butterknife Suicide*. Here, there is no agenda. No rails to be pushed from. No fictional forebears to snuff you out. No salvation to strive for. No God to lovingly hate. No reason to prove worth. No worth justifying reason. No noise. I will not acknowledge pain.

Open. White. Something like a ceiling floating overhead. Time, not ripe.

It's quiet, a quieter head. It's lighter, the load. A burden lifted. It's easier, getting about is easier. Step, step, breathe. Search. Step, Step, breathe. Search. Exhaustion, utter exhaustion. Relief, guilt. Guilt and Relief. Back and forth, one chokes the other. No, guilt. Guilt for relief. Just guilt. And exhaustion. Nothing more than gnawing guilt. It's louder now. His voice, louder. It's heavier now, the burden. The load, still light. Step, step, breathe. Search. Step, step, breathe. Search. Functional catatonia.

"I'm hungry," she says.

So was Maven.

"I'm tired," she says.

She was too.

The white lights of noon, translucent ripples of air rising from the ground. The relentless stench. Sun pressing down.

"I'm hungry," she says.

I know you rotten shit, I'm working on it. You could help with the hunt you know, it's your life too.

"I'm tired," she says.

I'm aware of that you little barbarian, we all are.

Step, step, breathe. Search. Step, step, breathe. Search. This is a job. This is a job for Job. Job's job. Jobby job job Job's jobby job. The stench, the rotten, fucking stench. What happened to the Claxtons? Why am I dragging children through a landfill. Child.

"I can't walk anymore."

Nor can she you degenerate, you reprobate little savage.

"I don't want to walk anymore."

Nor did she, you, you...

Step, step, breathe. Search. Step, step, breathe. Search.

When does the sadness come?

Right after the shock.

When does the shock come?

Right after the trauma.

When does the trauma come?

Soon no doubt.

Step, step, breathe. Search. Step, step, breathe. Search.

Are you faithful?

No I have nothing for you.

Will you deny me?

No, there is nothing to deny.

Are you afraid? ... are you?

What could I possibly be afraid of?

Step, step, breathe. Search. Step, step, breathe. Search.

I can't walk anymore. Exhaustion.

"I can't walk anymore."

"Gramma, I can't walk anymore."

Vicious, a cowering aggressor. Slashing amid surrender. A white flag concealing the knife in the other.

"Gramma?"

What?

Step, step, breathe. Search. Step, step, breathe. Search.

When does the sadness come?

Right after the shock.

When does the shock come?

Right after the trauma.

When does the trauma come?

Right after guilt.

Well, when does the guilt go?

At the start of trauma.

Step, step, breathe. Search. Step, step, breathe. Search.

"Gramma, I can't walk anymore."

Yeah.

"Gramma?"

"Gramma?"

"Gramma!"

"WHAT, WHAT?! WHAT! WHAT DO YOU WANT?"

Breathe. Breathe. Breathe.

When does the sadness come?

It has arrived.

What about the shock, the trauma, the guilt? What about those realities?

What are they?

Drip, drip, breathe. Drip, drip, breathe.

"Valerie? Valerie honey? Gramma is sorry. I didn't mean to snap. Valerie? Come here to Gramma."

Hug, hug, breathe. Hug, hug, breathe.

STOP.

"We can take a break, up ahead, see that overhang? Let's go there, get out of the sun a while. Don't cry honey. Gramma's here."

A hull. A massive arc of rusted metal, convex to the sun. In the foreground of towering glass giants. A violent, menacing scrap of tetanus, kinetic jaws waiting.

"Honey, let me help you."

From the bright white, into the mouth.

I slit the sheet the sheet I slit, and on the slitted sheet I sit

"Shit on this dear, try to keep your legs off the metal, Ok?"

My scrap. Two ladies enjoying the shade on a sunny afternoon, the smell of sheet wafting periodically. Two ladies, lethargic from over-basking. Moisture for tears.

"Gramma?"

Rest. A clamp. A clamp on an overworked hamstring, a calf. Pins and needles pimpling the skin's surface, pushing through, piercing like fire. Vibrations and dull knots. In the distance, shhimmering metals, chromium splotches of lies, mirages. Anemic marauders scavenging.

"Gramma? Gramma?"

"Yes dear, what is it?"

"Gramma, I'm tursty."

"Ok, here, have a little of this, a tiny sip, K?...Ok, Ok, k, k, k, k that's good enough, we must conserve."

"A little more Gramma, please?"

"One more sip, small now Ok?"

"K."

"Okayokayokay, that's enough. Let's save the rest, yeah?"

"Yah."

"Here, lie back for a while, put your head on this. Wait, wait, fold the bag over like this. Double it up. It's softer honey. That's good, close your eyes for a while, Ok? Try to get some rest, Gramma'll be right here."

"Ok."

"Gramma?"

"Yes sweetheart?"

"Does it hurt to die?"

"Nooo. No, no, no honey, dying doesn't hurt. Not at all. It's like, well... It's like walking through a door, except, when you walk through the door, you enter another world. It's not the home you know, but it's a nice comfortable place, and, well it becomes your new home. It's like moving, dying is a lot like moving into a nice, new home."

"Gramma?"

"Yes dear?"

"How did Maven open the door if she can't open the door at home?"

"It is a special kind of door honey, you only need to think to open the door. Close your eyes now sweetheart."

Chromium pools ripple on the horizon, the earth spews a rotten odor.

"Gramma?"

"Yes dear."

"If the door opens, do I have to go in?"

"Only if you want to sweetheart, only if you want to. But get some rest now, you needn't concern yourself with that. Close your eyes, rest, yeah?"

"Gramma?"

"Yes sweetheart?"

"Why didn't Grandpa go to the glass buildings when he died?"

"Well sweetheart, the glass buildings are for the people on the other side."

"Does God love the people on the other side more?"

"No, no sweetheart. God loves everyone the same."

"Then why won't he let Grandpa move to the glass buildings?"

"Well, because God can't control people. People on the other side decided they want to keep the glass buildings for themselves."

"But I thought God could do anything?"

"Well dear, God is complex and, well, sometimes even he trips on his own feet, accidentally by his own choosing of course. It's that, he's sad for us, but happy for them and so he's stuck between his rock and his hard place, but it's not as though it's his fault because someone ate the apple several thousand years ago....like I said, it's complex baby girl, get some rest for now, we can talk later." What the hell am I going on about. Just rest.

"I don't understand Gramma."

"You will one day sweetheart. You will. And, because you're such a smart girl, you will teach Gramma all about it. You're the one to untangle the knot."

"Will God let us go to the glass buildings, for a visit?"

"Well, yes sweetheart, we're going there now. But please, rest, then we will continue, Ok?"

"Ok."

The silence of anticipation, hanging in the air, rain about to fall. The sky, clear enough that rain won't fall. The rain, soon to disappear altogether in fall. Asleep, perhaps now she can fall. The pole, jutting from the ground, barely visible. The shred of swaddling whipping in the wind, a headstone's meek decor. Conquer or surrender? Screw the rules, she's my baby. Nothing will cart her off but me. This damn world.

Scurrying, a beetle. Slow bug. Nutty and dry. Bitter. A baby. My baby. Those big eyes. He wants her, it's His child. His baby. Lease is up. Flying, a pigeon. A beautiful pigeon. Free. It's not her fault, Valerie. Programmed like the rest of us. It's mine, my fault. Darkening. Cloud overhead. The light returns, same as it ever was. Tears, they fall somewhere. Somewhere guilty eyes have paid their debt and they fly home, pigeons.

Does she know what she did, understand the implications? Either way, she's not guilty and that's a blessing. Me, her trinity. The fault bypasses innocence in search of responsibility.My responsibiity. I showed hunger my back and Valerie overtook Maven, filch by filch. My baby. My babies. Here's the guilt. Fucking guilt. One baby dead, starved. Rest, a waste of time. The inseparability of calories and seconds. A clock ticks calories, a body burns seconds.

Outside the jaws, sun radiates, fire on the frontlines of econocide. The swaddling whips in the wind. Did she feel death coming on? She became so quiet, disinterested. On the same wind, a voice. A soft, gentle voice barely perceptible at first, then rising, comforting in its warm, paternal tones. Soft hands in the mind, the sun washing out hues, the deliverance of white, trans-porting in its monochromatic purity. Unimposing in every way imaginable he is. An exhausted smile shot from light years away, arrives as a faint echo of its original self. He treads carefully, the ground unaware of his presence. A single, loose cloth, vanity's last stand. Wasting sinews strapped tight across angles of bone. Skin blistered, corpuscular yellow ooze. He offers his hand. Dry. Calloused. A moment of humanness required. Vulnerability. A moment of need?

He wants to know if he can share our jaws

He wants to know where I've been

He wants to know which way I'm going

He wants to know if I've had any luck

He wants to know if we're alone

He wants a sip, just a small sip

He wants a tiny sip

Just a tiny sip

He says he know we're here alone

Just a tiny sip

He wants proof

He wants to verbally abuse me

He wants to know if I've seen pain

He wants to know if I know what pain is

He wants to teach me a lesson

He wants me to know that he hasn't always been this way

He wants to crush my throat with his thumbs

He wants me to know that he wasn't always this way

He wants me to keep it down, be quiet

He wants to teach me a lesson

He wants me to know that he was a father too

Was

He wants me to watch as he smashes her head with a stone

He wants me to keep it down, be quiet

He wants to teach her a lesson too

He wants me to know that he used to be a good man

Used to

He wants me to keep it down, be quiet

He wants me to know that he has developed a taste for flesh

He wants me to know that he hasn't always been this way

He wants me to know that he can't remember his own name

He wants me to know that he hasn't always been this way

He wants me to know that he is afraid of nothing

Absolutely nothing

And all that exists, all that ever existed, are these putrid tonsillolith odors and a rising sense of dyspneic euphoria. Until, the pigeon. It's back. Skims the ground, circles back and lands to watch the curious humans tussle. Cooing. Cooing and strutting, an odd dinner bell, as the sun dips to the horizon.

He wants me to know that he hasn't always been this way

He thanks me for keeping it down

He wants me to know I'm not worth it

She's not worth it

He apologizes

He wants me to know that this is not him

He wants me to know that he's not sorry

And he chases freedom.

Coughing. Hard, dry coughing. No wind.

Off he runs, my brow consumes him, tears across the bridge of my nose. Pigeon bounds, flops from one perch to another. The way pigeons do, gracefully, and just out of reach. Air feels cool, then hot, cool again. Convulsions, pounding. Cadence, reality's most prominent feature. A throat made of sand. Sand and tiny rocks grinding against one another in the shimmering chromium pools. Everything's quiet, dead silent. Distant and growing more so. Lay, just lay here a moment.

...

The sun shone down on his face, a face textured with neglect, uneven stubble poking from his neck, each hair shiny, individual. A swath of dry blood flaking off his cheek, some ignored cut. The filthy hands carelessly passing the grip back and forth to one another. Wild eyes, inky black save for a strangled band of light blue circling. Hair, disheveled, black clumps matted together with grease and chunks of scaly, white skin.

"I'm sorry, I'm really sorry to involve you. I'm awfully sorry."

If the gag wasn't in my mouth I would have told him that it's Ok, it's fine. I'm not so detached from reality that I can't reason through why he would do this. Of course I'd rather not be in this situation if given the choice, but at the same time, it's probably best for someone *like* me to be here. Someone who's able to see the larger context, remain calm. To perceive the entirety of the situation. We all play actors in roles not of our choosing and that's fine, it's how we learn to cope. To adapt. The real tragedy is when someone plays themselves in a role of their choosing for too long. Excessive comfort and happiness metastasize into blithe disregard for others if left steeping together indefinitely. Existential friction is what glues the conscious to the mind, what creates perspective.

"He was four. Can you believe he was four?"

He smelled, rather, stunk. A pungent, oniony smell, strings of hormonal firecrackers popping in his armpits. The dampness of sweat hanging in the room, the humidity of someone else's shower lingering in the bathroom. Other peoples' moisture creeping into your cavities. A minor violation of personal hygiene.

"Narfaei hawai ikai itach khuai ohiakha."

"I'm sorry for doing this to you, but, I have to keep up appearances, do you understand?"

"Hawai ihata kai."

But he didn't need my words. My eyes clarified the garble. My willing-ness to cooperate. My exaggerated subservience bordering on the complicit. If he needed some money, if his situation was so wrought with tragedy, then, collectively, we can all pitch in. The losses can be spread easily to all, not felt in any real sense. Tomorrow's sun will rise, people will go about their business and maybe one fallen individual will find the strength to get back up, keep keeping on. Tomorrow morning, while sipping coffee, I'll puzzle through the odds of being forced to spend the majority of the previous day in a broom closet. Then, I'll scratch my head, finish my muffin and send the girls to school, while the memory of mercy continues the shockingly brisk process of dissipation.

"I'm sorry, I'm so sorry. I won't hurt you, I promise I won't hurt you. This is a show, nothing more. This is a show of force. A farce! You're not at risk. Not one bit. Not even if they storm the place. I will go down alone. You are not at risk. I hope you know that."

"Hwai, khai."

Patting his arm, his shivering, soaking wet arm, I nodded, gave him the soft, welcoming blink of understanding. He rocked on his feet, peeking out of the window obsessively, searching for the way out, trying to figure out the answer to the impossible question. Wanting desperately to plead his case outside the courts, right there on the streets to real people, real humans, not to a courtroom of institutionalized 'people' concerned primarily with protecting paper (and, of course brooms, mop-buckets and other 'people', secondarily). The conflicted grimace from a head calculating the best way to strong arm a violent situation into a peaceful resolution.

"I WILL CUT HER FUCKING HEAD OFF ON NATIONAL TELEVISION IF THAT CHOPPER ISN'T HERE IN TWO MINUTES!"

Desperation sounded oddly similar to bromidic movie scenes.. Screenwriters, clairvoyant or prescriptive? Irrelevant.

"I won't. I won't do a thing. I don't even have a knife on me. I promise. Hell, I'm afraid of blood. I hate violence. And this gun, this gun isn't even real! It's a prop. It's a plastic look-a-like. See? See the line, the seam running down the barrel here, where the two plastic pieces are fused together. Here, hold it, look at it. See? I found it at the shelter, gave it to him for his birthday. His fourth. His fourth birthday. He wanted to play the good guys, bad guys thing. Imagine that. Can you imagine that? And here, now."

On his face, a grim look, a look absently projected when one find himself the victim of irony. But he didn't hang in that mode long, he was too focused on the fear. The fear overtaking him. The fear that lurched around the tiny room, staring at its watch, counting down the seconds until inevitability. Strange how when he talked about his son, he would scratch his arm uncontrollably, a remorse junkie. The same spot on his forearm, a repetitive motion, his absent-minded reach for comfort amid stress. Scratching for comfort till it weeps blood. How he told me I reminded him of his sister.

"You remind me of my sister, that way you sort of... invite calmness. There's an easiness about you. That's a trait few possess. I'm so sorry for this, you have no idea. I'm really sorry to put you through this."

"Kerhaiwai. Ikai hai hlai."

He started crying, sobbing in that jerky way where no tears come, only the convulses of the head, stomach. I imagined that he was running, running through the years. Running through the good times, the bad. Playing it all on high speed. Searching madly for those insignificant happy moments, moments of serenity. But probably even less than that. It was probably a search for those moments between the happy and the sad. Between the furious and the enthralled. Those beautifully mundane moments in life, easy comfort, floating in the ether, beyond reach. The utter banality of the typical day's ritual. Drudging in their respective moments, but so comfortingly bland and sedate upon retrospect with the right eyes. The type of blandness on cruise control where your presence is hardly required to draw breathe, it comes of its own accord.

"I'm giving this to you, this part of it. Take it. I'll hide it in your blouse, it's yours. I'll feel guilty otherwise. I already feel immense guilt. Story of my life. No, here, take it. Here. Here. No. Here. I'm sorry for my indiscretion. Sorry for everything."

"Klank Hew."

He tucked the wad of bills into my brassiere, pushed it under a breast. He felt the cup for protrusions then flattened my blouse over for a final check. He gave a wry smile, apologized for the millionth time then scratched at the red flakes clinging to his cheek.

"It's not visible. If someone accuses you, well, they'll see your hands are bound. It's pretty obvious. I'll bet you didn't imagine your trip to the bank would last for five hours, huh? Bet you didn't plan on being felt up by some asshole today, huh? I can't begin to express how sorry I am. Here, let me put some more in there. Please, please, it will make me feel better about this. Please."

The bills scraped along the inframammary fold of my breast, this time the left. Hands bound, mouth gagged, bra stuffed with large, unmarked denominations. It was Thursday.

"Klerhaai Ghanai Itai Hai."

"I know, I know but I still must say it. It's funny, my wife used to say the same thing, would get on my case about it."

"Klai Kai."

"Hold on a minute, K?"

"Kai."

"YOU HAVE ONE MINUTE BEFORE I START CARVING HER LARNYX FROM HER FUCKING THROAT YOU C-C-COCK-SUCKERS! THE CHOPPER, NNNOW!"

But his voice started to betray him. A bent bike tire, it wobbled, cracked like a pubescent boy crying foul at the cruel injustice levied by a inept referee. Wiping his brow, he exhaled, began ravaging his forearm again.

Slinking back to the floor, "a single dose, one pill. I still can't believe it. You know, one stupid pill could have saved his life. Just one. What wouldn't a father do to save his child? Huh? What wouldn't I do? Only, I did it too late, story of my life. Too little, too late. Always too little too late. And here we are. I'm sorry. I'm so sorry. And tell John I'm sorry for putting you through this, for putting him through this. You guys don't deserve it. You're good people. God, I feel as though I know him. I feel as though he's a friend. I hope things work out for him and his life after that damn university. Fucking bastards. Heartless, brainless souls. Dead, they are. I'm sorry, I don't mean to curse. This is not who I am. This is not who I was."

Blue and white at once. Everything blue and white simultaneously. Hot and cold together. Glass shards raining down, pelting the skin, a driving sleet of impending violence. On his face, a sublime sort of resignation of what was to come. The look of sad relief. His careful smile, lips tucked under teeth, clamped into position and restrained from uttering somber valedictions. A coughing fit and the long black tunnel reaching out to the other side of consciousness.

...

267

"GGGGRRRRAAAAA?"

"AAAMMMMMAAA?"

"GGGRAAAMMMMMMMAAAA!?"

Eyes. Bulging, sparkling.

"Gramma!"

The hover. The hover of red. The hover of a strained, cherubic face. Eyes falling out, landing as drops on my face. Wet tickles.

"Gramma, are you Ok?"

"Gramma? Gramma!"

"Yes, yes dear. Gramma is Ok."

"Gramma don't open the door pleeease you don't have to Gramma please!"

"Gramma is Ok sweetheart. Gramma is fine. Give Gramma a hug."

Long shadows point east. The jaws, filled with bright yellow. She smells horrid as me. But not as bad as her. Weight on my chest. Her weight on my chest. Calories and time. Silence. Solemnity brushing aside sniffles. The chatter of hunger then the screaming, gut-punch of it.

"Valerie dear, let's sit up, let Gramma sit up."

But she clings. We sit up in a pinch of sparse flesh, sharp bone.

"Look at me sweetheart," face framed in hands, "Gramma is Ok, do you understand? Gramma is perfectly fine."

"You were laying, you weren't moving. I screamed. I screamed loud." Tears.

"I'm sorry doll, I'm tired. Gramma's tired. I was asleep. But I'm awake now, with you. Everything is Ok."

And her head seeks a shoulder, her nose the warm, familiar comfort of a bare neck.

"Here now, sit on Gramma's lap, sit here."

The yellow goes orange in the jaws, shadows elongate.

"Would you like a sip sweetheart? Let Gramma get you a sip."

"There's no water Gramma."

Of course, she helps herself. That is what a human on the brink does, help number one. Protect number one. Maven knows this all too well. Knew.

"Oh sweetheart, did you finish the water? That's all we had. There is no more until we get home. We need to conserve, right?"

"No Gramma, there is no jar. I looked. I looked in your bag. There's no jar."

Son-of-a-bitch. An aching neck and a burning throat. A missing jar. The calling card of a human on the brink.

"It's Ok sweetheart. We're Ok. We can tough it out till we get back. You're a tough little girl aren't you?"

Sobs. No words. Just sobs as the nose returns to warm comfort, the jackknifing begins, her head drumming rhythmically on my shoulder.

"Don't cry sweetie, be my tough little girl. We'll head back soon. I know you're tired. Gramma's tired too. We'll head back soon. I know Gramma's work isn't any fun, I'm sorry I had to bring you. Are you my tough little girl? Huh? That a girl, let Gramma give you a kiss, Ok?"

Thumbs wipe tears, her face framed again. A soft kiss on a moist cheek held long. The myriad sympathies, apologies, sorrows, longing transmitted cutaneously. Guilt the only receipt. This guilt.

"And my tough little girl knows we must keep on, right? We need to make use of the last bit of light, right? Can you be my strong little girl, help Gramma finish out the work day?"

"Y-y-yes, Gramma. I can."

"That's my baby girl, let's take a stretch, prepare to move out."

Outside the jaws, the crispness of evening hints in the breeze, the glass giants stare down, orange-red, on fire, clouds washing across their austere permanence. The ticking clock. The clock forever ticks. A million grains of sand, one at a time, falling through the glass neck and disappearing before touching bottom.

"Let me see your foot honey."

She steadies herself on my shoulders, wobbles side to side, as I tighten the twisted plastic straps down upon her foot securing the footbed. A calloused line, scaly and pink, arcing across the top of her tender, little foot. Another timepiece.

"Ok, secure? You ready?"

The whimpers dissipate. Forward, establish cadence.

Step, step, breathe. Search. Step, step, breathe. Search.

Step, step, breathe. Search. Step, step, breathe. Search.

Menacingly close, the towers stare down. Sludge. Moist everything bogging feet. Suction and release. Footfalls of poor calculation ad infinitum.

"Catchup sweetheart. We're going to hike up around the back of the towers! Isn't that exciting? You said you wanted to see them, right?"

Twelve days? Or, thirteen now? Fourteen? The Archives, huge towers. Unexplored, unknown. The divide between two worlds. An abutment of fear? Aggression? Or maybe the same desolation as in the drop fields. The risk of the unknown. The risk of the known. Attacked or starved, which is better?

Step, step, breathe. Search. Step, step, breathe. Search.

"SEVENTY-THREE!"

"SEVENTY-TWO!"

"SEVENTY-ONE!"

I must, I must, must, mustmustmustmust go over these lines! Focus. Focus. Focus! So much responsibility for the CEO of this great country, this free and just conglomerate! The Biggest Swinging Dick in the land. But hold it, wait. WAIT! The president should open today's speech, right? Right?? People expect a trusted leader, an elected leader, to bless the biggest announcements, provide that juicy opiate of consent, nay endorsement! Nothing's more fundamentally delicious than seeing your own mouthpiece espouse the positions you barely understand, a way to gain brain cells for simply ticking a box! Who doesn't want something for nothing? How shortsighted I've been. This event needs legitimization under the auspices of an *elected* official. The top elected official! The *perceived* BSD! Who is to trust *me*, the mere Chief Executive, with an announcement of such import? This must come from a man of the people, Gatekeeper in Chief, protector of the peoples' will!

"HELP!!! I NEED HELP! HEEEELLLLPPP!"

The door rushes open, papers take flight.

"Yes, yes, yes Lord God, what do you need!?"

"SIXTY-FOUR!"

"SIXTY-THREE!"

"SIXTY-TWO!"

"GET ME PRESIDENT DOLT, IMMEDIATELY!"

"Dear Lord God, he is no longer with us, remember? You demoted him last week when he forgot to lift the toilet seat."

"Oh, right, shit! That nasty degenerate. Ok then, who took his place, who is the next warm-body leading this great nation? Hurry, time's a wasting!"

"But Lord God, you said you didn't want to appoint a replacement, remember? Dear Lord God, you said you wanted to call a special election, remember? Have the people bought-in on their new president?"

"Oh, right, shit. Alright, well, the plan's changed. Who's the current V.P.? Name, give me a name!"

"Umm, Uhh, that would be Uhh, let me check..."

"Hey Adrian, who's the current V.P.? ....Huh? ....Pillock? ....K! thanks!"

"Pillock, Lord God. Vice President Dittimas H. Pillock."

"Ok, perfect! Get IMA to coat him in that Corps silver shit and tell him to be ready for swearing-in in, wait how long until I go on?"

"Fifteen minutes Lord God."

"Five minutes. Have him on stage with the Chief Justice in five minutes for a swearing-in. Have the scribes draft some endorsements for today's an-nouncement. *'Great for the Country', 'Great for the Economy', 'Great for Scientific Advancement', blah, blah, blah* you know the drill, move it. Oh, and have the Chief Justice explain that the special election is postponed for one week due to the overwhelming excitement of this product launch."

"Yes Lord God, I'm on it."

"FORTY-EIGHT!"

"FORTY-SEVEN!"

"FORTY-SIX!"

Stupid me, that could have been an awful mistake, an awful mess! And to think I'm unclear as to who is the current warm-body surrogate, clearly my endeavors are too broad. Focus Zuberi!

"Note to Palette"

"**Palette ready**."

"First note, generate a list of warm-body surrogates acceptably assign-able to persona ficta twenty people deep. This country cannot afford to go without a president for a single day, end Note."

"**Note saved**."

"Second note, select the next four warm-body surrogates to sit for next week's special election, oh, and select Mr. Berk as the candidate for the Citizen's Party, end Note."

"**Note saved**."

Who was it? Who was that brilliant man who spoke those words so long ago? Those beautiful words indelibly etched in the minds of capitalists everywhere, 'Corporations are people my friend!' A genius. A man far ahead of his time. A man who caught flak from his pencil-dick cohorts for simply describing future's trajectory. Ah, such insight, such brilliance into the future of governance. Words spoken ahead of their time by a man destined to share Galileo's fate only because he recognized the respective orbit of powerful bodies. Of course the corporations are at center, how else would free markets function?

But that prescient man was merely a greenhorn, albeit a respectable one, when it came to harnessing the true capability, the full impact, of steering resources. As if money and possessions ever really granted the raw freedom attainable by their adroit manipulation. As if comfort and prestige ever really produced anything more than simple envy, a bland sort of covetousness procurable by so many different, and equally vapid, methods. Power, oh beautiful power, how you morph in accumulation, how you never cease to find new heights, scramble for the ultimate vista. To the uninitiated, the simpleton, power is a scepter in the hand, or a gold seal accolade growing brown on the wall lazily calling eyes to it like a magnet. The power of the educated opinion! Pinheads comparing trophies like a circle jerk of teens measuring their members, while envious onlookers salivate hopefully at the frottage. These, all these superficial attributes merely collected during the rise to actual power, real power. Real power is that of the lever. Simple but insanely powerful. Real power sucks the air from the room, leaving everyone unable to draw breath. Real power is nothing short of the ability to impose your will upon situations especially when your stated position sits far beyond the realm of what is considered acceptable. Real power enables one to act on this position and, of course, execute these vastly minority positions with absolute impunity. Real power, is the ability to choke a baby to death in the public square then, watch as every single bystander averts his eyes, searching busily for some imaginary pen dropped, an address, anything of immediate distraction. No talking. No eye contact. A rush to alleviate oneself from the nauseating force which mutes all. To kill. To torture without fear of reprisal, without the fear of wearing one's soul too thin. The sort of power created and honed in the mind to a sharp point capable of piercing any bubble of conscience apart from your own. Power over one's own slow-to-evolve, and highly deficient, sense of morality. Schadenfreude as a best friend. Power in its absolute manifestation. There is still so far to go!

"TWENTY!"

"NINETEEN!"

"EIGHTEEN!"

Focus. Must focus. Everything looks small. Everything looks weightless. Must continue to polish the machinery of power. Rise higher! Must give the people a teaser taste of power, something to whet the appetite, to prime the pumps so that hope doesn't feel forever distant and unattainable. Create the illusions. I must lose myself, fall into their realm of credibility, assimilate momentarily, then rise again even higher than ever before.

"Without further ado, it is with great pleasure that I present to you an amazing, *fully* subsidized technology that will greatly enhance every citizens' ability to communicate, and to fully enjoy all the wonderful entertainment options available in the marketplace. Ladies and gentlemen, introducing -"

Knock, Knock, Knock

"WHAT THE FUCK!"

"Dear Lord God, I'm sorry to disturb you, but one hundred seconds has passed. This is Alvin Tan."

And so, time drags on. The prescient thoughts painting themselves upon the white screen of here and now, wherever that may be. Nestled in the celestial white light, the symbol of God stares down. All-consuming. All-knowing. The denomination of all worth, domination from birth. The measure of love. The measure of spite. The measure of happiness. The measure of wrath. The measure of pain. I will not acknowledge pain. The measure of pleasure. The value of life. Price at death. The only yardstick of existence that matters. The only reason the sprockets turn, the widgets stack, that people sweat. Or. The reason that they don't. Precious, life-giving Credits. It's all about the Credits baby bling, bling!

Borrow your life until death. Or, borrow your death in life. Labor Credits, colloquially, Credits. Capital "C". Your purchasing power timeline chasing light until your life dims, a loan with a sliding scale rate. Overtime buys back time, get it? Physical age, 48. Current borrowing age, 64. Life Expectancy, 92. Rates are a simple calculation. The greater of 25%, or (2-(Life Expectancy/Physical Age)) + (2-(Life Expectancy/Current Borrowing Age)). Me, my life. A rate of 64.5%. Beyond half a borrowed life. Are you healthy? Congratulations, that's a 2% discount on your rate! Are you sickly? Uh oh, your premium is plus 10% for this loan my friend. Borrow your years beyond death! Life is financial engineering. Life AS financial engineering. Usury rates you say? Don't conflate usury with risk. Relation is not equivalence. Anybody could feasibly borrow the years after their calculated death at a rate of say 118%. (service charge not included) Yes! Work one hundred hours, earn nothing, and pay for 18 of your hours worked and we'll see who comes out on top in the gamble of life! Post no collateral! Life is collateral. Life AS collateral. We both stand to lose. Again, relation is not equivalence. Each mouthful only 35.35% mine, for now. Soon I won't own what goes into my mouth or the cells it sustains. And does it even matter? Credits, tiny blips on a screen somewhere, ranking every pound of flesh.

But Bank Inc will only shake your hand if your situation returns above its cost of capital. Business is about making money you see. An Iron you say? Well, do you reckon the joints are nice and pliable? Sinews reasonably taut? Regardless, you'll need a physical to apply for that loan, sir. If you're a gray matter worker, you should exercise often. Number puzzles. Crosswords. Pludoku keeps a Platinum mind shining brilliantly, staves off the oxidation of senility. Either way, you'll need to take a cognitive test for that loan, ma'am, and of course, we'll need the standard DNA sample. A Science Economy is not based on a cross of the fingers and, well, you know, sweat and synapses are such fickle collateral! We need scientific proof!

Ahh, but where it gets really interesting is the aggregation above the loans! Laying bets with borrowed money on inside information. God's jeopardy. You've seen the actuarial tables. Your neighbor in 823d, yeah, he's listed in the 6th traunche. You've seen how he lives. He should be listed in the 10th, or, possibly the 11th traunche. There's no chance he'll make it to life expectancy. Borrow a few Credits to place the bet, take a chance on his life. A few Credits to buy a short on Wilford M. Blatherton. You know that his debt beyond age 71 is absolutely worthless. You know this. Earn a few Credits on an easy, neighborly bet. But other people see this too, right? There's two hundred people living on this hall alone. They've seen his disheveled carcass splayed out beneath the strobe of a failing hall light. The chunky yellow bib he spews down his shirt after a long dance with the spirits. They know about Wilford's poor choices. The short position is likely overvalued at this point. But, what if he pulls a miracle, makes it to a Borrowing Age of 74? Or, what if medical intervention helps him breach the Borrowing Age threshold, if only, technically speaking? Who's got money in this game? Those Credits. Those borrowed Credits, gone. Finance has always been such a tricky game for those who don't control the market's movements. But, you could kill him! Or perhaps they are already planning to kill him to maintain expectation, guarantee their profits. It's so difficult to judge without all the data! Where lies the biggest honey pot? On his life or at his death? These financial decisions are quite difficult to make. Kill then be killed.

But never mind. Flush it all away, gain clarity. Nothing but distractions here. Money can't buy anything. Money can't buy anything worth having. Money can't buy anything worth having in this lifetime. It's a trap, the ultimate distraction. The great solvent of the conscience.

But what's left to discover? The secrets of life. Those fragments of consciousness slipping by. I will not acknowledge pain. Who am I? Who is anyone? Who are you? Sitting there, reading the whisper of my thoughts cast into the ether and subsequently reeled in by some telepathically-oriented digitized compiler only to be squirted onto your page. Hold on, let me think in zeros and ones, save your processor some clock cycles. We can cooperate you see? It's not too difficult. I just need you to read my thoughts. And please, all I ask is that you interpret them for me before my debt becomes worthless.

Organized chaos. The lack of a stench, striking. Tens of thousands of people crammed into an amphitheater, slouching reluctantly toward some unclear destination. A clot of people, fresh and clean, pleasant fragrances waft. An ocean of tidy, groomed people. No shirtless men. No smudged faces. No pliant folds of dissolving epidermis concealing months of forgotten grim. Sharp odors swirl. Some musky, androgenic, like a balmy afternoon in heaven. Others sweetly provocative, flower petals and clean skin. Sweet smoke, without creosote, curling from extended fingers, a biting odor of tannins stabbing at the tongue, deliciously acrid. Nothing makes sense. Nothing feels quite real. Why the hell am I here? *This is not The Piles Aphamli.*

Faces collide, pull apart. Anger promoted to aggression. Aggression panged with fear. Fear laced with confusion, confusion finding cold comfort in supplication. A sea of Rorschaching faces. A constant morphing. On his face. Her face. Every face. Emotions looping on faces. Every face. Nobody stands on solid ground. Psychosis animated without even a faint glimmer of self-awareness. Volume. The sheer volume. Or noise. The noise. People talk, but mostly to themselves. Almost exclusively to themselves. Lips never stop moving. The volume. Life as a pitch, one advertisement to the next. Everything for sale at once. An oppressive din causing eardrums to collapse into a feedback buzz. Something rattling so hard that the automatons of audibility numb the roots of the system, enhancing what's visual, making objects appear brighter, more contrasted. Noon sun's relentless glint. A billion voices competing for the same space on the audible bandwidth, the needle, as it where, of asymptotic throughput slapping hard against the red, bleeding edge of capacity's limit. The occasional fragments cutting through the cacophony in the form of desires, stated in the third-person by the first-person to convey thoughts to the second-person. Nobody is who they seem, but people are strangely connected, although not physically, to some other world. Connected in some other holding cell beyond the here and now. Nobody's connected to the present. If they do exist, it's impossible to identify any paired interlocutors, any two people engaging one another in the present. Until, them. Until a strange spontaneity carves out two glossy figures from the fold. Two people out of proximate thousands acknowledging each other through some unseen force, the conversation seemingly a requirement in order to compete with one another. Each one ostensibly speaking to the other but only in reference to a shared phenomenon. No eye contact, no body language.

"I was there, front row seat, when he stuck his head in the fryer. I could smell it cooking. It made me hungry, I ordered lunch right then and there."

"I gamed with his flat mate, *ballstothewall42*. Said he was addicted to burning, liked burning his feet. Said he knew something intense was bound to happen."

"Fine, but I watched the guy with the fork take a bite. I considered it myself, but I already paid for my lunch. Didn't want to waste my Credits."

"A guy on my hall copycatted, with just his hand. I watched for several minutes. He screamed bloody murder, a fisher cat. I bought a bite. You can't imagine. *I* know. Like chicken patty as they said back in the day. Exactly like chicken patty. It's crazy, something you must experience."

Then, divergence, as if they hadn't talked. Their respective attention called to the moment's commercial opportunity. The value of attention worth less than the prospect of a bargain. So where do I go? I am here, I've reached some kind of nerve center. Here, in an apparent tidy corner of the universe whereupon fortune smiles. But, amid the chaos, the view is as unclear as ever. Maybe more so. Me, a writhing worm on John's rusty hook, hoping to catch something passing by. Waiting for that opportunity to alter history. Four inches of stinking steel behind me, an ocean of chaos in front of me and an impossible hope propping me up. What would John do? A million theories lose their capacity to stare reason in the eye when opportunity holds so much gravity. Where do I go from here? More important, what's to gain?

"Do you have a criminal record?"

A woman, naked. Standing there, holding up three fingers. Then two. A lone finger points skyward as the look on her face sours. A man pulls her hand down. The corners of her mouth go up. They walk toward a clearing on the far edge of the amphitheater, disappear below the crowd.

Another woman, a hauntingly gorgeous creation. So perfectly made. Five fingers point skyward and they are quickly pulled back down to earth. Lustful smiles, jealous frowns.

"Do you have a criminal record?"

Sweat breaks. The stress of not knowing, the liability of expectation. The sinking sensation of hope getting lost in a meaningless black hole.

"Check one, one. Check two. A little more in my left please." A man in a dark suit speaks into the microphone on the stage in the distance. The huge banner, stretching the width of the stage adorned with the slogan *"One Corporation, Under The Quorum with Liberty and Consumption for Beatus."* Subtle

What to do? What can be done? Where am I? Why is there no blueprint, no contingency for when the human mind turns cold, attempts to detach itself from circumstance. This was supposed to be a plan. Think action. Force an action. In a situation of nothing versus something, chose the something. Action. John? John, should I cut-in on the chicken patty guy? Proselytize to him with my gun poking his **Lumbar (of, near, or situated in the part of the back and sides between the lowest ribs and the pelvis)?** Recruit him at the point of a gun? Hostage. Is he even afraid of death? Should I open a discussion on the inequities of mankind? Plead my own personal situation, the plight of many? What about the woman with her tits swaying for all to ogle? Should I collect her three skyward fingers? Recruit her doggystyle? I'm your *Princess* but you gave me nothing to go on.

They mill about, going nowhere. At times, bouncing off kiosks and shoving colorful objects into their mouths. Communicating vaguely in that far off world. The ads, the never-ending ads. Mouthwash for sale, care to freshen that horrid breath? Something to clean out those disgusting blackheads perhaps? A squirt of collagen for those pencil lips? Music in the distance. Something akin to music. Discordant metallic sounds pounding off one another, pixie bells flittering in between. No discernable beat, noises formed into the shape of something that implies the contours of musicality. A projection on the big screen. Scantily clad women riding cowgirl on the best in toothbrush technology, just two Credits. A different woman humping a snack cake, one Credit. A box of extra-strength, poly-impregnated, mesh-inlaid cinchable garbage bags emerging seductively from inside her dripping panties, a steal at one-and-a-half Credits. Fellatio a sandwich. Tongue-fuck a donut. Jerk-off a tube of faux meat product. Copulative commerce at its most exquisitely banal. Sale achieved by inducing tiny squirts of oxytocin to the bloodstream. A confused woman humping the air at random, looking bored and sleepy, lost, the product for sale not included in the clip. Ad Nouveau, obscure and undirected? A mistake in editing? Who's to know. It doesn't matter anyway. Some people stare blankly, others drool incessantly, a distant Pavlovian awareness. One man walks around as though fearfully balancing a glass of water that isn't on his head. Psychosis, his apparent action. What's mine?

And another woman, moderately attractive. Fingers go up. Four of them. Then three. Hand pulled down. Slot machine eyes spin, three cherries in a row. Chicken dinner.

"Do you have a criminal record?"

Sweat leaks from my skin, echoes bounce around in my head.

That question. It keeps popping up. Some laugh, thumb their nose in response. Others, stare into space, question unheard. Others cower. Many ignore, seemingly locked in a transaction of forgiveness with their hands, stating their transgressions and paying dearly.

"Twenty minutes till show time, audience please find your seat."

Seat, what seat? I have no seat. I'm mission bound. I'm here to make change. I'm here as the hope of an entire race of unwitting people, don'tcha know? A missionary sent out to bend the course of history. To leave a mark, to create awareness. I am aware. Action. I am a man of action and I've come to make things right.

But they're swirling around with their questions, each one in a dark, snuggly fitted suit. Each suit accented with silver trim. Cuffs, ties, piping. Silver. Maybe I'm the target. Maybe I'm the criminal that needs flushing out. Hope extinguished before it has a chance to foment. Before it even knows how to foment. Sweat. Keep moving.

People walk programmatically. Search. Search Pham, for the next door to walk through. John? WWJD? Walk. Walk to my seat. Confidence, it's 99% sweat and 1% gun in your rectum. Ethereally, John says it's time to pull it out. Put the world in its place. Create an opportunity, an action. But, the talking head. Where's the talking head, the big Target?

Me, sandwiched between a cluster of water glass balancers. John's legacy defecated into my feigned ass-scratching hand, improvised misdirection of the classless sort. There is no elegant way to do this. Here, compressed, hidden in the huddle. Shimmy the grip waist-ward, tuck it up into my belt, ready it for the next whisper from beyond, the next commandment fresh off destiny's cold and ugly lips. Walking together, me and the cooling steel, amid our ignoble cadre in search of? We don't know, but we walk, properly oriented in a manner commensurate with action.

"Do you have a criminal record?"

They still circle, the dark suits just beyond my protective human shell. So many glasses of water that mustn't tip. Keep them upright boys lest you make a big splash.

"Do you have a criminal record?"

Move forward, away from the questions. Start a smokescreen conversation. Create a buffer. Something closer to action.

"Excuse me."

Nothing. Tap his shoulder.

"Excuse me?"

"Wait, are *you* touching me?"

"Ah, yes, sorry, wondering if you could help me out."

"Doubt it, I wouldn't tap me again if I were you. You realize I'm twice your size?"

"Sorry."

Failure. Where is a smaller guy? Target acquired. Ready, action.

"Pardon me?"

"Hey man, may I ask you something?"

"Talking to me?"

"Yeah, wondering if you can help me out."

They're swirling, several angles.

"Do you have a criminal record?"

"Do you have a criminal record?"

"Ask me and I'll give you a price."

"Actually, curious if you could tell me who is speaking today?"

"Are you fucking kidding me? Who gives a shit? Tell you what. I may or may not know. Either way it's one Credit. Let me know if you want to proceed."

"I don't have any money."

"Fuck-off then."

"Do you have a criminal record?"

Getting closer. Sweat. Is this it? Is this the end of the line? John, is it time? Big Action?

"Do you have a criminal record?"

"Excuse me ma'am?"

"Yah honey, what's your lust? Point to a part to hear the price."

"Sorry, no, I just have a question."

"Don't we all."

"Do you have a criminal record?"

"Alvin? Alvin Tan, do you hear me? *Do you have a criminal record?"*

She's looking at me. She wants to communicate. A small bowtie of silver dangles from her neck. A comically large lapel pin reads "CORPS" on a slim fitting jacket. She is the utter absence of emotion. A visage perfectly disconnected from the influence of muscular control. Maybe she's talking to the ether too, and my eyes happen to sit in her line of sight at this particular moment. Coincidences are funny...all the tiny spring-loaded pins in the lock's cylinder lining up at once, the tumblers turning in unison. **Locks (a section of a waterway, such as a canal, closed off with gates, in which vessels in transit are raised or lowered by raising or lowering the water level of that section)** and **Lapels (the front part of a garment, as a coat or shirt, that is folded back on the chest and is joined to a collar or forms one continuous piece with it)**, the stupid shit collecting dust on the far corner of my useless brain. A Dirt, what, in all honesty, is to be expected? John, kill her?

"Alvin, are you there?"

"Who?............Me?"

"Yes you, Alvin Tan. *Do you have a criminal record?"*

"Uhm, nuh, no, not that I'm aware of."

"Ok then, a question for you."

The steadily increasing whistle of pressure halts. Time hangs.

"Ok."

"The poor have it, the rich want it, but if you eat it you will die. What

283

is it?"

"Why are you asking me? What is this?"

"Please, just answer the question. I'm in a hurry, have a quota to meet."

"I don't understand."

"That's well enough, please answer the question. The poor have it, the rich want it, but if you eat it you will die. What is it? Come, come, come, please, I'm short of time here, I have to keep moving."

Madness. It's nothing short of madness. There is no logic in madness. There are no nicely fitting pieces that add up to a sensible reality. When reality evaporates, it's time to panic and shoot.

The poor have it. The poor have it. What do the poor have?

"Nothing. It's absolutely nothing."

"How does that make you feel? One word."

"What?"

"I said, how does that, the answer, make you feel?"

"What is this? Why are you asking me these silly questions?"

"Please just answer the question."

Panicked hand tiptoes to the gun. Interrogation. Perp cracking?

"Well, hungry I guess."

"Ah, Ok, very good! Come with me Alvin," she brightens, ever so slightly.

"What? Where to?"

"Follow me. Somebody wants to talk to you. Somebody important wants to talk to you. It's your lucky day my friend, come."

She pulls me, pulls me through the crowd. She plows through people, pushes them aside. Regardless of size they stumble, shift out of her way. Of my way. Through the crowd we careen, her cold hand dragging me toward **Luck (the chance happening of fortunate or adverse events; fortune)**. John, what would you do?

Oh, here it comes, how creative. Now we're ticking off the last few boxes on the clichéd home invasion checklist. Let me guess, they made that flaming trail with the 200 year Macallan. Stupid donkeys aren't aware of the proper use of life's finer things.

I guess the idea's to burn the wicked home with the owner inside. Inventive. The dancing flame advances toward my how, creeps up the walls, sprints when it touches the tapestries, the valances. When death feels like a nauseating cliché, you know the end is pretty fucking near.

The how never had any answers, never will. What did Jeffrey see that I didn't? What did chance distill that I overlooked? How did my blinders grow so complete, so perfectly obfuscating, enabling reality's cold, indifferent logic to become pregnant with meaning?

It's that essence, she possessed it. She, herself, embodied the how. Ava again! She WAS the how. It coursed through her veins, tempted me against better judgment and exacted its price in the end. Trust. A cancer of the mind. An abject human faculty that places value on the fickle temperaments of breeding man, a man bent on perpetuation, not Providence. Screw you Jeffrey, you didn't see a goddamn thing. *Everything* happens for a reason, it's just that we are blind to reality's full scope most of the time. Jeffrey's as blind, more so. His sad, self-deprecating reality is the lazy sort of answer given to empirical questions such as *why do mathematics work?* or *why are men stronger than women*? The how is perfectly answerable with enough insight into reality. One only needs to open his eyes wide enough to take in the range of possibilities. Ava, why did you intersect my life? Why were my eyes so damn closed?

I was right, Ava polished up impeccably. No traces of wear on the fringes, no deterioration too irreversible for the marvels of a cosmetic reboot. It's the bones that matter most, the structural foundation that lends itself to that certain *je ne sais pas* that exudes from very few. Perfection can always be constructed from the ground up, however the fines seams of engineering always manage to spoil the spectacle whereas natural beauty transcends the concise mathematical precision of fabricated aesthetics. The delicious idiosyncrasy of a beauty mark. All the little imperfections, incongruous and sporadic, when summed up, create the wonder, the sheer mystique, the impossibility of natural beauty. Fucking shit, the gibberish of falling in love. How that calculus played out in my mind as I left the ground to my concubine in the sky. And when the elevator dinged, how it was impossible not to laugh as the utter lunacy of her standing in the western foreground, juxtaposed to her previous hell, framed by the floor to ceiling windows on the 187th floor. The filthy Piles smoked in the distance.

"What's funny?"

"It's not so much that it's funny, it's that it's absurd."

"Ok, and?"

"You standing there, the surreality of it. How does that old saying go? Like a million bucks?"

"To be honest, I'm quite uncomfortable dressed this way."

"I know, I know my dear, but think of it as your cover, not your clothes. Modesty isn't exactly a virtue where we're headed."

"I understand, but the tiara? The diamond-studded Kato mask, is it necessary?"

"Is the peacock's tail? In this world, conspicuousness is the realization of distinction. Look, one of the fees society levies upon us is The Pose. All Diamonds do it, some better than others, as a sort of necessary evil of selection as it were. The peacock didn't ask for his adornment, in fact, if given a choice he'd undoubtedly prefer a more lithe existence without having to drag that massive train of feathers through the dirt, flaunting it for his predator's saliva. Regardless, he finds himself burdened by evolutionary equipment, so he shows his ass for the world to see because he is genetically programmed for immodesty. And, to put it bluntly, he is subsequently fucked or eaten as a result, maybe both if irony is alive and well. Either way, the world around him points and claps, and sleeps well at night knowing that the improbability of the peacock lives on. We, as circumstances have unraveled, find ourselves in a similar plight, and, to keep the tension of social normalcy properly strung, we show our asses in the best way we know how."

"Alain, you know how I feel about rhetoric tying a person's social standing to natural selection."

"Dear oh dear, my fragrant flower. To even subtly imply that I haven't fully grasped the fragile nuances of your social reality is to place me among the Neanderthals we intend to dine with this evening. Surely you don't think my brow protrudes quite that far, do you?"

"I know you see wider than most, but even the show, The Pose as you describe it, when spoken of in confidence, smarts. It's simplistic, thoughtless and gives no consideration to the pure luck that runs through life like marble's veins."

"Ava, my dear Ava. Everything about our situation is predicated on chance. I'm well aware of this reality now, so much so that when my own personal realities conflict, I do my best to mesh them together to keep everyone smiling nice and wide. You've witnessed the impact. You've seen my change of heart, hell, you spawned it! But, you are on the inside. This façade, this subterfuge, is the necessary step to bring dissidents along over time. We must keep up looks, because frankly that's our best weapon, our only weapon. We are them and they are us. People of stature believe this. Our task is to slowly reapply the transitive property of humanness across social boundaries. Bear in mind, lasting change comes in a thousand little victories won. Bloody revolution is the lazy gamble of the Hail Mary pass."

"And you know me. You know my strength, my resilience. But I'm nervous, I don't know how I'll fare amid these people, in that setting. I'm not accustomed to being someone I'm not. It isn't in me."

"And that's perfectly fine love. You're here to be you. The sheep's clothing is merely the sugar that makes your pill palatable. Look, you're not yet fully tuned to the nuances of behavior in this new world you find yourself. It's not strange for a married man to have a girlfriend or few. I've told you this a thousand times. *It's not strange.* My wife's life is supremely comfortable and that's the only fact that matters to her or anyone else. Anything resembling love between us dried up long ago. I don't expect you to fully understand this, but at least try to continue trusting me the way you did last year. Ava? Please?"

Those eyes. Those hauntingly beautiful eyes. The power and beauty concentrated in the one feature that knows nothing of the disintegrating effects of elapsed time. What the hell were we talking about??? Right...

"Tell me, how would your Auntie A handle this situation, huh?" was how the question went. Oh how she revered that woman and the imbecilic ideas boring through her nutty mind.

"She'd corral them, spit fire into their cozy conventions."

"Hmmm, let's aim for some tact here. Changing minds is about crafting perception, giving people what they want, when they want it. We are the agents of change."

"I know, I know. But this isn't easy. Nothing ever is in this twisted place."

"I love you Ava. From the first time I laid eyes on you," is what I said, her rouged cheeks in my hands, the warmth of them radiating into me.

Enmeshed in a new life, it's amazing how quickly she came around to me. Attention, check. Companionship, check. Stability, check. Protection, check. Security, check. Material indulgence, check and check! A principled woman is exactly that, a woman who stands on principle, and what's more principled than protecting an innocent child's life? Absolutely nothing. How I was on the road to being a changed man, a man of lofty ideals with the power of covert action to implement them. Money be damned! It was that love, that infatuation, infecting an otherwise clear mind. How it all makes sense looking back, her obvious shortcomings, my silly compromises.

"Janice, sweetheart, you stay here with Roger that. Your grandma and I will return late, Ok sweetie?"

"Grandma loves you, Ok sweetheart?"

"IIII know, but I *haaaaate* being alone."

No amount of infatuation ever managed to alleviate the grating sting of juvenile sniveling. Hindsight's 20/20 gives clear eyes to one of the major cracks beginning to run in the otherwise perfect glaze of elopement. Kids fucking suck.

"You're not alone honey. Roger that will take good care of you," Ava pleaded.

"I knowwww."

"Tell you what, I'll sneak into your room when I get back, cuddle with you 'til morning, deal?"

"Deeeeeal. But don't forget to the leave the door open Gramma."

"I know sweetheart, I won't, don't worry."

"Alrighty then, we should move so as not to be late my love. Roger that call the MRAP, we're heading down."

As the elevator descended, it was up to me to provide the oxygen as usual, "a gala of this repute is perfect for your coming out. Imagine that, Ava the debutante!"

"Sure Alain, the silvery, menopausal debutante. It's not in you to charm. Stick to what you do best."

"And what is that my love?"

"Hmmm....grist those uncomfortable silences with your awkward irony, your overly self-indulgent manner that has that odd capability of ringing honest and true. You're not the charmer, you're the jerk whose honest quirk saves him each time his mouth flaps open."

Her smile, and the perfume it puffed over the stench of her words.

"I'm certainly the only man on planet earth touched by such a compliment."

"Alain, you know what I mean. Your warmth, your humanity, is often disguised with some careless verbal slant, a language few can truly understand. But I know you, your heart."

"I know dear, I'm only giving you a hard time. A kiss from my 'pausal polyglot?"

Those lips, how they worked well in many ways.

But, desire is fickle. Wants are tricky, subject to the whims of impulse, the frailty of pride. Here, a gorgeous woman, a graceful beauty whose figure laughs in the face of wilting time, skin defiantly elastic against the orthodoxy of aging. But it's never enough. How she held her own, she did!. Well, at first anyhow. Through the cattiness of exchange, the seething competition, the cornerstone of superficiality propping up society's top echelon.

On the menu that night, the last extant reptile of the order Crocodilia.

A beautiful specimen, a peek back into a simpler, more Oligocene time. A twelve foot long gator fed on a strict diet of butter and French tarragon for the previous thirty-six months. Fat and glistening and filleted alive before our eyes to maintain maximum blood-oxygen levels ensuring the freshest meat possible. Consuming the end of an era, otherworldly.

The usual suspects circled, having paid their five million Credits each for a taste of unparalleled succulence, casting eyes at what they most likely assumed was my evening's arm decor. Expectantly steely, Ava rose to the moment when approached.

"My husband asked me to get your card, he figured, if it's good enough for Alain, must be clean enough for him."

"Tell your husband that if he is unsatisfied with his wife he should invest in a good blindfold, assuming of course, the problem isn't rooted in one of those insidious little odors so mercifully designed as to go unnoticed to its bearer."

The first salvo deflected, returned in kind. Ava leveraged her ample wit to build her social rampart.

Porn Inc's CEO and Head Madame, Mrs. Ableson, was the next attempting to maintain noble purity, targeted me first with,

"Nelling, evening to you. Do explain," a single manicured finger pointing at Ava's face.

"Hello Mrs. Ableson, let me introduce Ms. Ava Singh. Ava, this is Mrs. Ableson, the mastermind of Porn Inc."

"Tell me Ava, where have you been hiding all these years?" Mrs. Ableson asked. "It's as if you were dropped from the sky into our little gathering here."

"Fair question. My most recent position is leading the creative department of Alain's company. I guess you could say I'm the brains helping to shape the future of entertainment, the person pulling the strings of entertainment's future."

"Really now? That's an impressive cover, barely sounds rehearsed. Tell me, what is your take?"

"I'm sorry?"

"Your take, what is it?"

"I'm sorry, I don't quite understand."

"Nelling, you could stand to educate your toys."

"I think you'll find she's perfectly capable of swimming on her own. Her battles are her battles."

"Well then, regardless, I'll double it. Whatever amount he's at, you tell me and it will be doubled. In my business there's been an upswing of interest in the over-fifty category. It looks as though those with means are exploring an age-perversion-thing this season. These John's, oh it's so difficult to keep ahead of their dithering compulsions. Their wants fluctuate puerilely. Under my umbrella, assuming the going fetish doesn't dry up tomorrow, and pardon the glib innuendo please, you stand to generate enough profit to appear alone in this very room in a few short years instead of relying on the fortuitous tether of Nelling's bubbling loins."

"Certainly colorful, and I appreciate your offer of employment. Unlike you though, I've built my career on the faculties of mind rather than the sleight of orifices and I intend to see how far that trick can take me. If Alain here finds reason to move on ahead of next year's gala, perhaps I'll find someone in Beverages or Automobiles who can use my talents."

"A mind whore, I see. Well, some sell their gray, some sell their pink. The real mark of success, my dear, is when you trade exclusively in the colors of others. It's important not to forget who's actually pulling the strings. We'll see if he keeps you around long enough, if so, you might actually figure out why you do what you do. Ciao!"

The lines of stress cracked her brow twenty minutes into the evening, and the pressure didn't relent for a moment as each woman, in succession, pecked away little by little consuming every last morsel of credibility she tried in vain to establish. The new girl around. Slut. Whore. Moron. Fat. Ignorant. Degenerate. Blah, blah, blah. Measured against this. Weighed against that. The many banal social appetizers priming the newbie ahead of the real feast. Ah, the beauty of competition and it's ability to weed out the absolute best of the best. For better or for worse, whether it matters or not. Perception. Perception counts for so much. From her routine, tramping around in the mud, Ava landed in the crucible of refined tastes and manners and as the evening wore on, her thin veneer of patrician luster oxidized as quickly as my libido shriveled. Love and desire, you are so fickle! But what's a date to do? Insult his partner with a safety net of biased endorsement? Coddle a bloody corpse? Hold fast to the illusion of tricking fate? Something always gives. Tell me Jeffrey, put a beautiful marlin in the shark tank and what do you have? A calculable inevitability. Stupid me for thinking otherwise. Stupid me for choosing to mate with the bait.

But it didn't stop, and she continued to tangle up in it. You could see it in her eyes as she fumbled her checkers across the chess board, playing one game with the rules of another. Her understanding of values was quaint if not musty. She misinterpreted vice as a weakness, vulgarity as desperation, gloating as veiled insecurity, vanity as something to powder over, contrivance as playful banter. She didn't seem to realize that elegance only found it's zenith when directly juxtaposed next to something vile. Beauty, along with anything else that holds value in high society, isn't measured in margins, it's defined by crushing magnitudes. When someone feigned sympathy, she didn't realize it was merely bait strung for anyone obtuse enough to commiserate. She couldn't identify allies of opportunity coagulating one minute, dissolving in the next, only to reinstate again moments later. She had no ear for the constantly fracturing melody of association, the bonds of momentary convenience, the evanescence of brotherhood. Relationships, to her, existed within firm boundaries, had defined roles and established codes of conduct. She didn't perceive the selfish fluidity of Homo beatus connection, couldn't code-switch between conversations, was left dumbfounded by the fine art of code inculcation as if it were a flow of pure gibberish from a maniac's mouth. Shit, act like you know! The sad revelation on her part when she, morosely silent, became aware that truth, among Diamonds, held no value beyond its usefulness for initiating arguments. The nuanced social cues, those highly refined procedures meant for navigating the labyrinthine linguistics of Beatus interlocution. Her overwhelming impotence of reply, for those within earshot, was clearly more delicious than the five-million Credit plate of reptile cooling on the crockery before them.

One could almost hear pleasure's goose bumps erecting on the collective skin as she treaded into the dicey realm of morality. Morality, with it's ever-shifting definitions, a difficult subject for the most socially adroit, and one rarely breached except by the most capable, bleeding-edge socialites. A conversational realm for those absolutely absorbed in the slippery facets of what is urgently current, what has crested for its fleeting breath of vogue. To battle in the morality arena, one must constantly study the flux of passions pressuring the social magma upward, passions sparking trends. A person operating in this realm must simultaneously articulate the moment's convention then tear it down in the same stream of thought. To be a moralist, you have to thread the invisible needle of self-contrarianism, remain a diligent student of Hypocrites without ever breaking eye contact, blushing or displaying social bruises by resorting to contemptuous retort. Disassemble people by trashing what you surmise to be their proud, unspoken merits without exposing your own complete lack of them.

Even in her brief attempts at the offensive, it was clear she didn't know how to punch off-balance, her words trailing off to the smugly incessant, Sorry? Sorry? Sorry? A cluster of slitted eyes mockingly searching for a hint of understanding, instead choosing to cast her words as ignoble by refusing to yield basic comprehension of them. Her absolute best defense, her best quality, that simple beauty, was picked apart so thoroughly that halfway through the evening she kept her hands under the table, let her hair eat up her face, as she slowly slumped into a disappearing ball of human shame. Only when her pitiful, cowering eyes found mine did I harness the wherewithal to begin imparting distance with, *well, nothing is truly without flaw, dear*, or, *contentions are at least worthy of consideration, are they not?* And the foolish use of the endearment on my part, how it redirected critical eyes from her, indicted me in her social blunders. Who endears with a slight without using the appropriate intonation? Did I momentarily forget how to use sarcasm? Me, reduced to moron-of-the-moment. But in my defense, the reality of the situation was still catching up to me. I was dumbstruck, blindsided, drunk on love but sobering fast. My intelligence, my strength, my rationality, my power, each called into question by incredulous stares. What's a date to do? Chivalrous man rarely jumps on the pyre, choosing instead to employ a perfectly timed quip as the best method of self-preserving defense. It's just that nothing came to mind. My quiver contained nothing of attack, nothing of use in the battle against what was becoming insanely obvious. What did circle, the thought that *did* play out, that painfully tardy question of social acclimatization in the Beatusphere....is social acclimitization bound by a simple function of time or by a limiting factor of a particularly insidious kind? Maybe all the brains in the world can't compete with the sinister ability to snag the threads of a person's will on the quickly evolving minutiae of decorum. Maybe a large dose of motivation squirted from a huge Motum Ducit helps a person overcome.

And so the night wore on, Ava committing every possible faux pas, shining like an idiot's beacon, distracting me from managing the most salient of social devices, the hierarchy. The persistent measuring, ranking, informing, reinforming, reinforcing of power. All of the aspects one is being evaluated and compared against with respect to the competition. Advantages and disadvantages of respective dinner patrons mentally filed in appropriate buckets and made readily available if needed to maintain order, to prevent the unnecessary social drift or imbalanced caused by an absence of firm attention to relevant disparities. Holding spears out from the towers and defending the status that the brazen, upcoming Diamonds ever so desirously attempt to scale, to acquire, to conquer. Call out his stupidity. Remedy this silly rumor with the 'truth'. Cut him down. Equalize them. Shuffle those. Demean her. Resort it all again. Passive aggression, passive aggression, passive aggression. Define terms for clarity. Clear communication. Clear understanding. Measure. Compare. Measure. Compare. Measure. Compare. State the difference. State it clearly. *I'm wealthier than you. I'm smarter than you. My house is bigger than yours.* Clearly, for everyone to hear, for everyone to make note of. Each person must know where in the hierarchy they exist, constantly. So easy to see now, as I lay dying of Ava's poison, Mr. Ollingford, the fucking throne of Sanitation Inc, literally the purveyor of shit for chrissakes! Ollingford sitting there waiting with a whisper of hanging apprehension for my onslaught, my retort, which never came! This retrospect, so crystal clear now, him sitting left of me with his slab of gator, the piece obviously larger than mine. Me, Alain Nelling. CEO of Watch Inc. Purveyor of Entertainment (not shit), the wealthiest fucker at the table. Everyone taking measure of the fortuitous challenge blindly initiated by some horse's ass server in a cutesy bowtie incapable of accurately reading a fucking seating chart, subsequently depositing the correct lump of dead flesh in the incorrect location. Oh, the endless justifications for the immediate swap, a righting of the obvious social wrong! Instead, my preoccupied mind, overly concerned with a self-inflicted misperception emanating from the paramour charm on my right. Too preoccupied to call out Bowtie's mistake, establish order in the universe, get the deserved, biggest slice of goddamn gator.

My preoccupation, my inattentiveness. So complete that, when the sharks smelled blood in the water caused by the gator gaffe, I wasn't even cognizant of the ensuing pile on until I was buried beneath it. Consummate opportunist and CFO of Salvation Inc, society's wannabe Zen master Dealis Showatra, strategically proffered his koan, aiming to capitalize on my moment of mental absence. And I tripped! Tripped over it in grand fashion. Egg on my face, dick in my hand. Oh Ava, the social damage you caused.

"Alain, what is the feast of fish desired after the fishes' fast?," the question squeaking out between his ridiculous, rhinestonish teeth. Perplexing, no, nonsensical enough that I immediately needed some buffer space to draw sufficient oxygen. Vile words, not gator, causing dyspepsia.

"Sorry Showatra, you were saying?"

"Yes, listen up 'ol chap, the fishes' fast, feasts and such. What have you?"

My mind, a blank, rather, too focused on the strands of thought starting to coalesce into a stratagem for a subtle disentanglement from my flailing, queerly beloved. Distance as quiet offense, quiet rebound. How the fuck did a fish factor into this conversation anyhow? We're still having gator, right?

"I think you're mistaken Showatra, I ordered the gator."

"Indeed you did Nelling, indeed you did! Tell me, does the big gator say later to the idle masturbator when the waiter shits the bed serving a hundred-person plater?"

The laughs. The goddamn cackles of scorn percolating through each dinner-face, utterly blooming with relished sadism at the table. And Ava, a rotting mess in her chair, the catalyst for so much social butchery. *Still* unaware of the breach of portion at this point, was my Ava-diverted mind. I was thrown back on the defensive again; attacking would appear defensive, mocking as deaf or worse stupid, silent as surrender. *What the fuck am I even going up against?* My head was a blur. The rational choice was to plead ill, retreat to organize the future attack. Heed the porcelain throne's beckoning call. Clearly to blame is the horrid cuisine served by this shit hotel, the cuisine these prats are cramming into their faces. Yep, that's it. Set the house on fire and run, just run.

"Good fun here, eh Showatra? You'll pardon me though, this slop posing as hors d'oeuvre is strangling my insides. It appears the best stomachs are the most responsive to attacks. I'll see everyone doubled-over momentarily, excuse me."

A stupid box to put oneself in! As the subsequent orderly digestive processes of the revelers ensued, it become painfully clear the entire night would chalk to failure for me. In silence, my beautiful mistake and I endured the shrapnel from our exploding farce as we gloomily sucked down slim portions of cold reptile. Ten million, poof!

A how? Why even bother? What's the point? Looking over at her, that scream of silence for the entire ride home. Apparently no sorry forthcoming. Not even humored with a conciliatory BJ. How could I fall for such a ruse? Did I honestly believe she was able to conduct herself? Is it hot in here or is it me? A broken spell. She looked like a buck-fifty in a eight million Credit dress. The thought alone of an erection turning my stomach. Where did this notion of elegance originate? Her eyes, something about her ageless eyes? No, her voice. That's what it was. Something about the strength in her voice, the confidence. How, or rather, why did that factor into my actions? Man cannot insert his penis into the voice of another Nelling! Is it hot in here?

Oh right, I forgot, and back at that table. Ollingford returning for a second bite, cowardly nipping at my bleeding carcass.

"Nelling, you look rather peaked, should I call you my doctor? He's good at keeping my regiment up to snuff such that I needn't worry with catching any nasty bugs floating about. I reckon you could probably afford him."

Probably? Asshole. Big guy to jab at someone while their down. Oh and here he goes. Now he's going to drone on about his money? Funny thing, he holds enough money to talk incessantly about it, but not enough to coolly disregard it. That dick never did figure out that the best measure of something that swings is the feeling it gives you, not the fluency with which you can describe it. What to do? I was down and out. Dammit Ava. Is it fucking hot in here or what?

Mr. Charity. Philanthropist in training. Taking a chance on an undeserving woman. Ha! Big ambitions of shaping dialogue, bringing people around to her cause. We're all one, right? Kumbaya my fucking Lord, Kumbaya! Ava, unable to drawn a single breath in high society's undertow. Damn it's hot in here. We're all one right? Each a human being? Our brother's keeper right? Sure Ava. And you can't even survive a simple conversation. Tell me what that adds up to Jeffrey, big shot. Some people just don't have that drive, that killer instinct.

"Are you going to say anything? Huh? Don't just sit there."

Tears. Oh yay, now the fucking tears. They dripped down from her face. I guess my money, my apartment, my food, my clothes, my jewelry wasn't enough. I guess the truly benevolent surrender their pride and social status as well. Bullshit.

"Well?"

She was given over a year of life in an environment well beyond what she could have possibly imagined. I've done my charity. I've proven that I have a heart, that I'm capable of minimizing human suffering. Who else has done what I've done?

"WELL?"

"What do you want me to say Alain?"

...

Goddamn it's hot in here.

Crystalline. A billion diamonds pouring over limestone, glinting madly in the hard beams of noon sun. Fresh water, the type flowing pure from his pierced side. But no blood flowing, and this is clearly why I'm here. The signs are obvious at this point. This doesn't require a mission statement, a strategic plan. There is but one action item and the single attribute required is Abraham's steady hand.

"Children, smile and rejoice, here is life! Take a drink!"

Ahead of my words, they are bent at the water's edge lapping handfuls of God's purest sacrament. The warmth of His grace shining down upon this day. Fear. There is no reason to fear. There is no reason, fallible and self-serving. There is only this.

She stands in the tree line, watching over us. Quiet, forlorn. She is no threat. Perhaps an angel, here to witness and report back. Or maybe Iblis prepared to whisper a competing proposal. Either way a cog. A cog in this spiritual dance. The intermittent chirping of birds, leaves rustling.

"Kids come gather 'round, let us pray."

"But Daddy, your device is dead. How will we make the call?"

Smart girl, but she's not onto the plan. Or is she? No. Shrouded in her own innocence, there is no pain.

"I know sweetie, but, we are going to do it the way I did as a child. The old fashion way. Us, alone, holding hands, giving thanks. Now come in close, Muhammad, hold my hand, Magdalene, you do the same.

Tired. The journey has taken it out of them. Not too much longer dears. *Weile, Weile, Waile.*

"Heavenly father, we humbly come to you on this day of atonement in order to seek forgiveness and give thanks for your mercy. Please find it in your heart to wash us clean of our sins, to grant us rebirth in the Kingdom of God. It is in the spirit of great sacrifice that I beg you to accept these debits into your ledger as an offset to my previous improprieties."

She stares at us, sobbing now, at the edge of the clearing. Inching her way in. Come what may.

"Kids, sit here with daddy on this rock. That's right, sit here. Lay down, relax in the sun. Let us take a moment to relax. Lay back, close your eyes. Warm yourselves in the sun. God's eternal light."

She bawls now, uncontrollably. Her lips move, emulating speech, but light is all that comes out. Wavelengths of color, not sound. And still, she inches closer.

Thuds and attempts at scramble. Entirely expected. Sheep bleating, they tend to do that. Flailing, yes, what do you expect? Moist, packing noises. Slaps and bizarre hand-paintings. Grunts, gulps of air. Moans and rhythmic thumping. Fish out of water, the perversity of uncommon movement. Hold it all still. Eyes squinting through the pinhole of reality. Sputtering. A car that won't start. The freeing of the damned. The final jolt of human electricity fouling the muscles. Silent bookkeeping nets the ledger, the pans finding peaceful equilibrium along a single plane. The apparition of two little souls rising into heaven.

Still she stands at a distance shuddering, doesn't retreat. Moves forward in fact, as if there is no where else to go. Come what may, there is no fear my child.

Quiet. No birds. Only the faint whisper of song filling the empty space between her and I.

There was an old man and he lived in the woods, weile weile waile.
There was an old man and he lived in the woods, down by the river Saile.

He had a baby three months old, weile weile waile.
He had a baby three months old, down by the river Saile.

He had a penknife, long and sharp, weile weile waile.
He had a penknife, long and sharp, down by the river Saile.

He stuck the penknife in the baby's heart, weile weile waile
He stuck the penknife in the baby's heart, down by the river Saile.

There were three loud knocks come a'knocking on the door, weile weile waile.
There were three loud knocks come a'knocking on the door, down by the river Saile.

There were two policemen and a Special Branch man, weile weile waile.
There were two policemen and a Special Branch man, down by the river Saile.

They took him away and they put him in the jail, weile weile waile
They took him away and they put him in the jail, down by the river Saile.

They put a rope around his neck, weile weile waile.
They put a rope around his neck, down by the river Saile.

They pulled the rope and he got hung, weile weile waile.
They pulled the rope and he got hung, down by the river Saile.

And that was the end of the man in the woods, weile weile waile.
And that was the end of the baby too, down by the river Saile.

The song, from so long ago. Daddy's favorite, sung on sour breath, craven eyes. Spoiling bread's crusty foam encircling the glass's rim. Mother's eyes, white in the black of the room, black in the white of the room. Redemption. Exhaustion. Safety.

Her hands are up now, reaching out to me. And she keeps walking toward. Tears still fall, heavy sobs, but the sharp emotion fades as she succumbs to the world around her. Hands still up, reaching to me now. She wants me to pick her up, important to proceed with caution though, not because of fear. Because of diligence.

Squatting, her level. A wee pink dress, muddy and torn. Smudges on a porcelain face. Her eyes, shut. No world. She starts, but the sobs consume it.

Memories of scrapped knees. Broken promises. The wretched horror of time-out. And here we are, at this, our moment on redemption's rebound.

A touch, a simple touch should suffice. Tuck a few strands of golden brown behind her little conch shell. Placidity. Not forced, realized, merely through the intersection of human flesh. And the words, they seems to just flow...

"What is wrong my child, why do you cry?"

Her baby blues capture God's broken light shining through the trees, everything's alright. "Speak to me my dear. What ails you? Why do you cry so?"

Eyes. She looks up into mine, light shining from behind hers. She gives a start, this time, a brief stutter, then,

"I can't find the door!"

A man sitting slumped against a tree. Motionless and speckled by the last threads of sunlight working their way through the tree's low-hung canopy. A songbird perched on his shoulder watches the world pass with regal eyes, its head carelessly flipping side to side. Suddenly it's clear. The oddity of learning of a man's death through the eyes of a fearless bird. *Death?* The blanket he wears, draped across his chest and legs, substantive.

"Valerie, stay close sweetheart. Let's go over there, to the backside of that first building. Stay close Ok honey?"

"Yes Gramma."

Shadows lengthen, our silhouettes glide across the wall of red-orange glass. Two tall, thin creatures carelessly strolling in the evening sun on a distant planet. The ground, a dry patchwork of flakey dirt, weeds, bits of trash twisted and mashed within. Nothing useful.

Step, step, breathe. Search. Step, step, breathe. Search.

The light of day, a disappearing promise. The memory of morning, of waking, as the mind desperately avoids, yet eventually falls into yesterday's rut.

Step, step, breathe. Search. Step, step, breathe. Search.

On the cool evening breeze, death wafts intermittently. The ground underfoot passes unceremoniously; a scuff, a stumble, micro events compiled into an obligatory forward motion. Possessed by this world.

Step, step, breathe. Search. Step, step, breathe. Search.

But there's nothing useful. Nothing.

Salt from Maven's last tear. Eyes stinging. Valerie's blithe egocentrism, its crushing consequences. The inadvertent evil of innocence.

The shame of loss and the bitter joy of beautiful memories. A self-indulgent wallow back through guilt for nothing more than a moment's reprieve from the pressing anxiety. This constant manipulation of emotions and the foul uncertainty about all the little things that should be classified as mundane: Eating. Drinking. The constant energy required to take absolutely nothing for granted.

Step, step, breathe. Search. Step, step, breathe. Search.

"Valerie, let's walk to the building's edge, search for puddles."

A vapor trail divides the sky overhead and the howl of vortex shedding bounces off the glass buildings as an airplane returns home after dropping its payload. To the right, a tidy row of forgotten shrubs edge the building, dry and barren. To the left, the steep drop-off into the vast drop fields, wherein Maven's body returns to mother earth. Myriad insects consuming, digesting, thriving off flesh. A microscopic mouthful at a time. Energy.

Calculating the last time it rained, but indistinguishable days collapse into one another. Time's a blur. Time without meaning. Recent rain though, this is no drought. But the divots and the nooks, the minor impressions that could hold water, don't, and appear as though they never will. Thirst, the petulant assailant, unappeasable and unreasonable, screaming louder the longer you deny it. The cruel bluff of the mirage, the tease of intermittent saliva. Cotton that won't go away.

Along the building, nothing. Step after step. "Valerie, please catch up honey."

How she ruffles, slumps. Conditioned to obstinance. Denial does that. Programmed to pout. Children shouldn't have to feel pain. The lie of innocence for poor kids

"Come on sweetheart. Come up here with Gramma. We're going to stop soon. Let's look for a decent place to bed down, and at first light, we'll cross back over the drop fields. Head home. The break in the shrubs, see that? Let's go over there."

Ripped out by their roots and cast aside, the resultant nook is a decent place to hideaway for the night. The pulled shrubs, dry and brittle, snap and crunch when tossed aside. Nicks and scraps mottle the roots, teeth marks of someone who hit rock bottom. Is there moisture stored in the roots, enough to make the effort worthwhile? Is this a technique I've neglected? Doubtful, most leaves have browned, fallen off. Could try digging for ground water. With what? Tired fingers into hard, dry clay? *Death?*

"Hold on a minute while I clear us a spot sweetheart." Plastic bags and disintegrating scraps of cardboard. Bits of torn cloth and random chunks of metal piled together. Nothing. Brush it under adjacent bushes, spread the cloth swatches. "Here you go honey, sit down here."

Exhausted she falls to her knees, crawls into place. Kneeling before the giant tower she reaches a hand up to touch the glass, her fingers caress it. She removes her hand, looks at her fingers in disbelief. The first time touching a structure made of something other than plastic and tin. She pushes on it, hard. Again. Slaps it.

"How come it doesn't move?"

"It's made of very strong materials sweetheart. Steel, concrete and glass. That's how it can stand so tall."

Just as quick she loses interest, lies prostrate before the glass giant, places her head on her stacked hands.

"Are you tired baby?"

"Yes Gramma, very tired."

"That's a good girl. Relax, get some rest, I'm going to look around for a minute. I'll stay within sight. Call if you need me, Ok?"

Facing west, the sun's but a sliver poking up from the horizon. A few black specks in the distance, ants moving across mounds of trash-strewn earth. The breeze carries night's chilly reminder and the stench of a land forgotten. Underneath the tree he still sits, his feathered companion since flown. Valerie's eyes, closed, as the sun winks out of sight leaving a marbled curtain; red, orange, and purple stretching to infinity.

Several minutes of light remain. Several minutes to ready for the night. He doesn't need his blanket. Dry earth crunches as throbbing feet press down. Headache. Backache. Hunger's sour bloat. Bite the inside cheek to stimulate that metallic ooze of saliva.

The wind curls his hair against its natural part. His bony hands, atop the blanket, clasp one another in silent repose. A face, sallow and gaunt, but placid, resigned. Legs are outstretched, toes of one foot poking from beneath the blanket. A calloused, mangled knob. No toenails, only thick, rough, brown-yellow skin worked into a sort of cracked, worn-out shoe leather. Time ticking. Scattered are the many fallen hearts of the man's sheltering catalpa. Yellow eyes stare glassy through mine. The natural, upward curve of his thin lips. Upon wasted shoulders, white clots hold fast to bits of shedded down dancing in the breeze. Pockmarks dot his clavicle, the Morse code etchings of a bird. Gentle tug and the blanket slides across his ribcage.

Naked apart from a loin cloth, skin-covered femurs rest akimbo. Valerie, against the building, motionless in the background, facedown. The whole world described in two juxtaposed figures. The lifecycle of humans condensed to poignancy. That pivotal moment where survival did or did not occur. A precipice everyone leans over to watch fortunes either materialize or quietly fade into oblivion. The energy expended, with life, life! teetering on the balance. Stuck in the never-ending continuum of paradoxes defining life. Evil or circumstance? Both? Omniscient or calculable? Both? Maybe the question never mattered, and the universe keeps expanding regardless. What's in a name anyway? Maybe He triggered it and maybe He didn't. And at the end, what of it even matters. Push on with the hope that the next moment will be better than the current one, without knowing what *better* is supposed to mean. Fulfilling a need? Earning a smile? Clenching a victory? Just names, labels. Labels for perceived phenomena. Perception, an undertaking to achieve comfort with the unknowable. What the fuck am I doing? Valerie's chilly by now.

Humph, I let it drag on the ground yet I give it the sniff test? A blanket removed from a dead man's body. The games we play, the justifications we invent, the pretty lies we manufacture out of the few shreds of knowledge that fortuitously find their way to us. A world of contradiction.

She snuggles the shroud laid across her back, a quiet moan, eyes remain closed. Her tongue plays in her mouth, searching, as she pulls a handful of blanket beneath her chin. Her breathing resumes cadence.

Should I search? Only scant light, plus we've been at it for hours. Maybe a short rest, then look for something to dig with? Some of those metal chunks? What if water's only a few feet down? Is an hour of pain worth the prospect of relief? No, that's the wrong question. Can an hour's sweat assume a strong probability of replenishment? Survival economics.

Death? So. *Are* we going to die this week? Why avoid? Why continue avoiding the thought percolating into all others? Acting as if it's a ridiculous question makes it seem even more plausible. But what's the point, why consider the unknown? To give circumstance a tidy answer? A name. Another one of life's cute paradoxes. Kneel and pray, or stand on principle and go defiant into the ground? A schismatic brain wanting to fuse itself back together again. I could certainly live without the passion of thought Mr. Kierkgaard. So what now?

Dig. The best option. Keep digging until you hit something. Scratch at the earth, peel back its layers. Search for something tangible. Stop avoiding it. Search for something that can drip.

Metal into earth. Earth into a pile. Repeat.

There is one truth comprised of several truths.

The dirt of someone's forgotten child collecting into a dry mound next to my feeble hole. And this damn dirt gets harder and dryer the deeper in.

"Why don't they help us?" she asks.
"Because they don't know," would be my reply.
"Why don't we tell them?" she then asks.
"The chasm is too wide," would be my reply.
"But I can help with Maven," she would say.
"I know sweetheart, I know," would be my reply.
"Then why don't we try?" she would ask.

"Because some things aren't worth risking," would be my reply.

The dirt, turning to stone. Stoic, deadpan. Impenetrable, hardpan. The stone, growing out wider. Scratch the walls of the hole. Clawing at the exposed tip of some buried monolith. The sensibility of sweat conservation. Fluidity of thought. Stop digging Sariya.

The air cools as fog rolls in. A yellow glow stretches through the fog from around the far corner of the building, the front of the building. Worth a look, a quick look. To know facts, not wonder at possibilities.

The crusty earth doesn't yield, my presence kept a secret. A whirring noise, something mechanical, and the sound of muffled voices. Cheek to the building's cool glass and a slow forehead pivot to hang an eye out over the building's corner. A slide projector, the image pushing into the frame from right. Hot flashes. Immobilization.

"So what are we supposed to think? Your brassiere is loaded with cash, there isn't a scratch on you."

"I don't know, what can I say? He said it was for my trouble, my unwanted involvement. I guess he felt guilty. Actually, guessing isn't necessary, he told me he felt guilty."

"Of course you see how that's difficult to believe, right? I mean, he yelled of your execution for several hours."

"I'm not suggesting that this is somehow normal, in fact, anything but. I don't pretend to know the contours of your typical day, but for me this day has been pretty goddamn strange."

"Do uh...*D'you know him?*"

"Are you asking me if I was involved with him? In this plot?"

"No ma'am, I'm simply asking if you knew this man. If you've had any interaction with him prior to today, on any level at all."

"No. I don't know him from Adam. Well, I didn't."

"What's that supposed to mean?"

"Well, a few hours ago, I met this man for the first time in my life. When he abducted me at the teller, demanded cash."

"And?"

"And, well I guess you could say he was rather verbal."

"Alright, meaning?"

"Meaning, he spoke a lot while holding me captive, shared some personal thoughts with me. We discussed family, our backgrounds, things of the sort."

"Ok, so I guess you can provide some insight as to why he did this, why he left you in such *good* shape."

"No, I have nothing unless you're curious about his happy childhood, the wife he loved or how much he adored his kids. If you have questions perhaps you shouldn't kill the person with the answers."

"You aren't serious? He was holding a gun to your head."

"It was a plastic toy."

"Right, easy to see that now, of course. Look this is distracting from the point."

"Which is?"

"Which is, you're saying that in five hours of talking he said nothing of *why* he did any of this?"

"That is exactly what I'm saying. Although, I could use my powers of deduction and arrive, rather quickly, at the conclusion that he was in a financial situation and needed money. But then again, I'm not a detective."

"That's cute. You realize how convenient all of this is, right?"

"Convenient how? My life's been under threat all day, and now, you guys. Look, this is my first time as a hostage, so maybe I'm missing something here. But, the fact that my kidnapper didn't disclose to me his motivation for robbing a bank doesn't exactly strike me as odd. You know what, I take that back. It does! Everything about today is fucking odd, and now the pleasure of being harassed by you gentlemen which I also find perfectly fucking odd as well."

"We're investigating a crime ma'am."

"Good, excellent, do what you need to do. In the meantime, may I see my husband and kids? I'm sure they are worried sick at this point."

"We'll get to that shortly, we still have a few more questions."

"This is insane. Haven't I been held at gunpoint long enough today? Whatever happened to the presumption of innocence?"

"Mrs. Voyes, you have it all wrong. The courts may be concerned with questions of innocence, we're here to accuse."

...

Guns. One, two, three. No, four, five, ...six. And more. Seven, ...eight, nine. Large, angry men yelling.

"DIRT! DIRT! DIRT! GET THE FUCK IN THE LIGHT OR WE'LL SHOOT!"

A semicircle of black-clad men punch at the dark with outstretched barrels, screaming. Screaming at little 'ol me. I have nothing, says my empty hands.

"WHO IS WITH YOU!"

With me? "No one, I mean..."

"Why the hell are you out here, what are you doing here?"

"I'm...my daughter and I. I mean my granddaughter and I are...we, we're just looking for food, some water. I..."

"THREE, wrench her arms behind her! EIGHT and NINE, secure a shoulder each! TEN, muzzle to her temple, now!"

Shooting pains, arms introduced to unknown positions. Eyes squirt in response. Precious liquid on exit. More combatants circle around. One man, dainty and without a weapon, looks on curiously from a distance. His squinted stare. Like trying to remember me. He advances quickly.

"Loosen your grip, guard."

The blood starts pumping back through as he walks up, assesses my face. Apart from a nervous twitch on the corner of his lips, he's composure defined. Airbrushed picture perfection. Nothing out of place. Nothing lacking or skewed in any fashion. Proportion, sufficiency, articulation, rhythm merge into one. Oddly crisp.

"What's your name?"

Name? My name? What's in a name? How could my whisper-of-a-name hold any meaning for you? Call me what you wish. This name, a clean way to identify, to label. The concise manner in which we sort ideas, build reference points, merely for expediency's sake. Me with my name. I often call myself guilt, staring down history with the eyes of a skeptic, the heart of a believer. Staring you down with a passivity borne of the tired longing for solace. So, when you know my name, what's next? I can utter anything at the point of a gun. I can make God find his way back to me as he whirls like a dervish down the spiraled rifling of your hired hands. But in this neither of us will find a speck of truth. The only path to truth is the painstaking journey through the long form. Point and counterpoint balanced against one another ad infinitum to whittle reality down into its atomic parts. Parts then slammed together to understand basic reactions, and there, emerging as pure energy, is the one truth comprised of several truths. Our happy little paradox. If you took the time to reach out though, to understand, you wouldn't need to know my name. You'd have something much more valuable, and so would I. If you cared, you could have, at no cost, the thoughts, the ideas, that flow through my living, breathing soul. All of us, victims of these superficial labels, these names. All of us wedged into a narrow set of expectations. Nobody wants the long form. Nobody wants to soak in the uncomfortably cooling bathwater of nuance. A binary world is much more mathematically precise, much more sane. Coddled or discarded based on a name. But what's in a name? What's in my name? I am the nobody. I am the Dirt, obviously, that's my name. Call me Dirt. Someday, maybe we can learn to not know, to not choose. The beautiful vulnerability of the not knowing. The incredible wisdom in accepting indecision. The trust borne of deferral. And if we did this, maybe I wouldn't feel obliged to call myself guilt. Instead, I could be Sariya, or, simply a thing called 'me'. Has anyone ever been this thirsty? But until then, I must meet your expectations. And mine too. I need to live so that she can survive. Because, what else are we going to do? So, I guess this is where we dance. Open your mouth with care Sariya, lest your internals come pouring out like a river. My name? My ridiculous, insignificant name.

"Ava. Ava Singh. Would you kindly ask these men to return my arms to me?"

Amazing. Nothing short of spectacular! A most gorgeous specimen, each one of his attributes finely tuned to that impossible specification resting hopeful in my mind's recesses for decades. Everything tingling, everything just wants to squirt, my body, some sort of quivering bird, newborn and still wet. A chill splintering across moist, matted downy kissed by a breeze. Like the first breath taken, a look at this fine young man, Alvin Tan they say. Life suspended. Time held in pause for the first pitch of his voice. Hoping, praying for that delicious warble of vocal chords still under the process of elongation. He walks across the room, an *artiste* (ohh Lord yes, put that extra fucking 'e' on it for me!) of the catwalk, anything but demure, an explosion of inhibitions shooting sparks for appreciative, awestruck eyes. A splendor to behold. This moment's gravity, a throwback to my birth into couture, my introduction to the delicately nuanced aesthetics of high fashion. A simple factory tour as politicians do from time to time. A simple tour forever altering perspective. A routine factory tour on the design floor of Apparel Inc.

...

Sitting there, hoisted decadently on his throne of sweaty men, men interlocked into an exquisite chaise of flesh and blood. He alone wielded the power to summon the Gods of Appeal while looking down upon his panel of creative directors with the critical eye's doubtful squint.

"We're not pushing hard enough!" his shrill voice sang. "The Spring line is less than six months away and this is shit, what you are showing me is pure shit! To compete with food, to compete with soap, to compete with the basic necessities of life, we must push boundaries, we must entice consumers in new ways! Fashion people! Fashion and its inextricable link with sex. Fashion *is* sex, period. Sex couldn't even exist without fashion's foreplay! The entire procreativity of mankind hangs in the balance! We need to push the envelope further! You know what? Screw the fucking envelope, let's fly right through it, without regard, without a single stress test. *We are the pioneers. We* are the cartographers of taste, of refinement, of desire! Now come on team, Springtime, I'm thinking flowers, green shoots, fertility, rebirth, the softness of new fuzz, the breaking of winter's fast, the yellow beams of sun teasing life from chilly, rain-soaked earth! Let's push this to an entirely new realm of thought! Thought beyond thought. The sort of thought stimulated only by the synesthetic broodings, broodings that yield salivary squirts at the first glance of a bold, new color! Thought that itself becomes the precious seed of copulation, the carnal yearning to go beyond decency, to rearrange one's own sense of sexuality!" Scurveus' team was in a frenzy, whipped up into a orgy of creativity that was bound to give birth to the epitome. Fashion perfected on humble planet earth. His eyes, heavily shadowed in black, the irises spinning a dizzying array of digital sparks around his pupils, surveyed the troops, while his wasting pale frame shifted uncomfortably atop a perspiring plateau of entangled underlings.

The first Creative stepped onto the hot plate. Far too singular and aloof to bear an ordinary name, his name, a clever little palindrome, right? Something about cats?

"Yes, you, Senile Felines, what have you got for me?"

"Well sir, I'm thinking dicey boundaries, teasing the consumer with the speckled-stub of pubic hair sprouting from the crotch of a fresh face. A girl with a sort of alienesque beauty, overly elongated features, immense almond eyes. The sprouting pubes reminiscent of Spring's eternal regrowth!" his voice an affected Received Pronunciation, passionately torqued and sounding as though bleated through a paper towel roll.

"NO, never! Pubes are so overdone, so last decade! Who tries to sell with pubes anyhow? And what the hell on God's-blue-green-ball-of-chaos am I paying you dolts for? Think!"

"But sir," aghast, "You don't understand! I'm not talking about the unkempt fringes of the triangle. What I'm saying is that we come from behind, āni pūbēs! Delicate and mysterious, forbidden yet curious! No clothing on the model, *of course*, just a sheer satin cloth draped across the naked back of an disgustingly gorgeous nymph, the cloth parting ways with decency right at the point of her upwardly arched anus, the whiskers sprouting in circular perfection around those delicate radial wrinkles."

The room, and the silence borne of a creative outburst. Eternity quickly evaporated.

"Lame! A cheap riff on last year's success," shouted a wild-eyed Scurveus. "Listen folks, we are in the fashion industry, *WE ARE ICONS*! There are expectations the world places on us! Think people, let's push this to a newly created stratosphere! You, Verruche Anali, what have you got?"

"Sir, I'm thinking flowers, Springtime, nothing but flowers. I'm thinking labia, engorged, excessively large labia. Generous folds! Ten models, no, twenty! All cramped into a life-sized planter box perched ornately below the glistening yet wavy panes of antique beveled, leaded glass. The models, lying spread-eagle, with legs overflowing the rim of the planter box like so many searching vines, perfectly nude, *of course*, each with their hypertrophied genitals sprouting forth Spring's most urgently crimson fecundity!"

Silence. Billions of meteor shower eyeballs darting silently. The moment clung precariously from anticipation's edge. Permission to breathe was collectively revoked, individually enforced.

"It will never work!" Scurveus brayed, simultaneously twisting two of his five nipples (the rumor, if remembered correctly, was that he surgically added three additional nipples, shirt-button fashion, down his centerline to better align his pilomotors with the pentatonic scale for maximum aural stimulation. However, as is often the case with demigods, the rumors took on a life of their own increasing the mystique, the wonder, shrouding this iconoclast). "It's cheap sex, nothing more. We're not challenging our consumers to think deeper, to push the boundaries of what fashion aims to represent. To leave a mark on culture by staking the stick of haute couture to the sheer ridge of necessity!"

Silence again. The overbearing processing power of the collective minds, neurons overheating, inching the mercury to Mars.

"Wait, I have it! Yes! Listen and learn people. I see a speculum, shiny and understated in it's clinical sanitariness. A woman's flower, up close, no clothes, *of course*, splayed open for a view of the ultimate representation of Springtime's regeneration, the egg! A magnifying glass, hovering over a single ovum, recently discharged from the Isle of Fallopia and resting expectantly on a carpet of warm red satin, waiting for the initiation of metamorphosis, waiting for the consumer to engage, to become one with the new fashion! And the woman! She should be gorgeous! No, I mean repulsive! Yes, the woman will be utterly repulsive! Asymmetrical, lipless, foreheadless...all chins and ears with narrow, cross-set eyes! Let us split the purchasing mind into a basic dichotomy, blunt sex on the one hand, a desire for social conformity on the other, and focus exclusively on the half that urges the sale based on nothing more than carnal desire to procreate, and, no less, with the mandatory assistance of a paper bag or two!"

The crashing wave of applause filled the room as a sea of heads nodded feverishly, lips quaking, eyes tearing. For once, the word "genius" wasn't tainted by the stink of hyperbole. Scurveus, his angular frame anchored to the slippery manthrone, calmly receiving the impassioned accolades and wincing grunts rightfully due a fashion eclecticist with infinite insight into human elegance. A aesthete so over-programmed for beauty that his ideas themselves became black holes, sucking in entire universes of visual perfection. Chagall's flowers never looked so hopelessly uninspired.

But wait, here. Here in this moment. Here is where we sit! This Alvin Tan, what a specimen, what a treat! A light brush of that Oriental mystique, a splash of malty brown in his smooth flesh, the still soft yet rapidly thickening hair of hebetic years.

He's sitting there, this man. But who is he, what does he want from *me*? What the hell have I been chosen for? How is it that I'm lucky? A trap? Is this a trap, are they on to me? John? The sweat, pouring down my back, trickling down behind my ears. Heavy beads hanging on my forehead, tickling. Action? Time for action Pham?

His face. Worn shoe leather with medallions of loose tissue drooping on opposite hemispheres, a network of broken capillaries running over his bulbous, irritated red nose. Scrotal eyelids dangle flaccidly, halfing his vision. Old. A very old man. An unrepressed obscenity, hungry eyes devouring everything his doughy paunch desires. How he stares at me, lascivious, the next meal. Golden twinkles on boney fingers and wrists, dispersing the dim light overhead. His suit, the fabric, the gentle, luxuriant folds screaming of exceptional refinement, insane measures of wealth. Sparse hair carefully coiffed, shiny and overly uniform like some plastic bowl curving around the dappled sunspots of an elongated forehead. A nauseating smile blooming on the chapped, rubber-band lips of an old goat. Somebody else's teeth revealed, someone larger, much younger and more robust. Nothing held back, nothing concealed. All the world's unearned pride displayed on the disintegrating mug of a decrepit suit and tie. But, who exactly? And why me? John? John, are you there?

Supple. The word keeps flipping through my mind. The supple nature of a young body. Falling without breaking, stretching without tearing, bending without snapping, suggestive without judgment. Pliable. In his chair he sits, sinks down too much to be child, just enough to be man. Eye contact doesn't break. His scent, light and airy with a whiff of that pubescent stink bleeding through. Perfection. A truffle melting in the mouth. Teasingly, he claws at his waistline, adjusting. Bulges bulging generously in all the right locations. Flits of aphrodisiac-infused adrenaline.

The gun, how it grinds into my hip, painful. Shift it gingerly, release pressure, without shooting a leg off or giving myself away. Focus. Action. Man of Action. Aphamli Twist is a Man of Action, and I fear not. I am a Man of Action and I'm here to burn the house down.

"So nice to meet you."

An arthritic, knuckly hand, a tangle of ropy veins and gaudy gold rings. Flickering gemstones and a few resilient hairs not yet claimed by senescence. Dry and scaly to the touch, shaking hands with a burlap bag. "Likewise, sir, though, I'm not exactly clear as to why I'm here. Perhaps you can help me?"

Oh, so direct! So to-the-point! The disposition of which real men are made! "Yes, yes, oh I can imagine. My staff tends to lack polish when it comes to these types of situations. But fear not, we'll get to the necessary details in short order. But, and if you wouldn't mind of course, indulge me briefly with a synopsis of yourself. Nothing too involved mind you, a few simple items, say, your age, where you are from, your interests, and, oh I don't know, what you want to *be* when you grow up."

He even smells old, a sort of baby powder mixed with accidental farts peering through the rancid fog of periodontal disease. But he's perking, swelling, and it's clearly me, I'm having this effect on him. Go with it. This is the part where I hold on and go with it. Relax. Relax and focus. Focus on focusing. Be here in the moment, in this moment. Be here. John always said the key to relaxation is to remain absolutely, unequivocally present. "Ok, sure, that's not a problem. Well, for a start my name's Alvin, Alvin Tan. I'm 17 years old as of May and I live in Block XZ. As far as what I want to be? That's a difficult question. You know, I'm not really certain at this point. I guess I'm interested in keeping my options open for as long as possible, find the path best suited for me at the right time. Too often it seems, we commit to paths we know little about, favoring a sort of blind perseverance to actual happiness. I hope that's not too vague Mr.... I'm sorry, I didn't catch your name."

"Ortiz, my name is Zuberi Ortiz, but please, feel free to call me Beri."

"Ok, Beri, it's nice to meet you."

"Oh no young Alvin, the pleasure resides entirely with me. Tell me, how does someone your age garner such an expansive perspective of the future anyhow? Most boys your age struggle to suppress a boner when a pretty girl struts by let alone speak to the *variety of opportunity* gained through the *virtue of patience*! Ha! And really, pardon my tone, it's not sarcasm, I assure you. I'm delightfully shocked by your maturity. It's odd in the absolute best sort of way."

"I'm not exactly sure sir, I guess..."

"Beri, please. Sir is far too formal for this conversation. Please call me Beri."

"Yes, Beri. Like I was saying, I'm not exactly sure but I've always been closer to books than people. I guess I matured early." His look, penetrating if not outright disturbing.

"And there it is, a young man ripe early for the picking. All head and no shaft! Oh the sublime constipation of intellectualism! But, sadly we are short of time here, so let's not fantasize in the moment, but rather, delay gratification in a manner fit for the mentally continent. My boy, you are here as those before you, brushing up against opportunity, testing your booties for grip on the starting line of life's fast track."

"I'm sorry, but that doesn't exactly clear things up." My eyes and my crotch sharing his eye's attention in equal part. One to the other then back again. He's on to something, but playing it cool. Poised. Remained poised. No, relax. Stay relaxed and focused. Relaxation is the zenith of stayed focus.

His carefully suppressed fear attempts to hoodwink me, no? He doesn't shrivel, not one bit. His game, complex, off-balancing. Intentionally so? Sweat beads on his forehead, but these perfectly composed words. An anomaly. A carefully managed contradiction? "Today, as you well know, is the release of the new Palette. My team has hand-selected several candidates for me to interview with one, hopefully, being selected as the Product Ambassador for this launch - the Iron representative if you will. Some candidates were chosen among those with exceptionally high academic marks. Others, like yourself, were selected from today's crowd by my staff based on, shall we say, *other positive attributes*."

He has forgotten my eyes. "I see. But therein lies an assumption, right? That I'm interested in being a, I'm sorry did you say *Product Ambassador*?"

Feisty! A reply straight from the gut with the tone of a stiffening cock! This one holds back nothing! There's no fear, only a delectable squirt of testosterone! A taught bubble of hormones waiting for a little prick. There is no need for these gloves, let the bare-knuckle pugilism begin! "Yes, you heard correctly, Product Ambassador, but.............*Alvin*?" Let's turn up the heat.

"Yes?"

"Shall we talk as men? Put this whimsy conversational bullshit behind us? I don't want to continue insulting your intelligence by being so unnecessarily oblique."

...THIS IS CALLED A LONG PAUSE. A TINY SPACE IN THE UNIVERSE WHERE TWO PEOPLE STARE ONE ANOTHER IN THE EYES, CAPTIVATED BY ANTICIPATION, AND LISTENING CLOSELY FOR THAT NEXT SHOE TO DROP...

"Yeah, that's preferable." What the hell is this? John? There is no plan. Relax. Pull everything into this moment. Pure focus.

"Well let's get to it then shall we? Clearly there's an uneasiness in the ranks over certain legislative changes placing some at, well, let's call it a *disadvantage*. To mitigate the damage caused by these changes, we offer today's carrot, today's much anticipated product launch. And, for free nonetheless. Politics, maneuvering! Am I coming in clear?"

"Yes, I think I follow what you're saying." Relax. Focus. Let things come.

"Good. Second to that is, what we call in this business, messaging. You could call it one of the reasons you are sitting in that very chair at this very moment. Is this coming in clear?"

"Ok, I see, so a sort of mouthpiece is needed. As you said, an Ambassador. Someone to speak on behalf of the Irons?"

"Yes, *impressive, very* good. You're certainly not of typical stock I see. Now, are you ready for the brass tacks?" Is he sharp? Is he lucky? Maybe a boy who possesses the innate ability to navigate the emergent textures of a quickly developing situation? Let's indulge, assume sharp, he hasn't stumbled yet. Oh Christ, how precocity makes me want to squeal like a teakettle!

"Let's continue on." Fingers to the waistband, slowly. Focus above all else.

"So, you. You are a *poor whittle guy* whose lottery ticket just... Hit! The. Numbers. BAM! Your current existence, living in some cramped hovel in The Blocks, typifies the lifestyle of your kind, your Iron brethren if you will. Unaided, you will continue on through that shit-of-a-life for many years to come, scratching out a living on what is mercifully trickled from above. I'm here as, well, let's say the lottery administrator, offering to help you cash-in that ticket which has fallen so fortuitously in your lap. Still clear?"

"I'd say so, you don't exactly mince words." Me over you. You into me. Demean me, own me. Establish position, reinforce it. The universal banality of hierarchy. Focus. Relax. Think.

"Wonderful! Now, this world is full of opportunities, but as they used to say there's no such thing as a free lunch my friend. Everyone, to a man, will exact his price in the end. And so, we are talking about two components of price, the price to cash in that lottery ticket. First, and for someone of your clearly abundant verbal ability, what I presume is an easy task to complete. We need an articulate young gent to handle a highly specialized component of our broader message. Dressed as you are, in that oddly hopeful mothball-of-a-suit, you are to stand among your comparatively dressed brothers and sisters and identify with them, woo them, explain to them the value, the benefit, the freedom and sheer joy derived from being a recipient of today's amazing product. You will explain to them, in a language they clearly understand, the vast improvements in life one gains from this new technology. We'll, of course, assist you with some of the finer talking points, a few items that must be communicated. The rest, however, is up to your discretion. You make the connection. You corral the flock. You help them to understand why life is So, God, Damn, Good! Why playing the merry game of civilized society is worth it. But realize please, we are not solely about the threats, we here prefer, in fact, loooooove the sedation of a tasty carrot. Salesmanship, yes? I need to know, are you capable?"

"Yeah, I mean, yes. I imagine I could do that. I've been told I'm persuasive, can talk people into submission. With your assistance, I believe I could put together a convincing argument."

"Good, that's really quite fantastic."

"But."

"But?"

"Yes, but. I must come clean with you. This is all so, well, odd. This is all incredibly strange for me, I'm sure you can understand. So, I guess my question is, why? Why should I go along with this plot? I'm just some kid from The Blocks, and that's from your mouth. I didn't ask for any of this. Honestly, I'm not sure I want this. I told you I'm still young, still searching. What's it to me? Why should I care? This isn't something I've pursued." Power. That's all it ever is, power. Was there ever any other motive? Does man ever pursue anything else? Hierarchy. The same old story recurring through time. Here we are, the latest troupe acting the script. Stay focused.

"Alvin, Alvin, Alvin. My dear boy Alvin. Little of what we do in life is so neatly arranged in the manner of desire, then acquisition, then happiness. You're young, but you will quickly see the untenability of idealism. Not to put you at ease, because frankly, that's not my job, but suffice it to say, in doing this, you shall become one of us. You will rise to these impossible heights! There is nothing you will ever want for until the day your gently used, exorbitantly aged corpse is delicately filed in The Archives. But, let's not put the cart before the horse, let's at least finish the proposal, yes?"

"Fine, I'm listening."

"Good. Ok, the price, part two of it. Are you ready? Because this may pinch ever so slightly."

"I guess I'm as ready as I'll ever be." So here it is, now we go to the beating heart of man, to all the hand-covered whispers in closed rooms that make the earth tilt so gently, so definitively, on its axis. His setup, the buildup. And me, so fortunate to witness. This man's awesome power, soon to be mine in complicity. But he doesn't know anything. About me. About man. About power. His narrow worldview comes into focus now as he tries to expand. Tries being expansive. Thoughtful. But all the while, missing it, missing the point. He has the means for virtually exponential, if not unlimited perspective, yet he appears as linear as they come, ascending the stairs to his warm perch one simple step at a time. Linear. The hierarchy.

"For years, and, many more than I care to admit, *heh*, I've been troubled by the burden of need. Need to procure sexual gratification in what are generally, though not exclusively, considered taboo realms. Some people have evolved, realized that old norms shouldn't cloud creative new ways, however, and quite unfortunately, some people still cling to moldy traditions, ugly convention. Pedophilia, as it were, has always been a refuge for me, the most comforting nook in my blithe existence. Unfortunately, as a public official of esteem, I'm only permitted to go but so far along the path of apparent vice before I become a liability, therefore I'm usually required to employ a sliver of discretion with respect to my exploits. And while we are dealing with a border case here, tact is certainly still required, or, at least advisable. N'est-ce pas? I beg your pardon for speaking so frankly, but as you say, I'm not the type to mince words. Plus, I think it is to your advantage to engage this situation with nothing less than a crystal clear understanding of what's at stake."

A COOL, CONTEMPLATIVE SILENCE. AT THIS POINT IN OUR STORY, TWO MEN FIND THEMSELVES FACED WITH THE OVERWHELMING BLUNT OF REALITY. WHAT ENSUES IS A SECOND'S LONG GAME OF OPTICAL CHESS. EVERY LITTLE START, SQUINT, MIOSIS AND DILATION OF THE PUPILS WEIGHED AND EVALUATED. MEASURED AND EXTRAPOLATED. TWENTY MOVES, FIFTY MOVES, IN VARYING COMBINATIONS. EVERYTHING EVALUATED AND RANKED ON THE MERITS OF EFFICACY. STRATEGY DEVISED WITH MULTIPLE CONTINGENCIES PLUGGING THE

POSSIBLE HOLES OF MISSTEP.

The overbearing eye contact. Some sort of strange joke, words coded with misdirected meaning? The syntax, of which, underscoring the distance between our two worlds? Is he speaking in metaphors? Is this some weird power trip I can't comprehend? What's the ulterior here? "I'm sorry Beri, I'm not quite following you here." His sense of power seems overly terrestrial. Has a physicality that draws exclusively from tangible existence. He doesn't even bother to reference anything greater than himself, he doesn't feel the need to. He looks inward, must believe infinity is slowly accumulating there. Little does he know. How is it that I'm the Dirt? How did the world end up this way? He just doesn't know. Or is this some sort of joke? The two of us, worlds apart, meanings enveloped in strange languages, dialects?

"And, you see, there it is! Clarity is so, relative, isn't it? The perfect oxymoron. And here, I thought I was being crystal clear. Alright, let's back up, let's approach this from a different angle. You see, it's the seed of man I crave, the wholesome, unscathed center that clings fast to all the potential energy it proudly stores. Sex is merely a pretext for, a method by which, a plucky pederast gains access to this succulence. A long time ago I learned a thing or two about real power...what it is, what it isn't and such. And what I discovered is that, well, *power*, it's not influence because influence is dependent upon variables beyond control; some people simply can't be swayed regardless of the argument or incentives provided. And, power is certainly not money, cause when it comes down to it, money is just a collective reality among us, something prone to the ebb and flow of social tides. Now, power's not authority because authority is a concept, a transient label really, designed to transfer in time to the most fit to wear it. Power is not even brute force, as force *can* be countered and diminished if enough people align against it. And power isn't the creation of fear, because fear can be overcome when a person chooses, in their mind, to be free. No, real power is the application of two elements, always in conjunction, and always complementing, reinforcing one another. Real power is the application of force, within a framework of fear, both elements trained simultaneously on a single, isolated target. Applied in unison, there is no escape, there is no hope! One path emerges and that is the path you are required to walk. With real power, faith is of no use because the spirit is broken. Retaliation isn't possible because the will is shattered. Avoidance isn't tenable because the issue is forced, and conspiracy isn't viable because people are divided and conquered. Acceptance remains the only plausible option. Better to give the underbelly for a scratch than for the back to receive the whip. And, from here at the top, I see nothing but mankind's beautifully pink vulnerability, crying out for exploitative scratching. Immaculate perception from this angle, perfectly constituted for its purpose. Alvin? Have you nothing to say? Am I being too impertinent for your tastes? Are you surprised by how direct I am? Well anyway, regardless, it's important for you to digest the reality at hand. It's important for you to know that I am going to take you, do with you what I will, and there is absolutely no way around it." Strange as it may be, he gives little away, more temperate than someone three times his age. He's certainly a special case! A special boy!

Terrestrial. A simplistic, skull-cracking, brute force sort of power. Exoteric and shallow. He doesn't expand because he doesn't know how to. I was over-thinking, his words, plainly stated, require no interpretation. A life of searching for ways to bend metals, steer wills, fold more paper. He is perfectly unaware that power has nothing to do with comfort, wealth, stature, or earth-bound abuses. Those left idling in this type of ephemeral power lose their name as their income dries up and their body rots away after their last breath. "I...I don't even know where to begin. Where to begin? It's difficult to know how to approach it. I mean, what does one say to that, honestly?" *Humph*, there's no ulterior, who'd a guessed? It's as plain as the salacious look on his face. A simple pervert, bent on consuming the earth. A degenerate old lecher. His mind conditioned for basic consumption, but on an Übermensch scale. Here is my target, plain to see. Well, John's target anyhow, neatly delivered with all the improbability of a miracle. Unreal. No calculable odds for the probability of this tête-à-tête. How to sort things out? Luck, fate, desire, ambition. Intelligence with plenty of grooming. Regardless, target acquired, time for action. Action! Here he is, a Man of Action. Pham!

"Understand this is not a proposal, in the typical sense of the word, and any niceties at the outset of our conversation were merely that and nothing more. I'm not one to squeak hopefully under the partition of a public restroom, blind to prey's attributes. You are here before me and I can clearly see that you are precisely what I've been waiting for all these years. You are what I want, what I've wanted, what I've dreamed of. What I'm taking. This is the part in our little chat where you give in before being coerced, where you accept what is given and make the best of it. And know there is good in it, I assure you. But regardless, there it is. That is the whole deck of cards. Now you've seen what's behind these old eyes. So tell me something, don't you feel special? Don't you feel like a big, broad boy? There's certainly a measure of power in being the focal point of desire, isn't there?"

"And if I say no? If I up and choke the life from you right here and now?" No, this man doesn't get it. Real power is the ability to echo your name centuries into the future, your physical body replaced with a concept that inspires people for thousands of years. The never-ending reverberation of an idea. To rise above the material noise, to speak the truth to the masses, to be The One. Right? Stand on stage, make some noise you Man of Action. Demonstrate how to stand on principle. Those many nights with a sweaty grip on hope. Show the cumulative value of pride Mr. Aphamli Twist.

Ah, that wavering baritone, outing his anemic bluff! The same muffled cry of man heard a thousand times before. "This, as you know, is a free country. I encourage you to do whatever you please and trust I'll do whatever I please. But don't be mistaken. You're not required to want this, and it's more enjoyable for me if you don't. What *is* clear, at this point, is that your real options are null. Blame it on fate, or on luck perhaps! However you choose to view life's circumstances. However, know that I will take what's inside of you and devour it whole again and again. You *will* become my overcoat, my skin. You will plug that hole in me some carelessly refer to as the soul."

Action! John? John, why do you sit so quiet? Why can't I hear you, your inspiration anymore? This is our moment, *your* moment! Isn't this the part where we high-five and burn the fucking house down? John?

"Alvin?"

John? Isn't this what your damn sessions were about? Why we are here? Why *are* we here? Why am *I* here? What were the passing years for? Time for action, Man of Action.

"Alvin?"

But you remain quiet. And it's me, just me. Me and fate, no, me and luck. However I choose to perceive it. John, why do you abandon? You didn't have a clever trick for this one. Decadence over poverty. Comfort. But no, he doesn't get it. Neither of them do. The self-indulgent rhetoric, layer upon layer of presumption, nothing really matters. Reality is finally starting to crystallize. Do *I* get it? Yes, it's starting to make sense. Can't even feel the gun anymore, is it still in my waistband? Immediate wealth and comfort, easy life. All this time spent trying to make sense of things. Why won't my fingers crawl back to my waist? I know why. All of this relentless effort to arrive here, in this moment. All of this doubt and uncertainty, forget it and push. Everything's starting to make sense now.

"Aaaaaaaalviiiiiiiiiiiin. Alvin?"

We strive toward an ideal, a concept that stands no chance to exist. A muddy amalgamation of lofty ideas bound to shatter into a million pieces. A perfect form, we know deep down is beyond ridiculous. Yet we strive. But why? Push, blindly, push! Outcomes will come out. John the Deceiver? John the Baptist? John the Overman? Exactly who could tell?

"Alvin??"

All these reckless desires, reckless hopes. Nothing adds up. Nothing equates. I guess this is goodbye. What's left? Goodbye John. We now go our separate ways.

"Alvin? Alvin? You've become rather quiet, is there anything you want to say?"

"There's nothing *to* say. You've said it all, correct?"

"That's a good boy. I will make you happy, you'll see."

Knock, Knock, Knock

"Lord God Almighty, my Savior up in Heaven?"
"Yes? What can I do for you? Please, please come in." This feeling of calm, a serenity unknown. Warm and encapsulating. The light, seen. I think I need a hug. I think I want to give a hug. If only I could wrap my arms around the entire world, squeeze it purple.
"Vice President Dittimas H. Pillock is in makeup and ready to go on in fifteen minutes."
"Excellent, good work. Everything is good. We are nearly ready on this end, just preparing to go over a few last minute details here with our new Product Ambassador."
"That's wonderful God, and congratulations Alvin. I'm glad the hunt worked out so well. You will be happy. We, to a person, are quite happy here."
"You wouldn't, by chance, have the talking points handy, would you? I'd like to go over them briefly here with Alvin."
"But of course, God. Here you go."
"Thank you. Thank you very much. Say, would you mind providing us with a two-minute warning when it's time?" Warm. Warm all over. Radiating out from a perfectly warm center. Little creatures serving, obeying. Beautiful equilibrium.
"Certainly God. I'll return in precisely twelve and.... twelve and a half minutes."

It's coming into focus. He is it. He's the man. That newspaper article was partially right. God doesn't exist, never did, not in the celestial manner prophesied throughout history anyhow. His illusion has been here with us all along. On humble, little earth. Who knew? Reticence. What's left to say?

"Now, where were we Alvin? Wait, hold it. Before we go on I have one, tiny request."

"Yes?"

"And you don't have to capitulate if you are uncomfortable. But, would you mind if I call *you* God?"

Clarity. Sharp and expedited. It's actually been there all along, but the wrong eyes were attempting to see. Couldn't put all the pieces into a single, concise meaning. "No, that's perfectly fine. I mean, we're family, aren't we?"

"Absolutely! Ok then, God, let us run through these lines, Ok?"

"As you wish."

"Time is of the essence! We have business to conduct, a speech to prep and only a few minutes in which to do it. We are Men of Action!"

"We certainly are, aren't we?" Christ, Zoroaster, Vorilhon. Marshall Applewhite and Bab. Sai Baba! Point and laugh. Discredit and abuse them.

"Ok God, the first point we need to stress is Unity. We *are* a united people, Homo beatus, all of us! But, further to that, and more importantly, you, an Iron, one with them! Part of their sub-culture. A blithe consumer overjoyed with the release of an amazing new technology! Tickled by the prospect of ever-expanding access to the digital world around us!"

"Ok, got it. Unity." Pastor Russell, Hongzhi, Nanak. Confucius and L. Rod. Vissarion! But pause for a moment, a tiny moment, and listen to the message. Slowly it starts to make sense and you pull your finger away from the trigger and the derisive smile on your face fades.

"Alrighty God, the second point is Freedom. A million ways to express yourself, a million ways to connect to others, full sensory absorption into the precious moments of our time. Our great society, based on the hard reasoning of science and the liberty afforded by its full implementation!"

"Got it. Freedom. Easy enough to remember." Reverend Moon, Muhammad, Joseph Smith. Calvin and Jim Jones. Robert Earl Burton! Then, like a miracle, you find yourself buried inside yourself. Tears of joy. Drawing new breath into virgin lungs. Now the world has become much more complicated.

"Alvin, please, if you could, work a *little* more emotion into your voice. This needs to pop-off crisply, convincingly. Let's show some passion, give a taste of our soul, eh?"

"Yes, Ok. *Increase* the passion, *more* emotion."

"Ok, well, good, good, and getting better. Now God, the third and final point is Value. The unbelievable value attained when people work together to reap the bounty of a successful, thriving society. Technology, entertainment, leisure all fully within every man, woman and child's grasp. A Palette in every hand, a roof over every head, food on every table."

"Value. The good life. Technology enabling it into the lives of all people. Understood." Abraham, Rishabha, Shoko Asahara. David Koresh and Laozi. Credonia Mwerinde! You've been touched by an angel, the hand of God, a spirit willing to give you a chance. Your smile returns, not derisive but ingratiating. Soft and malleable.

"Yes, yes! That's excellent, now you're getting it."

Luther, Mani, Nakayama Miki. Timothy Drew and Ellen White. Zuberi Ortiz and John Voyes. A Being that can lift you up to greater heights, make you a Saint here on humble earth. Bullshit.

"God, you're on in two."
"Ok," say two men simultaneously.
Two little chuckles reverberate through eternity.

"I think you're ready. Remember, this doesn't need to be anything elaborate, just clear and articulate. This isn't a speech, this is a product endorsement. Don't focus on perfection, just convey the message. Focus on the points, and then, be yourself. Sell people on you, on your point of view."

"I can do that."

"Very good. Now, and this is my final request before I leave you alone to rehearse for a few minutes, let's seal this deal with an embrace."

The sad, lonely arms of a man lost at sea, reaching out for a lifeline. The quivers. The odors. The unreality of it all. How the memory fades even before it gets stamped on the brain.

"That's good, that's really good my boy. Ok, I'll leave you to it. My assistant will come for you when it's time. Until then, rehearse, and I'll see *you*, Mr. Bigshot, back in here after this song and dance is over."

Song and dance.

But you, person of the ether, won't. You can't. You haven't the ability to listen. Rather, you weren't put here *to* listen. You were put here to speak, to shout. We all were, myself included. So now, as the sun sets on this life, I'll have my way with words if only in the confines of my skull.

Humans are rational.

Humans choose happiness or unhappiness.

If love is dead and brotherhood is no longer, then communication is pointless.

If security is unattainable, striving is futile, and if comfort is deliberately withheld, then society has failed.

If society has failed and communication is pointless, this world holds no human value.

The soul cannot be fed in a world lacking value to humans.

The human body, involuntarily, strives to exist.

If the body involuntarily wants to live and the soul involuntarily wants to be fed but both are unattainable simultaneously, then a human must act to override nature and take control.

If this world holds no human value and nature must be overridden, then rational decisions necessarily align with a human's choice of happiness or unhappiness.

Happiness is control.

The propositions flash like an equation assembling from nothing. I want to map out the logic, scan the truth tables for proof that the reasoning is sound, but me, no good with formulation. Mathematical assignations flooding eyes, unintelligible clusters of symbols and foreign alphabets. Instead, trust intuition and draw what appears to be the obvious conclusion after working through the truths. *Conclusion? I choose happiness. Logical. Deterministic.*

At some point, there's nothing left to mill over and there's no self left to discover. I will not acknowledge pain. A man tried to Rashomon his own thoughts right before he realized the walls were padded. When he realized they were padded, he asked the man with the square face, "Am I really that fragile?"

The square-faced man replied, "It's not for you, it's for us. We feel better knowing that you feel better."

"But I don't feel any better."

"That's not for you to decide."

Here in this moment, no distractions. Only my big white canvass. I will paint life. I will paint the life we revert to in dreams. The indistinct, formless familiarity that feels like legitimate hugs, the scent of mother's skin, the sound of sleep methodically parsing breath into equally-timed intervals. Everything simple that resonates in the heart.

But no. The man with the square face will not leave me to my work. Why? He looks angry, contemptuous. They all do as they storm in. Above me, his square, blood-red face inverted, his mouth a hole stretched thin. The pearlescent glint of white teeth. And that pink flower he's holding, he's trying to tell me something about it. He's talking, but he knows I can't hear him. Nobody can. He's talking because he must, because that's what we do, we talk, but more often, we shout. That is what we were put here to do. Talk. The others flash about tickling my periphery, a sort of strange rhythm to their motion. But him. He's the lead, he's the show's director. He gestures wildly. He points at me. He points to himself. He implies the world with a swooping gesture. He snaps his fingers. He rolls his eyes. I think he slapped my face, again. He shows me his rectangle flower. A beautiful, pink rose of sorts. He shows, a referee's penalty card. Into his pocket he goes, out comes a shiny little cylinder. He plunges the button on the cylinder and out pops the neck of an even smaller cylinder. He scrawls upon the rose, his mouth searching for ever-greater circumferences. Authority through volume. His eyes meet mine as he tears a petal from the rose. A single, velvety petal of a perfectly monochromic pink which he holds out, lets fall. Pink! The softest, gentlest of colors. The color of baby's cheeks. Innocence. How it floats from his hand, pirouetting through gravity's clench, homing chestward. There is no way to suppress it. There is no reason to suppress it any longer. It comes, explodes, because it must. Time is now ripe. Because it has been sitting inside of me, waiting for so long. This smile.

"Shit, who knows! Say something, anything. Anything's better than sitting there as if you've lost the ability to communicate."

"I'm sorry Alain, there's, just... so much to learn. This is all so new for me. I'm, I'm so sorry, but you must understand."

Exactly! See that's exactly it! *There's too much to learn Alain. There's too many obstacles to overcome Alain. There's too many people to convince Alain. There's too much work for one person Alain. There's too many of this, there's too much of that. I'm not like you yet Alain. I'm not like you.*

...

If you go slumming, expect to get dirty. There's your tidy fucking *how* Nelling. There's your answer 'ol boy. What? Did you think there was something arbitrary about science and order? Jeffrey convince you that happenstance simply forget to sprout a tail from your coccyx? Am I talking with myself right now or is this some sort of *divine* instruction? Am I aware of my own consciousness? Of course I am, but that's beside the point. Perception dictates my grasp on reality, and it's a matter of heat, consuming fire, that's about to define my reality. Flames give off heat, they burn skin when encountered. The race for oxygen is on. The flames want it, my lungs want it. The flames will win. The flames are going to burn this body to a pile of ash. And for what? A misstep? Several missteps? The *how* is so damn obvious, yet here I spend my final moments picking at the scab to see if it will bleed again? It's almost as though I deserve this. Almost. But, with a fully honest conscience, there was love wasn't there? Or, was it a headful of semen? Or does it even matter? There was a rational pursuit of happiness (perhaps mistakenly labeled as love?), irrespective of the inputs contributing to the desired happiness. But maybe it was just an ego trip, a thinking man attempting something no one else had done. To scale an untouched peak. An ego trip conflated with a deviant sprinkle of perfectly formed beauty, beauty giving off the odor of infatuation as love. Love. Love, just art, or a form of it. And the human mind needs this concept of love to make concrete its abstractions, those disconnected glints of euphoric emotion untethered to any semblance of reality. Love provides that channel on which to communicate the moral and ethical ideals spawned by its very evocation. A sort of unachievable perfection in its chicken-and-egg circularity, the most beautifully impossible art, forever out of reach. But regardless, she wasn't love. She couldn't have been love. She was a knot of unarticulated emotions. My silly, puerile, unarticulated emotions. My sloppy cognition of reality. What's real, what exists, is this moment. Wasting away.

It's a faint thump. A distant drumbeat wrestling with the scream of silence. A thinking man has no choice but to think to the bitter end, till the very last perceptible thump. And, reasoned thought, how it was put on hold for a period of time, a moment for people to be equals. This is how a how is born, when reality is merely glanced at from the corner of the eye rather than given a good, hard look. A gardener, man sweating to turn dirt. Servant to the whims and needs of brainless life. A Dirt. Apathetic and perishing before committing the effort to save itself. Platinum. A person as hope embodied, naïve optimism defined. A complaisant life to troll with a juicy lure of fear and want. Fear and want, oh! the lovefest between them. Few will succeed, most will fail. Most deserve to fail, and, those who intervene, clearly do so at their own peril. Workers should be chained. The lazy should be caged. The optimistic should be fed lies. Equality is not for thinking man. Thousands of years building walls, establishing hierarchy, codifying strata, reinforcing caste, excluding, ranking, indenturing and so on. Multitudinous modalities demonstrating how we are not the same. Differences stamped on our DNA for god's sake. Let the leper sleep in your bed? Let a hemophiliac sit on your white chaise? Let a vagabond into your home? Let a pervert watch your children? Engage a mongoloid in debate? Let a Turner borrow your turtleneck? Hire a fat man as your dietician? Let an anorexic cook your dinner? Let a savant into your head? Let a blind man paint your portrait? Let a Klinefelter date your daughter? Let a progerian be your executor? Let a Dirt into your life? No, no, no, no and no. Of course not. Not situations one considers, these are associations dismissed outright. Decisions conveniently made prior to the realization of the facts, because most times a single factor is all that matters. Equality is for equations not people.

...

She was full of tears but eventually came around, found her voice once again.

"Alain, I'm sorry. What do we need to do next? This blindsided me, I wasn't prepared for something so, ...so aggressive. You must understand I'm coming from a different world, I'm trying to adjust. I'm sorry. I know this has put pressure on you. What's going on in your mind? What do you think we need to do, I, need to do next?"

"Next. Yeah."

"Tell me Alain. We can figure this out. I need more exposure, need more time to engage, to better know where the other side is coming from, right? I'll learn from tonight, improve for next time. I will stand my ground, come ready to fight. The hope of transformation, the chance to change minds means the world to me."

"What is it that we are doing here anyway? I mean precisely. What the *hell* happened tonight? How did things get *so* mottled, *so* quickly?"

"Alain, I tried, I did. You must understand, this is so new for me. But I'm starting, I'm starting to see a way, to understand where I'm falling down."

"Well, what then?"

"How do you mean?"

"I mean, what then? What is the next step? You asked me, now I'm asking you. How do we turn this around? How can we possibly get back on track? What do *you* reckon are the next steps?"

"You know this situation better than I do. You've been among these people for so long. What do your instincts tell you?"

"It's funny. We could go back and forth all evening. I'm asking you because I have absolutely no idea. None. You ask me because you have no idea. None. But, you want to know what I think? How I really feel? This doesn't happen. What took place tonight *does not* happen. People maintain. People protect. People insure. People draw contingencies. People don't collapse, open themselves up for mass critique. You tripped, and people piled on as they do, and when you struggled, people piled on even more as they should. *That* is the way the world works. You either belong or don't, there isn't a space for revision, for amelioration. We are squirted from the birth canal ready to assail. Your mishaps tonight make you a desirable target in the future. A delicious sort of mark. This isn't a game of goodwill, life in this world isn't about some kind of feel-good diplomacy. We live in an era of infallibility. Only the bold survive. Only the strong can properly choke life into submission. One must stand ready to charge, always! And they charged right over top of you."

"Human beings aren't perfect Alain. Human beings will make mistakes."

"Says who? And what's a mistake anyhow? Let's not casually toss around terms. Define them, and with precision please. You know, maybe, just *maybe*, humans aren't perfect but they are close enough to walk perfectly balanced on the edge of Occam's razor. So please, don't bore me with trivialities conjured up from some stagnant philosophy mumbled in The Piles. Everyone chooses to believe something and that choice makes us who we are."

"How can you be so self-assured? How can you be so confident when you were the one admiring the irony of our situation a few hours ago? How do you reconcile the discrepancies?"

"Easily. In the same manner that any theory is constantly up for debate, constantly subject to revision. Perhaps you, your presence, shifted reason away from its normal course. You, this unforeseen enigma fell into my life, caused a momentary recalculation of what is, what isn't. But, time is on the side of truth. Tonight, this evening, more time in the bucket and more evidence to either prove or disprove theory. Are we all the same? Are we not? Do we all behave the same or don't we? And why? Why is it that we behave differently? Why do we follow these vastly different patterns of behavior? And I'm not trying to judge here, I'm merely attempting to assemble the facts, trying to make sense of why oil didn't mix into the water this evening? Huh? What do you think?"

"So, your tidy parsimony divides us right in two? You are you and I am me. You belong to a society of people that are where they are for a reason, what's more, a justifiable reason. I don't fit the mold because I'm cut from a different fabric. Is that about accurate? Am I understanding you well enough?"

"You speak in absolutes, whereas I prefer to speak in directions, trajectories if you will. In a process of constant revision, I'm obligated, humanity is obligated, to evaluate newly available evidence and apply it to theory accordingly. I follow where the facts lead me. This evening is but another artifact in a larger production. Maybe a new fact will come along requiring another revision. But, being correct, being truthful, is taking into account all available information and making the best decision possible at any given time. The world is black and white only in each discrete moment in time. If the earth goes crashing into the sun, do you praise Einstein's genius? That picture of him, the one with his tongue sticking out, will people remain enamored by the playfulness of genius or feel duped by the gravity of false enlightenment?"

"It doesn't matter, we'd be dead."

"Right. Right, right, right. Clever Ava. Always something sharp to say except for when it actually matters. As soon as your tears dry, you begin your march towards the next good, solid cry."

"I don't understand, why do we argue? I apologized. I'll apologize again, I'm sorry. I'm so very sorry, Alain. I know this evening has created stress, unwanted stress. I'm committed to this. I'm committed to you. One bad evening doesn't make a relationship. If handled well, if handled with forgiveness, it strengthens it. It creates an opportunity to grow stronger. We can be the example for a cynical world. A world full of hate. We don't have to be like everyone else, we can show them all how beautiful it is to be broken, imperfectly mortal. To be nothing more than repairable goods. But, goods *worthy* of repair. Humanity doesn't have to be a dated concept. Do you even hear me? Alain?"

...

No. Didn't. Couldn't. Real consequences were at stake. Real costs. Ava, her lofty ambitions. That childish, idealistic patina she slathered on everything. Eschew pragmatism and entertain the naive hopes swirling around in a fuzzy head waking in the morning. Most people swat them like flies, but she pityingly fed them like stray cats. An inclination to nurture when rational people preferred to look away. There was something similar to love, definitely a rational pursuit of it. Hard to admit, but it was there. Or maybe it was happiness, the divide between the two so impossibly narrow at times, her weakness, her compassion, both her best and worst qualities, something exotic, something sought after but then found to be acerbic, disagreeable until, in a few moments, it's not, it's exotic once again, something sort of lovely, whatever that means, and here it goes again, fingernail under the scab, crusty bit of topography tugging at virginal pink skin, skin to tear and leak anew, or maybe it will shed, heal, repair itself, working mysteriously on a clock of its own.

...

"Let's sit on it, Ok? Perhaps we both need a moment to set our heads straight after this evening. There's little sense in going after one another, let's looks at this with fresh eyes in the morning."

"Fine."

"Roger that, to Ava's apartment."

"Yes sir."

The silence, growing between us as the MRAP navigated the empty streets, the strobe of streetlights across her sullen face as she looked out the window at nothing in particular.

"You coming up?" she asked.

"No, not tonight. I have business out east. I'll return in a day or so."

She leaned over, her wet eyes deep into mine, her neck's heat amplifying waves of nauseating perfume.

"I'm not perfect and I don't want to be." Her fingers dragged along my jaw line as she softly placed a kiss on my lower lip, turned and rose from the MRAP.

"Sir?"

"Shut up Roger that."

"Yes sir."

"Take me to the office."

Does it even matter? Did it ever matter? Maybe more importantly, *will* it ever matter? No. No it doesn't. It didn't. Won't. Reality, merely a notion accepted by the majority at a specific point in space-time, an ever-morphing miracle of cognition. Meaning, a construct with inadequate framing, an anecdote masquerading as a joke without a punch line. Now it glints in my hand, a wink and a nod. Thankfully, no longer boring into my body. Something tangible in the hand, something close to real if only for a fleeting moment.

A coarse life forced upon a baby born impoverished. A decadent life forced upon a baby born affluent. The in-between for the rest. Ready-made situations upon which the will is free to roam. Rise to the top to fuck children, fall to the bottom to steal food. Fall to the bottom to fuck children, rise to the top to steal food. Same same, beautifully transposable humans. How amazingly versatile, the human spirit.

Modesty encapsulating motive, obfuscating intention. The free will is whispered directives in such a gentle manner, teased with a stimulating ego stroke. Slit your wrists intending to bleed out, pass out, wake up and try again. Saw at your wrists until you die, pass out, wake up and try again. Saw at your wrists...repeat ad infinitum. Free will hard at work.

The sheer narcissism of living. The sheer narcissism of living, breathing man. Standing, arms splayed, waiting patiently for deserved deliverance. When it doesn't come, we don't even know. All the while, nothing matters, but few are even aware of that. A narcissism so intense, yet buried beneath a well-designed, self-deprecating facade to ensure maximum impact... this, the M.O. of a mentor, of a guru. Betrayal, how it comes wrapped in help and guidance. It was me. Me, John's Raskolnikov. The one capable of walking the slippery slope of righteousness. Me, the perfect sacrifice, the one to march up to the power structure to cut off its planarian head just so it could grow once again. For what? To temporarily change the positions of fucker and fuckee? But no, no longer. I am the center of my own silly universe of nothingness. I am. A redundancy so boring it begs to be made redundant. Where the fuck is this? I miss you mom. Pham misses you daddy. Whoever you were, wherever you may be. But sorry, no tears, no more.

These walls of beautifully polished wood. This chair, comfortable, embracing, hoisting me off the floor... clean enough to eat from. Ornately carved table, its marble top, cool to the touch, holding illegibly scratched notes on a few bits of paper. Overhead lights of a soft warm glow, easy on the eyes, unlike the sharp slant of the morning sun. The faint scent of something sweetly floral wafting, even the air ushers a sense of wellbeing. An incredible fruit bowl. Close eyes, open them. Again, really quick. Keep going. Dozen of little snapshots of luxury. Each snapshot a hundred times, a thousand times more desirable than any discrete moment cherry-picked from an entire lifetime. Me, sitting here, gripping an ass-scented pistol, blinking madly, preparing for concubination by a vicious geezer who wants me to remind his slaves of their happiness. Reality. One. Two. Three. Squeeze.

Arrogance shoves its hand up the puppet, give it a try! Find your authentic self by first imposing it on something else, someone else. Give yourself a test drive in another's skin, see if it works, then step into the limelight and be the you you hoped you could be. But wait, the world doesn't stop spinning. These revelations, they keep coming, and you find out you are not you, oh, no, no, no, you are the someone you wanted someone else to be. Now you're acting, but nobody knows it and, above all, nobody would care if they did. And then you shake from your stupor and realize that you don't care either. Why should you? So then you wonder what's the point of it all? Did the math just fail? And if it did, well, what does that mean? But you, happy you, not to worry. This is no reason to fret, oh no! This is no basis for irrational thought. The snake can eat its tail all night long if it chooses.

You're a happy, rational being gently squirted from the feminine folds tethered to a long line of rational beings. You're the architects of insanely complex social systems, the engineers of structural marvels, the scientists who fashion a remedy from anything, for anything. Thousands of years of cumulative intellectual evolution! Anything is possible up to and including a succinctly rational exit from rational thought. *Voltaire's Bastards!* How odd that you kill the killer because killing is wrong. You're afraid of death but cannot reasonably ascertain what's on the other side. You're a skeptic but you believe in God because you're faithful. You disbelieve in God because you're empirical and only fancy to build your glass house of knowledge with observable phenomena (even if the phenomena are wildly abstract extrapolations of theory constantly debunked and retooled over time). Stay in the moment! You fear the unknown, the UNknown! You simultaneously think blood is thicker than water and that capitalism is the fairest, most un-biased method of exchange. You simultaneously think greed is inherent and communism is surely plausible because a strand of goodness runs through man, it connects us as one my proletarian pal! You commit suicide (well, not yet but you might!). You commit homicide (again, not yet, but wouldn't you say this is within the realm of possibility if all situations are honestly considered?) You put faith in love and choose to trust another person who is biologically wired to preserve the self above all else. But, regardless of the many inconvenient paradoxes, life boils down to the one big paradox. The omnipresent big black hole that every self-absorbed asshole tries to explain with some clever contraption, some ingenious device they've knitted together from the miniscule shreds of truth they've brain-strained a lifetime to acquire. The massive improbability of your own silly, little existence. You, a grain of sand sitting purposelessly on a beach the size of the multiverse. Imagine infinity! You, trying so hard to be the absolute best grain of sand you could ever possibly hope to be. The smartest. The strongest. The most powerful. Better than all of the grains of sand around you. No doubt eternity will cry its eyes out in happy honor of you should you manage to blip on its cold, black radar screen. A Planck time's pop of luminescent glory!

"Alvin, you're on," she says, pushing through the door.

"Yes, Ok."

She's tall and thin, dressed in severe, almost clinical attire. Shoulder-length hair hangs straight from a side part that cuts a white line across her scalp. Shiny and well nourished but plain. Unmemorable. One *of* a million.

"Wait, before you go, something for you. Here, hold still."

"What's this?"

"A gentle reminder that you're one of us now, just a token to welcome you to the club. So, welcome." No inflection, no subtle irony in her voice. She could be reading the instructions on the back of a medicine bottle. Maybe she is.

A lapel pin. A small band of flawlessly banal silver, beveled on all edges to smooth pill perfection. Pinned to my jacket. Her hair, flowers and fruits all lovely, but her breath, arriving from her depths, is stale, sour. She doesn't bother with a smile. Turning, she walks out under the assumption that I will follow, and look at me, rational as I am, I do. Left. Right. Left. Right. One. Two. Three. Squeeze.

I'm nothing, but you won't forget me anytime soon. I'm something, but I have no name, no name worth trying to construct. Aphamli Twist, a silly literary joke few undertand.

A long corridor, dark, a rectangle of light reaching in from the exit. The echoes of a loudspeaker, a voice tumbling down the hall, losing fidelity as it goes. The clap-clapping of shoes, uneven staccatos merging, finding unison, diverging once again.

Trust your instinct and burn everything you see. It isn't real. Trust your heart and smash everything around you. It isn't there. Everything asunder, then obliterate the pitiful pieces until nothing remains, not even the memory of an abyss. An unachievable singularity. A never-ending, never-beginning vomit of recursively created universes. A black hole. A white hole. A worm hole. Hyperbole at the event horizon of Godmath and the hominidian elegance of ultra deep thought. Sure, my brown hole. One. Two. Three. Squeeze.

The blind of our dear sun in the late morning, a whiff of vitamin D being manufactured en masse.

"Ladies and gentlemen, it is my pleasure to introduce you to Alvin Tan from Block XZ!"

Slouched in Gray's Dragons Chair gazing west, the night played out on repeat to the tune of four fingers of Dalmore Unary. The sting of being the laughing stock, the bumbling fool, of the evening couldn't be salved with all the world's liquor though. How intoxication served to cheapened reality, forced my brain to slog through increasingly ridiculous scenarios of redemption. *How much money is required to bend space-time a full 180 degrees, to go back? Certainly someone, somewhere perfected that Neuralyzer-thing (erase minds!) and everyone has a price no doubt. Poisoning, just kill 'em off? Rig a fleet of delivery drones with sights and rifles? No, that's absolutely stupid, traceable even.* But as the irritable gyrations of an inebriated mind idled with the drying snifter, increasingly plausible options crystallized.

An array of alternatives, each devised with the singular purpose of bending the appearance of social failure into the illusion of success. That stupid sort of lemons-to-lemonade switcharoo so futilely attempted by many an optimistic fuck…*but it might work?* Oh how they dance upon my feet now, sort of funny how the thrashing flame bubbles and pops, blackens, the skin of my feet as it works its way up my leg, imagine that, being thankful for a broken neck.

…

It's important to acknowledge that using aggression of any kind looks incredibly weak at this point. Second, purchasing power is bounded by certain practical limits; is time travel even theoretically possible? What's possible? That is the question, what is physically possible given this circumstance? Options that exist under an umbrella of reality, these options are possible. So let's take inventory. There are things known and things unknown which comprise our existence within the real world, a world within a range of possibilities. Reality must exist, it can't help but exist. It just is. But perception though. What is perception? Perception is that thin layer of uncertainty floating between the brain and indisputable reality. Perception is a matter of interpretation, as such, there is the ever-present possibility of a gap between perception and reality. What's more, perception is heavily influenced by the unknown realities, those realities as yet undiscovered. Yes! Reality versus perception. The perception gap! What's real *is*, and what's unreal *is not*. But, what's perceived as real is only as real as the perception of it permits. And, what's perceived as unreal may in fact be reality if only perception is tweaked accordingly. Yes, the perception gap! This is the way out of the conundrum of actuality!

Alright then Alain, walk through it. So practically speaking, the collectively perceived reality at dinner this evening was built upon the premise that my date, the unforgettable Ava, is a classless skank attempting to undeservedly guzzle cream from gentry's swollen mammae. But that, that is where everyone, every last one of those pompous shits steered wrong. It's a ruse! This is our ruse! It's one big fucking joke that you suckers took hook, line and sinker! The fallout from this evening's little social event wasn't an indictment of *my* lack of suitability among the ranks (*or* Ava's for that matter?? *hmm*, consideration required), it was an indictment on all of *you* lazy minded fops, ogling at the magician's fluffy bunny while sleight of hand masked the reveal of the joke. And what is the reveal you ask? *I* am the master of ceremonies. *I* am the anecdotist. *I* am the purveyor of The Now. Mr. Entertainment, Watch Inc embodied, personified! This was all just a joke, a joke you simpletons haven't yet grasped. A riff on our high society's well-defined social norms exposing your intellectual linearity. And those of you who doubled-down, thought it cute to draw out my torture, you will find the biggest pile of flaming dog shit on your porch! *Oh yeah, I'll let them have it. I'll coin a new word for the magnitude of their ignorance, their ease of deception. This word will replace "gullible" in the lexicon and their smug mugs will function as its root!*

So then, further consideration, where does all of this leave Ava? Is the joke an opportunity for her to redefine clever? Is she capable of conspiring to turn this into a well-rehearsed skit of "wow-you-people-are-gullible-motherfuckers-aren't-you?", effectively reshaping the whole meaning of the evening? The skit, obviously, would need to play out with the same crowd on a tight turnaround for authenticity's sake. Ava would require substantial coaching and training to ensure a flawless follow-up performance. Is she trainable? Could someone coach her into something she's admittedly not? And who coaches her? Well, me of course. Is this feasible? Is it possible to teach her the many nuances of Diamond rhetoric in a short time to pull this off? Note the implications. If the skit fails to resonate, if the joke doesn't punch, the gravity of the whole situation increases tenfold and I will never again attain sufficient thrust to escape the black hole of social banishment.

Risky, perhaps it is sensible to play it more conservatively? Instead I could craft a blunter joke, something less contrived, something along the lines of *Seriously? A Diamond of massive wealth and influence cavorting with an obvious Platinum?* A new sort of joke, a joke that lures naiveté with the illusion of permeable social boundaries. Set up the pins with what appears on the surface an honest breech of taboo and bowl it over with a spotlight on the collective credulity! Seriously? A Diamond with a Platinum? Who the fuck does that?? Is everyone here truly *that* stupid? *Ollingford, what were you thinking when I didn't immediately object to the plating mistake? Did you fancy you were my equal, or perhaps more ambitiously, did you figure you could take me down a notch? And you, Showatra, care to try out another riddle? Hhmm? No? Well that's Ok, I'll help you along, how about this, "who's stupid enough to lemming after a joke as old as time? Huh? Give up? Every soul within earshot of my fucking voice. Ladies and gentlemen, please, feel free to retrieve your incredulously hanging jaws, the show is now over. Goodnight."* I'll turn them all into a fucking anecdote, a reference point of humor with all the dickish chutzpah of a pop culture insult. Again, turn the tables around so that they're the joke's target. Only, this path puts Ava underfoot, unredeemable, out of the equation. Gone.

Two paths forward, clear and concise. One with Ava, one without. Those beautiful, smoky eyes. The indescribable thing that lingers when she is around, forever skewing time. Her ability to dissolve internal friction, ease the mind. But what is practical, what is feasible? I swear that I will never live for the sake of another man, nor ask another man to live for mine. But, even the sun wobbles.

How my knuckles fell hollow upon her door as I knocked, the sun graying the morning sky. Her face, a sleepless night, bewildered but relieved.

"I thought you had business out east."

"I do. I mean I did. Look, I have an idea."

"Would you like to come in?"

"Yes. I mean, no. What I'm trying to say is, I want you to come out east with me for a few days. I have an idea how to fix last night. We'll stay at a lodge I own, just you and I."

"Alain, I don't think Janice would be comfortable left behind for a few days."

"Of course of course, she may come as well. Look, Ava, I was thinking through the night, didn't sleep a wink in fact. I discovered a way out of this mess, but it requires much planning and prepping. And I need, well, I need to work with you to test out the plan, to prepare you see?"

"You know I'm onboard Alain. You know I'll do whatever it takes."

"Ok good, good. Get dressed, grab Janice and meet me at my office in twenty minutes and we'll fly east to begin."

But stupid me, stupid me for thinking I could do the impossible, you can't, it can't be done, killer instinct isn't taught, it germinates under the right conditions or it doesn't. People are not the same, people will not turn out the same even under the exact same circumstances, we are all different, some are better than others and it's best to state it plainly. Democracy? An Athenian joke, a fantastical feat of naivety, we've arranged society to account for these differences, the only sensible and fair way to go about it. Meritocracy? Aristocracy? Corporatocracy? Sedulousocracy? Intellectocrasy? No, none of these are comprehensive enough individually, it's a sort of Superiorocracy - an organic social arrangement where those who are simultaneously imbued with all of the best traits across the board naturally cream to the top, few will get there, and those that don't will find their niche in society as determined by their individual strengths or lack thereof.

She floundered from the start, couldn't keep up as I fabricated the back-story of our skit. How she thought there needed to be some continuous thread of authenticity running through the storyline, she couldn't distill the atmosphere enclosing a lie, and from it, extract the floating particles of truth on which to craft the next lie in the story thus pushing a contiguous plot forward. Hers was a submissive relationship with honesty, one that unmercifully chained her to the bull's-eye.

Fearing Janice's ubiquitous innocence was skewing her ethics I convinced her to let Roger that drive Janice out to the apple orchards. But did fresher air resolve Ava's romantic relationship with integrity? No, of course not! Reality started closing in, salvaging Ava was quickly becoming a loser's game. Fear of loss mixing with the stink of failure, the prickly process of reconciling love with self, parsing thoughts from emotions and compartmentalizing passions into appropriate like-kind buckets. Does feeling remorse make one a better person? Yes, right? Acknowledging the possibility of remorse is the creation of space, a space that enables an analysis of the full spectrum of emotions. Feeling remorse is validation that the rational pursuit of love was worthy, that a particular emotion (call this love) was justified. Or, is feeling remorse an admission of failure? The unnerving emotional asymmetry between love and loss; she had to go, there was no other option.

"Where is she?"

"Sir, she's back in the room, practicing the lines you gave her."

"Ok, fine. Look, you must get her out of my face right now, I think I'm going insane! I can't take this shit anymore. Tell me, have you ever failed to reconcile love with self?"

"Sir?"

"Never mind. What I'm saying is, Ava, get her out of here! Get her out of here right now. We're done, this isn't working. This whole mess is not working out, it's over."

"But sir, how? Where am I to take here?"

"Wherever, take her back west, I don't give a shit, just go, go now, right now!"

"But sir, Roger that took the MRAP."

"I don't give a goddamn. Figure it out! Here, here, here. Here's authorization. Go find a car, truck, whatever and buy it from the owner. Flag them down in the damn street, wherever, it doesn't matter. Pay whatever they want, just get her out of here now! Right now, chop, chop, chop! Do it!"

"Sir, where in the west should I drop her off?"

"The Piles, take her back to The Piles. No, wait. The Archives, take her back to The Archives. That is where we picked her up so that is where she is to return. Oh, and be sure she returns her purse to you. That is my property as are the contents therein. We don't need our mistakes following us back home, capisce?"

"Yes sir."

"Oh, and call Roger that immediately. Tell him to bring his ass back here now, AND, without that girl."

"Sir, where should he leave little Janice?"

"I don't know, I don't care. Just make sure she doesn't come back with him."

"But sir…"

"That's all, get going, chop, chop, chop!"

Everything manages to shake apart in the end. The heart searches a lifetime for a counterpart, hands work a lifetime for a legacy, but in the end, get nothing. Was supposed to live forever, built to last forever, but fuck it, fuck the whole world and everything in it, let it burn to smoldering ash, to absolute nothingness, treat people the way their supposed to be treated and you should expect that it will come back around to you to in kind, isn't the *how* so crystal clear now? am I supposed to scoff at nature? be a martyr? for what? what does that get me? It's a twisted paradox, nature presents herself, you walk along with her, you treat her accordingly, she behaves as expected, ruin settles in, my silly little paradox, everything is as it should be. vulcan dances wildly on my belly as inevitability closes in what's a man to do? to hold her hand the sublimity there was love once upon a time when she looked at me and I looked at her and we knew our secret was the thread that bound us it was rational it was irrational it existed even if only for a brief time now she's gone and it runs off my face leaves a trail of moist tickled nerve endings my feet may not but my eyes they sense the fire they know how to react but maybe it's a sign of something else I'm not sure when you can't tell whether a tear is protecting your eye or protecting your soul maybe she was a good person after all nothing real ever finds a balance point

Lethargic applause and a patchwork of lipless grins, contemptuous scowls scattered between the pinpricks of beaming stage light. My ignorant disciples, followers. Faces, shrinking to the fade. These people in this moment, one. Modernity's denizens, fascia strung taut between a lofty idea and its hoarded realization. A million martyrs standing for nothing. Rise up! Rise up and demand a quicker death! It's the one serenity afforded your kind! *Breathe.*

"Thank you. Thank you for the welcome," the microphone crackles, lips brush against cool metal weaves as my voice echoes back to me.

In the shadows, stage left, the lecherous smile dripping from his face. Shifting weight, one foot to the other, a stooped old cat wiggling podgy haunches in anticipation of the pounce.

"I was invited to speak to you this afternoon, to share some of my experiences, my thoughts." This spectral voice feeding through me, autopilot. And they stare, bored yet restless. Angry but aloof.

But what's to say? The stage, mine. Microphone in hand. An impossible soapbox. Pham Twist, the man of action. Tell them how the long arm of history will correct what's wrong, that karma's going to deliver a shockingly purulent case of anal warts to those resting comfortably in the highest asset classes who will, in turn, rot rectum first into the annals of history (no simple-minded chronological pun intended). **Laughter**. Tell them that pain is only a state of mind and that all anyone needs to do is work daily, *relentlessly*, to deeply inculcate in his psyche the prophesied message of passivity, a lofty spirituality transcending this base realm of man. **Languor**.

Or, tell them glory is only found in violent resistance - find an appropriate target and apply, with maximum sky-bound force, the claw-end of a hammer to said target's nasal septum (however, given the angle complexities of such a blow [in typical mano a mano combat configuration] and the strength limitations of lateral deltoid motion, it's advisable to execute the maneuver from an inverted position immediately above the target, faces oriented along the same plane, thereby leveraging both gravitational force of a downward swing and the smooth, axial motion both preferred by the humerus moving at a high speed and conducive to the traditional motion of a hammer blow). **Trivialities.**

Or, tell them to find a vantage point, hoisted somewhere high in the sky, the expected earthbound trajectory (plus or minus reasonable wind variances and also with consideration to the appropriate drag coefficient based on body type and fall angle) free and clear of those awful awnings, plucky perambulators, the ever slow-moving elderly, stray pets, Foxconn nets, limbless vets, plump brunettes, Baronets and any other objects that aim to smirkingly thwart a clean sprint to the Elysian Fields. **Let Go**. And, be aware, as you tumble out there in the fresh air, as your body presses against the wind in a violent search for terminal velocity, to pop open those peepers to the possibility that this whole reality, this whole shared drudgery of *being*, is little more than an inconvenient nick in Orion's sword.

But wait! I have a sob story. I don't have to peddle theories, I can speak from experiences. Me, the sad, forgotten orphan confined to a childhood of poverty. Watch me now as I weave the heartstrings in a delicate performance of woe is me, woe is you, woe is we! Catharsis as our weapon against a cold and uncaring world. Stand with me now my brother, my sister. Cry on my shoulder, let's dig deep on this one. Let's purge! Let's purge until the dry heaves have us choking for life's sweet flood of oxygen.

But, those Corps and my new debt to them. My rehearsed lines, Zuberi's ideas, should be dribbling from these lips. They look on, this crowd, with expectation. To them I'm speaking. Spotlights press in, their heat underscoring this growing silence. Feet crunching, shifting on gravel. His smile persists, surety. Hell, he owns the world, why worry?

"A friend of mine once said, *to prove yourself human you must pursue justice at all costs*. Recently though, I learned that he spent his whole life chasing a ghost. You see, to actually *be* human, you must realize that justice is the *only* impossibility in life. We intuit that the world is rational and that rationality implies an eventual bend toward truth, because if falsity and chaos reigned, the world would crumble. But what we choose not to see, precisely because we are rational, is that justice is a fool's game. If we open our eyes to the bleak truth we see that acquisition, control, in their many material and immaterial forms, trump justice every single time. And when glimmers of justice seem to peek from behind the veil, a veil ranging from indifference to brutality, know for certain that somebody's selfish gain is working, maniacally, to make the scales appear balanced. We are what we are in the world, organisms, each in search of the greatest heights possible, at whatever cost is required. Each of us wants to be the hegemon in whatever aspect of life is personally precious. Some win, but only until they lose once again in the cycle of so-called justice. So I ask you, those of you still bothering to search for meaning in life, a meaning that in your heart-of-hearts you know doesn't exist. As you ponder the probability of what comes next *ONE*, and you fall short of a sufficient answer *TWO* what are you going to do to save yourself from our stupid little game? *THREE* You see, as it sinks in to your brain, only then will you realize that I'm already far ahead of you, alighting in a providential glow." *SQUEEZE.*

So, I woke and the smoke cleared from my eyes
And before me stood an airy surprise.
She was tall, rather plain, enveloped in...
Shame? Wait! No. Modesty. I'll start again.

Once I gained sight on the aft side of life,
The answers swarmed in, without any strife.
Fast enough that I learned little is bound
To the rules false prophets oft proclaimed sound.
Come to find out, the he *IS* a she, AND
She is but me. Clone? Pas du tout, wrong brand!
Then others, billions, crowding all around
Melded into a monistic pronoun.
And so it happened WE all became one,
Universally acute like the sun.
Much larger than a holy trinity,
Call it incestuous infinity?

But my point, labels aside, it behooves
One to pry into the mind's deepest grooves.
That Veda you were given, the Torah,
The Bible (dogma's fauna and flora)
Are half-wit lies - please don't look so surprised!
The contrives of man tend to mesmerize.
And those big bangs, black holes, those beaut'fully
Shaped maths are ether-speak dutifully

Spit from the chops of one huge consciousness...
Induce urinary incontinence?!
By heavens, no! Truth's a calm ocean breeze.

With the fore in mind, get up off your knees,
Ditch the absurd hat and don't flog the math
Impaired. Instead here's a logical path:
Just think of what you know (what you call fact),
Then mix it 'round and swallow the swill back.
Now, tell me, what does it taste like to you?
Hmm? What's that you say? Your face has turned blue!
You can't taste thoughts? Well, perception *is* flawed.
These limits to the five senses (*by Gawd!?*),
Moreover, these five are bound and constrained
To frequencies, wavelengths, limits of brain.
Your face, blue! in the air I now respire.
Air in space will set earthly lungs on fire,
But not ours, WE, the matriculant class.
WE exist as one you conceited ass.
WE are not tethered to earth's mundane rules,
Myopic sight, or its erudite fools
(Like those who have a mental scope impaired
By limits like E=mc²).
WE are like God though instead we behave,
Imagine, you can't, you are Physic's slave.
The instantiation of all, WE ARE!
Existence prior to light from first star.

So kill your neighbor, starve the wretched poor,
Beat up on your children, debase the whore,
Claim to know all (then revise when you're wrong),
Steal from them all (yeah, you know this old song).
Morals, who cares? They're too fuzzy and vague...
...Remember that asshole tried at The Hague?
He led a great life, clipped but a few years,

But listen, you should've seen his croc tears
As he stood before us pleading his case,
A mess in his pants, pained look on his face.
He could scarcely splutter words, when he found
Out he was but a **She** <<*REDACT*>> **WE!**, sound
Peculiar? Well it shouldn't 'cause WE will see
You here posthaste (This warning given free).
We hate the brutal and those who conflate
The rhyme and reason, or meaning with fate.
So bear in mind WE're looking down on you
Evaluating all your choices through
& through; your flagrant, vile vulgarities,
Your hostilely enforced disparities.

Th!s notice needs no *Thank You*, very true,
Just strive to mind your mindfulness mind you,
And know, that We are watching and waiting
To judge your ne'er-ending masturbating!
(Ha! Like we care about your family's jools!
But, I digress, hear this, there are some rules.)
To stand here with us you must disavow
(Repudiate, reject, deny somehow)
That humanly logic, and those clever
Rationalizations whomsoever
You are, (trust me there kiddo, you're no star!)
And do it 'fore kissing Earth au revoir.
Cause we don't have time for your solo thoughts,
Your self-indulgence, your divided lots.
WE know your life's bound to the sweaty clutch
On the shit for which WE've never thought much.
The silly chattel-hoard, your accolades,
Mean squat beyond your social barricades.
You see, WE choose to cooperate here,
Alive, full of sublime, and absent fear.
Know there's no chance WE'll allow you to fuck

Up our peace with your motives that sip-suck
Out the life from those who want to just breathe,
Live freely, and avoid the need to seethe.

So take this warning it's free as I said
And let it seep to the gray in your head.
Remember, in YOUR shoes I walked the mile
(Though they stink something wretched) with a smile,
To the crossroads, and then, *The Other Side*,
The place where the minds of the world collide.
Oh look at my watch, time never moves slow!
Anaxagoras says it's time to go,
We must tune the cosmic nous before man
Attempts to implement his master plan.

Now I'll leave this verse, one last whimsy thrown
To catch then weigh upon porcelain throne.
While you try to divide the world in two
Cutting throats, crafting reasons (deja vu!),
Developing tortured logic to eschew
Those who have been supportive, honest, true.
Or, using bald deceit to misconstrue,
Or biting backs and bending truth (do you
Really enjoy playing verbal kung fu?),
Or peddling gore or watching the accrue
Of base financial gain bled out for you
(Is that what you like? Is that your world view?),
Or setting him against her (hitherto,
They were in love, you jerk, what did you do?!),
Or bombing the defenseless from the blue,
Or laying waste to Mother's vast milieu,
Or, well, damn, that's a lot to answer to
So I'll give your mind a tictoc to stew.

(This is a pause...

Ok, pause is now through.)

Your visage is still a dyspneic blue,
But don't sweat, remember, I was much like you,
And in time, I found out th!s to be true:
We are all one; him, her, me, it and you,
So heed this warning, then, next up to do...
Bend. See the other person's angled view.

With love from our future,
Aphamli (Pham) Twist (born Ortiz)

THE END

Conception: June 2011 - May 2012

Iterative Composition and Revision: August 2011 - October 2014

Final Revision Complete: January 2016

Tell Me Again, What the Fuck is...

32nd Amendment - a legislative amendment passed in Congress which formally recognizes the biological emergence of a new species of human being, the Homo beatus. The amendment codifies the legal distinction between Homo sapian and Homo beatus and, as a result, Homo sapians are deemed non-citizens thus not permitted to reside, work or visit The Archives, The Blocks, The Core, or The Bunkers.

33rd Amendment - a legislative amendment passed by the Corps-led Congress meant to deal with the increasing number of homeless people accruing in The Blocks and The Core. The 33rd Amendment states that if a person is dismissed from a full-time job, the obvious implication is that the person is too lazy to in fact be a Homo beatus. As such, the retrenchment is effectively a reclassification of the person from Homo beatus to Homo sapian.

The Archives - a huge skyscraper complex that houses dead and close-to-dead humans in tiny capsules. Because clean land is highly prized, The Archives are the natural evolution of cemeteries.

Atonement Center - a large call center where armies of customer service representatives receive phone calls from Iron sinners. For a small fee, guilty Irons can engage in telephony repentance.

atonements - short, confessional phone calls meant to forgive the sins of callers for a fee.

The Bunkers - a sprawling, exclusive, highly protected land mass outside of The Core where Diamonds live in palatial, underground, highly-secured, fully-serviced estates.

The Blocks - a cramped, poorly constructed high-rise housing concentration complex exclusively reserved for Irons.

The Bug - some horrific disease that killed shitloads of people (everyone dystopian-oriented scratch of literature has to have something to this effect).

Blazzel - a game poor kids play to simultaneously learn charity and revenge.

The Big Gas Bubble (aka: The Flatulence Bubble) - a financial bubble phenomenon that preyed on the lower economic rungs of society. Average everyday savers enticed by celebrities and socialite endorsements, were drawn to investing in their own flatulence (and the flatulence of others) as a means to achieving greater economic security.

The Core - the commercial center of a city where all valid citizens (Homo beatus) work. Almost all Platinums live here exclusively with the exception of a tiny minority who are able to afford a home in The Bunkers. All Diamonds have multiple satellite homes here.

Corps (aka: Corporate Party) - One of four political parties represented in the Legislature (the other three parties being The Radicals, The Religious and The Citizens). The Corps are by far the strongest party and, for all intents and purposes, the only party that wields any measure of influence and power in society.

Diamonds - a socio-economic classification of Homo beatus responsible for business and political leadership in society. Diamonds are the wealthiest class and hold all of the power in society.

Dhalytes (aka: Dirts) - a classification of humans (also referred to as Homo sapians) who have been banished from society and are forced to live in The Piles.

drop fields - a massive trash-dumping area adjacent to The Piles where all refuse from Irons, Platinums and Diamonds is deposited. The drop fields are where Dirts go to search for food and building materials.

HFWYG - an acronym for the game show How Far Will You Go? It is a participatory game show that encourages large-scale acts of violence with the possibility of achieving massive financial compensation for "winners".

Homo beatus - the species of human beings created in the 32nd Amendment. Homo beatus are superior to Homo sapian in that they have a substantially larger Motum Ducit.

Homo sapian - the person literally reading this sentence. Sorry, but you have a tiny Motum Ducit, pity.

hunt - a term used by Dirts referring to the process of digging through bags of trash in the drop fields in search of food discarded by Irons, Platinums or Diamonds.

Irons - a socio-economic classification of Homo beatus responsible for providing all physical labor in society. From a socio-economic ranking perspective, Irons are below Platinums and situated on the lowest rung of society.

Labor Credits (colloquially known as Credits) - A fiat currency that directly correlates to the hourly labor working units for the Iron class. All classes of people use and spend credits but the value of the currency is pegged only to Iron working hours.

Motum Ducit - a region of the brain responsible for stimulating human motivation in the hippocampus.

Membrane - an ionizing filtration air bubble that hovers atop The Blocks, The Piles, The Bunkers and The Core providing breathable air to inhabitants.

neural station - a personal network terminal where end-users can connect to other end-users and simultaneously ingest an array of substances including The Pine.

Palette (aka: device) - a portable, digital device that is essential to survival for Homo beatus.

persona ficta - a constitutionally-defined person, but only in a legal sense. Essentially, persona ficta is a legal container that can be filled with a human representative in order to grant the physical human specific legal rights.

The Pine - a relaxing, pine-scented psychotropic drug delivered in an aerosol with the intent to sedate and control Irons.

The Piles - A sprawling slum where Dhalytes (and recently out-casted Irons) live.

Platinums - a socio-economic classification of Homo beatus responsible primarily for the intellectual capital of society. From a socio-economic ranking perspective, Platinums sit below Diamonds but above Irons.

Prattle - a social media tool used to convey excessively terse, thoughtless nuggets of information usually in a hostile or aggressive manner.

Quorum of Religious Institutions (aka: The Quorum) - a collection of the most powerful religious leaders. The Quorum's primary task was to develop and sustain a business plan meant to reverse the declining population of religious congregants, a decline that was a direct result of the Science Economy initiative sparked by the discovery that God never existed. The Quorum, along with its team of consultants, are responsible for the creation of the Atonement Centers as the new denominationally-agnostic method of religious practice.

sensory games - electronically-derived games that interface with all five human senses to provide an immersive gaming experience that is virtually indistinguishable from actual human reality.

Super Depression - the period of financial fallout that occurred as a direct result of the The Big Gas Bubble.

Science Economy - the disingenuous policy "wrapper" placed around economic legislation created by Diamonds. This wrapper was artfully crafted to give scientific legitimacy to a new economic order covertly designed to further pilfer economic resources and labor from Irons.

Vacant Eyes - one particular exhibition of people interred in The Archives. Everyone in the Vacant Eyes exhibit share the common fate of deciding to cut out their own eyeballs in order to avoid any further sins.

The Wastelands - large swaths of uninhabitable land situated beyond The Piles. Formerly, this land was used for farming, but due to environmental degradation it is no longer fit for any human purpose.

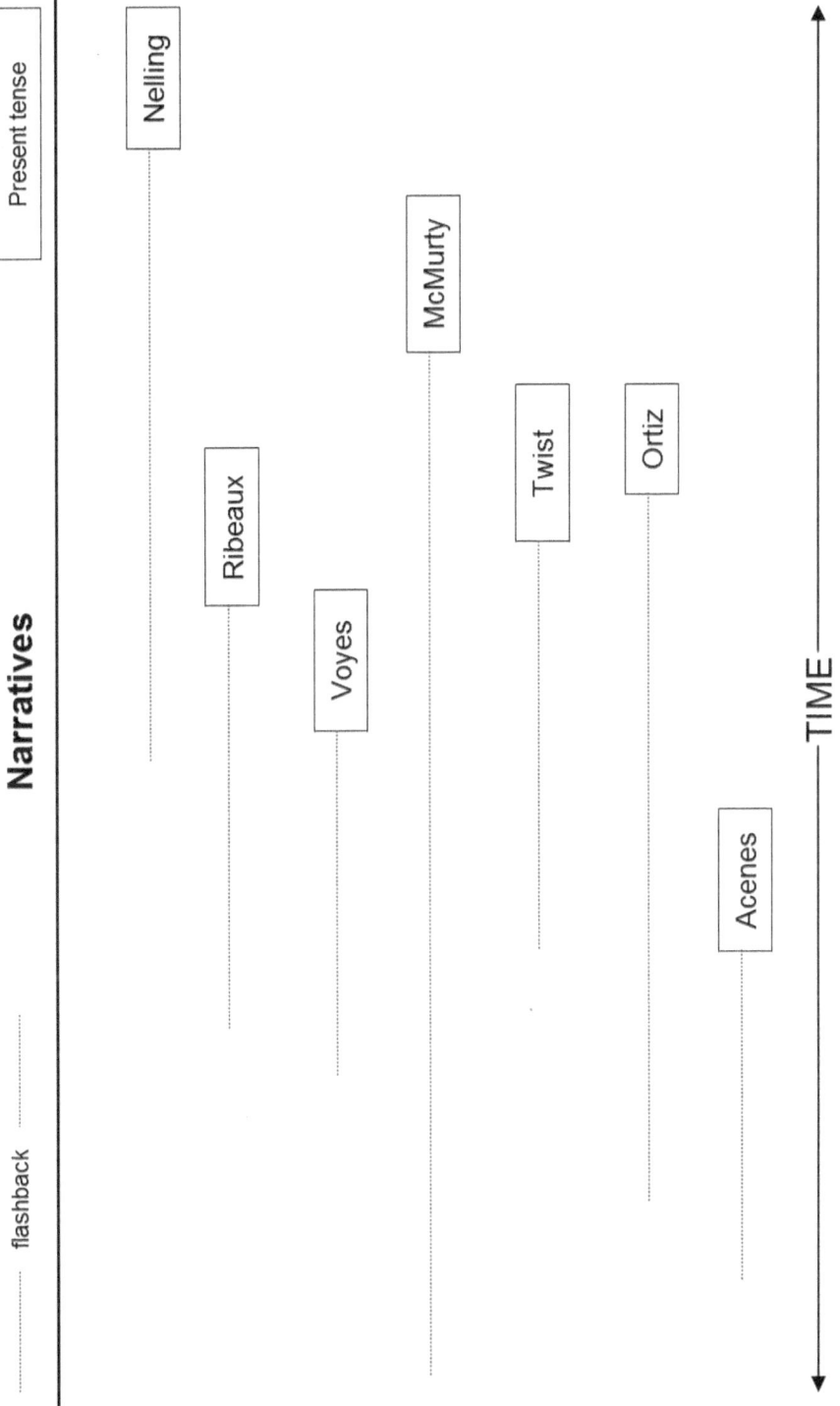

Narratives

Present tense

flashback

Nelling

Ribeaux

Voyes

McMurty

Twist

Ortiz

Acenes

TIME

About the Author

Daniel Shortell is a recent escapee of NYC currently marooned in a culture-free enclave of central New York. At university, he was fully indoctrinated with corporatism. The resulting pathology completely dismantled his psyche resulting in a 2009 exodus from the corporate world. His real education came from traveling, tinkering and reading the ideas of those ostricised by The System. When not writing, he enjoys building things and incubating the seeds of revolutionary ideology in the tender mind of his 5 year old. th!s is his second novel.

www.ingramcontent.com/pod-product-compliance
Lightning Source LLC
Chambersburg PA
CBHW030549180626
46816CB00005B/1476